Rhoda Broughton

Doctor Cupid

Rhoda Broughton

Doctor Cupid

1st Edition | ISBN: 978-3-75232-734-2

Place of Publication: Frankfurt am Main, Germany

Year of Publication: 2020

Outlook Verlag GmbH, Germany.

Reproduction of the original.

DOCTOR CUPID

BY
RHODA BROUGHTON

CHAPTER I

What the Big House Owes to us.	What we Owe to the Big House.
1. As much of our company as it likes to command.	1. Heartburnings from envy.
2. As much dance music as it can get out of our fingers.	2. Headaches from dissipation.
3. The complete transfer of all the bores among its guests from its shoulders to ours.	3. The chronic discontent of our three maids.
4. The entire management of its Workhouse teas.	4. The utter demoralisation of our boot-boy.
5. The wear and tear of mind of all its Christmas-trees and bran-pies.	5. The acquaintance of several damaged fine ladies.
6. The physicking of its sick dogs.	6. A roll of red flannel from the last wedding.
7. The setting its canaries' broken legs.	7. The occasional use of a garden-hose.
8. The general cheerful and grateful charing for it.	

'There! I do not think that the joys and sorrows of living in a little house under the shadow of a big one were ever more lucidly set forth,' says an elder sister, holding up the slate on which she has just been totting up this ingenious debit and credit account to a pink junior, kneeling, head on hand, beside her; a junior who, not so long ago, did sums on that very slate, and the straggle of briony round whose sailor-hat tells that she has only just left the sunburnt harvest-fields and the overgrown August hedgerows behind her.

'We have had a good deal of fun out of it too,' says she, rather remorsefully. 'Do you remember'—with a sigh of recollected enjoyment—'the day that we all blackened our faces with soot, and could not get the soot off again afterwards?'

To what but a mind of seventeen could such a reminiscence have appeared in the light of a departed joy?

'I have left out an item, I see,' says Margaret, running her eye once again over her work; 'an unlimited quantity of the society of Freddy Ducane, when nothing better turns up for him! Under which head, profit or loss'—glancing with a not more than semi-amused smile at her sister—'am I to enter it, eh, Prue?'

'Loss, loss!' replies Prue, with a suspiciously rosy precipitation. 'No question about it; no one makes us lose so much time as he! Loss, loss!'

Margaret's eyes rest for an instant on her sister's face, and then return not quite comfortably to the slate, upon which she painstakingly inscribes the final entry, 'An unlimited quantity of Freddy Ducane's society, when nothing better turns up for him!'

"'The acquaintance of several damaged fine ladies!'" reads Prue over her sister's shoulder. 'I suppose that means Lady Betty?'

'I name no names,' replies Margaret gravely. 'I keep to a discreet generality—

> "'If it do her right,
> Then she hath wrong'd herself; if she be free,
> Why, then, my taxing like a wild-goose flies,
> Unclaimed of any man.'"

'Dear me!' repeats Prue, under her breath, in a rather awed voice; 'I wonder what it feels like to be damaged!'

'You had better ask her,' drily.

'I suppose she says dreadful things,' continues the young girl, still with that same awed curiosity. 'I heard Mrs. Evans telling you that she "stuck at nothing." I wonder how she does it.'

'You had better ask her,' more drily.

'Damaged or not damaged,' cries Prue, springing up from her knees and beginning to caper about the room, and sing to her own capering, 'we shall meet her to-night—

> "'For I'm to be married to-day, to-day,
> For I'm to be married to-day.'"

Or if I am not to be married, I am to go to my first dinner-party, which is a step in the right direction. Do you remember your first dinner-party, Peggy? How did you feel? How did you look?'

'I looked very plain, I believe,' replies Peggy sedately. 'At least, I was told so afterwards. I remember that I felt very swollen. I had a cold, and was shy, and I think both combined to make me feel swelled.'

'It is a pity that shyness has not the same effect upon me,' says Prue, stretching out a long girlish arm, whose thinness is apparent even through its chintz muslin covering. 'The one thing that would really improve my appearance'—stopping before the only looking-glass that the little room boasts, and putting her finger and thumb in the hollows of cheeks scarcely rounded enough to match the rest of the pansy-textured child face—'the one thing that would really improve my appearance would be to have the mumps.'

Peggy laughs.

'*Unberufen!* I should catch them, and you cannot say that they would improve me.'

'Never mind!' cries Prue, turning away with a joyous whirl from the mirror. 'I shall do very well. There are people who admire bones! I shall pass in a crowd.

> '"For I'm to be married to-day, to-day,
>   For I'm to be married to-day."'

Her dance and her song have carried her out into the garden—the small but now opulent garden; and, partly to look at her, partly to pasture her eyes upon a yet more admired object, Peggy has followed her as far as to the French window, and now stands leaning one handsome shoulder against the door-post, and looking out upon her kingdom of flowers.

'We owe the Big House one good thing, at all events,' she says, a smile of satisfaction stealing into her comely eyes. 'I never knew what peace of mind was until I had a garden-hose.'

At this moment, in the hands of Jacob the gardener, it is playing comfortably on the faces of the tea-roses, and a luxurious drip and patter testify to their appreciation.

Prue has come back panting, and sunk out of breath on the window-sill. The briony garland has fallen from her hat, and a little hairy dog is now galloping about the lawn boastfully with it, his head held very high. Something in his attitude gets on the nerves of the other animals; for the parrot, brought out to sun himself upon the sward, raps out his mysterious marine oath, which he generally keeps for a crisis; and the white cat forgets herself so far as to deal him a swingeing box on the ear as he passes her.

'I met the brougham from the Big House as I came up the lane,' says Prue, trying to cool herself with the inadequate fan of a small pocket-handkerchief; 'it was on its way back from the station. How tired those poor horses must be of the road to the station! It had three people inside it—Lady Betty, Mr. Harborough, and some third person.'

'Her maid, probably.'

Prue shakes her head.

'No; the maid followed in a fly with the nurses and children. Dear me, Peggy, what a number of servants they take about with them—maid, one; valet, two; footman, three; two nurses, five!'

'Nurses, five!' repeats Margaret inattentively, not thinking of what she is saying, and with her eyes still riveted on the hose; 'surely that is a very unusual number, isn't it?'

'I could not see the third person distinctly,' continues Prue narratively; 'but I think it was the man whom Lady Betty brought with her last year. She seems always to bring him with her.'

'More shame for her!' replies Peggy severely.

'Mr. Harborough was very fond of him, too,' says Prue reflectively. 'He called him "John."'

'More fool he!' still severelier; then, with a sudden and happy change of key, 'That is right, Jacob. Give it a good souse; it is covered with fly.'

'Do not you wonder what we shall do to-night?' cries Prue, her mind galloping gaily away from the blackness of Lady Betty's deeds to the splendid whiteness of her own immediate prospect. 'Charades? dancing? I prophesy dancing.'

'"For Willy will dance with Jane,"'

bursting out into song again—

'"And Betty has got her John."'

She breaks off, laughing. Margaret laughs too.

'Betty may have got her John, but I am sure I do not know who Peggy and Prue will have, unless Freddy can split himself up into several young gentlemen at once. He can do most things'—with a touch of bitterness—'possibly he can do that too.'

'Or perhaps we shall go out star-gazing in the walled garden,' interrupts Prue, hurriedly and redly shying away from the name thus introduced. 'I always think that the stars look bigger from the walled garden than anywhere else in the world.'

'Was it there that you and Freddy went to look for Cassiopeia's Chair?' inquires Peggy drily; 'and were more than an hour and a half before you could find her?'

'It is so odd that I had never noticed her before,' cries Prue hastily. 'She is such a queer shape, more like a long straggling W than a chair.'

'And, after all,' continues Margaret slowly, with an uneasy smile, and not paying any heed to her sister's interpolation, 'she turned out to be in the kiosk.'

Prue is silent. The little hairy dog has brought her ruined garland back to her feet; and, holding it between his fore-paws, is painstakingly biting off each leaf and tendril, and strewing them over the close-shaven sward. The parrot is going to sleep, standing on one leg, and making a clacking noise with his beak; not a posture that one would have thought *à priori* conducive to slumber.

'It was not a place in which one would have expected to find a large constellation, was it?' asks Peggy, still with that same rather rueful smile, and stroking her sister's childish head as she speaks—'the darkest corner of a kiosk.'

But at that Prue leaps to her feet; and having, in the twinkling of an eye, twitched the hose out of Jacob's hand, she points it at her sister.

'Mention the word kiosk once more,' cries she desperately, and winking away a couple of tears, 'and you will not have a dry stitch upon you.'

CHAPTER II

'Ave Maria! 'Tis the hour of prayer!
Ave Maria! 'Tis the hour of love!'

Ave Maria! 'tis the hour of dinner, too; and towards that dinner, about to be spread at the Big House, the inmates of the little one are hastening on foot through the park. Brougham have they none; goloshes and a lanthorn their only substitute. The apricot sunset and the harvest moon will be their two lanthorns to-night; but upon the goloshes Peggy has, in the case of her sister, sternly insisted. Hastening through the park—alternately hastening, that is to say—and loitering, as Prue's fear of being too late, and Peggy's better-grounded apprehension of being too early, get the upper hand.

'How calm you are!' cries the young girl feverishly, as Margaret stops for a moment to

'Suck the liquid air'

of the ripe harvest evening, and admire the velvet-coated stags springing through the bracken. 'How *can* you be so calm? Were you calm at your first dinner-party?'

'I cannot recollect,' replies Peggy, honestly trying to recall the now five-years-old dead banquet referred to. 'I can only remember that I felt swelled.'

'Do not you think that we might go on now?' asks Prue, anxiously kicking one golosh against the other. 'We cannot be much too soon; our clocks are always slow. It would be awkward, would not it, if we sailed in last of all?'

Though inwardly convinced that there is very little fear of this catastrophe, Peggy good-humouredly complies; and still more good-humouredly refrains from any 'told-you-so' observation upon their finding themselves sole occupants of the flamboyant Louis Quatorze chairs and Gobelin sofas in the large drawing-room, where the housemaids have evidently only just ceased patting cushions and replacing chair-backs.

'Never mind!' says Prue joyfully; 'we shall have all the more of it, and we shall see everybody come in. I shall love to see everybody come in. Who will be first? Guess! Not Lady Betty! she will be last. I remember your saying last year that she was always late, and that she never apologised.'

'That was very ill bred of her,' replies Margaret austerely.

'And that one night Mr. Harborough scolded her, and you saw her making a face at him behind his back. Oh! how I wish'—breaking out into delighted

7

laughter—'that she would make a face at him to-night, and that he could catch her doing it!'

Her laughter is checked by the thrilling sound of the folding-doors being rolled back to admit some new arrivals. It is nobody very exciting, however; only Mr. Evans, the clergyman of the parish, whom they see every day, and that household angel of his, upon whose testimony lies the weight of Lady Betty Harborough's conversational laxities.

A stranger would be thunderstruck to hear that Mrs. Evans is in her wedding-dress, as the sable rook is less black from head to heel than she; but to those who know and love her, it is *le secret de Polichinelle* that her gown—through having since taken an insignificant trip or two to the dye-pot, and been eked out with a selection of funeral scarves and hat-bands—is verily and indeed the one in which she stood in virgin modesty beside Mr. Evans at the altar, fifteen rolling years ago. During a transition stage of red, it has visited the Infirmary Ball for five years; it had an unpopular interval of snuffy-brown, during which it did nothing remarkable; and in its present inky phase it has mourned for several dead Evanses, and for every crowned head in Europe.

'I am so glad we are not last,' says Mrs. Evans, relaxing her entrance smile, and sinking into an easy conversational manner, as she sees that she has only her two young parishioners to accost; 'not that there is ever much fear of that in this house, but Mr. Evans could not get the horse along. Have you any idea'—looking curiously round—'whom we are to meet? Lady Roupell's note merely said, "Dear Mrs. Evans," or "My dear Mrs. Evans"—I forget which —"will you and Mr. Evans come and help us to eat a haunch of venison?" She knows that Mr. Evans would go any distance for a haunch of venison.'

To this somewhat extravagant statement of his appreciation of the pleasures of the table the pastor is heard to make a captious demurrer; but his wife goes on without heeding him.

'Of course that gave one no clue. I think people ought to give one some clue that one may know what to put on. However, I thought I could not go far wrong in black; never too smart, and always smart enough, you know.'

Peggy assents, and, as she does so, a trivial unbelieving wonder crosses her mind as to what the alternative 'toilette,' which Mrs. Evans implies, but upon which the eye of man has never looked, may be.

'And you are no wiser than we?' pursues the vicar's wife interrogatively. 'I wonder at that, living so near as you do. Have not you heard of anybody at all?' with a rather discouraged intonation.

'I am not sure—I think—the Harboroughs——'

'The Harboroughs?' cries the other eagerly. 'Mr. and Lady Betty? Her father died last winter; he was the second duke; succeeded by his eldest son, her brother. The Harboroughs!—and Mr. Talbot, of course?' with a knowing look.

'I do not know,' replies Margaret cautiously; 'perhaps.'

'I am afraid it is more than perhaps,' rejoins Mrs. Evans significantly. 'I am afraid it is——'

But her sentence dies unfinished, killed by the frou-frou of silk that announces the approach of a smart woman, and of the white-waistcoated gentleman who has bought the privilege of paying for the silk. Then follows an unencumbered man, whose speech bewrayeth him to be a diplomate, and who has a great deal to say to the smart woman.

After five minutes more frou-frou is audible, heralding the approach of a second smart woman—Lady Betty herself this time—with her lawful Harborough stepping somewhat insignificantly behind her.

Lady Betty is so exceedingly glad to see the two girls that Peggy asks herself whether her memory has played her false as to the amount of intimacy that existed between them last year. She has not overheard the aside that passed between her ladyship and her husband as she sailed up the long room:

'Who are they? Have we ever met them here before? Are they all one lot?'

Nor, indeed, would it ever have entered into the guileless Peggy's mind as possible that a woman who took her by both hands, and smiled into both eyes, could have clean forgotten, not only her name, but her very existence.

Once more the folding-doors roll wide, to admit this time, at last, the hostess, Lady Roupell, and her nephew, Freddy Ducane, who—both chronically late for everything—arrive simultaneously; the one still fastening his sleeve-link, and the other hastily clasping her bracelets.

'I beg you all a thousand pardons, good people,' cries the old lady, going round and dealing out hearty handshakes to her injured guests. 'I am sure you must all have been blessing me; but if you had seen me five minutes ago, you would wonder that I am here now—ha! ha! Well, at all events we are all assembled at last, are not we? No! Surely we are short of somebody; who is it? John Talbot, of course! Where is John Talbot?' looking round, first at the general company, who are quite unable to answer her; and turning, secondly, as if involuntarily, towards Lady Betty. 'Where is John Talbot?'

But at this instant, in time to save Lady Betty's blushes, which indeed are in no great hurry to show themselves, John Talbot appears to answer for himself —John Talbot, the third occupant of the brougham, the 'man whom Lady

Betty always takes about with her.'

His entry is not quite what is expected, as he enters by no means alone. Clasped in his embrace, with her fat arms fastened round his neck, and her face buried—a good deal to its detriment—in his collar, is a young person in her nightgown; while running by his side is a little barefoot gentleman, with a long dressing-gown trailing behind him.

'We hope that you will forgive us,' says the young man, advancing towards his hostess; 'but we have come to say good-night. I suggested that our costume was not quite what is usual, but I was overruled.'

As he speaks his fair burden makes it clear by a wriggling movement that she wishes to be set down; and, being obliged in this particular, instantly makes for her mother, and, climbing up into Lady Betty's splendid lap, begins to whisper in her ear. The boy stands shamefaced, clutching his protector's hand, and evidently painfully conscious that no other gentleman but himself in the room is in a dressing-gown.

'Do you know what she is asking me?' cries Lady Betty, bursting into a fit of laughter. 'Freddy, I must congratulate you upon a new bonne fortune. She is asking whether she may kiss Freddy Ducane! There, be off with you! Since'—with a look of casual careless coquetry at Talbot—'you have introduced my family, perhaps you will be good enough to remove them.'

Mr. Talbot complies; and, having recaptured Miss Harborough—a feat of some difficulty, as, unlike her brother, she enjoys her *déshabillé*, and announces a loud intention of kissing everybody—departs in the same order in which he arrived, and the pretty little couple are seen no more.

CHAPTER III

It is obvious that, whatever else he may be, John Talbot is, with the exception of Mr. Evans, the man of smallest rank in the room, since to him is assigned the honour of leading Peggy into the dining-room. She had not at all anticipated it; but had somehow expected fully to see him, in defiance of precedence, bearing off his Betty. Nor is she by any means more pleased at, than prepared for, the provision made for her entertainment. John Talbot, the man whose name she has never heard except in connection with that of another man's wife! John Talbot, 'the man whom Lady Betty always takes about with her!' In Heaven's name, why does not she take him about with her now, and not devolve the onus of his entertainment upon other innocent and unwilling persons?

With thoughts such as these, that augur but ill for the amusingness of his dinner, running through her mind, Margaret lays her hand as lightly as it is possible to do, without absolutely not touching it, upon the coat-sleeve presented to her, and marches silently by its side into the dining-room, inwardly resolving to be as laconic, as forbidding, and as unlike Lady Betty to its owner as politeness towards her hostess will allow, and to devote as nearly as possible the whole of her conversation to her neighbour on the other side. Nor does her resolution flinch, even when that other neighbour reveals himself as Mr. Evans. It is certain that no duty compels her to take the initiative. Until John Talbot begins, she may preserve that silence which she would like to maintain intact, until she rises from the feast to which she has but just sat down. Doubtlessly he is of the same mind as she; and, maddened by separation from his idol, irritated against her, who, for even an hour, has taken that idol's place, he will ask nothing better than to sit mute in resentful pining for her, from whom Lady Roupell has so inhumanly parted him. As to his intentions to be mute, she is soon undeceived; for she has not yet finished unbuttoning her gloves when she finds herself addressed by him.

'I think I had the pleasure of meeting you here last year?'

Nothing can be more banal than the observation; more serenely civil, less maddened than the tone in which it is conveyed. He is not going to leave her in peace then? She is so surprised and annoyed at this discovery that for a moment she forgets to answer him. It is not until reminded of her omission by an expectant look on his face that she recollects to drop a curt 'Yes.'

'I came'—thinking from her manner that the incident has escaped her memory, and that he will recall it by becoming more circumstantial—'I came with the Harboroughs.'

Another 'Yes,' still more curt and bald than the last. H'm! not flattering for him, certainly; but she has obviously not yet overtaken the reminiscence.

'It was about this time of year.'

'Yes.'

What is the matter with the girl? there is certainly something very odd about her. He has noticed her but cursorily so far, but now gives her an attentively examining look. She appears to be perfectly sane, and not in the least shy. Is that handsome mouth, fresh and well cut, absolutely incapable of framing any syllable but 'Yes'? He gives himself some little trouble so to compose his next question that the answer, 'Yes,' to it shall be impossible.

'Do you happen to recollect whether it was this month or September? Lady Betty Harborough and I had an argument about it as we came up from the station.'

Lady Betty Harborough! With what a brazen front he himself has introduced her! She, Peggy, would as soon have thought of flying in the air as of mentioning that name which he has just so matter-of-factly pronounced.

'I am afraid that I do not remember,' she answers frostily.

He looks at her again, in growing wonder. What *does* ail her? Is it, after all, a mysterious form of shyness? He knows under how many odd disguises that strange malady of civilisation hides itself. Despite his thirty-two years, is not he shy himself sometimes? Poor girl, he can feel for her!

'Not only did we meet here,' pursues he, with a pleasant friendly smile, 'but Lady Roupell was good enough to take me down to call upon you at your own house.'

'Yes?'

Well, it is uphill work! If he has to labour at the oar like this from now until dessert, there will not be much left of him at the end. Well, never mind! it is all in the day's work; only he will ask Lady Roupell quietly not to inflict this impossible dummy upon him again.

'We came down upon you in great force, I remember—it was on a Sunday— Lady Roupell, Freddy, the Bentincks, the Harboroughs.'

He pauses, discouraged, despite himself. She has been leisurely sipping her soup, and now lays down her spoon, looking straight before her. He heaves a loud sigh, but not even that induces her to look round at him.

'Lady Roupell often brings people down on Sunday afternoons,' she says, in an indifferent voice, which implies that it is a quite impossible feat for her memory to separate the one insignificant Sunday to which he alludes from all or any others. In point of fact, she remembers it perfectly, and the recollection of it adds a double chill to her tone.

On that very Sunday afternoon did not this man and his Lady Betty flagrantly lose themselves for an hour in an orchard six yards square? Did not Lady Betty, without leave asked or given, eat all the mulberries that were ripe on Peggy's one tree? Did not she, in rude horse-play pelting a foolish guardsman with green apples, break a bell-glass that sheltered the picotee cuttings cherished of Jacob's and of Peggy's souls?

Ignorant of the offensive reminiscences he has stirred up, Mr. Talbot blunders on:

'I remember you had a tame——'

He stops. He cannot for the life of him recollect what the tame animal was that he was taken to see. He can only recall that it was some beast not usually kept as a pet, and that it lived in a house in the stable-yard. Of course if he pauses she will supply the word, and his lapse of memory need never be perceived.

But he has reckoned without his host. She has indeed turned her face a little towards him, and says 'Yes?' expectantly.

It is clear that she has not the least intention of helping him; and is it, or is it not, his fancy that there is a slight ill-natured tremor about that corner of her mouth which is nearest him?

'A tame—badger,' suggests he desperately.

But the moment that he has uttered the word he knows that it was not a badger.

'A tame badger!' repeats she slowly, and again gazing straight before her; 'yes, what a nice pet!'

She is not shy at all, nor even stupid. She is only rude and malevolent. But he will not give her the satisfaction of letting her see that he perceives it.

'Perhaps Lady Roupell will have your permission to bring us down to see you next Sunday, when I may have an opportunity of stroking my old friend the badger's' (he smiles, as if he had known all along that it was not a badger) 'head once again.'

'I do not know what Lady Roupell's plans for next Sunday are,' replies she snubbingly; and so turns, with a decided movement of head and shoulder, towards her other neighbour, Mr. Evans, who, however, is not nearly so grateful for her attentions as he should be.

Mr. Evans has the poor and Peggy Lambton always with him, but he has not a haunch of fat buck-venison more than three times a year. In everyday life he is more than willing to give his share of the Vicarage dinner to such among the sick and afflicted of his flock as can be consoled and supported by underdone shoulders of mutton and batter-puddings; but on the rare occasions when the opportunity offers of having his palate titillated by the delicate cates of the higher civilisation, he had very much rather be left in peace to enjoy them. He has no fault to find in this respect with Prue Lambton, to whom, as having taken her in to dinner, he might be supposed to have some conversational obligations.

Why, then, cannot Peggy, to whom he owes nothing, be equally considerate? Perhaps Peggy's heart speaks for him. At all events, after one or two vain shots at the harvest-home and the Workhouse tea, she desists from the futile effort to lead him into chat; but subtly remains sitting half turned towards him, as if talking to him, so as to baffle any further ventures—if, indeed, he have the spirit to make such—on the part of her other neighbour. Her tongue being idle, she allows her eyes to travel. It is true that the thick forest of oats and poppies which waves over the board renders the sight of the table's other side about as difficult as that of the coast of France; but at least she can see her fat hostess at the head of the table, and her slim host at the foot. Freddy Ducane is in his glory—something fair and female on either hand. On his right Lady Betty, who, being a duke's daughter, takes precedence of the other smart woman, who was only a miss before she blossomed into a viscountess; on his left, to ensure himself against the least risk of having any dull or vacuous moments during his dinner, he has arranged Prue Lambton—'his little friend Prue.' Beyond the mere fact of proximity—in itself, of course, a splendid boon—she does not, so far, seem to be much the gainer by her position.

However, he snatches a moment every now and then to explain to her—Peggy knows it as well as if she heard his words—how entirely a matter of irksome duty and hospitality are his whispers to Lady Betty, his tender comments upon her clothes, and long bunglings with the clasp of her pearls. And, judging by her red-stained cheeks, her empty plate (which of us in his day has not been too superbly happy to eat?), and the trembling smiles that rush out to meet his lame explanations, Prue believes him. Poor little Prue!

Margaret sighs sadly and impatiently, and looks away—looks away to find John Talbot's eyes fastened upon her with an expression of such innocent and genuine curiosity that she asks involuntarily:

'Why do you look at me?'

'I beg your pardon a thousand times!' he answers apologetically. 'I was only wondering, to be quite sincere—by the bye, do you like people to be quite sincere?'

'That depends,' replies Peggy cautiously.

'Well, then, I must risk it. I was wondering why on earth you had thought it worth your while to snub me in the way you have been doing.'

She does not answer, but again looks straight before her.

How very offensive in a woman to look straight before her! She ought to be quite certain of the perfection of her profile before she presents it so persistently to you.

Shall he tell her so? That would make her look round pretty quickly.

'I was trying to see whether I could not regard it in the light of a compliment,' continues he audaciously.

'That would not be easy,' replies she drily.

'It was something that you should have thought me worth wasting your powder and shot upon,' he answers.

Certainly her profile is anything but perfect; her chin projects too much. In her old age, if she had a hook nose (which she has not), she would be a mere nut-cracker.

Shall he tell her that? How many disagreeable things he might tell her! It puts him into quite a good humour with her to think of them.

'Now, about that badger, for instance,' says he.

But at that, against her will, she laughs outright.

'Dear little beast!' she cries maliciously; 'so playful and affectionate! such a pet!'

She has laughed. That is something gained, at all events. It is not a nice friendly laugh. On the contrary, it is a very rude, ill-natured one: she is obviously a rude, ill-natured girl; but it is a laugh.

'You can see for yourself,' pursues he, holding out one of the *menus* for her inspection, 'that we are only at the first *entrée*; we shall have to sit beside each other for a good hour more. Lady Roupell does not want to talk to me; and your neighbour—I do not know who he is, and I will not ask you, because I know you would not answer me civilly—but whoever he is, he will not talk to you. I saw you try to make him, and he would not; he snubbed you. I was avenged! I was very glad!'

Peggy would much rather not have laughed; but there is something that seems to her so ludicrous in the fact of her abortive advances to Mr. Evans having been overheard and triumphed at, that she cannot help yielding to a brief and stifled mirth at her own expense. And, after all, what he says is sense. He is a very bad man, and she dislikes him extremely; but to let him observe to her that the news from Afghanistan seems warlike; or to remark in return that she has never seen the root-crops look better, need not in the least detract from the thoroughness of her ill opinion of him, and may make the ensuing hour a shade less tedious to herself than would entire silence. So she turns her candid eyes, severely, serenely blue, for the first time, full upon him, and says:

'I think you are right; I think we had better talk.'

But of course, at that sudden permission to talk, every possible topic of conversation flies out of his head. And yet as she remains, with her two blue eyes sternly fixed upon him, awaiting the question or questions that she has given him permission to put, he must say something; so he asks stupidly:

'Who is your neighbour?'

'Our vicar.'

'What is his name?' (How infinitely little he cares what the vicar's name is; but it gives him time.)

'E V A N S,' replies she, spelling very distinctly and slowly, afraid that she may be overheard if she pronounce the whole name.

'Oh, thanks; and the lady opposite in mourning is Mrs. E V A N S?' (spelling too).

'She is Mrs. Evans; but she is not in mourning; she is in her wedding-gown!' replies Peggy, breaking into a smile.

She never can help smiling at the thought of Mrs. Evans's wedding-dress, any more than Charles Lamb's Cheshire cats can help laughing when they think of Cheshire being a County Palatine. She is smiling broadly now. Well, if her smile come seldom, there is no doubt that it is a very agreeable one when it does come. What sort of thing could he say that would be likely to bring it back?

'I did not know that people were ever married in black.'

She shakes her head oracularly.

'No more they are!'

She is smiling still. (What a delightful wide mouth! and what *dents de jeune chien*!)

'It is made out of an old Geneva gown of his?' suggests Talbot wildly.

Again she shakes her nut-brown head.

'Wrong.'

'I have it!' he cries eagerly. 'I know more about the subject than you think; it has been dyed.'

The mirth has retired from her mouth, and now lurks in the tail of her bright eye.

'You did not find that out for yourself,' she says distrustfully; 'some one told you.'

'Upon my honour, it is my own unassisted discovery,' replies he solemnly, and then they both laugh.

Finding herself betrayed into such a harmony of light-hearted merriment with him, Margaret pulls herself up. After all, she must not forget that there is a medium between the stiff politeness she had planned and this hail-fellow-well-met-ness into which she finds herself somehow sliding. Nor does his next sentence, though innocently enough meant, at all conduce to make her again relax her austerity.

'I should not allow my wife to dye her wedding-gown black.'

His wife! How dare he allude to such a person? He, with his illegal Betty ogling and double-entendre-ing and posturing opposite! How dare he allude to marriage at all? He to whom that sacred tie is a derision! She has frozen up again.

Without having the faintest suspicion of the cause, he is wonderingly aware of the result. Is it possible that she can object to his introducing his hypothetical wife into the consideration? She is more than welcome to retort upon him with her supposititious husband. He will give her the chance.

'Would you?'

'Would I what?'

'Dye your wedding-gown black?'

She knows that she would not. She knows that she would lay it up in lavender, and tenderly show the yellowed skirt and outlandish sleeves to her grandchildren forty years hence. But in the pleasure of contradicting him, truth is worsted.

'Yes.'

'You would?' in a tone of surprise.

She must repeat her fib.

'Yes.'

'Well, I should not have thought it.'

He would like her to ask him why he would not have thought it; but she does not oblige him.

'I think it would show a want of sentiment,' pursues he perseveringly.

'Yes?'

Good heavens! If she has not got back again to her monosyllable!

'Do not you?'

'No.'

'I should think it would bring ill-luck, should not you?'

'No.'

'Should not you, really?'

'I do not think that it is worth arguing about,' replies Peggy, roused and wearied. 'I may dye mine, and you need not dye yours, and we shall neither of us be any the worse.'

'And yet——' he begins; but she interrupts him.

'After all,' she says, turning once more upon him those two dreadfully direct blue eyes—'after all, I am not at all sure that it is not a good emblem of marriage—the white gown that goes through muddy waters, and comes out black on the other side.'

There is such a weight of meaning and emphasis in her words that he is silent, and wishes that she had kept to her monosyllables.

CHAPTER IV

'Yon meaner beauties of the night,
That poorly satisfy our eyes,
More by your number than your light;
You common people of the skies,
What are you when the moon shall rise?'

'Oh, Peggy! I have had such a dinner!' cries Prue, in an ecstatic voice, drawing her sister away into a window as soon as the ladies have reached the drawing-room.

'Have you indeed?' replies Margaret distrustfully, and wilfully misunderstanding. 'Had you two helps of venison, like Mr. Evans?'

'Oh! I am not talking of the food!' rejoins the other impatiently. 'I do not know whether or not I ate anything; I do not think I did. But they were so amusing, I did not want to talk. He saw that I did not want to talk, so he let me sit and listen.'

'That was very considerate of him.'

'She was so amusing; she told us such funny stories about Mr. Harborough—no harm, you know, but rather making game of him. I do not know what Mrs. Evans meant by saying that she stuck at nothing. She said one or two things that I did not quite understand; but I am sure there was no harm in them.'

'Perhaps not.'

'And she was so kind to me,' pursues Prue, with enthusiasm; 'trying to draw me into the conversation, asking how long I had been out.'

But here the sisters' *tête-à-tête* is broken in upon by the high-pitched voice of the subject of their conversation.

'Who would like to come and see my children in bed? Do not all speak at once. H'm! nobody? This is hardly gratifying to a mother's feelings. Miss Lambton, I am sure you will come; you look as if you were fond of children. And you, Miss Prue, I shall insist upon your coming, whether you like it or not!'

So saying she puts her hand familiarly through the delighted little girl's arm, and walks off with her, Peggy following grudgingly. She has not the slightest desire to see the young Harboroughs, asleep or wake; though she has already had to defend her heart against an inclination to grow warm towards them, upon their rosy nightgowned entry before dinner. She has to defend it still more strongly, when, the nursery being reached, she sees them lying in the all-gentleness of perfect slumber in their cribs. Even that not innumerous class who dislike the waking child, the self-assertive, interrogative, climbing, bawling, smashing, waking child, grow soft-hearted at the sight of the little sleeping angel. Is this really Lady Betty bending over the little bed? recovering the outflung chubby arm from fear of cold, straightening the coverlets, and laying a light hand on the cool forehead? Peggy ought to be pleased by such a sign of grace; but when we have formed a conception of a person we are seldom quite pleased by the discovery of a fact that declines to square with that conception.

'You are very fond of them?' she says in a whisper, that, without her intending it, is interrogative; and through which pierces perhaps a tone of more surprise than she is herself aware of.

Lady Betty stares.

'Fond of them! Why, I am a perfect fool about them; at least I am about him! I do not care so much about her; she is a thorough Harborough! Did you ever see such a likeness as hers to her father? He' (with a regretful motion of the head toward the boy's bed) 'is a little like him too; but he has a strong look of me. When his eyes are open he is the image of me. I have a good mind to wake him to show you.'

'Oh, do not!' cries Margaret eagerly; 'it would be a sin!'

But the caution is needless. The mother had no real thought of breaking in upon that lovely slumber.

'Did you ever see such a duck?' says she rapturously, stooping over him; 'and his hand!'—taking the little plump fist softly into her own palm—'look at his hand! Will not he be a fine strong man? He can pummel his nurse already, cannot he, Harris? And not a day's illness in all his little life, bless him!'

Her eyes are almost moist as she speaks. The colour would no doubt come and go in her cheeks, only that unfortunately it has contracted the habit of never going, unless washed off by eau-de-Cologne. Against her will, Peggy feels her ill opinion melting away like mist; but happily, on her return to the drawing-room, she is able to restore it in its entirety. For no sooner have the men appeared than Lady Betty disappears. The exact moment of her flight and its companion Peggy has been unable to verify; as, at the moment when it must have taken place, she was buttonholed by Mrs. Evans on the subject of rose-rash, an unhandsome little disorder at present rioting among the Evans's ranks; and for which Peggy is supposed to have a specific. But though she did not actually see the person who shared Lady Betty's evasion, she is as sure as to who it was as if her very bodily eyes had looked upon him,—John Talbot, of course. With John Talbot she is now dishonestly philandering under the honest harvest-moon; to John Talbot she is now talking criminal nonsense, with those very lips that five minutes ago were laid upon the sacred velvet cheeks of her little children. With a curling lip Margaret looks round the room.

Why, Prue is missing too, and Freddy! Prue, the prone to quinsy, to throats, to delicacy of all kinds, straying over the deep-dewed grass without cloak or goloshes! For it would be expecting something more than human of her to suppose that when invited out by her admirer to hear all that the poets have said of Orion and Arcturus and the sister Pleiads, she should stop him in the full flow of his inspiration to inquire after what the Americans prettily call her 'gums.' If she will only have the sense to keep to the gravel paths! The elder sister has walked to the window, and now stands straining her eyes down the long alley to see if she can catch any glimpse of the little figure that, since its wailing infancy seventeen years ago, has caused her so many anxious hours. Shall she take upon herself the invidious office of spy, and follow her? or trust to the child's common sense, and to the possibility of her occasionally dropping her eyes from the enormous moon, now queening it in a great field of radiance above her head, to her own thin-shod feet? She is still hesitating when a voice, coming from behind her, makes her start.

'What a night!'

She turns to find that the utterer of this original ejaculation is none other than John Talbot. Is it possible that they have already returned from their lovers' ramble? But no! there is no sign of Lady Betty. It is clear that *he* could not have been the companion of her stroll. For the second time this evening Margaret has found herself in error.

'*You?*' she says, in a tone of rather vexed surprise.

'Why not?'

'I thought that you were out.'

'*I!* no!'

A moment's silence. Whom then could she have lured into her toils? Freddy? But Freddy must be with Prue. Mr. Evans? the diplomate? There is not much choice.

Her speculations are again broken in upon by the voice:

'Will not you take a turn?'

'I think not; that is to say'—correcting herself—'I shall only go a few steps, just to find my sister.'

'May I help you to find her?'

'I do not know why I should give you that trouble.'

A moment's silence, spent by both in reflections. This is the outcome of his.

'I do not think that I have done anything fresh.'

'Anything fresh?'

'Not since we parted; nothing to earn me a new set of snubs.'

She smiles a little. 'You have not had much time.'

'And I will not do anything fresh.' Then aside, 'I am blessed if I know what I did.'

'That is rather a rash engagement,' smiling again.

It is fortunate that her teeth are so good, for she shows a great many of them.

'But if I keep it I may come?' pertinaciously.

'I suppose so;' and out they step together.

It cannot be helped, but it is a little perverse of fate that, after all, it should be she who, in appearance at least, is the one to philander in the moonlight with this despiser of the marriage law. And whether or no it is his presence that brings her ill-luck, it is some time before she succeeds in the object of her search. The grounds are rather large, with meandering walks and great clumps of shrubs that hide them from one another.

Each of Prue's favourite resorts has been visited, but without result. The walled garden, hushed and sleeping; the trellised wall, where ancient brick has disappeared beneath the thronged faces, diversely dazzling, of the brown, orange, tawny and sulphur nasturtiums; the retired seat beneath the tulip-tree. All, all are empty. Nothing remains but the kiosk, and Peggy feels sure that Prue is not in the kiosk.

Thither, however, they bend their steps; but before they reach it a turn of the walk reveals to them two seated figures. One is certainly the Prue whom they seek; Prue sitting upon an uncomfortable garden bench, on which nobody ever sits—on which she herself has never sat before. But is it conceivable that, since dinner, Freddy can have doubled in size, can have lost all the hair off the top of his head, and have exchanged his cambric shirt-front and his diamond and turquoise studs for a double-breasted waistcoat buttoned to the chin?

With a feeling akin to stupefaction Peggy realises that it is Mr. Evans, and not Freddy, who is Prue's companion. As they approach he rises reluctantly. He had much rather that they had not come. Prue never wants to talk to him. She lets him sit and silently ruminate and dream beside her; a cigarette between his lips, and a blessed oblivion of dissenters, boys' schooling, girls' ugly faces, rickety baby, Christmas bills, invading his lulled brain. Prue neither rises nor changes her position. Her arms lie listlessly on her lap, and she is staring up at Cassiopeia, the one constellation for ever exalted above its fellows by having had Freddy Ducane for its exhibitor.

'Do you think you are quite wise to sit out here, with nothing over your shoulders?' asks Margaret, stooping over her sister, and speaking in a tone of such exceeding gentleness as positively to astound Talbot, who had not calculated upon the existence of such tones in a voice which has conscientiously employed only its harsher keys for his benefit.

'I am not cold,' replies Prue dully.

'How long have you been here? Long?'

'I do not know.'

'We were too comfortable to take note of time, were not we, Miss Prue?' says Mr. Evans, with a sigh for his lost peace. 'A southern moon, is not it?' to Talbot.

'Quite long enough, I am sure,' rejoined Peggy, putting her hand persuasively on her sister's shoulder. 'Come with us! come!'

Talbot cannot help hearing that 'Come!' even while exchanging original remarks upon the stars of the southern hemisphere with the vicar; nor can he further help speculating as to whether, if that 'Come!' were addressed to himself, and were inviting him to follow it to Lapland, to Hong Kong, or to some yet hotter place, he should have the force of mind to decline. But at all events Prue has.

'I had rather stay here,' replies she, *sotto voce*, with an accent of miserable irritation. 'Why should I come? Nobody wants me; nobody misses me! Please leave me alone.'

There is nothing for it but to comply. With a heavier heart than that with which she reached it, Margaret leaves the bench and its ill-sorted occupants. She takes little heed as to the direction of her steps until she finds herself and her companion approaching the kiosk, whence is plainly audible the sound of voices, which, as they advance nearer to it, grows hushed. It is too dark to see into the interior, as above the little gimcrack temple, memorial of the bad taste of fifty years ago, rises a brotherhood of tall, spruce firs that project their shade over and before it.

Just in front of it Talbot stops her to point out to her a shooting-star that is darting its trail of glory through the immensities of space. Has he not heard those voices—he must have been deaf if he did not—nor observed that

marked succeeding silence? He shows no sign of uneasiness
  or curiosity. His eye is resting apparently, with a
calmer enjoyment than she can bring to it, on the gold mist rolling its gauzy-
billows in the hollows of the park.

It is only to those who come to her with a tranquil and disengaged mind that
the great mother gives the real key of her treasure-houses; and Peggy's mind
to-night is too ruffled to give her any claim to the great endowment.

They are standing silently side by side, when a noise, proceeding from the
inside of the kiosk, makes itself audible—a noise apparently intended to
counterfeit the mewing of a cat, followed by the crowing of a most
improbable cock.

Talbot does not even turn his head.

'We are not at all frightened, and not much amused,' he says, in a clear
matter-of-fact voice.

'You had not an idea that we were here, had you?' cries Lady Betty, springing
out of the temple, followed by Freddy Ducane. 'Did not I mew well? and did
not Freddy crow badly? Freddy, you have no more idea of crowing than a
carp.'

'I can do better than that,' replies Freddy, in self-defence. 'I am not in voice
to-night.'

'But you had not a notion that we were here, had you?' repeats Lady Betty
pertinaciously.

'As we had heard you talking at the top of your voices for half a mile before
we came up to you, we had some slight inkling of it.'

Peggy wonders whether the cold dryness of his tone is as patent to the person
to whom it is addressed as it is to herself. She supposes that it is, since she
instantly takes possession of him; and, under the pretext of showing him a
plant which can scarcely be distinguishable from its neighbours under the
colourless moonlight, walks him off into a dusky alley.

Margaret remains alone with Freddy.

> '"Why so dull and mute, young sinner?
> Prithee, why so mute?"'

says he familiarly, approaching her.

She looks him fully and gravely in the face. Most people find it difficult to
look at Freddy Ducane without smiling. Peggy feels no such inclination.
Between her and this image of youth and sunshine there rises another image

—a poor little image, to whom this gay weather-cock gives its weather—a little image that expands or shrinks as this all-kissing zephyr blows warm or cold upon it.

'Because I have nothing to say, I suppose,' replies she shortly.

'Come with me to the walled garden'—in a wheedling voice—'and show me the stars.'

'Thank you, I can see them quite well here.'

> "'My pretty Peg, my pretty Peg,
> Ah, never look so shy!'"

cries he, breaking into a laugh, which she does not echo.

'I am not your pretty Peg; and I have told you several times that I will not be called "Peg."'

'*Peggy*, then. Personally, I prefer *Peg*; but it is a matter of opinion. Peggy, are you aware that you have been poaching?'

'I do not know what you mean.' But she does.

'Her ladyship did not much like it, I can tell you,' continues he delightedly. 'She manifested distinct signs of uneasiness. I could not keep her quiet, though I went through all my little tricks for her. She *would* make those ridiculous noises; and she whipped him off pretty quickly, did not she? Ah, Peggy'—tenderly—'you would have done better to have kept to me! *I* would not have left you in the lurch.'

To this she deigns no answer.

'Where is Prue?' asks he, a moment later, with an easy change of topic. 'What have you done with Prue?'

'I have done nothing with her,' rather sadly.

'You have sent her home with her nurse to bed, I suppose?' suggests he reproachfully. 'I sometimes think that you are a little hard upon Prue.'

Hard upon Prue! She, whose one thought, waking and sleeping, is how best to put her strong arm round that fragile body and weakling soul, so as to shield them from the knocks of this rough world! This, too, from him, who has introduced the one element of suffering it has ever known into Prue's little life.

'Am I?' she answers quietly; but her cheek burns.

'There is no one that suits me so well as Prue,' says the young man sentimentally, looking up to the sky.

> "'She's like the keystone of an arch,
> That doth consummate beauty;
> She's like the music of a march,
> That maketh joy of duty!'"

Peggy's eye relents. He may mean it—may be speaking truth—it is not likely, as he seldom does so; but after all, the greatest liars must, during their lives, speak more truth than lies. One is prone to believe what one wishes, and he *may* mean it.

'There is no one that I am so fond of as I am of Prue,' pursues he, with a quiver in his voice.

'You have an odd way of showing it sometimes,' says she, in a softened tone.

'Are you alluding to *that*?' asks he, glancing carelessly over his shoulder at the kiosk. 'Pooh! I hated it. I shall get milady to pull it down some day. I was so glad when you and Talbot came up: it was so dark, and I felt the earwigs dropping on my head.'

'Then why did you go there?' inquires she.

He bursts into a laugh, from which sentiment and quiver are miles away.

'The woman tempted me; at least' (seeing his companion's mouth taking a contemptuous upward curve at this mode of expression)—'at least, she seemed to expect it. I always like to do what people seem to expect.'

And Margaret's heart sinks.

CHAPTER V

'To one that has been long in city pent,
'Tis very sweet to gaze upon the fair
And open face of heaven—to breathe a prayer
Full in the smile of the blue firmament.'

It is the next day. John Talbot has spent a very happy morning. He is a countryman at heart. Fate has put him into the Foreign Office, and made him a great man's secretary, and tied him by the leg to London for ten months out of the twelve; but the country, whose buttercups brightened his childhood, keeps his heart—the country, with its little larks upsoaring from its brown furrows; with its green and its russet gowns; with its good, sweet, innocent noises, and its heavenly smells. He has been lying on the flat of his back on the sward, with his hands under his head, staring in luxurious idleness up at the sky, and listening to the robin's song—in August scarcely anybody but the redbreast sings—and to the pleasant swish of the wind among the lime-tops. Lying there alone on the flat of his back—that is to say, at first. Afterwards he has plenty of company. Not, indeed, that either his host or his fellow-guests trouble him much. From the lair he has chosen he has a view of his lady's window. It is true that he looks but seldom towards it, nor do its carefully closed casements and drawn curtains hold out much hope of a descent of the sleeping goddess within. Lady Roupell lets it be understood that she does not wish to be seen or spoken to till luncheon; and the rest are dispersed, he neither knows nor cares whither. And yet he has companions. They are in the act of being escorted out to walk by their nurses when they catch sight of him. In an instant they bear down upon him as fast as their fat legs will carry them.

'Just think!' cries Lily, beginning to shout at the top of her voice long before she reaches him—'just think what Franky has been doing! Is not he a naughty boy? He took the water-can and emptied it over Nanny's skirt! She says she will ask mammy to whip him!'

'Which mammy will most certainly decline to do,' says Talbot *sotto voce* to himself.

He has raised himself on his elbow, the more safely to receive their onslaught. He is aware of an idiosyncrasy of Miss Harborough's—that of narrating hideous crimes as having been committed by her little brother, which have in reality been executed by herself.

'If it was Franky who upset the water-can, how is it that it is your frock which is wet?' asks he judicially.

27

She does not answer, beyond putting her head affectedly on one side, and rubbing her shoulder against her ear.

'Are you sure that it was not you, and not Franky?'

Instantly, with the greatest ease and affability, she acknowledges that it was she; and the nurses at that moment coming up, she is about to be walked off for chastisement, when weakly interceded for by Talbot, who has the further lunacy to request that both children may be left in his charge. After that he has a very eventful morning. He is in turn a pony, a giraffe, a hyæna, a flamingo (unhappily for him the little Harboroughs have lately visited the Zoological Gardens), a rabbit (about the natural history and domestic life of which animal he hears some very startling facts), and the captain of a robber band. Finally, he has to take part in a terrible game—the one most dreaded by their family of all in the little Harborough repertoire—Ingestre Hall destroyed by fire, done with bricks. And the odd thing is that he likes it—likes it better than Downing Street and the great statesman.

When the luncheon gong sounds he can hardly realise that it is two o'clock. He is so much dishevelled by his transmigrations—which, indeed, have been as numerous as Buddha's—that, after having repaired the injuries to his toilette, he finds that everybody is already in the dining-room—finds the inevitable chair left vacant for him beside Lady Betty. He has sat by Lady Betty through so many luncheons and dinners that it has lost the gloss of novelty, and they speak to each other scarcely more than a husband and wife would do. It is her voice that he hears prevailing over those of the rest of the company as he enters the room, for she has not Cordelia's gift.

'Lambton? Are they any relation to Lord Durham?'

'I do not think so,' replies the hostess carelessly. 'Their father was a small squire in these parts, who over-farmed himself, and died very much out at elbows. And their mother—well, their mother was nothing but a very poor creature' (with a shrug), 'who was always fancying herself ill, and whom nobody believed until she proved it by dying! Ha! ha! Poor soul! I do not think that anybody cried much, except Peggy; she cried her eyes out.'

'Not quite out,' thinks Talbot, remembering the severe blue darts that shot at him over-night; and to his own soul, at this testimony to her tender-heartedness, he says, 'Nice Peggy!'

'Which was Peggy?' asks Mr. Harborough, looking up from his cutlet; 'the big one? Yes? I like Peggy. I do not know when I have seen such a good-looking girl.'

His wife bursts into a laugh.

'I knew that Ralph would admire her. Did not I tell you so?' turning to Talbot. 'She is just his style; they cannot be too big for Ralph; he admires by avoirdupois weight.'

'As to that, my dear,' retorts Mr. Harborough tranquilly, 'we all know that you are not much in the habit of commending your own sex; but I think you will find that I am not alone in my opinion.'

There is a moment's silence. Men are cowardly things. Not one of them is found to take up the cudgels for poor Margaret.

'She would be good-looking perhaps if she were bled,' pursues Lady Betty; 'she looks so aggressively healthy!'

'You cannot make the same complaint of poor Prue, at any rate,' says Lady Roupell, in a voice that betrays some slight signs of dissatisfaction with her guest's observations, for she likes her Lambtons.

'No; she is a high-coloured little skeleton!' rejoins Betty, looking with pensive ill-nature at her plate. 'What a pity that they cannot strike a balance! The one is as much too small as the other is too big; they are like a shilling and sixpence!'

And having thus peaceably demolished the sisters, whom nobody defends, she passes smilingly to another subject.

After luncheon Talbot is lounging before the hall door, with a cigarette, thinking, with a sort of subdued disgust (engendered, perhaps, by the fragment of conversation but now related) of himself, his surroundings, and his life in general, when he is joined by his hostess, dressed for walking—as villainously dressed as only a female millionnaire dares be: a frieze jacket like a man's, a billycock hat set on the top of her cap, and a stout stick in her hand. She tells him that she is going down to the farm to see how the stacks are getting on, and he strolls along aimlessly beside her. He knows that he ought not—he knows that his unwritten laws bind him for all the afternoon to the side of the hammock where Lady Betty is swinging; and yet he goes on strolling along by the side of an old woman to whom no laws, either God's straight or man's crooked ones, bind him, simply opening his nostrils to the pungent perfume of the hot bracken, and his eyes to the sight of the gentle doves watching him from under Queen Elizabeth's oak.

Arrived at the farm, he is slowly making up his mind to return to his duty, when his companion addresses him:

'Will you go a message for me?'

'With all the pleasure in life,' replies he, a slight misgiving crossing his mind as to how he will be received on his return after so prolonged a truancy.

'It is only just to run over to the Lambtons'.'

'The Lambtons'?'

'Yes—Peggy and Prue.'

'Of course, of course; but—but how am I to find them?'

'I thought you knew the way; I took you there last year. You cannot miss it; a hundred yards down the road'—(pointing)—'just outside the park; a little old red house. You cannot miss it.'

She is turning away back to her ricks and her reapers when he recalls her.

'But what am I to say when I get there?'

'Pooh?' she says, laughing; 'what a head I have! I forgot the message. Tell Peggy we are all coming down to-morrow afternoon, Sunday, as usual; and bid her have plenty of muffins for us.'

As he walks along the road he ponders with himself whether, if Margaret looks at him with the unaccountable austerity of last night, he shall ever be able to give her that insolent order for unlimited muffins.

Lady Roupell was right. There is no missing the way. He almost wishes that there was. He has rung the bell—how much too loudly! It seems as if it would never stop clanging. And yet the odd thing is that he has produced no result by his violence; nor does the stout Annian door show any signs of rolling back on its hinges. He stares up at the face of the house; every window wide open, and above each a little century-and-a-half-old decoration of Cupids and cornucopias, and apples and grapes; a broken arch over the relentless door, and on either hand of it a great bush of traveller's joy, with its pretty welcoming name; and a Virginia creeper, in its dazzling decay, showing the stained and faded red brick what red can be. Is that one of the windows of the drawing-room on the right-hand side—that window into which he has so much difficulty in hindering himself from looking—with the green earthenware cruches and the odd-shaped majolica pot crammed with corn marigolds on the window-ledge? It is certainly very strange. He rings again, more mildly, but still very distinctly, without any further result than before. A third time; the same silence. A ridiculous idea crosses his mind that perhaps Margaret has seen from an upper window who her visitor is, and has forbidden any of her household to admit him; and, though he dismisses it as incredible, he is so disheartened by it, and by his thrice-repeated failures to attract attention, that he is turning away towards the entrance-gate, when, at last, something happens. A figure appears, flying round the corner of the house; a figure so out of breath, so dishevelled, so incoherent, that it is some seconds before he recognises in it the younger Miss Lambton—the 'high-coloured little skeleton,' as his gentle lady had sweetly baptized her. High-coloured she is now with a vengeance!

'Oh! it is you, is it?' she cries pantingly. He has never been presented to her, nor have they ever exchanged a sentence; but, in great crises like the present, the social code goes to the wall. 'Oh, I wonder could you help us? we are in such trouble!' Her tone is so *navré* that his heart stands still. Peggy is dead, of course. 'The fox has got out!' pursues she, sobbing; 'got out of his house, and we do not know what has become of him!'

'*The fox!*' repeats he, relieved of his apprehensions, and with a flash of self-reproach—'of course it was a *fox*! of course it was not a *badger*!'

Surprise at this observation checks Prue's tears.

'No!' says she; 'who ever thought it was?'

And at that moment another tumultuous figure appears round the corner of the house. This time it is Margaret; Margaret nearly as breathless, as scarlet, as tearful as Prue. On catching sight of Talbot she pulls herself into a walk, and with a laudable, instantaneous struggle to look cold and neat and repellent, she holds out her hand.

'I hope you have not been waiting long,' she says formally. (The little unconquerable pants between each word betray her.) 'Did you ring often? I am afraid that there was nobody in the house; we were all, servants and all, about the fields and garden. Oh!' (nature and sorrow growing too strong for her) 'have you heard of our misfortune?'

'That I have,' replies Talbot, throwing as much sympathetic affection as that organ is capable of into his voice; 'and I am so sorry!'

'He has never been out except upon a chain in all his life, poor little fellow!' says Peggy, sinking dejectedly upon a large old-fashioned round stone ball, one of which ornaments each side of the door. 'He will know no more than a baby how to take care of himself!'

'Have you searched everywhere?'

'Everywhere.'

'The hen-house?'

'Yes.'

'Stables?'

'Yes.'

31

'Coach-house?'

'Yes.'

'Hayloft?'

'Yes.'

'Boot-hole?'

'Yes.'

'Cellar?' growing wild in his suggestions. 'Once I knew a hard-pressed fox run right into a cellar.'

'Even there.'

Talbot is at the end of his ingenuity. But at least there is one thing gained—she has spoken to him as to a fellow-sufferer.

This is no great advance perhaps, since were a new Deluge to cover the earth, which of us would not cling round the neck of a parricide if he were on a higher ledge of rock than we?

'If he is once away in the open,' says Margaret desperately, 'he is sure to get into a trap or be worried by a dog; he has no experience of life. Oh, poor little man!'

Her eyes brim up, and her voice breaks.

Prue has fallen, limp and whimpering, upon the other stone ball. Talbot stands between the mourners.

'Come,' says he stoutly, 'let us be doing something. Let us rout out every possible hole and corner once again; and if he does not turn up, I will go and tell the game-keepers and the farm-labourers to be on the look-out for him.'

Something in the manly energy of his tone puts new life into the dispirited girls, and the search recommences.

The procession is swelled by the three maids, with their aprons over their heads; by the stable-boy, and by Jacob with a pitchfork. It is led by Talbot, whose zeal sometimes degenerates into ostentation, as when he insists on exploring chinks into which the leanest lizard could not squeeze itself, and on running his stick through little heaps of mown grass where not a field-mouse could lie perdue.

The party has gradually dispersed in different directions, and Talbot finds himself alone in the tool-house, which has been already twice explored. In one corner stands a pile of pots of all sizes, reaching almost to the roof, and with its monotony enlivened by a miscellaneous stock of rakes, pea-sticks, and scythes leaning against it. The whole erection looks too solid to admit of its being a hiding-place for anything, but it is possible that there may be a hollow behind it.

After prying about for a few moments on his knees, he finds indeed an aperture, which has been hidden by a pendent bit of bass-matting—an aperture large enough to admit the passage of a small animal. To this aperture he applies his eye. What does he see? Two things like green lamps glaring at him from the darkness. Aha! he is here!

CHAPTER VI

Talbot looks round apprehensively. Heaven send that no one, neither meddlesome Jacob, nor gaping boy, nor screaming maids, nor—worst of all— Peggy herself, may come up till he has got at his prey, may come up to rob him of the glory of safe recovery and restoration. In his haste he incautiously thrusts in his arm, feels something warm and woolly, but feels too, at the same instant, a smart stinging sensation as of little teeth fastening on his finger. He draws his hand away quickly, and shakes it, for the pain is acute.

'You are there, my young friend, that is very clear.'

But he cannot be stopped by such a trifle! He hastily binds up his wound with his pocket-handkerchief, and begins quickly to enlarge the opening. As it grows, he has to fill it with his body, to obviate the danger of the fox making a dash past him. In the course of his labours, several little pots fall about his ears; a dislodged spade-handle gives him a brisk blow on the shoulder; old cobwebs get into his mouth. But he is rewarded at last. Through the breach he has made daylight pours in, and shows him a little red form crouched up against the wall, and showing all its dazzling white teeth in a frenzy of fear. Poor little beast! Probably some indistinct memory of the cruel hounds that tore its mother limb from limb is giving its intensity of terror to that grin. But if he is suffering from fear, he is also perhaps at present a little calculated to inspire it. It just crosses Talbot's mind how exceedingly unpleasant it will be, if, in these very close quarters, the companion of his *tête-à-tête* makes for his nose. There is nothing for it but to take the initiative. It occurs to him that he may have a pair of dog-skin gloves in his pocket; and this on examination, proving to be the case, he puts them on. The right-hand glove will of course not go over the handkerchief that binds his finger. It—the handkerchief—has therefore to be removed, and the blood spurts out afresh. What matter? Thus protected, without further delay he makes a bold grab, past that grinning, gleaming row of fangs, at the scruff of the fox's neck, and having got a good grip of it, proceeds to back out of the hole, dragging his booty after him; the booty snapping, and holding on to the ground with all his four pads in agonised protestation.

To back out of a hole, with all the blood in your body running to your head, smothered in cobwebs, with dusty knees and barked knuckles—this is hardly the way in which a man would wish to present himself to a woman with whom he is anxious to stand well. And yet it is under these conditions that Peggy, at whose feet he finds himself on having completed his retrograde movement, first sees anything in him to admire.

'So you have found him?' cries she, dropping on her knees, and turning a radiant face towards the procession on all-fours which has now quite emerged into the daylight; 'behind the pots? and we thought that we had searched everywhere so carefully. How clever of you!—but' (her tone changing) 'you have hurt him!' her glance falling on a few drops of Talbot's blood which, stealing from under the glove, have dropped on the fox's fur.

'I do not think so,' replies the young man drily; but he does not more directly claim his own property, nor protest against the—as it happens—rather ingenious injustice of this accusation.

'Then he has hurt you!' says she, drawing this obvious inference; and her blue eye darts like lightning at his hand. 'He has bitten you! oh, how shocking of him! Not badly?'

'He mistook me for a hound, I suppose,' replies John, smiling.

'He was determined that you should not forget a second time that he was a fox,' says she, breaking into a charming mischievous laugh, lapsing, however, at once again into grave solicitude; 'but it is not a bad bite, is it? Let me look! Here, Prue! take this little villain home, and shut him up, and let us hear no more about him!'

Prue complies, and the two young people remain in the tool-house alone.

'Let me look,' says she, beginning very delicately to pull off the glove, so as not to hurt him. 'How did he manage to get at you through this thick glove?'

'I did not put it on till afterwards,' replies Talbot. 'Of whom does that trait remind you? If it is Simple Simon, do not mind saying so!'

They both laugh.

'But it is a dreadful bite!' says she, holding the wounded finger with two or three of her slight yet strong ones—fingers a little embrowned by much practical gardening, and down which he now feels little shivers of compunction and concern running. 'Almost to the bone! oh, poor finger! I feel so guilty. Come with me into the house, and let me tie it up for you.'

He is in no great hurry to have it tied up. He likes the dusty tool-house, and is not at all alarmed at the sight of his own gore; but, consoling himself with the reflection that Prue will probably pass some time in weeping over and fondling their amiable pet, and that he has a good chance of, at all events, some further *tête-à-tête* over the rag and oil-silk, he follows her docilely, and presently finds himself inside the little room into which he had had so much ado to hinder himself from peering during his long kicking his heels at the hall door.

It proves to be not a drawing-room after all—to have more of the character and informality of a little sitting-hall; a room where dogs may jump on the chairs with as valid a right as Christians; a room with an oak settle by the chimney-corner, and a great cage full of twittering finches in a sunny window, and into which half the flowers of the field seem to have walked, and colonised its homely vases; a room with nothing worth twopence-halfpenny in it, and that yet is sweet and lovable.

He has not many minutes in which to make his explorations, for she is promptly back with her appliances, and silently binding round his finger her bit of linen that smells of lavender.

As she stoops over his hand he can look down on the top of her head, and admire her parting—a thing which not many ladies possess nowadays. Hers is as straight as a die; and on each side of that narrow white road rises the thick fine hair, bright and elastic.

It is many years since Betty has owned a parting. On the other hand, she has two very nice toupets—a morning and an evening one. Talbot has once or twice seen one of these toupets off duty, and has regretted his knowledge that it came off and on. Well, there is nothing about Peggy that comes off and on.

How quickly and daintily she has dressed his wound, and—oh! if here is not Prue already back again!

'Have you shut him safely in?' looking up from her nearly finished task.

'Yes.'

'And given him his dinner?'

'Yes; but he will not eat it. I think he is seriously vexed; he tried to bite me, too!'

Talbot laughs.

'What could have made you choose such a pet?'

'We did not exactly choose him,' replies Margaret gravely; 'he was sent to us; all the rest of the litter were killed. He was the only one the huntsman could save. He brought him to show us. He was a mere ball of fluff then. One could not turn away a poor little orphan ball of fluff from one's door, could one?'

'He was a very tiresome orphan then, as he always has been since,' says Prue drily. 'No one but Peggy would have been bothered with him; he was far more trouble than a baby. She had him,'—turning towards Talbot—'to sleep in her room for a whole fortnight, and got up every two hours all through the night to feed him.'

Margaret reddens.

'He would have died else!'

'But no other person on earth would have had the patience, would they?' cries Prue, warming with her theme.

'Prue!' says Peggy severely, 'is my trumpeter dead, and are you applying for the situation?'

At this moment the door opens, and one of the three neat maids whom John has already seen careering about the pleasure-grounds in pursuit of the fox, enters with a tea-tray.

The sight of a covered dish of hot cakes recalls to Talbot the original object of his visit.

'Oh, by the bye, I was forgetting! I have a message for you from Lady Roupell.'

'Have you?'

She is standing, straight and lithe as a young poplar, by the tea-table, brandishing a brown teapot in her hand.

'Yes. She bid me tell you that they are all coming down to see you to-morrow afternoon.'

Is it his imagination that a sudden slight stiffening comes over her as he speaks—a stiffening that seems to extend even to the friendly teapot?

'And also,' continues he, not much liking his errand, and hastening to get it over, 'she desired me to say that, as she is particularly fond of muffins, and as yours are an exceptionally good——'

'Are you sure that she said all that?' interrupts Prue, with a sceptical gaiety. 'She is not generally so polite. She generally says only, "Girls, I'm coming; have lots of muffins!"'

Talbot laughs, convicted.

'Perhaps that was nearer the mark.'

'I am so glad that they are all coming,' pursues Prue, with excitement. 'Will Lady Betty come? Oh, I hope so! How beautiful she is! What eyes! What a colour!'

Talbot looks sheepish. The alarmingly increased volume and splendour of his Betty's carnations of late have been the cause of several sharp altercations between him and her. And yet he cannot doubt that the child says it in all good faith. It is not at the corners of *her* mouth that that tiny malicious smile is lurking. To him how much pleasanter a topic was the fox! He relishes the change in the conversation so little that he scalds his throat in his haste to drink his tea and be gone.

As he walks home across the park he entertains himself with the reflection how he shall account to Betty for his finger.

CHAPTER VII

Next day is

> 'The day that comes between
> A Saturday and Monday,'

as the pretty old song obliquely puts it. Such of the parish as are not Dissenters, drunkards, or the mothers of young babies (it does not leave a very large margin), have been to morning church. The Vicarage, the Manor, and the Red House have all been represented. The Vicarage sits immediately below the pulpit, so that the preacher's eloquence may soar on stronger pinions, upborne by the sight of the nine ugly faces to whom he has given the light of day. The Manor, with its maids, footmen, and stables, spreads half over the aisle; and in one of its pews the Red House, pewless itself, is allowed to take its two seats.

On this particular morning Peggy's devotions are a good deal distempered by the fact of her having Miss Harborough for a neighbour—Miss Harborough without her nurse; Miss Harborough wriggling a good deal, bringing out of her pocket things new and old; and finally (the devil having entered into her), when the hymn begins, striking up in rivalry, 'Over the Garden Wall.' As, however, no one perceives this piece of iniquity except Peggy, who feigns not to hear it, she desists, and adopts instead the less reprehensible but still somewhat embarrassing course of closely copying Peggy's every smallest gesture—unbuttoning her glove, turning a page of her prayer-book, whipping out her pocket-handkerchief at the very same instant as her unwitting model. It is even a relief when this flattering if servile imitation gives way to loud stage-whispers, such as, 'Franky has got his book upside down;' 'Don't you wish you were as tall as John Talbot?' 'Evans is all in white;' 'Did you hear me say the Lord's Prayer?' etc. etc.

It is afternoon now. You need not be either a Dissenter, a drunkard, or a mother, not to go to church in the afternoon. Nobody goes—nobody, that is, except Mr. Evans and the children whom he catechises, asking them questions which they never answer, and which he would be very much embarrassed if they did. Luncheon is over.

'Let us give them all the slip,' says Lady Betty. 'I know what milady's Sunday walks are—she does not spare one a turnip or a pigsty; and as to going to tea with the Lambtons, I say, like the man in the Bible, "I prithee have me excused."'

Talbot, to whom this is addressed, follows her in silence, to where, beneath a great lime-tree only just out of flower, hangs the hammock, spread the wolf-skins, stand the wicker-chairs and tables, the iced drinks, and the Sunday papers.

'Now we'll be happy!' says Betty, sitting down sideways on the hammock, and adroitly whisking her legs in after her. 'As soon as milady's back is turned I will have a cigarette, and you shall talk me to sleep. By the bye,' with a slight tinge of umbrage in her tone, 'your conversation of late has rather tended to produce that effect.'

'And what better effect could it produce?' asks John ironically. 'I sometimes wish that I could get some one to talk me to sleep for good and all!'

'How tiresome!' cries his fair one, not paying much heed to this lugubrious aspiration, and feeling in her pocket. 'I have left my cigarette-case in the house; go, like a good fellow, and get it for me. Ask Julie for it.'

He goes with the full docility of a pack-horse or a performing poodle, and on his way indoors meets his young host, sent by his aunt in search of the truants, and to whom he imparts Betty's change of plans.

'So you are not coming!' says Freddy, in a broken-hearted voice, throwing himself into a chair. In his soul he is rather glad.

'So I'm not coming!' repeats she, mimicking his tone.

'May not I stay too?' travelling over the sward in his chair nearer the hammock, and lightly touching the pendent white hand.

'What! and leave your little anatomical specimen lamenting?' cries she ill-naturedly.

He winces.

'I do not know to whom you are alluding. But may not I stay?' with a slight tremble in his voice.

'Of course you may,' replies she cheerfully. 'Who hinders you?—stay by all means!'

He looks confused. He has not the slightest wish to stay. He has only followed his habitual impulse to say what he imagines to be the agreeable thing—an impulse that has already led him into many quagmires, and will lead him into many more.

'I would not be so selfish,' he says with a charming smile of abnegation; 'I know my place better,' with an expressive glance at the back of the disappearing John. And, suiting the action to the word, he disappears too; when she screams after him:

'Give my love to the sack of potatoes and the skeleton!'

By the time that Talbot returns with the cigarette-case the coast is quite clear, and Betty is at liberty to light her cigarette as soon as she pleases; a liberty of which she immediately avails herself.

There is a prospect before them of an unbroken *tête-à-tête* until eight o'clock. With how deep a joy and elation ought this reflection to fill him! A year ago it would have done so. To-day with how leaden a foot does the stable clock pace from quarter to quarter. And yet there is no lack of talk. He himself, indeed, does not contribute much; but Betty is in a fine flow. She favours him—not for the first time by many—with several unamiable traits in Mr. Harborough's character, with the dreadful things her dearest friend said of her last week— faithfully reported to her by her second dearest—together with various shady particulars in the personal history of both friends. She gives him the latest details of an internecine broil between two ladies, both candidates for the favour of a great personage. She makes some good jokes upon the death of a relation, and the approaching collapse of an intimate acquaintance's reputation; and, in short, dots her *i*'s and crosses her *t*'s, and calls a spade a spade, and enjoys herself famously. And *he*? He listens in a sort of wonder.

This, then, is what he has for five years sacrificed his career to. This, then—to be alone with this—he has manœuvred for invitations, planned risky rendezvous, abandoned the hope of home's sanctities. A heavy leaden sickness seems to steal over him. He is recalled to the present by a tone of very decided indignation in his lady's voice—his lady, who, by an easy transition, has slipped from scandal to the hardly dearer or less dear subject of clothes.

'Shepherd is a beast! Just fancy! he sent me out deer-stalking in a silk skirt! Why, you are not listening to a word I say!'

It is in vain for him to protest. On cross-examination he shows so culpable an ignorance as to who Shepherd is—though heaven knows that in his day he has heard enough of the great woman's tailor—that her ladyship's anger is heightened instead of appeased.

'You certainly are not amusing to-day,' cries she, flouncing out of the hammock.

'I never was much of a Jack Pudding,' replies he wearily. 'Was I ever amusing? I do not recollect it. I think that I left that to you.'

His tone is so dry that she reddens even under her rouge.

'Perhaps it is your finger that pains you too much,' says she, looking round her armoury for a weapon of offence, and rather cleverly hitting upon this one. 'We have never got to the bottom of that mysterious wound yet. I believe it is somehow connected with your Blowsabella. Perhaps you became too attentive, and she had to set her dog or her cat upon you in self-defence.'

There is such a horrible caricature of the truth in this supposition, and her tone is so insulting, that he turns pale, and it is a moment or two before he can speak; then:

'Do not you think it would be a good thing if you gave up this sort of joke?' he asks, with a rather dangerous quietness. 'They are not very ladylike. Had you not better leave them to Julie?'

He has no sooner finished these sentences than Betty bursts into tears. She had imagined that she was amusing him as much as herself; and, indeed, he has often before laughed heartily at things not less ill-natured or more harmless; now the disgust and *ennui* of his tone are a disagreeable revelation to her. And besides, as I have before observed, her paint is of that quality that she may confidently afford herself a few tears. But even if it were not to be done with safety she must give way to them now, anger and mortification forcing them from her eyes.

Now if there is one thing that a waning lover dreads more than a quarrel, it is the reconciliation that follows it. So, by the time that Betty has sobbed, and wished herself and him dead, and announced her intention of telling Mr. Harborough, and going away to-morrow and taking Freddy Ducane with her, and been apologised to and comforted, her admirer is reduced to such a pitch of flat lassitude of mind that there is no bidding of hers which he would not tamely execute. He therefore acquiesces dumbly when, her smiles being at length restored, she proposes that they shall go to tea with the Lambtons after all. They can easily overtake the others, and perhaps it will be more amusing than sitting here quarrelling—'though there is a certain charm in quarrelling too!' she adds sentimentally.

As he cannot echo this, he pretends not to hear it. His mind is occupied by the doubt, which he is unable to resolve, whether her proposal is dictated by a generous desire to make an *amende*, or by further malice. She is perfectly capable of either. They have not a very pleasant walk. Betty's preposterous heels turn under her at every three steps; and though she always says that she is very fond of the country, she generally forgets to look at it, while John loves it too heartily and deeply dear to say anything about it to such ears.

As they near the Red House his heart sinks lower and lower. He has never had the moral courage to confess his yesterday's visit, and the episode that marked it. There are ninety-nine chances to one against his escaping without some inquiry after his finger, some mention of the fox, some chance allusion which will betray him. And then? what then? Why, another quarrel, another reconciliation. Pah! No; sooner than face that he will be telegraphed for back to Downing Street.

They are not kept waiting at the door at all to-day, but are at once ushered through the house into the garden, where they are told that they will find Miss Lambton.

As she hears their footsteps she looks up, and sees them approaching—Betty stepping smartly ahead, and Talbot following sheepishly behind. He is conscious of there being a sort of false air of man and wife about them—a happy couple spending their Sunday afternoon in parading their domestic bliss before their friends. By an intuition that he would far rather have been without, he sees the same idea passing through Margaret's mind, and reflected in a sudden cloud, and as sudden honest redness on her face. Certainly any stranger coming in upon the scene would be more likely to credit him with the honour of being Lady Betty's owner than he would the insignificant figure kneeling and mysteriously bending over something on the top of the stone steps that lead down a gentle bank from the gravel walk to the sward and the vivid August borders—a figure whose manœuvres are interestedly watched by the rest of the company, and which does not take the trouble to turn its head an inch at the sound of its wife's voice.

'We have been quarrelling,' cries Betty, with a sprightly candour which grates horribly upon Talbot, 'and we have come to you to help us to keep the peace. Oh!'—making a face—'so Ralph is showing you some of his tricks. I would not look at them if I were you. He will never leave you any peace if you encourage him! The whole of the first year of our married life he spent in teaching me to tie knots in my pocket-handkerchief and swallow spoons; and I have never found that I have been much the better for either.'

Not a shadow of a smile shows itself upon Margaret's face, but Prue has smiles enough for the two.

'He is showing us how to mesmerise a hen!' cries she delightedly. 'Oh! it is *so* clever! I cannot think how he does it!'

In effect, upon closer examination, Mr. Harborough is seen to be grappling with a large barn-door fowl, which is squawking a good deal, and resisting his efforts to hold her nose down upon the stone step; while Freddy, with a piece of chalk, draws a straight line from her beak to the end of the step.

'You must none of you speak!' says Mr. Harborough, with authority. 'If you talk, you will prevent her going off into the mesmeric sleep.'

Dead silence. The protesting squalls have ceased. After a few moments the hands that hold her are lightly removed. She lies quite still.

'There!' says the operator, in a tone of subdued triumph; 'she will not awake until the chalk line is rubbed out. Curious, is not it?'

But even as he speaks Dame Partlet, to give him the lie, has struggled to her legs, and lustily screeching, makes off with her longest stride and fluttered wings. Instantly the whole company gives chase. John Talbot, Mr. Harborough, Freddy Ducane, Margaret, Prue, even Chinese-footed Betty, two collies, and a terrier, who have been standing officiously round, all off in full cry at once. Across the garden-beds; through Jacob's best potatoes; over the sunk fence into the open park, helter-skelter they go—John leading, closely followed by Freddy and Mr. Harborough, while the three women tear madly behind.

John has got her! Not at all! She has slipped between his fingers, and he has measured his length on the grass! Then it is Freddy's turn, but she runs between his legs, and down goes he too. Certainly she is a gallant hen! John is up again, and now both he and Peggy make an unsuccessful lunge at her as she passes; and if it had not been for Mink, who adroitly pinned her by the wing—a feat for which he was afterwards much blamed, though they profited by his discourtesy—they would probably still have been tumbling over each other in pursuit of that speckled hen.

At the moment when Peggy and John had made their joint and futile grab at the object of their chase, her hand had come with some violence into contact with his wounded one. Instantly she is off her guard, and down from her stilts.

'Did I hurt your finger?' very anxiously.

'Not in the least, thanks.'

'Are you quite sure?'

'Quite.'

'But I am afraid that I must have done.'

'I assure you no! How is the fox?'

He adds the last words with a hasty attempt to keep the conversation to the one topic over which alone they seem fated to be friendly.

'He is very well! better'—with a slight smile—'than he deserves.'

'I should like to see him, to tell him that I bear no malice.'

She looks irresolute for a moment; then, 'Would you? Come this way!'

Before they have made three steps Betty is after them.

'Where are you two making off to in such a hurry?'

'We are going to see the fox,' replies Peggy coldly.

'The fox? What fox?'

'Why, my tame fox,' rejoins Peggy, with a little air of surprise; 'the one that bit Mr. Talbot when he was here yesterday.'

The murder is out.

'H'm!' says Betty, in a very dry voice; 'so the mystery is solved!'

'What mystery?' asks the other, in a tone of ever colder and growing astonishment. 'There is no mystery; it is only that my fox escaped from his house yesterday, and Mr. Talbot was good enough to catch him again for me; and in so doing was unfortunately bitten. What mystery is there in that?'

Her displeased blue eyes turn in inquiry from one to the other, but neither has any answer ready for her. Nor does she again repeat her question; but Talbot, stealing one guilty look at her, sees that she has comprehended that he has been afraid to own his visit to her, and that she despises him heartily for it.

CHAPTER VIII

John Talbot spends a wretched night. He does not owe this to the fact of Betty's infantine gambols, her ogles and cats'-cradles with Freddy Ducane through the previous evening; nor yet to any physical ill. It is one ray of honest contempt from a country-bred girl's heaven-blue eye that kills his rest. It seems to shine in upon his whole life, as a beam of clear morning sunshine shines in upon some ugly over-night revel, bringing out into all their unlovely prominence the wine-stains, and the guttered candles, and the faded flowers. A desire, whose futility he recognises, but which is none the less real for the impossibility of its ever being gratified, to set himself right with this thrice-seen stranger, takes possession of him; a desire to tell her his story—to lay before her the reasons why she should be lenient with him. Would she think them very cogent? His memory, made acuter by the darkness, journeys back over the past five years, weighing, sifting, recalling—back to the beginning, that August when his chief's affairs kept him in London after everybody else had left; when, sick at heart from a recent grief, he had fallen sick in body too; and when Betty, also detained in London by some accident—Betty, whom he had hitherto met only as one meets in the world, hearing of his sad plight, had come out of pure kind-heartedness—yes, he is quite sure that at first it was only out of pure kind-heartedness—to sit beside his sofa; Betty, laden with sweet flowers; Betty, with compassionate eyes and a womanly smile; Betty, with less paint and a lower voice; with more clothes and fewer after-dinner stories; and last, fatalest of all, with that likeness, fancied or real, to the sister he had just lost. He remembers the day on which he first told her of that resemblance. In the dark night he recalls again many another little landmark in that first period of his passion, and grows half tender again as their dead faces rise before him. But what did that first idyllic stage lead to? To nothing, indeed, as criminal as the world, as Margaret probably gives them credit for, but to those unhandsome shifts and expedients which have made of his life since one long shuffle and evasion. The kotowing to people he disliked and despised for invitations to meet her; the risky rendezvous; the mad jealousies; the half-heartedness in his work; the entire disintegration of all his plans, liable to be upset at a moment's notice, in order to dovetail in with her convenience; the irrepressible senseless friendliness, which he dare not refuse, on the part of the stupid worthy Harborough; the genuine fondness of that Harborough's little children—he looks back upon them all with nausea. No! there is nothing to be said for him! She would say that there was nothing to be said for him! He has slidden down a precipice, it is true, whose first slope was easy and gentle; but there were many bushes at which he might have caught in his downward passage to save himself if he had wished; and he caught at none. And now he is at the bottom! The very passion which gave some slight tinge of a bastard nobility to his ignoble life is dead—dead as the roses that flushed its dawn, and he must still be tied to its lifeless body as fast as—nay, faster than—he was to its living charms. This is his conclusion; and it is one not much calculated to lull him into slumber.

To prove the difference between a bad conscience and a good one, Margaret sleeps calmly; but she wakes in the morning with the sense of something faintly disagreeable having happened. She shakes it off as she goes about her garden and her chicken-pens, the more easily as Prue is in bounding spirits, which is to be accounted for by the fact of Freddy having invited her to go out riding with him in the afternoon, and promised to mount her upon one of his own horses—a privilege often before accorded to her, but which never fails to lift her into Elysium. She is too excited to settle to anything more solid than jumping over the garden-beds and the tennis-net, to and fro with Mink. If you are in paradise, why trouble yourself with earth's sordid tasks? But Margaret, not being in paradise, is meditatively grubbing on hands and knees in the rather overgrown border, when a ring at the door-bell brings her somewhat quickly to her feet. A sudden thought sends the indignant blood to her cheek. Is it possible that it can be Talbot? After yesterday, is it conceivable that he can have the presumption again to force himself upon her? She moves hastily towards the house to forbid his admission, if it be he. But she is too late. The visitor has been already let in; and proves to be one to whom her door is never shut—only Freddy Ducane.

'Have you come to fix the time for your ride?' asks she cordially, beaming upon him. He, at least, has wrenched himself out of Circe's sty. 'Do you want Prue? She is in the garden.'

The young man looks a shade embarrassed.

'Yes,' he says; 'I do. No; I do not—at least, I have something to say to her, but I think'—insinuatingly—'that I had rather say it to you. You know, Peggy, how fond I am of saying things to you! There is no one to whom I can say things as comfortably as I can to you.'

At this preface her heart sinks a little.

'What is it?' she asks curtly.

'Oh, only my luck!' throwing himself into a chair. 'By Jove'—looking round the room—'how cool you feel! and how good you smell!'

'I do not suppose that you came here to say that,' rejoins she, still standing over him in expectant anxiety.

His answer is to try and get possession of her hand.

'Peggy,' he says plaintively, 'that is not a nice way to speak to me; that is not the way I like to be spoken to. The reason why I came here—it is very inhospitable of you to insist upon my giving a reason—was to say'—sighing profoundly—'that I fear dear little Prue and I shall have to give up our ride this afternoon.'

Her foreboding was a true one then!

'Why?'

'Oh, because—because—just my luck!'

'I understand,' replies she caustically. 'You are in the case of the man who telegraphed to the house where he did not wish to stay, "So sorry. Cannot come. *No lie ready*."'

Freddy colours.

'Peggy, if I were not so really fond of you,' he says, in an injured voice, 'I should not allow you to speak to me like that. There are days when you rasp one like a file. Prue never rasps one.'

'Is that the reason why you think yourself justified in always letting her go to the wall?' asks Margaret, with a bitterness that seems out of proportion to the occasion; but in her mind's eye she sees the poor little figure that has been frolicking among the geraniums with dog and cat—sees, too, the metamorphosis that will be worked in it.

Freddy rolls his curly head uneasily to and fro on the chair-back.

'You talk as if I were not quite as disappointed as she,' he says, in a lamentable tone. 'But what is one to do? When one has guests, one must entertain them. Somebody must entertain *her*.'

'Must entertain whom?'

'Oh, you know as well as I do! You are only asking out of ill-nature. Betty, of course!'

'Betty, of course!' repeats she after him, with an indefinable accent.

'Well, Peggy, I appeal to you. What could I do, when she asked me point-blank? You know that I never can refuse to do anything that anybody asks me point-blank.'

'Then suppose that *I* ask you point-blank to throw *her* over?' suggests Margaret, looking full at him with her straightforward blue eyes.

'But you would not,' returns he hastily. 'You dear thing, it would not be the least like you; and it would only make her hate Prue for life. Ah, you do not know Betty!'

'And, meanwhile, where is her *âme damnée*, pray?' asks Margaret with a curling nose.

'"Where is John Talbot? Where is valiant John?"'

Freddy shrugs his shoulders.

'Valiant John is a little slack of late; he wants poking up a bit. But'—with a coaxing change of tone—'it will be just the same to Prue to go another day, will not it? and you will tell her, will not you? I—I really am in a great hurry this morning; and I—I—think I had rather *you* told her.'

'I will do nothing of the kind,' replies Peggy severely. 'You may do your own errands.'

Nor do any of his blandishments, any of his numerous assertions of the reverential attachment he has always felt for herself, any of his asseverations of the agonising grief it causes him to give the slightest pain to Prue, avail to make her budge one inch from her original resolution. She watches him as, with a somewhat hang-dog air, he walks across the grass-plot to meet her sister, who comes treading on air to meet him. And then Margaret looks away. She cannot bear to witness the extinction of that poor short radiance. She does not again meet young Ducane; nor does Prue reappear until luncheon-time, when she comes down from her bedroom with red eyes, but an air of determined cheerfulness.

'It would have been much too hot for riding to-day,' she says, fanning herself; 'unbearable, indeed! We are going a far longer ride in a day or two. He says he does not think that they will stay long. He was so bitterly disappointed. I do not think that I ever saw any one so disappointed—did you?' casting a wistful glance at her elder.

'He *said* he was,' replies Peggy sadly.

The incident has made her own heart heavy; and it is with an unelastic step that she sets off in the afternoon to the Manor, summoned thither by one of Lady Roupell's almost daily cocked-hat notes, to hold sweet converse upon the arrangements of an imminent village concert. A casual sentence to the effect that everybody but the old lady herself will be out has decided Margaret to obey the summons, which, did it expose her to a meeting with Lady Betty and John Talbot, she would have certainly disregarded.

Prue accompanies her to their gate, still with that strained look of factitious content on her childish face; and, as she parts from her sister, whispers

49

feverishly:

'Find out how soon they are going!'

Dispirited as she was on leaving her own home, Miss Lambton's cheerfulness undergoes still further diminution before she reaches her goal; as, in passing through the park, has not she, in a retired and bosky dell, caught a glimpse of a white gown, and of a supine male figure, with a curly head and a poetry book, stretched beside it? She starts at the sight.

Freddy had certainly implied that he was going out riding with Lady Betty. On searching her memory, she found that he had not actually said so; but he had knowingly conveyed that idea to her mind. It is not the first time by many that Freddy Ducane has succeeded in conveying impressions that do not absolutely tally with the fact; but each fresh discovery of his disingenuousness gives her a new shock. Lady Roupell's boudoir is upstairs; and, following her usual custom, Margaret repairs thither unannounced. In doing so she passes the day nursery's open door; and, through it, sees Miss Harborough sitting on the floor, buttoning her boots. Peggy stops a moment to throw the child a greeting; but is instantly checked by the nurse.

'Oh, please, ma'am, do not speak to her! I am sure that she does not deserve it! she has been a real naughty girl!'

On inquiry, it appears that the enemy of man having again entered into Miss Lily, she has cut the string of her necklace, strewed the beads all over the floor, and then told a barefaced lie, and entirely denied it.

During this recital of her iniquities she continues her buttoning quite calmly; and merely says, with a dispassionate tone of indifference and acquiescence:

'Yes, I am bad.'

It is two hours later—so long does the discussion over the penny reading last —before Margaret again passes the nursery door. The interval has been filled by a discussion as to which of the local talent must be invited to contribute, and which may be, without giving too much offence, left out; but the larger part has been spent in a confederate consultation as to how best to prevent Mrs. Evans from singing 'Love, the Pilgrim.'

The matter is arranged at last; and Peggy puts on her hat and gloves again to depart. As she repasses the nursery door she finds that an entire change of decoration has taken place. Instead of the young cynic defiantly buttoning her boots in the teeth of the law, she sees a little pious figure in a white nightgown, kneeling by its nurse's side. The instant, however, that the saintly little form catches sight of her it is up on its bare legs, and rushing towards her.

'Oh, Miss Lambton, do let me say my prayers to you! it would be so pleasant! —No, Franky,' with a disposition to hustle her little brother, who is putting in a like claim; 'you are too little; you can say yours to Nanny!'

As she speaks she pulls Peggy by the gown into the room; and, placing her in a chair, kneels down at once—so that there may be no chance of her escaping —beside her, with hands devoutly folded, but a somewhat roving eye.

'Which shall I say?' asks she, with a wriggle of the back and an air of indifference: '"Our Father" or "Gentle Jesus"?'

'Say whichever you please,' replies Margaret gently; 'only attend and make up your mind which.'

'Oh, then,' with another wriggle, 'I will say "Gentle Jesus."'

After a pause:

'Do you think that there would be any harm in my praying for John Talbot?'

Margaret gives a little jump. It is, then, an hereditary passion! But she answers drily:

'Not the least.'

Another pause. The wriggling has ceased.

'Only,' pursues Peggy, quite determined not to supply the form of petition for Talbot's welfare, 'only you must say it out of your own head. I am not going to tell you what to say.'

'Oh, then,' with an air of resolution, 'I had better say, "God bless John Talbot; and I am glad he is here."'

She has pronounced this last somewhat eccentrically-worded supplication rather loud, and at the end of it her wandering eye takes in an object which makes her spring from her knees as hastily as she had done before.

'Oh! there is John Talbot!' cries she, tearing out barefoot into the passage, and flinging herself into his arms.

'I have been praying for you!' cries she, hugging him. 'Miss Lambton said that I might.'

At this unexpected colouring given to her reluctant permission Peggy reddens.

'I said that there was no harm in it,' explains Peggy hurriedly; 'there is no *harm* in praying for any one.'

'And the more they need it the greater charity it is,' replies he, looking at her with so sad and deprecating a humility that her anger against him melts.

CHAPTER IX

'God Almighty first planted a Garden. And indeed it is the Purest of Humane pleasures. It is the Greatest Refreshment to the Spirit of Man; Without which Buildings and Pallaces are but Grosse Handy-works: And man shall ever see that when Ages grow to Civility and Elegancie they come to Build Stately, sooner than to Garden Finely: as if Gardening were the Greater Perfection.'

I do not know whether Peggy had ever read Bacon, but she certainly endorsed his opinion.

'The garden is the only really satisfactory thing,' she says to herself, three days after that on which she had conducted Miss Harborough's devotions, as she stands beside her carnation-bed, and notes how many fat buds have, during the night, broken into pale sulphur and striped and blood-red flowers.

To few of us, I think, has not at one time or other of our lives the doubt presented itself, whether the people we love are not a source of more pain than pleasure to us, what with their misfortunes, their ill-doings, and their deaths. But despite frost, and snail, and fly, and drought, and flood, the joy in a garden must always enormously exceed the pain. The frost may shrivel the young leaves, but the first sun-kiss brings out green successors; the drought may make the tender herbs bow and droop, but at the next warm rain-patter they look up again. The frost that nips our human hearts often no after-sunbeam can uncongeal; and the rain falls too late to revive the flower that the world's cruel drought has killed.

'Did you find out how soon they are going?' asks Prue breathlessly, running down the road to meet her sister on her return from the Manor, in her eagerness to get her tidings.

It has been the one thought that has filled her mind during the three hours of Margaret's absence. Peggy shakes her head despondently.

'Milady did not know.'

'I suppose that they had gone out riding before you got there.'

This is not a question, so Margaret thinks herself exempted from the necessity of answering it.

'Had they gone out riding before you got there?' repeats Prue, with feverish pertinacity.

It *is* a question now, so she must make some reply. She only shakes her head.

'Then you saw them set off?'—very eagerly. 'How did she look? beautiful, I am sure!'

'I did not see them.'

It is a moment before the younger girl takes in what the last sentence implies; then she says in a changed low key:

'You mean to say that they did not go out riding at all?'

'No,' replies Peggy, softly putting her arm round her sister's shoulders, as if she would ward off the imminent trouble from her by that kind and tender gesture; 'they did not go out riding at all; they sat in the park together instead.'

There is a short silence.

'Then he threw me over for nothing?' says Prue, in a choked whisper.

'Yes,' in a whisper too.

Prue has snatched herself out of Peggy's arms, and drawn up her small willowy figure.

'He shall not have the chance of playing fast and loose with me again in a hurry,' she says, her poor face burning.

Alas! he would have the chance next day, if he chose to take it; but he does not even take the trouble to do that. Two whole days pass, and nothing is either seen or heard of him. And through these two long days Prue, with flagging appetite and fled sleep, rejecting occupation, starting at the sound of the door-bell, watches for him; and Peggy watches too, and starts, and is miserable for company.

During those weary two days Prue's mood changes a hundred times, varying from pitiful attempts at a dignified renunciation of him, always ending in a deluge of tears, to agonised efforts at finding excuses for his neglect, and irritation at her sister for not being able to say that she thinks them sufficing ones.

'He is so hospitable,' she says wistfully, as the sun sets upon the second empty day; 'he has almost exaggerated ideas of what he owes to his guests. And after all, there is no one else to entertain them. Milady does not trouble her head about them; he has such good manners; he is so courteous! Come now, prejudiced as you always are against him, you yourself have often said, "How courteous he is!"' Then, as Peggy makes but a faint and dubious sign of acquiescence, she adds irritably: 'Whether you own it or not, you have said so repeatedly; but there is no use in talking to a person who blows hot and cold, says one thing to-day and another to-morrow.'

The third morning has come. In the garden, dew-crisped and odorous, but whose spicy clove-carnation breath brings no solace to her careless nostril, Prue sits bent and listless, her fragile prettiness dimmed, and the nosegay of her choicest flowers—usually most grudgingly plucked—extravagantly gathered by Margaret five minutes ago, in the hope that their morning beauty may tempt her sick chick to a smile, lying disregarded on the grass beside her, and sniffed at by Mink, who makes a face of unaffected disgust at the mignonette.

'He has never in his life been so long without coming to see us when he was at home,' says Prue dejectedly; 'once he was thirty-six hours, but that was accounted for afterwards by his having had one of his neuralgic headaches. Do you think'—with a little access of life and animation—'that he can be ill?'

'It is possible, of course,' replies Margaret gravely; 'but I do not think it is probable.'

'If I could only *know*,' says the other wearily; 'if I could be *sure*; it would be something to be *sure* of anything! I am so tired of wondering!'

'I might go up to the Big House to find out for you,' suggests Peggy, magnanimously swallowing down her own acute distaste to this proposition, and speaking with a cheerful relish, as if she liked it. 'I could easily make an excuse to go up to the Big House; shall I go?'

The capricious poppy colour has sprung back into Prue's thin cheek.

'Oh, if you would!'

'Of course I will,' replies Margaret gaily; 'it will be a nice walk for me; the garden makes me so lazy about walking. What time shall I go? morning or afternoon?'

'Oh, if you did not mind, morning is the soonest.'

The words are scarcely out of her mouth before ting, tang! sharply sounds the hall-door bell. It is a bell that is hardly ever pulled in a forenoon, save by one person—a person who does not confine himself to the canonical hours of calling.

In a moment there is a light in Prue's dimmed eyes, and Margaret's great blue ones beam for company.

'I think that I need not go up to the Big House, after all,' she says, with soft gladness.

'Shall I go away,' asks Prue, in a trembling whisper, 'and not come back for ten minutes or so? Perhaps he would think better of me if I did not seem so eager to meet him. Shall I?'

'I think I would not,' answers Peggy gently; 'I would sit quietly here, just as if nothing had happened. I think it would be more dignified.'

They wait in silence. What a long time Sarah is in putting on a clean apron and turning down her sleeves! But he is admitted at last, has passed through the house, and is stepping across the turf towards them.

He! But what he? Alas for Prue! there are more he's than one in the world— more he's that call at uncanonical hours!

'Oh, Peggy!' she says, with almost a sob, 'it is only John Talbot! It is not he after all.'

Peggy does not answer. Her feelings, though nearly as poignant as her sister's, are a good deal more complex. An indignation for which she can perfectly account, and an agitation for which she can give herself no reason at all, make her disappointment, though not far from being as bitter, less simple than Prue's.

She advances to meet her visitor with an air that would make a more impudent heart than his sink. Over her face is written, though the words do not actually pass her lips, that least reassuring of salutations, 'To what are we indebted for the honour of this visit?'

A woman's anger is seldom wholly reasonable, and on this occasion Margaret's indignation against Talbot is called forth not only by his being himself, but by his not being Freddy Ducane, which is certainly more his misfortune than his fault. After all, he is, for a villain, not possessed of very much effrontery, since the austerity of so young an eye strikes him dumb.

The only person who shows him any civility is Mink, who, being of a rather superficial character, is glad of any addition to his social circle, and does not inquire too nicely into its quality.

It is probable that Talbot, being a man of the world, would have recovered the use of his tongue in time; but as he is rather slow about it, Margaret takes the initiative.

'Is it something about the village concert?' she asks.

He looks puzzled.

'The village concert! I am afraid that I have not heard anything about the village concert.'

'Oh!' returns she, coldly surprised. 'I thought that probably Lady Roupell had asked you to leave a message with me about it. It is not that, then?'

She continues to look expectantly at him. Since it is not that, it must be on some other errand he has come. She clearly thinks it an impossible impertinence on his part to have called on her at eleven o'clock in the morning without an excuse.

And yet such is the case. He has come because he has come; he has no better reason to give, either to her or to himself. A wild idea of trumping up the expected message, and another of feigning that he has come to inquire after the fox, cross his mind; but he dismisses both: the first because he knows he should be found out, and the second because Miss Lambton might take it as a fresh demand upon her pity for the wound got in her service.

'I am afraid I have no message,' he says boldly. 'I was passing your door, and I—I—rang. By the bye' (smiling nervously as the utter inadequacy of his explanation falls upon his ears), 'what a loud bell yours is! I was so frightened at the noise I made that I was half inclined to run away when I had rung it.'

She does not say that she is glad he did not; she does not say anything civil. She only asks him to sit down, which, when he has shaken hands with Prue, and wondered inwardly what she can have been doing to make herself look so odd, he does.

Again silence, and again it is broken by Margaret. After all, she cannot be conspicuously rude even to him in her own house. It is, indeed, one of the problems of life, 'When is it permissible to insult one's neighbour?' Not in one's own house; not in his. There is, then, only the open street left.

For the sake of saying something, and also because she knows that she is giving voice to her sister's unspoken wish, Peggy inquires civilly whether they are all well at the Manor.

'Yes, I think so,' replies Talbot slowly. 'I have not heard any of them complain of any disease beyond the long disease of life.'

His tone is so little what one would expect from the happy lover of a fashionable beauty, that Margaret, with that charity that thinketh no evil, to which we are all so prone, instantly sets it down to affectation.

'That is a disease that I daresay does not hinder you all from amusing yourselves,' returns she sarcastically.

'Amusing ourselves? Oh yes, very well. I do not complain.'

There is such an obviously true ring about the depression with which this announcement of his contentment with his lot is uttered, that even she can no longer doubt of its reality. So he is not happy with his Betty after all! And a very good thing, too! Serve him right! But perhaps the discovery tends to mollify a little the tone of her next observation.

'Are you thinking how badly we want mowing?' she asks, her eyes following the direction of his, which are absently bent upon the sward, to-day not shorn to quite its usual pitch of velvet nicety. 'So we do, indeed. But Jacob has unluckily fallen ill, just as milady lent me the machine, and there it and the pony stand idle, and we'—regretfully eyeing her domain—'are, as you see, like a hay-meadow.'

Talbot does not speak for a moment. A great idea is labouring its way to birth in his mind—an idea that may give him a better foothold here than any casually escaped fox or precarious porterage of messages can ever do.

'Why should not I mow?' asks he at last.

'*You?*'

'Yes, I; and you lead the pony.'

She looks at him, half inclined to be angry.

'Is that a joke?'

'A joke—no! Will you tell me where the pony is? May I harness it?'

Again she looks at him, waveringly this time, and thence to her turf. It is already an inch and a half too long; by to-morrow morning it will be three inches, an offence to her neat eye; and when Jacob falls ill he is apt to take his time about it. She yields to temptation.

'I will call the boy.'

But the boy is out—*marbleing*, vagranting after his kind about the near village, no doubt.

They have to harness the pony themselves; and by the time that they have put the bridle over her head, inserted her feet into her mowing shoes, and led her out of her dark stall into the sunny day, John has almost recovered the ground he had lost since that fortunate hour when, with three drops of his blood, he had bought a square inch of oil-silk and a heavenly smile.

They set off. Loudly whirs the machine. Up flies the grass in a little green cloud, which the sun instantly turns into deliciously scented new-mown hay; sedately steps the pony; gravely paces Margaret beside her; honourably John stoops to his toil behind. It is not a pursuit that lends itself much to conversation; but at least he has continuously before his eyes her flat back, her noble shoulders, the milky nape of her neck; and can conjecture as to the length of her unbound hair by counting the number of times that the brown plait winds round the back of her broad head. Every now and then they pause to empty out the grass, and each time a few words pass between them.

'Is Jacob very ill?'

'I am afraid that he suffers a good deal.'

'Is he likely to die?'

'Heaven forbid!'

'Because if he is, I wish you would think of me.'

He is half afraid when he has said this; it verges, perhaps, too nearly upon familiarity.

But she is not offended. Her eye, flattered by her shaven lawn, cannot rest very severely upon him who has shaven it for her. Her spirits have risen; exhilarated by the wholesome exercise, by the sunshine, by who knows what. Only when her look falls now and again upon Prue, still flung listlessly on the garden-seat, with her nosegay—not more flagging than she—withering on the ground beside her, does a cloud come over it.

'Should I get a good character from your last place?' returns she playfully.

'From the Foreign Office?'

'Was it the Foreign Office?' with a momentary impulse of curiosity for which she instantly pulls herself up. 'You know one always expects to get a character from the last place.'

'I do not know whether it is a good one. It is a nine-years' one.'

Then they set off again. Next time it is about Prue.

'I hope she is not ill?' his eyes following Margaret's to the little forlorn figure under the Judas-tree.

'No-o.'

'Nor unhappy?'

'We all have our Black Mondays'—evasively—'only some of us have Black Tuesdays and Black Wednesdays as well—ah!'

What has happened to her? Her gloomy sentence has ended in a suppressed cry of joy, and her cheeks have changed from pink to damask. He turns to seek the cause of this metamorphosis.

'Why, there is Ducane!'

In an instant his eyes have pounced back upon her face. It is settling again into its pretty normal colours, but the joy is still there.

'Yes, there is Freddy!' she acquiesces softly.

A sharp needle of jealousy pricks his heart. This, then, is why she received him so frigidly. She was expecting the other.

'We stop now, I suppose?' he says abruptly.

'What! tired already, Jacob's would-be successor?' asks she rallyingly.

'Hardly. But I supposed that you would wish to stop.'

'On account of Freddy?'—with a little shrug. 'Pooh! he is a fly on the wall; and besides, he—he is not coming this way.'

It is true. Straight as a die young Ducane is making for the Judas-tree; and from under that Judas-tree a little figure, galvanised back into youth and bloom, rises, walking on air to meet him.

The eyes of John and Margaret meet, and he understands. As he goes home he feels that he has made a real step in advance this time. He shares a secret with her. He knows about Prue!

CHAPTER X

'Our Master hath a garden which fair flowers adorn,
There will I go and gather, both at eve and morn:
Nought's heard therein but Angel Hymns with harp and lute,
Loud trumpets and bright clarions, and the gentle, soothing flute

'The lily white that bloometh there is Purity,
The fragrant violet is surnamed Humility:
Nought's heard therein but Angel Hymns with harp and lute,
Loud trumpets and bright clarions, and the gentle, soothing flute

'Well,' cries Peggy anxiously, as, the young men having taken leave, she sees her sister come running and jumping, and humming an air, to meet her, 'is it all right?'

'Of course it is all right,' replies Prue, vaulting over the tennis-net to let off a little of her steam. 'If it had not been for your long face, I should never have doubted it.'

'Yes?'

'It was just as I expected; he was too polite to leave them. He says he never in his life remembers spending two such tedious days; but he is so unselfish. He says himself that he knows he is full of faults, but that he cannot understand any one being selfish, even from the point of view of their own pleasure. He said it so simply.'

'H'm!'

'I was so sorry for you, Peggy—saddled with that tiresome John Talbot all morning. Of course I ought to have helped you; but you know I had not a word to throw to a dog. It was very provoking of him, wasting all your morning for you.'

'My morning was not wasted,' rejoins Margaret calmly. 'He may be a very bad man, but he mows well.'

'He might as well have finished it while he was about it,' says Prue, captiously eyeing the lawn. 'It looks almost worse than it did before, half mown and half unmown.'

For an instant Margaret hesitates; then, with a slight though perceptible effort over herself, she says:

'I suppose he thought so; for he has offered to come again to-morrow to finish it. He said one could not leave it half-shaven, like a poodle.'

She looks at her sister a little doubtfully as she speaks—as one not quite sure of the soundness of the comparison, and that would be glad to have it confirmed by another judgment. But Prue's wings have already carried her up again into her empyrean.

'We are to ride quite late this afternoon. He wants me to see the reapers reaping by moonlight as we come home. He says he always associates me with moonlight. I am to ride the bay. He says he quite looks upon her as mine —that it gives him a sort of turn to see any one else on her;' and so on, and so on.

Margaret smiles rather sadly; but as it is no use going to meet trouble half-way, she allows herself to be carried away by Prue's infectious spirits, on however rickety a foundation those spirits may be built. In her heart she is scarcely more pleased with her own conduct than with her sister's.

'One cannot touch pitch without being defiled,' she says to herself severely.

She says it several times—is, indeed in the act of saying it next morning, when, on the stroke of eleven, punctual to his minute, the poor pitch reappears. She sets him at once to his mowing, and allows him very short intervals for rest and conversation. Since he has come to work, let him work. No doubt as soon as he discovers that it is honest labour and not play that is expected of him he will trouble her with no more of his assiduities. And yet, as he bids her good-bye, leaving behind him a smooth sweep of short velvet for her to remember him by, he seems to linger.

'How is Jacob?' he asks.

'No better.'

'The garden looks a little straggly,' suggests he insidiously, knowing her weak side. 'A great many things want tying up. The beds need edging, and the carnations ought to be layered.'

'You are very learned,' says she, smiling. 'Does the F.O. teach you gardening?'

'Well, no; that is not included in the curriculum. That is an extra.'

'Who did teach you, then?' asks she, with an inquisitiveness which, as soon as the words are out of her mouth, shocks and surprises herself.

Can it be Betty? A Betty that loves her children and digs in her garden! If it is so, Peggy will have to reconstruct her altogether.

'My sister.'

His sister! What a relief! It would have been so humiliating to have had her strongest taste degraded by a community with painted, posturing Betty.

'You have a sister?'

'*Had.* There is a good deal of difference.'

And with that he leaves her abruptly. But he returns next day at the same hour; and, as there has blown a boisterous wind in the night, which has prostrated top-heavy plants, torn off leaves, and scattered flower-petals, she has not the heart to refuse his aid in a general tidying and sweeping up. Next day he clips the edges of the borders very nicely with a pair of shears; and the next day they gather lavender off the same bush. Gathering lavender, particularly off the same bush, is a good deal more productive of talk than mowing; nor is it possible to her to keep her new servant within the bounds of a silence to which she had never attempted to confine her old one.

But, indeed, by the time that they have come to the lavender day the wish for his silence has ceased. On the second—the general sweeping day—he had told her about his sister—had told her in short dry sentences how he had lost her; and she had cried out of sympathy for him who did not cry, and had said to herself, 'What if it had been my Prue?' On the third day, though assuredly no word or hint of Betty had passed his lips, somehow, by woman's instinct, sharpened by observation, she has sprung to a conclusion, not very erroneous, as to his garish mock-happiness and his shattered life. On the fourth day she asks herself why he never comes except in the forenoon; and herself answers the question, that it is because lazy Betty lies late, and until one o'clock has no knowledge of his comings or goings. On the fifth day she resolves that he shall come in the afternoon. She will be visited openly or not at all. So when, giving his bundle of lavender into her hands, he says with a valedictory formula, 'The same hour to-morrow?' she answers quietly:

'I am afraid not; I have an engagement with Mrs. Evans for to-morrow morning; we must give up the garden to-morrow, unless'—as if with an afterthought—'unless you could come later—some time in the afternoon?'

His countenance falls. What property has he in his own afternoons? His weary afternoons of hammock and scandal and cigarettes?

'I am afraid——' he begins; but at once he sees her face hardening. She knows. She understands. Cost what it may, he will not see again in her mouth and eyes that contempt whose dawning he had once before detected, to the embittering of his rest. He will not leave her with those tight lips and that stern brow. Pay for it as he may, he will do her bidding.

'At what hour, then?' he asks readily. 'Four? five? it is all one to me.'

She hesitates a moment. She has laid a trap for him, and he has not fallen into it.

'Shall we say five?'

He sees the surprise in her look, and is rewarded by it. But as he walks home he ponders. How is he to break to Betty the act of insubordination of which he has pledged himself to be guilty? For the last week he has been leading a double life; dissembling his happy mornings from the monopoliser of his weary afternoons. A sense of shame and revolt comes over him. He will dissemble no longer. Know as he may that from the tyranny whose yoke he himself fastened about his neck—from the chain which he himself has encouraged to eat into his life, only death or Betty's manumission can—according to honour's distorted code—free him; yet there is no reason why he should deny himself the solace of such a friendship as a good woman who divines his miserable story will accord him: a woman who lies under no delusion as to his being a free agent; in whose clear eyes—their innocence not being a stupid ignorance—he has read her acquaintance with his history; and whose strong heart can run no danger from the company of one whom she despises. Nor as the time draws near, though the natural man's aversion from vexing anything weaker than itself, coupled with his knowledge of his lady's unusual tear-and-invective power, may make him wince at the thought of the coming contest, does his resolution at all flag as to asserting and sticking to his last remnant of liberty. He might, as it happens, have cut the knot by flight, Betty having given him the occasion by forsaking him for a game of billiards with Freddy; but he is determined to fight the battle out on the open field. She has rejoined him now, and the weather being fresher than it was, and Betty the chilliest of mortals, they are walking briskly up and down the terrace, she wrapped in a 'fluther' of lace and feathers, and with her children frisking round her, a good and happy young matron. She is very happy just now, dear Betty. She has beaten Freddy at billiards, and made him break tryst with Prue. She is going to make him break another to-morrow. Is it any wonder that she looks bright and sweet? Little Franky has hold of her hand; and Lily is backing along the gravel walk before her. Betty laughs.

'Can you imagine what can be the pleasure of walking backwards with your tongue out?' asks she of Talbot. 'Franky darling, you are pulling my hand off; would not you like to run away and play with Lily?'

But the little spoilt fellow only clutches her fingers the tighter.

'No, no; I like to stay with you, mammy!'

'And so you shall,' cries she, hugging him; 'you shall always do whatever you like. But Lily'—in a colder key—'you may run away; we do not want you. What are you staring at me so for, child?'

Lily puts her head on one side, and hoisting up her shoulder to meet her cheek, rubs them gently together, with her favourite gesture.

'I was only thinking, mammy,' replies she pensively, 'what much smaller ears than yours Miss Lambton has. Do you think that she will grow deaf sooner than other people because her ears are so small?'

'Nonsense!' rejoins the mother sharply; 'do not get into the habit of asking stupid questions. Run away!'

'Out of the mouth of babes and sucklings,' etc. The way has been paved for Talbot in a way that he could not have expected. Miss Harborough walks away slowly, dragging her legs, and with a very deep reluctance. She scents an interesting conversation in the air.

'It is odd that Lily should have mentioned Miss Lambton,' says Talbot, taking the plunge; 'for I was just going to mention her myself.'

'It is what you do not often do,' replies Betty drily; '"out of the abundance of the heart the mouth speaketh," cannot be said of you.'

'Her gardener is ill,' continues Talbot, leaving unnoticed this little fling, and speaking in as matter-of-fact a tone as he can assume; 'and I promised to help her to water her garden. By the bye'—with an unnecessary glance at the stable clock—'if you could spare me for half an hour—I said I would be there by five—I ought to be off.'

There is an ominous silence. Then:

'How do you know that her gardener is ill? Did she think it necessary to write and communicate that interesting fact to you?'

'No.'

'She has not been here since Monday?'

'I believe not.'

'Then you have been there?'

'Yes.'

'What day?'

He hesitates. Shall he make a clean breast of it? Yes; 'in for a penny, in for a pound.'

'I have been there five days,' replies he slowly, and looking down.

Another pause. He keeps his eyes resolutely averted from her face, but he hears an angry catch in her breath.

'In the morning, I suppose, before I was up?'

'Yes.'

She breaks into a rather shrill laugh.

'What an incentive to early rising! The early Blowsabel picks the worm.'

Her tone is so inexpressibly insulting that he has to bite his lips hard to keep in the furious retort that rises to them; but he masters himself. Of what use to bandy words with an angry woman? And, after all, from her point of view she has some cause of complaint. Franky has altered his mind, and trotted off after his senior, for whose tree-climbing, cat-teasing, general mischief-doing powers he entertains a respect tempered with fear. They are alone.

Betty is walking along with her nose in the air, a smile of satisfied ire at the happiness of her last shaft giving a malicious upward curve to her pretty mouth.

'How I should have laughed,' says she presently, 'if any fortune-teller had told me that it would be my fate to be supplanted by a sa——'

'You are going to say "a sack of potatoes,"' says he, interrupting her. 'Do not. If you must call names, invent a new one!'

'Why give myself that trouble,' asks she insolently, 'when the old one fits so admirably? *Supplanted by a sack!*' (dwelling with prolonged relish on the obnoxious noun). 'What a good title for a novel! Ah! Freddy, my child!' catching sight of the young fellow, who is just stepping out of the window of the drawing-room. 'I was afraid you had gone to dry your skeleton's eyes. Come and dry mine instead: I assure you they need it much more.'

As she speaks she goes hurriedly to meet Ducane, and disappears with him round a corner of the house.

Talbot is free to pursue his scheme with what heart he may. The last ten minutes' conversation has taken all the bloom off his project. That the whole pleasure to himself has been eliminated from it is, however, no reason why he should break his word to Peggy, and, if he wishes to obey her with the punctuality that he has always hitherto shown, he must set off at once. He begins to walk towards a turn-stile that leads into the park!

CHAPTER XI

'Her cheeks so rare a white was on,
No daisy makes comparison
(Who sees them is undone);
For streaks of red were mingled there,
Such as are on a Catherine pear,
The side that's next the sun.'

He has not gone above a hundred yards when he hears a small thunder of feet behind him, and turning, finds Miss Harborough flying at the top of her speed to overtake him.

'Mammy said I might go with you,' cries she breathlessly.

He stops and hesitates. Is it possible that she has sent this innocent child to be an unconscious spy upon him?

'Mammy said I might go with you,' repeats Lily, seeing his hesitation, and beginning to drop her long lashes, and rub her cheek with her shoulder, according to her most approved methods of fascination.

'But I did not say so,' returns he gravely.

'Oh, but you will,' cries she, flinging herself boisterously into his arms; 'and I —I'll help you over the stiles.'

Who could resist such a bribe as this? Certainly not Talbot. They walk off amicably hand-in-hand. After all, he ought to be thankful for anything that distracts him from his own thoughts, which are certainly neither pleasant nor profitable enough to be worth thinking. To-day he is sad, not only on his own account, but on Margaret's. Short as has been the time of his acquaintance with her, he has got into a habit, which seems long, of being sorry with her sorrows. He knows that to-day will be a black day for Prue, and that Peggy will be darkened in company. Is it not better then, seeing that he cannot stir a finger to lift the weight from the three hearts he would fain lighten, that he should have his eight-year-old companion's chatter to be distracted by, that he should be initiated into the hierarchy of her affections, and learn the order and degree in which her relations and friends are dear to her? He is surprised and flattered at the extremely high place assigned to himself immediately after father, and some way above mammy; but is less exhilarated on finding out that he shares it with the odd-man, who has made and presented a whistle to her.

'And Franky? where does Franky come?' asks John, really quite interested in the subject.

'My dear little brother!' exclaims Lily, with an extravagant affection of sisterly tenderness. 'I am *so* fond of him! Poor little brother! he has *no* toys!'

John smiles rather grimly. He knows that Miss Lily squabbles frightfully with her little brother in real life; and how entirely mendacious is her statement as to his destitution of playthings.

'I have given him most of mine,' pursues Lily, casting one eye subtly up to watch the effect of her words, 'but he has broken them nearly all, and now we neither of us have any!'

John receives this broad hint in a silence which Miss Lily feels to be sceptical; but as her attention is at the same moment diverted by the sight of Miss Lambton's Red House, and of Mink's face looking through the bars of the gate, on the anxious watch for passing market-carts to insult, she does not pursue the subject.

Mink takes them for a market-cart at first, and insults them; but afterwards apologises, and shows them the way to the garden, jumping up at Lily's nose, with an affectation of far greater pleasure than he can really feel.

They find his mistress standing alone in the middle of her domain, a great gutta-percha snake lying on the ground behind her, and the hose directed at a thirsty verbena-bed.

As they come up with her, the chiming church clock, having finished its preliminary stave of 'Home, Sweet Home,' strikes five. Whether the chimes or her own thoughts have deafened her, she does not hear their approach.

'Is not that punctuality?' asks Talbot, drawing near. 'Which is better, to have only one very small virtue, and to have it in absolute perfection, or to have a smattering of several large ones?'

At his voice she starts, and turns, her eye falling upon him, and also, of course, upon the child. The latter instantly flings herself into her arms.

'Mammy and John Talbot said I might come!' cries she effusively.

'You did not give John Talbot much choice in the matter,' returns he drily.

'But mammy told me to come,' urges Lily in eager self-defence; 'she told me to run fast that I might be sure to overtake you!'

John feels a dull red rising to his brow; but he will not let his eyes sink: they meet Peggy's full and straight. She shall see that this time, at all events, he has been neither ashamed nor afraid to proclaim his visit to her.

Peggy has gently unclasped the child's arms from about her neck.

'What a dear little doggy!' cries Lily, chattering on, and deceived by Mink's manner, as all strangers are, into the belief that he has conceived a peculiar fancy for her. 'What is his name?'

'Mink.'

'And what kind of dog is he?'

'That is what no one—not even himself—has ever been able to make out,' returns Margaret, with a smile. 'Sometimes he thinks that he is a Yorkshire terrier, and sometimes he does not. I bought him at the Dogs' Home, because he was the most miserable little dog there, and because I was quite certain that if I did not, nobody else would. He has grown so uppish now that sometimes I have to remind him of his origin—have not I, Minky?'

'Mammy had a Yorkshire terrier once,' says Miss Harborough thoughtfully —'John Talbot gave it her—but he died. She had him stuffed: he looks horrid now!'

Talbot writhes. It seems to him as if he had never before tasted the full degradation of his position. He makes a clumsy plunge at changing the conversation by inquiring after Prue.

'She is lying down,' replies Peggy, while he sees a furrow come upon her white forehead. 'The heat tries her; at least'—her eye meeting his with a sort of appeal—'she is very easily tired; and she has been waiting all afternoon with her habit on. She was engaged to go out riding at three, and now it is five; people ought not to make engagements if they are not prepared to keep them!'

'I am afraid he had forgotten all about it,' answers Talbot sadly.

Margaret's only answer is a dispirited shrug; and Lily having by this time scampered off to visit the fox; if possible, with safety, pull his brush; eat anything that is eatable in the kitchen-garden; and make friendly advances to the stable-boy—Miss Lambton again takes up the hose.

'This,' says she, looking at it affectionately, 'is the one solid good I have ever got from the Big House!'

He does not answer. Though he certainly does not class himself under the head of a solid good, her words give him a vague chill.

'It sounds ungrateful,' pursues Peggy; 'but I often wish we could move this acre of ground, with everything that is on it, fifty miles farther away.'

'Do you?'

'Of course,' pursues she gravely, 'we get a great deal more society here than we should anywhere else; but I often think that that is a doubtful good. We grow to know people whose acquaintance we should be far better without.'

He winces. Does he himself come under this category? But she means no offence.

'You can have no notion how our lives are cut up,' she continues. 'We live in a whirl of tiny excitements, that would not be excitements to anybody but us. We never can settle to any serious occupation; the moment we take up a book there is a note: "Prue, come out riding;" "Peggy, come and look over the accounts of the Boot and Shoe Club;" "Peggy and Prue, come and dine to meet the—the——"'

Harboroughs is the name which rises to her lips, and which she suppresses out of politeness to him.

He knows, too, that the plural pronoun which she has employed throughout has been used only as a veil for Prue's weakness; that the picture she has drawn has no likeness to her own steady soul.

'I sometimes think seriously of moving,' she says presently. 'It would be a wrench'—looking round wistfully. 'The only two big things that ever happened to me have happened here: Prue was born here, and mother died here. Yes, it would be a wrench.'

He listens to her in a respectful silence. It would be impertinent in him to express overt sympathy in her trouble, the trouble she has never put into words.

'Sometimes I think that we should do better in London,' she goes on, looking at him almost as if appealing to him for counsel; 'there would be more to interest and distract us in London.'

'What, and leave the garden?' says he, lifting his eyebrows.

'She does not care really about the garden,' answers Margaret, forgetting herself, and using the singular pronoun which she might have employed all along. 'And as for me'—with a little laugh—'I would grow mignonette in a box; and buy a load of hay, as I heard of one country-sick lady doing, and make myself a haycock in the back-yard.'

'I cannot fancy you in a town,' says he, almost under his breath.

It is true. It is impossible to him to picture her except with a background of waving trees, a floor of blossoming flowers, a spicy wind to toss her hair, and finches to sing to her. His imagination is not strong enough to transplant her to the narrow bounds of a little South Kensington home, lost in the grimy monotony of ten thousand others.

'It is very difficult to know what to decide,' she says, almost plaintively, 'and I have no one to advise me. Though I am not very young—twenty-two—I have very little experience of life. There must be a best; but it is hard to find. Do you never feel it so?'

Her large pure eyes are upon him, asking him, as well as her mouth does, for an answer to this unanswerable question. For a moment he hesitates, then:

'Do not you know that there are some people who have arranged their lives so ingeniously that for them there is no best; that the only choice left them lies between bad and worse?'

'I do not believe it,' answers she solemnly. 'God gives us all a best, if we will only look for it; and' (in a lighter key) 'never fear but I shall find mine before I have done!'

After that they finish their watering almost in silence. When he bids her good-bye, having recaptured his Miss Harborough, who is restored to him a good deal smirched by a delirious half-hour in the hayloft with a litter of kittens, Margaret thanks him simply, yet very heartily, for his services to her.

'Why are you so grateful to-day particularly?' asks he, alarmed. 'You make me feel as if the band were playing "God Save the Queen," and everything was at an end.'

'Jacob comes back to his work to-morrow,' answers she, 'and you know,' with a smile, 'I cannot afford to keep two gardeners.'

'He must be very weak still.'

'Do not be afraid,' laughing again; 'I will not overwork him.'

'Then I am to consider myself dismissed?'

'With thanks—yes.'

'Out of work? Turned into the street?'

'Yes.'

'And without a character?'

'I daresay you will not miss it,' replies she, a little cynically. 'Many people do without one.'

He winces. She is not half so nice when she is cynical.

'Come along, Lily,' he says, in a vexed voice; 'we are not wanted here any longer. We are old shoes, sucked lemons, last year's almanacs. Let us go.'

'My child!' cries Margaret, her eye falling for the first time on a gigantic rift in the front of Miss Harborough's frock, 'what have you done to yourself? What will Nanny say to you?'

'I do not care what she says!' replies Lily swaggeringly. 'She is an old beast! Oh, Miss Lambton,' with a sudden change of key, 'may not I come again to-morrow? Alfred wants me to come again to-morrow.' (Alfred is the stable-boy.) 'May not I come with John Talbot again to-morrow?'

'You see that we are both of one mind,' says John, with a melancholy whine, walking off with his young lady.

CHAPTER XII

The Harboroughs' and Talbot's invitation to the Manor had been for a fortnight. Of that fortnight fully a week has already elapsed. To the house which comes next in the Harboroughs' autumn programme John Talbot has, by some strange oversight, not been asked. For this reason—to mark her indignation at so flagrant a departure from the code of civilised manners—Betty shows every symptom of an intention to throw up her engagement.

But for once Mr. Harborough's love of sport exceeds his pliability. From a house which possesses some of the best grousing on the Yorkshire moors, not even the fact that his wife's admirer is not bidden to share it can keep him; and what is more, as it is an old-fashioned house which expects to see husband and wife together, he will make Betty go too.

Talbot's engagements are more elastic. By an easy readjustment of them he might spare another seven days to his present quarters. It is true that Lady Roupell has not as yet definitely asked him to prolong his visit, but he knows that she is hardly aware whether he goes or stays; and as to Freddy, he is always brimming over with an easy hospitality which costs him nothing, and makes every one say what a good fellow he is.

A whole week of absolute freedom, afternoons as well as mornings; a whole week during which he need not pretend to be jealous—pretend to be fond—pretend to be everything that he once was, and is not, and never will be again! It is possible, too, that Jacob may have a relapse. In that case, a whole week of mowing, of clipping edges, of picking lavender, and gathering groundsel for the cage-birds! He knows that there must always be eleven bits gathered, because there are eleven birds, and she cannot bear one to be without. He smiles softly at this tender-hearted puerility of hers.

And meanwhile, since she has made it clear to him that she does not desire any more of his immediate company, he keeps himself away for two whole days. What business has he, who can never claim any rights over her, to expose her, by his assiduities, to the coarse gossip of a gaping village?

But though his eye is not enriched by her, her presence and her words are with him night and day. One of her sentences rings for ever in his ears—'God gives us all a best, if we will only look for it.' Look for it as he may, how can he find his best? and finding, how dare he take hold of and make it his? His best! The best for him—does not it apparently stare him in the face?

To shake off this chain that was once of flowers, and is now of cold eating iron, and to walk the world a free man, free for honest work and honest love. Ay, but to the riveting of that chain there went an oath, from which the mere fact of his having grown tired of wearing its fetters does not, in his opinion, release him. He is bound by an engagement the more perversely sacred, because none can hold him to it.

Only by her with whom it was made can he be emancipated from it; and for that emancipation how can he ask her? How can he go to her and say, 'I have grown tired of you; I have grown fond of another woman. Let me go!'

It is only as a free gift from her hand that he can accept his dismissal; and, of the improbability of her ever making him that gift, his sinking spirit assures him. It is not only vanity and habit that tie her to him. Deep in his heart he knows that, cold wife, partial mother, bad friend as she is, to him she has been, and is, a fond and faithful lover; that, if he were but to hold up his finger, she would toss to the winds position, diamonds, toilettes, admirers, everything that for her life holds of valuable, to face opprobrium and poverty by his side. He knows that he and Franky are the two things in the world she really loves, and for whom her foolish heart beats as truly under its worldly 'fluther' of lace and satin as did ever Cornelia's for her Gracchi, or Lucretia's for her lord.

It is absolutely impossible that he can cut her adrift. Bitterly unsatisfactory, wrong, senseless, and now oppressive as is the connection that binds him to her, he must hope for none other, none better, none dearer, as long as her and his lives last.

Such being the case, is not it the height of unwisdom to himself, perhaps of injustice to that other woman, that he should seek her company with the consciousness of a heart he dare not give, and a hand he dare not offer?

This is the question that dings perpetually in his ears, as he lies down and as he rises up, as he walks moody and alone in the park, as he answers Lily's startling questions, and evades her broad hints; or listens to Betty's anathemas of her man-milliner, or her petulant lamentations over the expected loss of his society during the ensuing week.

He has not yet answered it on the third day after his last visit to the little Red House, when he meets Peggy in the lane, staggering under a philanthropic load of framed lithographs, which he helps her to carry to the workhouse, and to hang up on the walls, whose dreary monotony of whitewash they agreeably and gaudily vary. He has not yet answered it the next day, when he carries a message to her from Lady Roupell, a message which must be preposterously long, since it takes two hours and a half to deliver; he has not yet answered it on the day after, nor on the day after that again, which is the last of the

Harboroughs' visit.

On the afternoon of that day some business has brought Peggy reluctantly up to the Manor, where she had not appeared for above a week. John and Lily, as is but civil, escort her home again! It is true that Miss Harborough has had a near shave, at the moment of setting off, of being recaptured by her nurse—a danger from which she has been rescued only by her own presence of mind, a presence of mind made all the acuter by her excessive desire to flirt with John, and to overhear what—unintended for Lilyan ears—he has to say to his companion.

'Oh, Miss Lambton!' cries she, pulling down Peggy's face in order to whisper importantly into her ear; 'do not you think I had better come with you? There are the stiles! I do not see,' with an affectation of excessive delicacy, 'how you are to get over the stiles with only John Talbot!'

Her plea is admitted as sound.

They all three spend a long dawdling afternoon at the Little House. They take the fox out for a run in the field on his chain; and in his joy he gallops round and round, tying all their legs together, even throwing Miss Harborough down —an accident which fills her with delight. He offers to play with Mink, who growls, and receives his advances with such hauteur that he has to be reminded of the humility of his own beginnings, and of the Dogs' Home. The snubbed fox throws himself on the sward and pants, swishing his brush from side to side like a cross cat. Then they restore him to his prison, at which he opens his red mouth wide, making little angry wild noises.

After they have done with the fox, they have still the garden to water; the kittens in the hayloft—to which they ascend, on the joint invitation of Alfred and Lily—to see; peas to throw to the pretty prosy pigeons, long-windedly courting in fans and pouts, and prism-coloured throats on the dove-cot roof. And when at length her guests take their tardy leave, Peggy is insensibly lured, step by step, into accompanying them more than half-way home.

Into what could not such an evening lure one? Through a barley-field first; all the pale spears slanting westward in the level sun; then a field of old pasture, knapweeds purpling, little hawkweed clocks telling the time in fairyland, loitering buttercups. Then a hedgerow with woody nightshade and long blue vetch; then the green night of a little wood. Though the sun is nearing his declension, the delicious smell that all day long he has compelled the grass and the flowers to bring him, in odorous tribute, still tarries, making the air rich—*âcre*, as the French say; a word for which there is no precise English equivalent. On the farther side of the tiny forest they part; if so short a severance can indeed be called to part. Are not they to meet again in an hour or so, at that dinner-party at the Manor, to which both Peggy and Prue are bidden? and even if it were not so, have not they to-morrow, and again to-morrow, and yet to-morrow again, to look forward to? This being so, why is it that such a curious last-time feeling clings to Talbot as he crosses the park with his little chattering comrade, making him turn his head again and again in futile seeking towards the sylvan gate whence his tall and white-gowned friend has already disappeared?

On entering the house, and going through an upper passage to his room, he is accosted by Betty's maid, who tells him that her ladyship's headache is better; that she is on the sofa in Lady Roupell's boudoir, and that she has expressed a wish to see him as soon as he comes in. He follows with a guilty conscience and a sinking heart. Has he for one moment of his long blissful afternoon remembered the headache, to which alone he owed his freedom; the headache genuine enough—though it took its birth from mortification and spleen—to keep her stretched in pain and solitary darkness the livelong day? She is in semi-darkness still, her windows closed (a headache always makes her chilly); not a glint of apricot cloud or suave blue sky-field reaching her. A sense of pity, largely touched with remorse, comes over him, as he takes her hand, and says softly:

'You are better at last? Come, that is well!'

She leaves her hand, languid and rather feverish, lying in his.

'It is time that I should be better!' she says, with an impatient sigh. 'What a day I have had!—our last day!' There is such genuine grief and regret in the accent with which she pronounces the three final words that his remorse deepens; but that increase of self-reproach does not make it the least more possible to him to echo her lamentation. 'I asked Julie how often you had been to inquire after me,' continues she, turning her eyes, innocent to-day of their usual black smouches, interrogatively upon him; 'she said she could not remember.'

Talbot blesses the wisely ambiguous maid; and, to hide his confusion, stoops his head over the hand, which he still—since it is evidently expected of him—holds.

'I wish my inquiries could have made you better,' says he, taking—and feeling with shame that he is taking—a leaf out of Julie's book. 'I am afraid that you will not be able to come down to dinner.'

'Oh, but I shall!' returns she sharply. 'Why do you think I shall not? Is the wish father to the thought?'

He laughs constrainedly, taking refuge in what is often the best disguise, truth.

'Yes, that is it!'

'Milady would never forgive me,' pursues she, rolling her head restlessly about upon the cushions, 'if I left her to struggle with the natives alone; I am sure I have not the heart to struggle with any one! Oh, how miserable I am! John!'—laying her other hand on his, and clasping it between both hers —'how *am* I to get through the next fortnight?'

Talbot wonders whether the burning blush that he feels searing him all through his body shows in his face, whether he looks the double-faced cur that he feels. Probably he does not, or else the faint light helps him; for she goes on unsuspiciously:

'You have never told me where you have decided to go to-morrow—to the Mackintoshes or the Delaneys? If you ask my advice,' with a rather showery smile, 'I should say the Delaneys; for you will be less well amused there, and have more time to think of me! Remember that you have not given me your address; give it me now, lest you should forget it!'

The tug of war has come. He would rather have put it off until her headache was gone—until he could meet her upon more equal terms. What chance has a man against a woman lying on a sofa with her eyes full of tears, and a handkerchief wetted with eau-de-Cologne tied round her aching brows? None. His hesitation is so obvious that she cannot but notice it.

'Well,' she says, with some sharpness, 'why do not you answer me? Where is the difficulty?'

He laughs artificially.

'The difficulty,' he says, trying to speak carelessly—'the difficulty is that there is no difficulty. You have my address already. I am going to stay here!'

He has deposited his box of dynamite: he has now only to wait for the explosion. But for twenty or thirty heart-beats she remains entirely silent, and, at the end of that time, only repeats his own words:

'To—stay—here!'

'Yes.'

Another silence. He begins to wish that the explosion would come. It would at least be better than this. She has sat up on her sofa, and pushed back the wet bandage from her damp and straightened hair. She has neither belladonna nor rouge. He has always strongly deprecated and even reviled the use of either; and yet he cannot help thinking, though he hates himself for so thinking, that she looks old and haggard without them.

'And this,' says she at last, speaking between her teeth in a low voice, 'is your delicate way of intimating to me that I am superseded!'

He has risen to his feet. They stand staring each at each in the twilight room, the one not whiter than the other. How much worse it is than he had feared! Close outside the window a robin is piping blithely. A stupid wonder flashes across his mind as to whether he is one of those for whom Peggy scatters crumbs on her window-sill.

'I think that that is a question not worth answering,' he replies, trying to speak calmly.

'But all the same it must be answered,' rejoins she, with symptoms of rising excitement. 'You shall not leave the room until it is answered.'

'Will you please to repeat it then in a more intelligible form?' asks he, with a forced composure.

For a moment she glares at him with dead-white face and shining eyes; then, rising from her sofa, flings herself into his arms.

'How can you expect me to say such words twice?' cries she, bursting into a tempest of tears; 'but if it is so, tell me the truth. You have always blamed me for not speaking truth; learn your own lesson: tell me the truth. Is it all over— all at an end?'

She has withdrawn herself again from him, and now stands holding him at arm's length, a hand upon each shoulder, her dimmed eyes fixed upon his face, searching for the least sign of faltering or evasion upon it. But she finds none.

'You know,' he answers, in a low quiet voice, whose gentleness is the cover for a bottomless depression, 'that there will never be an end to it until you make one.'

Something in his tone dries her tears.

'Then why do you want to stay here?' asks she, her voice still shaking from her late gust of passion.

He is silent. Her words find an echo in his own heart. Why indeed? Seen in the hell-light of his renewed bondage, his plan for that one little halcyon week ahead seems to him to have been a monstrosity of folly and unreason. How could he, for even a moment, have entertained it?

Betty has sat down again upon the sofa; and wiping rather viciously the eyes in which an ireful light is flashing, she says softly, as if she were saying something rather pleasant:

'I am sure you would not wish to hurt *her*, or blight *her* young affections; and yet it seems to me that you are on the high-road to do both.'

He writhes, but he could not speak, if flaying alive were to be the penalty of his dumbness.

'I do not think'—still in that silky key—'that you have any right to turn the poor thing's head with attentions such as she has probably never received before.'

At that he laughs out loud, and insultingly:

'Turn her head! Ha! ha!'

'It is very amusing, no doubt,' rejoins Betty, her false suavity giving way to a most real fury, breast heaving, and colour rising, 'and such hilarity becomes you extremely; but, as she has probably never seen any one more attractive than the village apothecary, it would be no great excess of coxcombry on your part to suppose that you might be his successful rival.'

But this taunt fails to extract any reply. Exasperated by her insuccess in driving him into angry speech, she goes on:

'I do not think you have had to complain of her rigour; how many days'— with an innocent air of inquiry—'has she allowed you to mow her lawn, and milk her cow, and feed her pig for her? Six? Seven? I suppose you have been with her to-day, too?'

At that he unwisely abandons his fortress of silence, and speaks:

'You had better ask Lily; you have set her on more than once as a spy. Have your child in and ask her!'

To this cold and withering taunt her own weaker sarcasms succumb; and again abandoning all self-control, she bursts into an agony of weeping, burying her head in the sofa-cushions, and convulsed from head to foot by her sobs.

'Is it any wonder,' she moans, 'that I do not want to see the only thing I have in the world go from me? What am I saying?'—pulling herself up suddenly —'how dare I say the only thing? have not I my Franky? I shall always have my Franky!'

The grief of her tone is so poignant and so real that his heart softens to her, despite her former gibes. He lays his hand upon her shoulder.

'What is all this about?' he asks kindly. 'You know as well as I do that you will have me—such as I am—as long as you choose to keep me!'

'Then you will not stay here?' cries she precipitately, quitting her desperate posture, and springing back with startling suddenness into life and animation again; 'then you will go to-morrow?'

There is a pause. He walks to the window. Through it there comes the peaceful sound of bleating sheep; and the distant sharp bark of a little dog. Can it be Mink? He has a sharp bark. Poor little Mink! He will probably never see Mink again. And to-morrow, according to Peggy, Mink had promised to tell them all about the Dogs' Home!

He smiles transiently at the recollection of her childish jest. How many things they were to have done to-morrow! Then he walks slowly back from the window and says:

'I will go to-morrow!'

Perhaps there is something in the tone of this concession which takes away from the value of it, for Betty begins to sob again; this time more in wrath than in sorrow.

'I do not think you need make such a favour of it; I do not think it is much to ask, considering all things—considering how I have com—com—compromised my reputation for your sake for the last five years!' cries she hysterically.

He does not defend himself; only a thought, whose want of generosity shocks him, flashes across his mind, that that was already a *fait accompli* when he had first made her acquaintance.

'*We* know that there is no harm in our friendship,' pursues she, a slight red staining her tear-washed cheeks; 'but nobody else knows it. The world is always only too pleased to think the worst, and in one sense'—again mastered by her emotion—'it is right! I would have given up *anything—everything* for you—you know I would! and you—you—will give up *nothing* for me, not even such a trifle as this!'

Once again pity gets the upper hand of him; but a pity crossed by such a bottomless regret and remorse at having let himself slide into this tangled labyrinth of wrong, when honour and dishonour have changed coats, and he does not know which is which, as the Lost Souls in Hell, if such there be, might feel in looking back upon their earthly course.

'You are right,' he says; 'we must do the best we can for each other! We must not make life harder for one another than it already is. I will do what you wish! I ought! I will! Such a trifle, too!'

CHAPTER XIII

'At length burst in the argent revelry,
With plume, tiara and all rich array,
Numerous as shadows haunting fairily
The brain new stuffed in youth with triumphs gay
Of old Romance.'

The 'argent revelry' has burst into the Manor in the shape of what Lady Roupell, with more vigour than elegance, is apt to call one of her 'Beast Parties,' *i.e.* one of those miscellaneous gatherings of the whole neighbourhood to which she thinks herself bound twice or thrice in the year— gatherings which, though dictated by hospitality, are not usually very successful. It is Lady Roupell's principle to override all the small social distinctions of the neighbourhood, to invite all the people who quarrel, all the people who look down upon each other, all the people who are bored by one another, all the people who are trying to avoid each other, to hobnob at her bounteous board.

'They all go to God's house together, my dear; why should not they come to mine?' asks she, with a logic that she thinks unanswerable. And so they do; but they do not enjoy themselves.

That, however, is no concern of milady's. The 'Beasts' *must* like to talk to one another, or, if they do not, they ought to like it.

Having thrown open her house to them, having given them every opportunity of over-eating themselves on her excellent food, and being exhilarated by her admirable wines, she washes her hands of them; and having enjoyed her own champagne and venison, sits down to her Patience-table, which is set out for her every night of her life, and would be were Queen Victoria to honour her with a visit.

Of the Beast Parties the Evans pair invariably form a constituent part.

'I always ask the Evanses,' says milady good-naturedly. 'It is quite pretty to see the way in which he enjoys his dinner; and she likes to wear her dyed gown, good woman, and smuggle candied apricots into her pockets for those ugly urchins of hers, and look out my friends in her "Peerage" next day!'

So the Evanses are here, and several harmless rural clergy; like them to the outer eye, though no doubt to the inner as dissimilar as each island-like human soul is from its neighbour. There are some large landowners with their wives, and some very small lawyers and doctors with theirs. There is a tallow-merchant, who to-day grovels in hides and tallow, but to-morrow will probably—oh, free and happy England!—soar to a seat in the Cabinet. There is a Colonial Bishop imported by one neighbour, and a fashionable buffoon introduced by another; and lastly, there are Peggy and Prue.

Never before has Peggy set off to a Beast Party with so light a heart. She knows how little chance of rational or even irrational entertainment such a feast affords; and yet, do what she will, she feels gay. Prue is gay too, extravagantly gay, for did not Freddy stroll in half an hour ago with a flower for her, and a request to her to wear her green gown for his sake?

Before setting off Peggy bids her eleven birds good-night, telling them that to-morrow they shall have a swinging ladder in their large cage to remind them of the swinging tree-tops. Has not Talbot promised to make them a ladder?

The girls have timed their arrival better than on a former occasion. The room is already full when they walk in with their breeze-freshened cheeks and their simple clothes.

Margaret has not even her best dress on. She had looked at it waveringly and hankeringly at dressing-time; but a sort of superstition—an undefined feeling that she is not going to meet any one for whom she has a right to prank herself out, prevents her wearing it. But she cannot help having her best face on. There is sunshiny weather in her heart. Even her repulsion for Lady Betty is weakened. Possibly she has been unjust towards her. Certainly she is not the human octopus from whose grasp no prey can escape alive, for which she took her. She herself has the best reason for knowing that from this octopus's arms prey can and does escape alive and well. After all, she has condemned her upon mere loose hearsay evidence. Henceforth she will trust only the evidence of her own eyes and ears. At present her eyes tell her that Betty is very highly rouged, and rather naked; and her ears—thanks to the din of tongues—tell her nothing.

For a wonder, Lady Roupell is down in time, her gown properly laced— usually, from excessive hurry, her maid has to skip half the eyelet-holes—and with her ornaments duly fastened on. She is following her usual rule, talking to the person who amuses her most, and leaving all the others to take care of themselves.

As soon as dinner is announced, and Freddy has walked off with his allotted lady, she turns with an easy smile to her company, and says:

'Will everybody take in somebody, please?'

At this command, so grateful and natural in a small and intimate party, so extremely ill-suited to this large and miscellaneous crowd, there is a moment of hesitating and consternation. The hearts of those who know that they are never anybody's voluntary choice, but whom conventionality generally provides with a respectable partner, sink to the soles of their shoes. The young men hang back from the girls, because they think that some one else may have a better right to them. All fear to grasp at a precedence not their due.

At length there is a movement. The tallow-merchant, true to his principle of soaring, offers his arm to the wife of the Lord-Lieutenant. The parsons and doctors begin timidly to exchange wives. The Colonial Bishop casts his landing-net over Prue. Margaret's is one of the few breasts in the room in which the order for promiscuous choice has excited a spark of pleasure. In the ordinary course of things she is aware that it is improbable that Talbot would be her portion. If it is a case of selection, the improbability vanishes. She smiles slightly to herself as she recalls the surly indignation with which she had discovered that he was to be her fate on the last occasion of her dining here. She is still smiling when he passes her by with Betty on his arm. For a few seconds it seems as if the handsomest girl in the room were to be left altogether overlooked and unclaimed; and, in point of fact, she is one of the latest to be paired. Usually such a blow to her vanity would have disquieted her but little, as her pretensions are never high. To-day she is shocked to find how much it galls her.

The ill-sorted party have taken their seats, precedence gone, natural barriers knocked on the head, reciprocal antipathies forced into close contact, in that topsy-turvy Utopia of universal equality and amity which it is Lady Roupell's principle to produce.

Margaret looks round the table to see how the principle has worked. Mrs. Evans has been led in by the doctor, to whom she is fully persuaded that she owes the death of the last Evans but one. The next largest squiress in the parish to Lady Roupell is made sulky for the evening by having had to accept the arm of her man of business. Prue's Bishop has innocently planted her as far as the length of the interminable table will allow from Freddy. Betty and Talbot, though distant, are in sight. She can see that they are sitting side by side in total silence. Is this their mode of expressing their sorrow at their approaching separation? Possibly; but, at all events, what a depth of intimacy does such a total silence imply! Margaret's own mate is the buffoon. She has often heard his name as that of the pet of royalty; the darling of the fine ladies; the crowning sparkle in each choicest social gathering. To her, whether it be that her mental palate is out of taste, he seems dull and coarse; his wit made up of ugly faces, elderly *double-entendres*, flat indecencies.

'It is clear that I am not made for good company,' she says to herself sadly and wearily. 'Jacob, and the birds, and the fox—these are my society! They are the only ones I am fit for.'

The long dinner ends at last, and the incongruous couples part—in most cases with mutual relief. Neither Margaret nor her merry man ever wish to set eyes upon each other again. In the drawing-room natural affinities reassert themselves: intimates gather into little groups. The squiress, escaped from her presumptuous solicitor, makes her plaint to her fellows. Mrs. Evans makes hers to Peggy.

'Did you see how unlucky I was?' cries she. 'I assure you it gave me quite a shudder to put my hand upon his arm! I declare I look upon that man as as much the murderer of my Natty as if he had stuck a knife into her. I could hardly bear to speak to him. However, I managed to secure some crackers for the children'—indicating a tell-tale bulge in the direction of her pocket. 'Their last word to me before I came away was, "Mother, be sure you bring us some crackers!"'

Then it is Prue's turn to make her lament, which she begins with almost the same words as Mrs. Evans:

'Did you ever see anything like my ill-luck? I was the farthest from *him* of anybody at the table. There were eighteen between us. I counted. But did you notice how he rushed to open the door? As I passed him he said to me, "Thank you, Prue." That was because I had put my green gown on. He is always so grateful for any little thing that one does for him.'

She pauses rather suddenly, for Lady Betty has drawn near.

'What a pretty frock!' says she, stopping before the two girls. 'As green as grass, as jealousy, as green peas! Come and talk to me, Miss Prue, and tell me what you have all been doing to-day. You may have been up to any amount of mischief for all I can tell. Do you know that I have been writhing on a bed of pain from morning to night? No? but I have. Are not you sorry for me?'

As she speaks she draws the childish figure down on the sofa beside her.

Margaret walks away. She would like to take Prue away too. There seems to her to be something unnatural and sinister in an alliance, however temporary, between these two, and from the distant corner to which she has retired her eye often wanders uneasily back to them.

Presently her view is obscured. It is no use her looking any longer. The sofa is shut out from her by a ring of black coats that has clustered round it. Only now and then, through the interstices, she catches the glint of one of the numerous hornets, lizards, frogs, flashing in diamonds upon Betty's breast. Bursts of laughter come from the group, which Freddy and the buffoon have joined. In the intervals of the other conversations buzzing around Peggy can hear Betty's high voice piercing. She cannot hear what she says; but apparently it is always followed by torrents of mirth, among which Prue's girl-tones are plainly audible. Oh, what is Prue laughing at? If she could but get her away!

As she so thinks, herself wedged in among a phalanx of women, she sees a stir among the band she is watching. It expands and moves, pursuing Betty, who has walked to the piano. Evidently she has been persuaded to sing.

As soon as this intention has become manifest in the room there is a polite hush in the talk. Wives look menacingly at unmusical husbands. The Bishop, who is fond of music, approaches the instrument. Betty has seated herself leisurely, her audacious eyes wandering round and taking in the prelate with a mischievous twinkle.

'I am not quite sure that you will like it,' Peggy hears her say. 'But, you know, I cannot help that—I did not write it. It is supposed to be said by an affectionate husband on the eve of his setting out for the wars.'

With this prelude she sets off—

>'Oh! who will press that lily-white hand
>When I am far away?
>Some other man!'

Two more lines in the nature of a chorus follow, but they are so drowned by a roar of applause that Peggy can't catch them. She can only conjecture their nature from the look of impudent laughing challenge which the singer throws at the men around her. Under cover of that roar of applause the Bishop turns abruptly away.

The second verse follows—

>'Oh! who will kiss those ruby lips
>When I am far away?
>Some other man!'

Again the two drowned lines. Again the chord and the applause; but this time it is very evident that the approbation is confined to the circle round the piano.

Betty has been well taught, and her enunciation is exceedingly pure and distinct. Not a word of her charming song is lost. She has reached the third verse—

>'Oh! who will squeeze that little waist
>When I am far away?
>Some other man!'

Again that roar of admiring laughter from the men round the piano—all the more marked from the displeased silence of the rest of the room.

But is it only men who are encoring so ecstatically? Is not that Prue who is joining her enraptured plaudits to theirs?—Prue, with flushed face and flashing eyes, and slight shoulders convulsed with merriment? If she could but get her away! But that is out of the question; Prue is in the inner circle, utterly beyond reach.

'Oh! who will pay those little bills?'

Peggy cannot stand it any longer; it makes her sick. A gap in the ranks of ladies that had shut her in gives her the wished-for opportunity to escape. She slips towards an open French window giving on the terrace. Before reaching it she has to pass Lady Roupell and her Patience. As she does so she hears the old lady saying, in a voice of tepid annoyance, to the man beside her:

'I wish that some one would stop her singing that indecent song. She will not leave me a rag of character in the county!'

CHAPTER XIV.

'Whilst she was here
Methought the beams of light that did appear
Were shot from her; methought the moon gave none
But what it had from her.'

Safely out on the terrace in the moonlight! Not, it is true, a great wash of moonlight such as went billowing over the earth when she paid her former night-visit to milady's garden; but such small radiance as a lessening crescent, now and then dimmed by over-flung cloud-kerchiefs, can lend. The stars, indeed, seeing their lady faint and fail, eke her out with their lesser lights. Peggy stands drawing deep breaths, staring up at them with her head thrown back, as they shine down upon her in their overwhelming, overpowering distance, and purity and age. But between her and their august and soothing silence comes again that odious refrain:

'Some other man!
…..'

She puts her fingers in her ears and runs, nor does she stop until she has reached the close of the long, broad gravel walk that keeps the house-front company from end to end. Then she pauses and listens. No, she is not far enough off even yet. Fainter, but still perfectly audible, comes the vulgar ribaldry:

'Some other man!
…..'

and then the storm of applause. Let her at all events reach some spot where she will be unable to detect any tone of Prue's in that insane mirth! But is there such a spot? To her excited fancy it seems as if in the remotest dell, the loneliest coppice of the park, she would still overhear her Prue's little voice applauding that disgusting pleasantry.

She walks quickly on, between flower-borders and shrubberies, until she reaches a wrought-iron gate that leads into the walled garden. She opens it and passes through, then stands still once again to listen. She has succeeded at last. Not an echo of Betty's high-pitched indecencies attains to this quiet garden-close to offend her ears. There is no noise less clean and harmless than that of the south wind delicately wagging the heads of the slumberous flowers.

The garden, as its name implies, is hedged in from each rude gust on three sides by stout walls, stone-coped and balled. On the fourth, towards the sun-setting, it is guarded only by a light decorated iron railing, now muffled in the airy fluff of the traveller's joy, and embraced by the luxuriant arms of the hop, the clematis, and the wandering vine. Between their tendrils, between the branches of the strong tea-rose and the Virginia creeper's autumn fires, one catches friendly glimpses of the church tower and the park, and the gentle deer. Inside, the garden is encompassed by wide and crowded flower-borders, but the middle is sacred to the green simplicity of the velvet grass.

Margaret draws a deep breath of relief, and begins to walk slowly along. A row of tall, white gladioli, nearly as high-statured as herself, looking ghostly fair in the starshine, keep her company, lovely and virginal as May lilies; and from the farther side of the garden comes an ineffable waft of that violet smell which we used to connect only with spring. As she paces to and fro the ugly din fades out of her ears and the ireful red out of her cheeks. A sort of peace settles down upon her—only a *sort* of peace, however! Her mind is still oppressed by the image of Prue, and by a vague misgiving of coming trouble, coupled with a sense, which she will not own to herself, of personal disappointment, and of a mortified covert self-gratulation upon not having worn her best gown, or in anywise tricked herself out.

To one, however, whose hand is on the garden-latch, as she so thinks, she looks tricked out enough, indeed, in her own fairness; enough to make his heart sick with the hopelessness of its longing as he goes towards her. After all, she is not much surprised at his having followed her! Possibly he may have a message of recall for her.

'Well!' she says, meeting him with a delicate moonlit smile.

Low as the light is, it is light enough to show that there is no answering smile on his face.

'So you escaped at last!' he says, with a sort of groan. 'I watched to see how long you could stand it.'

The shadow that the star-beams, and the violet breath, and Heaven knows what other gentle influence, have chased from her features, settles down on them again.

'I am never fond of comic songs,' she answers stiffly; 'and I do not think that that was a particularly favourable specimen.'

He makes a gesture of disgust.

'Pah!' Then adds: 'I should have followed you before, only that I wanted to get Prue away. I knew that you would be glad if I could; but it was impossible!'

He has never spoken of her as 'Prue' before; but in his present agitation—an agitation for which Peggy is at a loss to account—he has obviously clean forgotten the formal prefix.

She is too much touched by his thoughtfulness for her to answer.

'My chief motive for following you,' continues he, speaking in an unusual and constrained voice, 'was that I thought I might possibly not have another opportunity of giving you *this*.'

As he speaks he puts a small parcel into her hands.

'It is only the ladder for the birds.'

She breaks into a laugh.

'They are in no such great hurry for it,' says she gaily; 'they could have waited until to-morrow.'

He sighs.

'I am afraid that they would have had to wait longer than until to-morrow!'

'Well, I daresay that they might have made shift until Wednesday,' returns she.

The entire unsuspiciousness of her tone makes his task a tenfold harder one than it would otherwise have been.

'It is—it is better that you should take it yourself to them,' he says, hesitating and floundering. 'I—I—might be prevented after all from coming. There is a chance of my—my—being obliged after all to go to-morrow!'

The star and moonlight are falling full on her face, lifted and attentive: he can see it as plainly as at high noonday. It seems to him that a tiny change passes over it. But still she does not suspect the truth.

'What!' says she; 'has your chief telegraphed for you? What a thing it is to be so indispensable!'

Shall he leave her in her error? Nothing would be easier! Leave her in the belief that a legitimate summons to honourable work has called him away; leave her with a friendly face turned towards him, expecting and perhaps lightly hoping his return. The temptation is strong, but he conquers it.

'No,' he says, trying to speak carelessly; 'my chief is innocent this time of breaking into my holiday. I expect that he is enjoying his own too much; I am not going Londonwards; but—but—other reasons compel me to leave to-morrow.'

How unutterably flat and naked it sounds! There is no mistake now as to the change in her face—the change that he has dreaded and yet known would come—the hardening of eye and tightening of lip. Well, it is better that it should come! And yet, do what he may, he cannot leave her in the belief that, as he sees, has in one moment stolen all the frank sweetness out of her eyes.

'I—I—am not going north, either,' he cries, in miserable, eager stammering. 'I—I—do not know where I am going!'

'You are compelled to go, and yet you do not know where you are going! is that a riddle?' asks she ironically.

Her tone jars horribly upon his strung and aching nerves.

'Not much of a riddle,' he answers, with a bitter laugh. 'I do not know the exact road I am going to take; I only know the direction—downhill.'

She fixes her eyes steadily upon his for a moment or two, a ray of compassion stealing into them. So they are to pass each other, like ships upon the sea! After all, he has not been able to wrench himself out of the arms of his octopus! A transient flash of self-derision crosses her mind for having ever supposed it possible that he could, coupled with an immense pity.

This is to be their last speech together; for some instinct tells her that he will not return. Let it not, then, be bitter speech! Poor fellow! There are aloes enough, God wot, in the cup he has brewed for himself!

'Well!' she says, smiling kindly, albeit very sadly, at him, 'whether you go uphill or downhill, the birds and I must always have a good word for you. I do not know what we should have done without you; you have been so kind to us all—to me and my Prue, and my fox and my birds!'

He ought to make some acknowledgment of this farewell civility of hers; but to 'ought' and to do have, since the world was, never been one and the same thing. He receives it in a suffocated silence.

'And I was so rude to you at first,' pursues she, lightly brushing, as she speaks, her own lips with a bit of mignonette she has gathered from the odorous bed at her feet, perhaps to hide the slight tremble of which she cannot but be conscious in them—'so angry at being sent in to dinner with you! but, then'—with another friendly starlit smile—'you must remember that I did not know how well you could *mow*!'

He is still silent, his throat choked with words he dare not utter. Oh, if she would only stop! But she goes on in all innocence:

'You never took your bunch of lavender after all to-day. I thought of bringing it up for you to-night, but then I remembered that I should see you to-morrow, so I did not; I wish I had now.'

89

Cannot he find even one word? one word of prayer to her in mercy to be silent? Not one!

'Are you going by an early train?' continues she; 'because, if not, I might send up Alfred with it in the morning, if you really cared to have it.'

Perhaps it is that last most unnecessary clause that loosens the string of his tied tongue.

'Do not!' he says almost rudely; 'I hope I shall never smell the scent of lavender again!'

For a moment she looks at him, astonished at his discourtesy; but probably his face explains it, for her eyes drop. When next she speaks it is in a rather colder key.

'At all events I must send you back your books; you left some books with us to-day, if you remember.'

If he remember the Keats from which he was to have read aloud to her to-morrow, sitting beside her under the Judas-tree, with her little finches calling to her from the house, with Mink crouched on her white skirt, and the parrot waddling over the sward, with his toes turned in, to have his head scratched by her! *If he remember!* She must be the very 'belle dame sans merci' of whom John Keats spake, to ask him that! May not he at least beg her to keep his Keats to remember him by—laying here and there among the leaves a sprig of the lavender they together plucked? No! No! No! Out of her life he and his Keats must depart, as she and her lavender out of his. Who, in his place, will read her 'La Belle Dame sans merci'? As if in devilish mockery of the jealous anguish of this question comes Betty's disgusting refrain darting across his mind:

> 'Some other man!
> .....
> .....'

He grinds his teeth. It is some minutes before he can regain sufficient command over himself to answer with a tolerable appearance of composure:

'You are right; I will send for them!'

A little sighing gust has risen; sighing for him perhaps, he thinks, with a flash of imaginative self-pity, as he watches its soft antics among the lily-like flowers, and its light ruffling of Peggy's gown. It has mistaken her for one of the flowers! What foolish fancies are careering through his hot brain! There can be none in hers, or how could she be holding out such a cool hand and lifting such a suave calm look to his?

'I must be going,' she says, speaking in a rather lower voice than is her wont; 'good-bye! Since'—a wavering smile breaking tremulously over her face —'since you are so determined to go downhill, I suppose I dare not say that I hope our roads will ever meet again!'

Her hand slides out of his unreturning clasp. He feels that if he keep that soft prisoner for one instant, he must keep it through eternity.

'Good-bye!' he says.

He would like to bid God bless her; but he can no more do it than Macbeth could say 'Amen.' What right has he to bid God bless her? Will God be more likely to send her a benison for his unworthy asking? So he lets her go unblessed.

CHAPTER XV

The Beast Party is over. It has not differed materially from its predecessors, though it may perhaps glory in the bad pre-eminence of having left even more ill-feeling and mortification in its wake than did they.

The little Evanses, indeed, bless its memory, gobbling the bonbons and strutting about the Vicarage garden in the masks and fools' caps that they have extracted out of its crackers. And Lady Roupell, too, is perfectly satisfied with it. Her guests have come, have eaten and drunk, have gone away again, and she need not trouble her head about them for another six months. To-day she gets rid of all her friends except the Harborough children, and is left at liberty to waddle about in her frieze coat, and with her spud in her hand, in peace—a peace which, at the worst of times, she never allows to be very seriously infringed. But there are gradations of age and shabbiness in her frieze coats, and to-day she may don the oldest.

The peace of the Manor, like its gaieties, is apt to be reflected in the Cottage: an exodus from the one is virtually an exodus from the other; and, as such, is apt to be rejoiced over by Margaret as the signal for Prue to begin to eat her dinner better, sleep sounder, and engage in some other occupation than running to the end of the garden to see whether there is a sign of any messenger coming from the Manor. She is at her post of predilection this morning—the end of the garden that overhangs the highway—that highway along which all arrivers at and departers from the Big House must needs travel. She is looking eagerly down the road.

'Prue!' cries her sister from under the Judas-tree, where she is sitting, for a wonder, unoccupied.

'Yes,' replies Prue, but without offering to stir from her post of observation.

'Come here. I want to talk to you.'

'In a minute—directly—by and by.'

A few moments pass.

'Prue?'

'Yes.'

'What are you looking at? What are you waiting for?'

'I am waiting for the Harboroughs to pass. I want to kiss my hand to Lady Betty as she goes by; she asked me to.'

Margaret makes a gesture of annoyance, and irritably upsets Mink, who has just curled himself upon her skirt; but she offers no remonstrance, and it is a quarter of an hour before—the brougham with its Harboroughs, late as usual, and galloping to catch the train, having whirled past and been watched till quite out of sight—Prue saunters up radiant.

'She kissed her hand to me all the way up the hill!' says she, beaming with pleasure at the recollection. 'I threw her a little bunch of jessamine just as the carriage went by. She put her head out in a second, and caught it *in her teeth*!' Was not it clever of her? She *is* so clever!'

'Why should she kiss her hand to you? Why should you throw her jessamine?' asks Peggy gloomily.

'Why should not I?' returns the other warmly. 'I am sure she has been kind enough to me, if you only knew!'

'You were not so fond of her last week,' says Margaret, lifting a pair of very troubled eyes to her sister's face. 'Have you already forgotten the three days running that she robbed you of your ride?'

'I cannot think how I could have been so silly!' returns Prue, with a rather forced laugh. 'Of course, it was a mere accident. *He* says he wonders how I could have been so silly; he was dreadfully hurt about it. He says he looks upon her quite as an elder sister.'

'An elder sister!' echoes Peggy, breaking into a short angry laugh. 'The same sort of elder sister, I think, as the nursery-maid is to the Life Guardsman!'

'I cannot think how you can be so censorious!' retorts Prue, reddening. 'He says it is your one weakness. He admires your character more than that of any one he knows—he says it is—it is—laid upon such large lines; but that he has often been hurt by the harshness of your judgments of other people.'

'Indeed!' says Peggy, with a sort of snort. 'But I daresay that Lady Betty bandages up his wounds.'

'You must have noticed how kind she was to me last night,' continues Prue, thinking it wiser to appear not to have heard this last thrust. 'Of course, every one was longing to talk to her, but she quite singled me out—*me*, of all people! Oh, if you only knew!'

'If I only knew what?' inquires Margaret, struck by the recurrence of this phrase, to which on its first utterance she had paid little heed, as being the vague expression of Prue's girlish enthusiasm.

Prue hesitates a moment.

'If—if—you only knew the delightful plan she has made!'

'What plan?' shortly and sternly.

'She—she—I cannot think why she did it; it must have been the purest kind-heartedness—she asked me to go and stay with her.'

The colour has mounted brave and bright from Margaret's cheeks to her brow.

'She asked you to stay with her?' repeats she, with slow incisiveness; 'she had the impudence to ask you to stay with her!'

Prue gives a start that is almost abound.

'*The impudence?*'

'The woman who had the effrontery to sing that song last night,' pursues Peggy, her voice gathering indignation as it goes along, 'has now the impudence to invite a respectable girl like you to stay with her! Oh, Prue!' her tone changing suddenly to one of eager, tender pain, 'just think what I felt last night when I saw you standing among all those men in fits of laughter at her stupid indecencies! Oh! how could you laugh? What was there to laugh at?'

Prue has begun to whimper.

'They all laughed. I—I—laughed be—be—cause they laughed!'

'And now you want to go and stay with her!' says Margaret, touched and yet annoyed by her sister's easy tears, and letting her long arms fall to her side with a dispirited gesture, as if life were growing too hard for her.

'I am sure it would be no great wonder if I did,' says Prue, still snivelling. 'I, who never go anywhere. She—Lady Betty I mean—could not believe it when I told her I had only been to London twice in my life; and He says that the Harboroughs' is the pleasantest house in England!'

'What does He say?' inquires a soft, gay voice, coming up behind them. 'Why, Prue, what is this? Why are the waterworks turned on? It is early in the day for the fountains to begin playing!' and Freddy Ducane—the flower-like Freddy—with his charming complexion, his laughing eyes, and his beautifully-fitting clothes, stands between the agitated girls.

He has taken Prue's hands, both the one that contains the small damp ball of her pocket-handkerchief and the other. But she snatches them away and runs off.

'You seem to have been having rather a quick thing,' says the young man, bringing back his eyes from the flying to the stationary figure.

The latter has risen.

'Did you know of this invitation?' asks she abruptly, without any attempt at a preliminary salutation.

'I do not much like that dagger-and-bowl way of being asked questions,' returns Freddy, sinking pleasantly into the chair Margaret has just quitted. 'What invitation?'

'You know perfectly well what invitation!' retorts she, her breast beginning to heave and her nostril to quiver, while her pendent right hand unconsciously clenches itself.

Freddy has thrown back his curly head, and is regarding her luxuriously from under his tilted hat, and between his half-closed lids.

'I wish you would stay exactly as you are for just two minutes,' he says rapturously; 'I never saw you look better in my life! What a pose! And you fell into it so naturally, too! I declare, Peg, though we have our little differences, there is no one that at heart appreciates you half as much as I do!'

'I suppose that you suggested it?' says Margaret sternly, passing by with the most absolute silent contempt her companion's gallantries, and abandoning in the twinkling of an eye the admired posture which she had been invited to retain.

'*I suggested it!*' repeats Freddy, lifting his brows. 'Knowing my Peggy as I do, should I have been likely to call the chimney-pots down about my own head?'

'But you knew of it? You had heard of it?'

'I daresay I did. I hear a great many things that I do not pay much attention to.'

'And you think that Lady Betty Harborough would be a desirable friend for Prue?' says Peggy in bitter interrogation, and unintentionally falling back into her Medea attitude, a fact of which she becomes aware only by perceiving Freddy's hand covertly stealing to his pocket in search of a pencil and notebook to sketch her.

At the sight her exasperation culminates. She snatches the pencil out of his hand and throws it away.

'Cannot you be serious for one moment?' she asks passionately. 'If you knew how sick I am of your eternal froth and flummery!'

'Well, then, I *am* serious,' returns he, putting his hands in his pockets, and growing grave; 'and if you ask my opinion, I tell you,' with an air as if taking high moral ground, 'that I do not think we have any of us any business to say, "Stand by! I am holier than thou!" It has always been your besetting sin, Peggy, to say, "Stand by! I am holier than thou!"'

'Has it?' very drily.

'Now it is a sort of thing that I never *can say*' (warming with his theme). 'I do not take any special credit to myself, but I simply *cannot. I* say, "Tout savoir c'est tout pardonner!"'

'Indeed!'

'And so I naturally cannot see'—growing rather galled against his will by the excessive curtness of his companion's rejoinders—'that you have any right to turn your back upon poor Betty! Poor soul! what chance has she if we all turn our backs upon her?'

'And so Prue is to stay with Lady Betty to bolster up her decayed reputation?' cries Peggy, breaking into an ireful laugh. 'I never heard of a more feasible plan!'

'I think we ought all to stand shoulder to shoulder in the battle of life!' says Freddy loftily, growing rather red.

'I shall do my best to prevent Lady Betty and my Prue standing shoulder to shoulder anywhere,' retorts Peggy doggedly.

A pause.

'So that was what Prue was crying about?' says Freddy, with a quiet air of reflection. 'Poor Prue! if you have been addressing her with the same air of amenity that you have me, it does not surprise me. I sometimes wonder,' looking at her with an air of candid and temperate speculation, 'how you, who are so genuinely good at bottom, can have the heart to make that child cry in the way you do!'

'I did not mean to make her cry,' replies poor Peggy remorsefully. 'I hate to make her cry!'

'And yet you manage to do it pretty often, dear,' rejoins Freddy sweetly. 'Now, you know, to me it seems,' with a slight quiver in his voice, 'as if no handling could be too tender for her!'

Peggy gives an impatient groan. At his words, before her mind's eye rises the figure of Prue waiting ready dressed in her riding-habit day after day— watching, listening, running to the garden-end, and crawling dispiritedly back again; the face of Prue robbed of its roses, clipped of its roundness, drawn and oldened before its time by Freddy's 'tender handling.' A bitter speech rises to her lips; but she swallows it back. Of what use? Can the Ethiopian change his skin, or the leopard his spots?

Another pause, while Margaret looks blankly across the garden, and Freddy inhales the smell of the mignonette, and scratches Mink's little smirking gray head. At length:

'So you do not mean to let her go?' says the young man interrogatively.

'I think not,' replies Peggy witheringly. 'If I want her taught ribald songs I can send her to the alehouse in the village, and I do not know any other end that would be served by her going there.'

Freddy winces a little.

'I daresay you are right,' he rejoins blandly. 'I always say that there is no one whose judgment I would sooner take than yours; and, in point of fact, I am not very keen about the plan myself; it was only poor Prue's being so eager about it that made me advocate it. You see,' with a charming smile, 'I am not like you, Peggy. When persons come to me brimming over with pleasure in a project, I have not the strength of mind instantly to empty a jug of cold water all over them! I wish I had! it would,' sighing pensively, 'make life infinitely less difficult!'

'You are going to Harborough yourself, I suppose?' asks Peggy brusquely, brushing away like cobwebs her companion's compliments and aspirations.

He shrugs his shoulders.

'How can I tell? Do I ever know where I may drift to? I may wake up there some fine morning. It is not a bad berth, and,' with a return to the high moral tone, 'if one can help a person ever so little, I think that one has no right to turn one's back upon her!'

'Of course not!' ironically.

'And I have always told you,' with an air of candid admission, 'that I am fond of Betty!'

'I know,' returns Peggy, with a somewhat sarcastic demureness—'I have heard; you look upon her quite as an elder sister; it is a charming relationship!'

Freddy reddens, but instantly recovering himself:

'I am not so sure about that! I must consult Prue!' cries he, going off with a laugh, and with the last word.

CHAPTER XVI

She remains behind without a laugh. She is not, however, left long to her own reflections, for scarcely is young Ducane out of sight before Prue reappears. Her eyes are dried, and her cheeks look hot and bright.

'Well?' she says, in a rather hard voice, coming and standing before her sister.

'Well, dear!' returns Peggy, taking one of her hands and gently stroking it.

'Has he been talking to you about it?' asks the young girl, with a quick short breathing.

'I have been talking to him about it,' returns Margaret gravely, 'if that is the same thing.'

'And you have told him that I—I—am not to go?'

'Yes.'

Prue has pulled her hand violently away, which for a few moments is her only rejoinder; then:

'I hope,' she says in a faltering voice, 'that you told him as—as gently as you could. You are so often hard upon him; it must have been such a—such a bitter disappointment!'

'Was it?' says Peggy sadly; 'I think not! Did you hear him laughing as he went away? You need not make yourself unhappy on that score; he told me he had never been very eager for the plan!'

'*He said so!*' cries Prue, with almost a scream, while a deluge of carnation pours over her face. 'Oh, Peggy! you must be *inventing*. He could not have said that! I think—without intending it of course—you often misrepresent him! Oh, he could not have said it! Why, only last night, as we were walking home in the moonlight, he said that to have me there under those chestnuts—I believe that the Harboroughs have some very fine old Spanish chestnuts in their park—would be the realisation of a poet's dream.'

Peggy groans.

'If he did say it,' continues Prue, in great agitation, 'it was to please you. He saw how set against the plan you were, and he has such beautiful manners—such a lovely nature that he cannot bear saying anything that goes against the person he is talking to.'

'Perhaps you are right in your view of his character,' says Peggy quietly, but with a tightening of the lines about her mouth that tells of acute pain; 'in fact he told me that the only reason of his having ever advocated the project was that you were so keen about it.'

If Peggy imagines that the drastic medicine conveyed in this speech will have a healing effect upon her sister's sick nature, she soon sees that she is mistaken.

'And is it any wonder if I *am* keen about it?' asks she, trembling with excitement. 'I who have never had any pleasure in all my life!'

'Never any pleasure in all your life!' repeats Peggy, in a tone of sharp suffering. 'Oh, Prue! and I thought we had been so happy together! I thought we had not wanted anything but each other!'

Prue looks rather ashamed.

'Oh! of course we have been happy enough,' returns she; 'just jogging along from day to day—every day the same. But that—that,' her agitation gathering volume again, 'that is not *pleasure*.'

'*Pleasure!*' repeats Margaret, with reflective bitterness; 'what *is* pleasure? I suppose that the party last night was pleasure. I think, Prue, that pleasure is an animal that mostly carries a sting in its tail.'

'I—I should not be among strangers either,' urges Prue, with that piteous crimson still raging in her cheeks; '*he* would be there.'

'And he would be such an efficient chaperon, would not he?' returns Peggy, unable to help a melancholy smile. 'But from what he said to me, even his going seems problematical.'

'Oh no, it is not!' cries Prue hurriedly. 'There is no doubt about that; the very day is fixed. I—I,' faltering, 'was invited for the same one, too.'

Again Margaret gives vent to an impatient groan at this fresh proof of Freddy's unveracity, but she says nothing.

'Is it quite sure that I am not to go?' asks Prue, throwing herself upon her knees at her sister's feet, and looking up with her whole fevered soul blazing in her eyes. 'I do not feel as if I had ever wished for anything in my whole life before.'

Peggy turns away her head.

'I shall have to begin to live on my own account some time!' continues Prue, her words tumbling one over another in her passionate beseeching. 'I cannot always be in leading-strings! Why may not I begin now?'

'Are you going to kill me, then?' asks Margaret, with a painful laugh. 'Am I to die to be out of your way? I am afraid, for your sake, that I do not see much chance of it.'

'I have never in my whole life stayed in the same house with him,' pursues Prue, too passionately bent upon her own aim to be even aware of her sister's sufferings. 'He says himself that our meetings are so scrappy and patchy that he sometimes thinks they are more tantalising than none.'

'And whose fault is it, pray, if they are scrappy and patchy?' cries Peggy, bursting out into a gust of irrepressible indignation. 'Who hinders him from coming here at sunrise and staying till sunset?'

'You never did him justice,' returns Prue irritably. 'You never see how sensitive he is; he says he thinks that every one's privacy is so sacred, that he has a horror of intruding upon it. Ah! you will never understand him! He says himself that his is such a complex nature, he fears you never will.'

'I fear so too!' replies Peggy sadly.

There is a short silence.

'I—I—would behave as nicely as I could,' says poor Prue, beginning again her faltering beseechments. 'I—I—would not do anything that I was not quite sure that you would like.'

The tears have stolen again into her great blue eyes, and across Margaret's mind darts, in a painful flash, the recollection of Freddy's late reproach to her, for the frequency with which she makes his Prue cry.

'I am sure you would not!' cries the elder sister, in a pained voice, taking the little eager face, and framing it in both her compassionate hands. 'Oh, Prue, it is not *you* that I doubt!'

'But indeed you are not just to her!' returns the young girl, eagerly seizing her sister's wrists, and pressing them with a violence of which she herself is not aware, in her own hot, dry clasp. 'You should see her at home! He says that you should see her at home; that every one should see her at home; that no one knows what she is at home, and that she has a heart of gold—oh, such a good heart!'

'They always have good hearts!' rejoins Margaret, with a sad irony. 'These sort of women always have good hearts.'

'And every one goes there,' urges Prue, panting and speaking scarcely above a whisper. 'Last year the Prince of Morocco was there.'

'H'm! Nice customs curtsey to great kings!'

'And the Bishop.'

'What Bishop?'

'Oh, I do not quite know. *A* Bishop; and when he went away he thanked Lady Betty for the most delightful three days he had ever spent.'

'H'm!'

'*He* thought it so beautiful of him; he said it showed so large a charity.'

'So it did.'

'And if a *Bishop* visits her' (redoubling her urgencies, as she fancies she detects a slight tone of relenting in her sister's voice)——

'Do you think that she sang to him?' interrupts Margaret scathingly. 'Oh, Prue!' (as the vision of Betty with her song, her naked shoulders, bismuthed eyes, and dubious jests, rises in all its horrible vividness between her and the poor, simple face, lifted in such passionate begging to hers), 'I *cannot*; it is no use to go on asking me. Oh, do not ask me any more; it only makes us both miserable! I tell you' (with rising excitement) 'I—I had rather push you over that wall' (pointing to the one at the garden-end, which drops sharply to the road), 'or throw you into that pool' (indicating a distant silver glint), 'than let you go to her!'

There is such an impassioned decision in both eyes and words that Prue's hopes die. She rises from her knees, and stands quite still on the sward opposite her sister. Her colour has turned from vivid red to paper-white, with that rapidity peculiar to people in weak health. In a moment she has grown to look ten years older.

'I suppose,' she says in a low but very distinct key, 'that it is John Talbot who has made you hate her so!' Then she turns on her heel and walks slowly towards the house.

As long as she is in sight Peggy stares after her wide-eyed, and as if stunned; then she covers her face with both hands and bursts into a passion of tears, in comparison with which Prue's small weepings are as a summer shower to a lashing winter storm. Can it be that there is any truth in her sister's words?

———————————

A few days pass, and to a superficial look the Big House and the Little House wear precisely the same aspect as they did before the invasion of the former by its last batch of guests. It is only to a more careful eye that the presence of the little Harboroughs in the Manor nurseries, to which they are chiefly confined—milady having no great passion for the society of other people's children—is revealed; and it would require a still nicer observation to detect the change in the Little Red House. There is no longer any question there of the Harborough invitation. It has been declined, though in what terms the refusal was couched Peggy is ignorant. At all events the letter to Lady Betty has gone. Freddy has gone too. It had been understood, or Margaret imagined that it had been understood, that he, at least, was to have remained; that he had, in fact, been counting the hours until the departure of importunate strangers should leave him free to show the real bent of his inclinations.

However that may be, he has gone, having deferred his going no later than the day but one after that which saw the Harboroughs' exodus. He leaves behind him a misty impression of having reluctantly obeyed some call of duty—some summons of exalted friendship. It is a duty, a task that involves the taking with him of two guns, a cricket-bag, and some fishing-rods.

The Manor is therefore tenanted only by its one old woman, and the Red House by its two young ones. This is a condition of things that has existed very often before without any of the three looking upon herself as an object of pity in consequence of it.

Milady is far, indeed, from thinking herself an object of pity now. But the other two? Prue has made no further effort to alter her sister's decision. She has beset her with no more of those tears and entreaties that Margaret had found so sorely trying, but she has exchanged them for a mood which makes Peggy ask herself hourly whether she does not wish them back. A heavy blanket of silence seems to have fallen upon the cheerful Little House, and upon the garden, still splendid in colour and odour, in its daintily tended smallness. The parrot appears to have taken a vow of silence, in expiation of all the irrelevant and loose remarks of his earlier years; a vow of silence which the greenfinch and the linnet have servilely imitated. Even Mink barks less than usual at the passing carts; and though his bark, as a bark, is below contempt for its shrill thinness, Peggy would be glad to hear even it in the absence of more musical sounds.

Prominent among those more musical sounds used to be Prue's singing, and humming, and lilting, as she ran about the house, and jumped about the garden with Mink and the cat. Prue never now either sings or runs. She is not often seen in the garden: dividing her time between the two solitudes of her own room and of long and lonely walks. If spoken to, she answers briefly and gravely; if her sister asks her to kiss her, she presents a cold cheek; but she volunteers neither speech nor caress. She eats next to nothing, and daily falls away in flesh and colour.

By the close of the week Peggy is at her wits' end. She has spent hours in the hot kitchen trying to concoct some dainty that may titillate that sickly palate.

In vain. To her anxious apostrophes, 'Oh, Prue! you used to like my jelly!' 'Oh, Prue! cannot you fancy this cream? I made it myself!' there is never but the one answer, the pushed-away plate, and the 'Thank you, I am not hungry!'

One morning, when the almost ostentatiously neglected breakfast, and the hollow cheeks that seem to have grown even hollower since over-night, have made Peggy well-nigh desperate, she puts on her hat and runs up to the Manor. She must hold converse with some human creature or creatures upon the subject that occupies so large and painful a share of her thoughts. Perhaps to other and impartial eyes Prue may not appear so failing as to her over-anxious ones. She reaches the Big House just as milady takes her seat at the luncheon-table. Miss and Master Harborough, who have been given swords by some injudicious admirer, have been rushing bellowing downstairs, brandishing them in pursuit of the footmen. Nor has the eloquence of the latter at all availed to induce Franky to relinquish his, even when he is hoisted into his high chair and invested with his dinner-napkin. He still wields it, announcing a doughty intention of cutting his roast-beef with it.

'You will do nothing of the kind!' replies milady, who, on principle, always addresses children in the same tone and words as she would grown-up people; 'it would be preposterous; no one ever cuts beef with a sword. You would be put into Bedlam if you did.'

And Lily, whose clamour has been far in excess of her brother's, chimes in with pharisaic officiousness, 'Nonsense, Franky! do not be naughty! You must remember that we are not at home!'

'Bedlam!' repeats Franky, giving up his weapon peaceably, and pleased at the sound. 'Where is Bedlam? Is that where mammy has gone?'

Milady laughs.

'Not yet! Eat your dinner, and hold your tongue.'

Franky complies, and allows the conversation to flow on without any further contribution from himself.

'It was not such a bad shot, was it?' says milady, chuckling; 'I heard from her this morning.'

'Yes?'

'They are still at the B——'s. She says that the one advantage of visiting them is, that it takes all horrors from death! Ha!—ha!'

'Prue heard from her the other day,' says Peggy, speaking slowly and with an overclouded brow; 'she asked Prue to pay her a visit.'

'H'm! What possessed her to do that, I wonder? I suppose Freddy wheedled her into it. Well, and when is she to go?'

'She—she's not going.'

'H'm! You would not give her leave?'

Peggy glances expressively at Miss Harborough, who has dropped her knife and fork, and is listening with all her ears to what has the obvious yet poignant charm of not being intended for them.

'Pooh!' replies milady, following the direction of Margaret's look. 'Ne faites pas attention à ces marmots! ils ne comprennent pas de quoi il s'agit!'

At the sound of the French words a look of acute baffled misery has come into Lily's face, which, later on, deepens on her being assured that she and her brother have sufficiently feasted, and may efface themselves. Franky gallops off joyfully with his sword; and his sister follows reluctantly with hers. As soon as they are really out of earshot—Peggy has learnt by experience the length of Lily's ears—she answers the question that had been put to her by another.

'Do you think that I ought to have let her go?'

Milady shrugs her shoulders.

'Everybody goes there. Lady Clanranald, who is the most straitlaced woman in London, takes her girls there; one must march with one's age.'

The colour has deepened in Margaret's face.

'Then you think that I ought to have let her go?'

Lady Roupell is peeling a peach. She looks up from it for an instant, with a careless little shrug.

'I daresay that she would have amused herself. If she likes bear-fighting, and apple-pie beds, and practical jokes, I am sure that she would.'

'And *songs*?' adds Peggy, with a curling lip; 'you must not forget *them*.'

'Pooh!' says milady cynically; 'Prue has no ear, she would not pick them up; and, after all, Betty's bark is worse than her bite.'

'Is it?' very doubtfully.

'Why do not you go too, and look after her?' asks the elder woman, lifting her shrewd eyes from the peach, off whose naked satin she has just whipped its rosy blanket, to her companion's troubled face.

'I am not invited.'

'And you would not go if you were—eh?'

'I would sooner go than let her go by herself,' replies poor Peggy with a groan.

'She is looking very ill,' says Lady Roupell, not unkindly. 'What have you done to her? I suppose that Freddy has been teasing her!'

'I suppose so,' dejectedly.

'I wish that he would leave her alone,' rejoins milady, with irritation. 'I have tried once or twice to broach the subject to him, but he always takes such high ground that I never know where to have him.'

'I wish you would send him away somewhere!' cries Peggy passionately. 'Could not you send him on a tour round the world?'

The old lady shakes her head.

'He would not go; he would tell me that though there is nothing in the world he should enjoy so much, it is his obvious duty to stay by my side, and guide my tottering footsteps to the grave.'

She laughs robustly, and Peggy joins dismally. There is a pause.

'She *does* look very ill,' says the younger woman, in a voice of poignant anxiety; 'and long ago our doctor told us that she was not to be thwarted in anything. Oh, milady,' with an outburst of appeal for help and sympathy, 'do you think I am killing her? What *am* I to do? oh, do advise me!'

'Let her go!' replies the elder woman half-impatiently, yet not ill-naturedly either. 'She will fret herself to fiddlestrings if you do not; and you will have a long doctor's bill to pay. I daresay she will not come to much harm. I will tell Lady Clanranald to have an eye upon her; and if she fall ill, I can promise you that nobody will poultice and bolus her more thoroughly than Betty would; she loves physicking people.'

Even this last assurance fails very much to exhilarate Margaret. She draws on her gloves slowly, takes leave sadly, and walks heavily away. She does not go directly home, but fetches a compass through the lanes, on whose high hedges the passing harvest-waggons have left their ripe tribute of reft ears; over a bit of waste land, barrenly beautiful with thistles, some in full purple flush, some giving their soft down to the fresh wind. Singing to them, sitting on a mountain-ash tree, is a sleek robin. Peggy stands still mechanically to listen to him; but his contented music knocks in vain at her heart's door. There is no one to let it in. In vain, too, the reaped earth and the pretty white clouds, voyaging northwards under the south wind's friendly puffs, and the thistle's imperial stain ask entrance to her eye. Whether standing or walking, whether abstractedly looking or deafly listening, there is but one thought in her mind;

one question perpetually asking itself, 'Is it really and solely for Prue's good that I have prevented her going?' Neither the thistles nor the redbreast supply her with any answer. The only one that she gets comes ringing and stinging back in Prue's own words: 'I suppose it is John Talbot who has made you hate her so.' 'Can there be any truth in them?' she asks again, as she had asked with tears when they were first spoken.

Her aimless walk has brought her, when the afternoon is already advanced, to the gate of the Vicarage. It is open, swinging to and fro, with a bunch of ugly little Evanses clustered upon its bars. This slight fact of its being open just makes the scale dip towards entering. She enters. Mrs. Evans is in the nursery, as the nurse is taking her holiday. She is sitting with a newish baby in a cradle at her side, and an oldish one alternately voyaging on its stomach across the scoured boards, and forcing its sketchy nose between the uprights of the tall nursery fender. A basket of unmended stockings balances the cradle on Mrs. Evans's other side, and an open Peerage lies upon her lap.

'Why, you are quite a stranger!' she says. 'I have not seen you since the party at the Manor. I was just looking out some of the people who were there. I have not had a moment to spare since; and you know I like to find out who is who.'

Peggy sits down, and the old baby props itself against the leg of a chair to stare at her.

'How is Prue?' asks Mrs. Evans, discarding the Peerage. 'Mr. Evans met her yesterday on Wanborough Common, five miles away from home. Do you think it is wise to let her take such long walks?'

'I did not know that she had been so far,' answers Peggy dispiritedly.

'I do not like her looks,' continues the other, consulting Peggy's face with a placid eye, full of that comfortable and easy-sitting compassion with which our neighbours' anxieties are apt to inspire us. 'Do you ever give her cod-liver oil?'

'She has been taking it for the last two months.'

'Or malt? Malt is an excellent thing; the extract, you know—half a glass taken after meals. It did wonders for Billy. No one would have known him for the same boy.'

'I have tried that too.'

'I expect that what she wants is change of air,' says Mrs. Evans, shaking her head as she thrusts her hand into the foot of a stocking, running an experienced eye over the area of its injuries. 'Could not you manage to give her a little?'

For an instant Margaret is silent; then she says abruptly:

'Lady Betty Harborough has invited her to pay her a visit.'

'*Lady Betty Harborough!*' cries Mrs. Evans, dropping stocking and darning-needle. 'Dear me! what luck some people have! And you, too? No? I wish she had asked you too.' It is the measure of how low Peggy has fallen that she goes nigh to echoing this wish. 'Well, she must be a very kind-hearted woman,' pursues Mrs. Evans, resuming her darning-needle, 'as well as a very pretty one. And what a charming voice she has! That was a horrid song she sang; I did not hear the words very clearly myself. Mr. Evans says it was just as well that I did not; but how well she sang it! What spirit! When does Prue go?'

'I—I—am not sure that she is going at all.'

'I would not put it off longer than I could help, if I were you,' says Mrs. Evans. 'Do not you think that she has fallen away a good deal of late? And such an opportunity may not come again in a hurry. Dear me!' with a sigh and a glance towards the two babies and the stocking-basket, 'some people are in luck!'

It is evident that Margaret is not destined to draw much consolation from her visits to-day. At the gate Mr. Evans is waiting to greet her, having routed that numerous detachment of his offspring which was ornamenting it on Peggy's arrival. There are day's on which Mr. Evans's children appear to him intolerably ugly, and his lot unbearably sordid. On such days he lies under a tree, reading Morris's *Earthly Paradise*, and his family give him a wide berth.

'How is Miss Prue?' he asks, holding the gate open for her to pass through. 'I met her yesterday on Wanborough Common, looking like a——'

'Yes, yes, I know,' interrupts Peggy, almost rudely. 'Mrs. Evans told me.'

'Are you quite happy about her?' inquires he, not perceiving his companion's shrinking from the subject, glad to escape for a few moments from the contemplation of his own unpicturesque ills to the more poetic ones of other people, and walking a few paces down the road at her side. 'Had not you better take care that she does not slip through your fingers?'

CHAPTER XVII

A fortnight later, and Peggy is alone. Prue has gone after all—gone to that paradise, in yearning for which she seemed to be stooping towards the grave; she has gone to empty jugs of water over stairs on Guardsmen's heads, to put crackers into the coat-tail pockets of Secretaries of Legation, and set booby-traps for Members of Parliament. No wonder that even before entering upon these glories their mere prospect had restored her to more than her pristine vigour. She has gone, with Peggy's one string of pearls in her trinket-case; with Peggy's best gown, contracted and modified to her smaller shape, in her trunk. She has gone, nodding her head, waving her hand, and blowing kisses, altogether restored apparently to the blithe Prueship of earlier days. But at what price?

Peggy's repugnance to the plan has been in no degree diminished by the fact of her having consented to it. She has consented to it, driven partly by a suspicion that her opposition has been half-due to no solicitude for her sister's welfare, but to a resentment and an ache of her own; driven much more, though, by Mr. Evans's few light words, 'Take care that she does not slip through your fingers!' They pursue her by day and by night. 'Slip through her fingers!' There seems a dreadful fitness in the very form of the phrase. Other people may die, may be killed. Prue would just slip away! Oh, if he had but used another form of expression! As she lies on her wakeful, anxious bed, one couple of lines torments her with what she feels to be its prophetic applicability:

> 'Like a caged bird escaping suddenly
> The little innocent soul flitted away!'

Some day she will wake to find her arms empty of little Prue, whom for seventeen fond years they have girdled. That Prue has always been sickly and often forward, has from the moment of her birth caused her far more pain than pleasure, makes no sort of difference. The sea does not reckon how many little rills run into it. A great love has no debit and credit account; it gives vastly, not inquiring for any return. People in weak health, who can become genuinely moribund upon opposition, possess a weapon which the sound cannot pretend to emulate.

On the evening of the day of Margaret's visit to the Vicarage Freddy Ducane had unexpectedly returned to the Manor.

'I believe that that wretched little Prue is going to die on purpose to spite Peggy for not letting her go to the Harboroughs!' says milady crossly, vexed at her nephew's serene flower face. 'I cannot think what possessed you to put such an idea into her stupid little head!'

And Freddy looks mournful, and answers sweetly that he supposes it is useless his trying to explain that he had no hand in the matter, but that he is afraid he shall never be able to inflict gratuitous pain upon any one as long as he lives.

Despite his assertion of innocence, he has in his pocket a second letter of invitation from Lady Betty for Prue, which he reads with her next day under the Judas-tree while Peggy is away at the workhouse. She comes back a little too soon, before the reading is quite finished, just in time to see Prue stick the note hastily into her pocket. At this gesture her heart sinks—Prue is beginning to look upon her as an enemy.

'You need not hide your letter, Prue. I am not going to ask to see it,' she says, in a wounded voice, either forgetting or omitting to make any salutation to Freddy.

Prue reddens.

'I should not have hidden it, only that I knew it would make you angry,' she answers, with a sort of trembling defiance. 'Lady Betty has invited me again. I cannot help it; it is not my fault.'

Freddy has risen, and, scenting a coming storm, follows his instincts by beginning to edge away.

'How bad of you—you dear Peg!' cries he affectionately, holding out both hands—'to come back just as I am obliged to be off! That is the way you always treat me—is not it, Prue?'

'You needn't go,' replies Margaret, neglecting his hands, and looking rather sternly at him. 'I shall not be here a moment; and we are not going to quarrel, if that is what you are afraid of. Prue, since Lady Betty is so urgent, and you wish it so much, tell her that you will go to her.'

Then she leaves them with a steady step, but when she reaches her own room her tears gush out. That gesture of Prue's hand to her pocket has cut her to the quick; Prue, whose one first impulse through all her seventeen years' span has hitherto been to run to her sister with whatever of good or bad—be it broken head or new doll—fate has brought her. That one small gesture tells her that the old habit is for ever broken, and she cries bitterly at it. She may cry as much as she pleases during the silent fortnight that follows, certain that neither Mink nor the cat will ask her why; but she does not weep again. Through the gossamer-dressed September mornings, and the gold-misted September noons, she lives alone. Alone with her thoughts—thoughts none the less worth thinking perhaps for their new tinge of deep sadness—with her unpretending charities, with Jacob and her hollyhocks. It is a novel experience, since never before in all Prue's little life has she borne to have the child out of her sight for as much as a week.

Three months ago she would have thought it too hard a thing to have asked of her to forego Prue's songs and kisses for a whole fortnight; but of late Prue herself has so entirely robbed their intercourse of its old confident sweetness, has put such a bitter sting into it, that for the first few days after her departure Peggy (albeit with self-reproach) experiences a sense of relief in no longer meeting the small miserable face with its mute and dogged upbraidings. So little does she dread her own company that she avails herself but sparingly even of such society as is within her reach, *i.e.* that of the Manor and milady, with her spud and frieze-coat; that of the Vicarage with its stocking-basket and its *Earthly Paradise*. The only visitors of whom she sees much are the little Harboroughs, who still adorn the Manor nurseries, and call upon her almost daily, with that utter absence of misgiving as to being always welcome that few people—and those only the most consummate bores—are able to preserve in later life.

She likes them—the boy best; and even if she herself is not quite in tune for their chatter, there is always the red fox to pant at them, with pretty cunning face and hot wild breath, from behind the wire walls of his house; the pump to wet their clothes, and the stable kittens to scratch them. So no wonder that they come every day. She would enjoy their conversation more if it did not involve so ceaseless a reference to one whom she has neither the need nor the desire to have thus hauled back into her memory. But it seems as if John Talbot had been so inwoven with the very woof of their lives that no anecdote of their little past is complete without it. She could endure it, however, if they confined themselves to anecdotes. It is the perpetual appeal to her for her opinion about him that she finds so trying.

'Oh, Miss Lambton! do not you like John Talbot? When is he coming back? Do not you wish he would come and live with you here always? Do you like him better than father? Franky says *he* does. Is not it naughty of him?'

And the questions of childhood are not like those of a maturer age, which may be evaded or put aside. They must and will be directly answered. Peggy cannot help a vexed internal laugh as she hears herself, allowing that she likes John Talbot, asseverating that she has no wish that he should come and live with her always, and explaining that it is possible to appreciate him and father too. But she is always deeply thankful when the conversational charms of Alfred the stable-boy, or the chicken-feeding hour, or any other timely distraction releases her from this trying interrogatory. Of John Talbot, except through the too glib tongues of his little partisans, she has heard absolutely nothing. On the morning of his departure she had sent his Keats and one or two other of his books up to the Manor after him.

As she was neatly wrapping them in paper a sprig of lavender fell out of the Keats—a sprig which, as she remembered, he had put in as a mark into the unfinished 'Eve of St. Agnes,' on their last reading. She stooped and picked it up, looking hesitatingly at it. Shall she return it to its place? Why should she? No one could ever connect the idea of Betty with lavender. Gardenias would bring her image at once—gardenias wired and overpowering; but the clean and homely lavender—never! She throws it pensively away; and as she does so a foolish fancy comes over her, as if it were herself that she had just been tossing away out of his life! That he acquiesces in that tossing away is but too evident. He does not even send her a formal line to acknowledge the receipt of his restored property. So it is not his fault that his image walks beside her so often down the garden alleys; both at high blue noon and when, on fair nights, she steps abroad to look at the thronged stars.

One must think of something; and there are many interstices in her thoughts which cannot all be filled up by the one topic—Prue. Into them he creeps; the more so as she lives almost wholly in her garden; and with that his memory is so entangled that there is scarcely a plant that does not say something to her of him. She thinks of him always without bitterness; generally with deep compassion; never with any hope of pulling lavender with him again. But she thinks of him. Perhaps there was some truth in Betty's fleer, of her never having known any better company than that of the village apothecary. The only outward incidents of her life come in the shape of Prue's letters. These begin by being long and full of ecstasies; end by being short and full of nothing.

Before the first week is over they are hurried up, ere the sheet is full, with some excuse. She must go and get dressed to go out riding. They are just off to a tennis-party. They are to go out shooting with the men. The expressions of enjoyment grow fewer in each. Yet in not one is the slightest wish expressed for a return home. In fact, before the fortnight ends comes a feverish note, evidently written in hot haste and deep excitement, begging for a further reprieve of a week. It gives Peggy a little fresh pang to notice that this petition is urged as a criminal might urge some request upon his executioner, not as one would beg a boon of a tender friend.

But she is used to such pain now; rises up and lies down with it; and to-day puts it patiently aside. What she cannot put aside is her perplexity as to how to answer. She has a deep repugnance against complying; and yet the memory of her terror at Prue's rapid decline upon her former opposition makes her tremblingly shrink from adopting a course that may all too probably bring back that condition. She dares not decide upon her own responsibility. She will consult milady.

On her way to the Manor she goes round by the Vicarage, and looks in. Over the lawn there is a festal air. It is evident that the little Evanses have been drinking tea out of doors, in honour of a visit from Miss and Master Harborough. The Vicar is nowhere to be seen; a fact which does not surprise Peggy, as she knows that any signs of conviviality on the part of his children are apt to make him disappear.

On catching sight of her Franky Harborough precipitates himself towards her as fast as his fat legs will carry him. He is in wild spirits, and has evidently, on his own showing, been extremely naughty.

'Oh, we have been having such fun!—we have had tea out of doors! Mrs. Evans said that the next child who shook the table so as to upset anything should have no tea! I,' with a chuckle, 'had finished my tea, so I gave it a good shake!'

He looks so rosily delighted with his own iniquity, and is so flatteringly glad to see her, that poor Peggy, who feels as if not many people were glad to see her nowadays, has not the heart to rebuke him.

With her admirer's small soft hand tightly clutching hers, she advances to where, under a copper beech's shade, sits Mrs. Evans—the stocking-basket banished, and engaged upon some genteeler industry—in company with a female friend.

'We were just talking of you,' says the Vicar's wife, putting out a welcoming hand. 'Let me introduce you to my cousin, Miss Jones; she has been staying in the neighbourhood of the Harboroughs; she saw Prue.'

'Did you indeed?' cries Peggy, turning with anxious interest to the new comer. 'Was she well? Did she look well?'

'She looked extremely well.'

'She must have been very well indeed, I should think,' adds Mrs. Evans, with a meaning smile. It is a smile of such significance that, for a moment, Peggy dares not ask an explanation of it; and before she can frame her question Mrs. Evans goes on. 'How very oddly people seem to amuse themselves in smart houses nowadays!—one never heard of such things when I was a girl; but I suppose, as it is the fashion, it is all right.'

'Were they—were they doing anything very strange?' asks Peggy, with rising colour and wavering voice, addressing the visitor.

'They seemed to be enjoying themselves very thoroughly,' replies the latter, with a prim evasive smile.

'They were all driving donkey tandems full gallop down the main street of the town,' cries Mrs. Evans, taking up the tale; 'it seems that there is a town about three miles from Harborough Castle. Prue was driving one!'

'PRUE?'

'Yes, *Prue*! I was as much surprised as you can be; but it must have been Prue; there was no other unmarried girl there!' Peggy is silent. 'My cousin says it was wonderful how she got her donkeys along! She was at the head of the party; and they were all shouting—shouting at the top of their voices!' Still Margaret makes no comment. 'My cousin says that the whole town turned out to look at them; they were all at their doors and windows. I am sure so should I have been,' with a laugh; 'but it seems a childish romp for grown-up people, does not it?'

Peggy's answer is a slight assenting motion of the head, but her words are not ready. Her eyes seem fixed attentively on the distant gambols of the children —on Lily Harborough swarming a cherry-tree, and being pulled down by the leg by an indignant nurse; on Franky giving a covert pull to the end of the white tea table-cloth, in the pious hope of precipitating all the teacups to the ground.

'Another day,' pursues Mrs. Evans cheerfully, 'they drove into the town and bought all the penny tarts at the confectioner's, and pelted one another with them in the open street.'

Peggy has at length recovered her speech.

'It was very, *very* stupid,' she says, in a voice of acute annoyance; 'senseless. But after all there was no great harm in it.'

'Of course one does not know what they did indoors,' rejoins Mrs. Evans, as if, though a good-natured woman, unavoidably anxious to knock even this prop from under our poor Peggy. 'People said—did not they?' turning to her cousin—'that they sat up smoking till all hours of the night, and ran in and out of each other's rooms; and the ladies put things in the men's beds——'

'I am afraid I must be going on,' interrupts Margaret, starting up as if she had been stung; 'I have to see Lady Roupell.'

She takes leave abruptly. It seems to her as if she should not be able to draw her breath properly until she is alone. She pants still as she walks on over the stubble fields, across the park, under the September trees, whose green seems all the heavier and deeper for their nigh-coming change of raiment. She pants at the recollection of the picture just drawn for her of her Prue—*her Prue*—shouting, smoking, making apple-pie beds!

Her worry of mind must have written itself upon her face, for no sooner has she joined milady, whom she finds out in the shrubberies leaning on her spade, like Hercules upon his club, than the old lady asks sharply what she has been doing to herself.

'Nothing that I know of,' replies Peggy, 'except that I have been rather bothered.'

'Prue, eh?'

'Yes.'

'What about her now?' with a slight accent of impatience.

'She wants to stay away another week.'

'And have you given her leave?'

'I came to ask your advice.'

Milady is neatly squirting a plantain or two out of the turf. She waits until she has finished before answering. Then she says with decision:

'Have her back.'

'You think so? But if,' very anxiously, 'she falls ill again as soon as she gets home?'

'Pish!' rejoins the other in a fury; 'give her a dose of jalap and a whipping.'

But Peggy does not even smile.

'Have you—have you heard anything of the party?' she asks hesitatingly; 'of whom it consists, I mean? Prue is not very communicative. Is Lady Clanranald there still?'

'No, she is gone,' replies milady shortly, digging her weapon into a dandelion. 'She could not stand it. Betty is an ass!'

Could not stand it!

In a dismayed silence Margaret awaits further explanation, but none comes. Milady, whatever she may know, is evidently determined not to be diffuse on the subject.

'Have her home!' repeats she briefly, lifting her shrewd old eyes to Peggy's, and replacing her billycock hat on the top of the cap from which her stooping attitude has nearly dismounted it; 'have her home, and do it as quickly as possible.'

Beyond this piece of short but very definite advice, nothing is to be got out of her. She will explain neither why Lady Clanranald took flight nor why Betty is an ass.

In an uneasiness all the deeper for the vagueness of milady's implications, Peggy takes her way home to her little solitary Red House, and writes the letter which is to summon Prue back.

But with how many tears is that letter penned! How many fond and anxious apologies! Wrapped in what a mantle of loving phrases does the unpalatable fiat go forth! However, it has gone now, and there is nothing for her but to await its result. Between the day on which it was sent and that appointed for Prue's homecoming there is ample time for an answer to be returned; but none comes. The day arrives; the servant who is to be Prue's escort sets off in the early morning, and through the long hours, forenoon, noon, afternoon, Peggy waits. Not in idleness though. She is hard at work from dawn till sunset, cooking, gardening, rearranging, planning surprises that are her fatted calves for the prodigal. As she works her spirits rise. The small house looks so bright; perhaps, after all, Prue will not be very sorry to find herself back in it; and how pleasant it will be to hear her little voice singing about the garden, and to see her jumping over the tennis-net with Mink again! Mink has not jumped over the tennis-net once since she left. With a lightened heart Peggy stoops to ask him why he has not, but he answers only by a foolish smirk.

The expected moment has come. For half an hour beforehand Peggy has been standing at the garden-end straining her eyes down the road, and making up her mind that there must have been an accident. But at length the slow station fly with its dusty nimbus heaves in sight, rolls in at the gate, stops at the door.

Before Prue can well emerge her sister has her in her arms.

'Oh, Prue! how nice it is to have you back! How are you? Have you enjoyed yourself? Are you a little glad to see me?'

Prue's first remark can hardly be said to be an answer to any of these questions. She has disengaged herself from her sister, and stands staring round, as if half-bewildered.

Prue does not look like herself. She has an oddly-shaped hat; there is something unfamiliar about the dressing of her hair; and can it be fatigue or dust that has made her so extremely black under the eyes.

'What a squeezy little place!' she says slowly, with an accent half of wonder, half of disgust. 'Surely it must have shrunk since I went away!'

And Peggy's arms drop to her sides, and her hopes go out.

CHAPTER XVIII

A wretched month follows—a month of miserable misery—misery, that is, that springs from no God-sent misfortune; that has none of that fateful greatness to which we bow our heads, stooping meekly before the storm of the inevitable; but a misery that is paltry and reasonless—one of those miseries that we ourselves spin out of the web of our own spoilt lives. It seems such a folly and a shame to be miserable in the face of these yellow October days that by and by steal in, pranked out in the cheerful glory of their short-lived wealth, with such a steadfast sun throwing down his warmth upon you from his unchanging blue home; with a park full of such bronze bracken to push through at your very door; and with such an army of dahlias, ragged chrysanthemums, and 'Good-bye-Summers,' with their delicate broad disks, to greet you morning after morning as you pass in your pleasant ownership along their gossamered ranks.

So Peggy feels; but that does not hinder her from being wretched to her very heart's core. The inside world may throw a sunshine on the outside one, as we all know—may make June day out of January night—'the winter of our discontent' into glorious summer; but the outside can throw no sunshine on the inside unless some is there already. So Peggy's 'Good-bye-Summers,' though they never in their lives have flowered for her so beautifully before, smile at her in vain. She has no answering gladness to give them back. It has not taken twenty-four hours from the time of her return to prove that it has become absolutely impossible to please Prue. It is nothing that, on the first evening of her arrival, she has, as it were, walked over all poor Peggy's little planned surprises without even perceiving them; that she has turned her dinner over disdainfully, and remarked how much worse Sarah cooks than when she went away. These may be but the childish fretfulnesses engendered of fatigue, and that a good night's rest will sweep away. But when twenty-four hours have passed, when a week, when a fortnight have gone by, and find her still cavilling at the smallness of the rooms, the garden's confined space, and the monotony of their lives, then, indeed, Margaret's spirits sink as they have never sunk before.

The one definite property that Prue seems to have brought back from her Harborough visit is a sickly and contemptuous disgust for whatever had formerly given her pleasure; a standard by which to measure all the conditions of her own life, and find them grossly wanting. About the visit itself she is singularly reticent. Not a word does she breathe of her own prowess in donkey tandem-driving; not a hint does she let drop of any midnight gambols.

Once and again Margaret sadly fancies that she sees faint signs of the old lifelong habit of telling her everything trying to reassert its sway; but in a moment it is checked. Often Prue seems to her sister like a child who, engaged in some naughtiness, has been charged by its confederates not to tell. And Prue does not tell. Yet, from indications which she cannot help letting fall, Peggy gathers that the visit has not been all pleasure; that fits of bitter disappointment, sharp jealousy, grisly disillusion, freaked the surface of its feverish joy. And yet Freddy had been a co-guest with her through the whole fortnight! This fact Margaret has elicited by direct inquiry; it would never have been volunteered.

'Come, Prue,' she says coaxingly, on the morning after the young girl's return, as they stroll about the garden, whose flowers Prue notices only to disparage, 'I let you off last night because you were so sleepy, but you must tell me something about your visit now. Was Freddy there?'

'Yes.'

'All the time?'

'Yes.'

'Did you see much of him?'

A slight hesitation, and then an accent of impatience:

'Of course. Were not we staying in the same house?'

'And—and—did Mr. Harborough mount you? You know, don't you—I told you, I think,' a beam of pleasure shining in her anxious blue eyes—'that milady has lent you the little gray mare for the whole winter?'

'I do not think that I care for riding as much as I did,' replies Prue listlessly, plucking the seed-vessel from an overblown dahlia in the border beside her, and idly scattering the seeds over the walk. 'We did not ride much; there were so many more amusing things to do.'

'What sort of things?'

'Oh, they would not have amused you!'

'How do you know that, until you tell me what they were?'

'Oh, they would not have amused you; you are not easily amused. *He* always says so; and besides,' sinking down with a sigh on the bench under the Judas-tree, 'of what use to talk of them now they are over?'

For a second Peggy shrinks into herself in baffled discouragement, but immediately recovers. She will not be so easily disheartened.

'If they are so amusing,' she says cheerfully, 'perhaps we might adopt some of them here. We are not above learning, are we?'

Prue smiles disdainfully, curling her childish nose.

'In these extensive grounds?'

Nor as time goes on does she grow more communicative about her visit, though it is clear that its incidents occupy her thoughts to the exclusion of all other subjects, and though its influence may be traced in each fragment of her sparse talk. It is one of Peggy's severest daily penalties to recognise in her sister's languid speech continually recurring phrases of Betty's; thin echoes of her flippancies. Prue is even growing to have a dreadful likeness to her model. Possibly this may arise only from Betty's old hat, which she persistently wears; or from the mode of hair-dressing, slavishly copied from her original. That the now fixed bloom in her cheek may be derived from the same source as Lady Betty's, and cause the undeniable resemblance that exists between them, is a supposition too bad to be faced, and that Peggy drives away from her mind as soon as it presents itself. But it recurs. How many disagreeable things do not recur nightly as she lays her head on that pillow which is oftener than not wetted with her tears?

'Oh, why did I let her go?' she sobs. 'Why did I take any one's advice? What has happened to her? What shall I do? It is not my Prue at all that has come back to me!'

Now and again, indeed, there is a tantalising glimpse of the old Prue, hidden away, as it were, behind the new one. Once, twice, there is a curly head resting voluntarily on Peggy's knees; thin arms thrown—and oh, how thankfully welcomed!—round her glad neck; a little voice plaining to her of some small physical ill, with a touch of the old childish confidence in Peggy's power to kiss any wound well. But in a moment she is gone again; and the new Prue, the dreadful, new, cynical, imitation Betty Prue is back. It is this new Prue who daily steals with surreptitious haste to meet the postman, lest the eyes, whose love has enveloped her through life, should now dare to alight upon her correspondence. And yet Peggy knows by the after-mood of the day, as well as if she had scanned superscription and seal, whether or not the expected missive has come. Judging by this test, the postman is for Prue, far oftener than not, empty-handed. Once, twice, as Margaret learns from Lady Roupell, Freddy is expected at the Manor. Once, twice, at the last moment, some motive of exalted self-sacrifice prompts him to telegraph that he is unable to come. And now he can no longer be expected, for mid-October is here; the Universities have reopened their long-shut arms to their children, and Freddy has returned to Oxford. To add still further to the discomfort of the situation, the weather, hitherto so far beyond praise, becomes suddenly as much beyond blame. There follows a week of pouring, tearing, ruthless rain. The 'Good-bye-Summers' say good-bye indeed.

Three days after the fall of this final blow to Prue's hopes the two girls meet milady coming out of morning church; milady in her reluctant and temporary divorce from her spud and frieze-coat. They walk down the yellow, leaf-strewn church-path with her, as they always do, while she throws her brusque nods, and her good-hearted greetings to her fellow-worshippers. As she seats herself in the carriage she pulls a letter accidentally out of her pocket with her pocket-handkerchief.

'Oh, by the bye,' says she, 'I heard this morning from Freddy; I came away in such a hurry that I had not half time to read it. If I had been a little farther off the Vicar,' laughing, 'I would have read it during the sermon. (Poor dear man!' in a loud aside, 'he really ought to treat us to a new one.) Freddy says that he is ill.'

'*Ill*, is he?'

'So he says,' with a shrug. 'He says that he has caught a chill. Oh, I am not very much disturbed,' laughing again. 'I daresay that we are not going to lose him this time. You know he always cries out some time before he is hurt.'

She rolls cheerfully away, resuming the reading of her letter as she goes. Peggy turns apprehensively to her sister. The congregation have all issued into road and bridle-path, and they are alone. Peggy has time for an impulse of thankfulness that such is the case; for Prue is leaning, whiter than her pocket-handkerchief, against the lych-gate.

'*Ill!*' she says gaspingly, under her breath. 'Ill! and all alone! nobody with him!'

'Pooh!' replies Peggy lightly, and with a half tone of contempt. 'I daresay it is not much; he is always frightened about himself. Do not you remember the time when he thought he was going into a consumption, and bid us all good-bye? How white you look, darling! Had not you better sit down a moment? Take my arm.'

But Prue will not sit down—will not take her sister's arm. She walks home unhelped, and on getting there, refuses all Peggy's simple cordials. But she leaves her luncheon untouched, and is out the whole afternoon on a long aimless, solitary ramble. She comes in again a full hour after dusk has fallen, and, complaining of headache, goes to bed. The next morning she is up, and at her usual stand, lying in ambush for the postman. After he is gone Peggy catches distant glimpses of her walking up and down the kitchen garden, reading a letter. She has heard, then, from him. Thank God! Perhaps her heart will be more at ease.

With her own mind relieved, Margaret goes about her morning's work with a better courage; and it is eleven o'clock before she again thinks of her sister. The striking of the hour reminds her that Prue will probably forget to take her tonic, and that it will be safer to administer it herself. She pours it out, and opening the drawing-room door, calls 'Prue! Prue!' There is no answer. She moves to the foot of the stairs and repeats her call, 'Prue!' No answer. She sets the glass down upon a table, and runs into the garden. 'Prue! Prue!' There is an answer this time, but unfortunately it is not the right one. It is the parrot officiously replying, 'Yes,'m,' in the cook's voice. She re-enters the house. Possibly Prue may be in her own room—one of her new tendencies is to lock herself in there for hours together—and with the door shut Peggy's summonses may, though in so small a house it is not likely, have remained unheard. She runs up and knocks. No answer. She turns the handle, the door opens, and she looks in. In vain! The room is empty. She can see this at a glance. It is not likely that Prue is hiding in her own cupboard, or beneath her narrow chintz bed; and yet her sister, pushed by what vague suspicion she does not know, enters. A note in Prue's handwriting and addressed to herself, lying on the small writing-table in the window, at once catches her eye. In an instant she has sprung upon and torn it open. What is this? There is neither beginning nor ending; only a few unsteady lines straggling across a sheet of paper:

'I have not asked your leave, because I knew that you would not give it; but I could not—could not let him die alone. Oh, Peggy, do not be very angry with me! I am so miserable, and I could not help it.'

That is all. It has not taken Margaret two seconds to master the contents; and having done so, she stands vacantly staring at the empty envelope still held in her hand. It is a minute or two before she has recovered her wits enough to realise that it is not yet empty; that it contains a second sheet. This is in a different handwriting, one of those small, clear, clever handwritings affected by the cultured youth of the day.

'Ch. Ch. Oxford.

'MY PRUE,

'Send me a little word. I am suffering, and I am all alone. I am scratching you these few pencil-lines in case—as, I fear, is too probable—I may be too ill to write to-morrow. Oh, my Prue! "The whole head is sick, and the

120

whole heart faint." What would not I give for one of your little cold white hands to lay on my throbbing brow?

'Your

'FREDDY.'

It was only with a half comprehension—so stunned was she—that Peggy had read Prue's missive; but at the end of Freddy's the dreadful white light of full understanding breaks upon her soul. Prue has gone to Oxford!—gone to fulfil young Ducane's aspiration—to 'lay her little cold hand on his throbbing brow.' Can it be possible? Can even Prue's madness have gone so far? She snatches up her sister's note again, and greedily reads it afresh, in the wild hope of finding that she has mistaken its drift. Alas! there is no room for misapprehension. If she need further confirmation of her worst fears it comes in the voice of Sarah, who looks in, duster in hand, through the half-open door.

'Please, 'm, did you want Miss Prue? She has gone out.'

'Gone out!' repeats Margaret breathlessly. Then, making a great effort over herself for composure, she adds, 'Yes, yes, I know; how did she go? did she walk or drive?'

'She went in the pony-carriage, 'm.'

'Did she take Alfred with her?'

'No, 'm; she said she should not want him.'

'And how—how long ago did she set off?'

'Indeed, 'm, I did not much notice. I happened to look out of the passage window as I was dusting the stairs, and I saw her drive off; it must be the best part of an hour ago.'

The best part of an hour ago! Like lightning it dawns upon Peggy that a train leaves her station for Oxford at ten minutes to eleven. It is a slow one, as all must be which draw up at the little wayside platform; not so slow, however, but that a crawl of a hundred and twenty minutes will land Prue as hopelessly beyond her power of reach as if it were the 'Flying Dutchman' itself, at Oxford station. She is as little able to hinder her sister from forcing her mad way into the young man's room as she would be to stop God's lightning from splitting the tree it is appointed to rend.

With a gesture of rage and despair she dashes Freddy's note to the ground, and flings her own head down on the open blotting-book whose pages keep the imprint, scarcely dry, of her sister's insane words. But in a few minutes she has pulled herself together. There is only one thing for her to do—to follow and overtake her sister as quickly as possible. *As quickly as possible! But how quickly is that?* This is the first thing to be discovered.

She goes down into the cheerful hall, where the birds in their big cage are swinging on John Talbot's ladder, and chattering to each other as jovially as if no disaster had fallen on their roof-tree; where Mink is lying on his small hairy side in a sun-patch, with his little paws crossed like a dying saint's. Margaret searches for the *Bradshaw*, which apparently Sarah has tidied away. Her first impulse is to call to her, and ask where she has put it; but her second corrects it. Why should the household learn any sooner than is unavoidable that Prue has fled?

By and by she discovers the missing volume, and sitting down, buries herself in its pages. What she had feared is realised. There is no second train for Oxford until 2.15. Three hours of forced inaction stretch before her—three hours for Prue to carry out whatever cureless folly her burning heart and rudderless mind may dictate.

She starts up. To sit still with such thoughts for company is out of the question. She wanders back again to Prue's room, picks up Freddy's note which she had left in her ire lying on the carpet; tears both it and Prue's into small pieces, and throws them into the grate; then, misdoubting their being sufficiently destroyed, collects the fragments again and burns them—tears out even that sheet of the blotting-book upon which Prue had dried her words, and burns it too.

Then she goes downstairs, and looks at the clock. It has seemed to her as if she had been a long time over her burning. Yet the clock-hand points only to a quarter past eleven. She must force herself to some occupation. To read is impossible. Needlework and gardening both sharpen instead of deadening thought. It is the day for doing up the week's accounts. She will compel herself to do them as usual. But the figures swim before her eyes. The simplest addition baffles her. The names of Prue, Freddy, Oxford, force themselves into her record of expenditure, making nonsense of it, defacing her neat columns; and after half an hour's vain efforts, she desists with a sigh. When one o'clock comes at last she sits down to luncheon, calmly telling Sarah that she does not expect Prue back; and having obliged herself, for the sake of appearances, to eat something, she puts on her hat and jacket.

Leaving word with her household as indifferently as she can that they are not to be surprised if she and her sister are late in returning, she sets forth on her walk to the station. She has reflected that she would start early, in order to give herself plenty of time to walk slowly. But she does not walk slowly; she walks fast; towards the end she runs. Who knows whether her clocks may not be slow? whether on coming in sight of the little upstart red-brick house that constitutes the station, she may not see the train sliding away without her? She arrives breathless, to find that she has half an hour to wait—half an hour in which to admire the station-master's canariensis and his mignonette, which greets each dusty train-load with its whiff of perfume.

By and by another intending traveller or two arrive. The Manor omnibus drives up, and disgorges the little Harboroughs and their nurses. Peggy had known and forgotten that they were to return home to-day. She feels rather guilty at her own cold inability to echo their loud expressions of pleasure at this unexpected meeting with her. But they apparently detect no lack of warmth in her answering greetings, as they each at once take possession of one of her hands, and march up and down with her. In the intervals of a searching interrogatory as to the goal and object of her journey, they continue a quarrel apparently begun in the omnibus; putting out their red tongues at each other before her face, and executing agile kicks at one another's legs behind her back.

When the train draws up they insist upon deserting their own suite and getting in with her. She had rather that they would not have done so; and yet perhaps it affords a wholesome diversion from her own thoughts to be continually jumping up to grasp Franky by the seat of his sailor-trousers, and hinder him from breaking his neck by tumbling out of the window, or his legs by his endeavours to climb up into the netting. Lily is not nearly so troublesome. She is sitting quite still, and *showing off*; trying, that is, to impress by her remarks two quiet ladies who are fellow-occupants of the carriage with a sense of her importance.

'I hope,' she says, in a loud voice, 'that my large box is in;' as she speaks she turns her eyes upon the strangers to see whether they look awed; but as they do not, she adds, in a still louder key, 'because it is full of clothes!'

The train slides on through the bright-dyed autumn country; past the flooded flat meadows lying a-dazzle in the sun, blinding mirrors for the gorgeous October trees; across and then again across the broad ribbon of the silver Thames; past distant country houses, lifting their shoulders out of the gold and red billows of their elms and beeches; past big villages and little towns, till, after several previous stoppages, they come to a standstill at the platform of a small station, as destitute of importance as the one from which they set off. It is that at which the little Harboroughs are to get out.

'Mammy is coming to meet us,' Lily had announced; 'she will give Franky such a hug! She never hugs me—I am father's child.'

She throws one final look at her fellow-travellers, to see whether they are not rather struck by the last statement, before joining her brother at the window, and jostling her hat against his in the endeavour to have the glory of obtaining the first glimpse of their common parent. Of this, however, she is balked, as, whatever may be her after-assertions to the contrary, there is no doubt that the shrill cries of boy and girl, 'There she is!' 'There's mammy!' rang out absolutely simultaneous.

Their curly heads fill up the window-space so completely that Peggy, for a moment, hopes to escape detection and recognition. She hopes it the more, since, for the first minute, Betty has no eyes save for her boy, whom she has caught in her arms; relieving Peggy at length from her convulsive hold of his small-clothes, and burying him under a perfect smother of kisses.

'My blessing—my beauty! so I have got you back at last! You must never—never leave your poor mammy again! Well, Lily, how are you? Goodness, child, what a figure you are! You are one large freckle! Oh, Miss Lambton, is that you? Where are you off to? Is Prue with you? No? What fun Prue is! I had no idea until she stayed with me what capital fun she was. You must let me have her again before long.'

The train moves off, and Margaret, a little heavier-hearted than before, with it. Some impulse prompts her to pull back the curtain of the little side-window in order to watch, as long as it is in sight, that figure on the little platform. Yes, Prue is certainly like her; but, alas! it is to be not even a good imitation for which she has foregone her own woodland grace. Margaret had forgotten how pretty Betty was. How charming she looks now, with her face full of wholesome mother-love, perfectly unconscious, indifferent as to whether any one is looking at her or not, clasping her little rosy child.

CHAPTER XIX

'Ox—ford! Ox—ford!' Her goal is reached; and as she has no luggage, and is therefore independent of the scanty-numbered and not particularly civil porters, in two minutes after the stopping of the train she is in a hansom, spinning up to Christ Church. At Tom Gate she gets out, and rather timidly entering the archway, bends her steps to the porter's lodge. He comes out politely to meet her.

'Can you tell me where Mr. Ducane's rooms are?'

'Certainly, ma'am. Peckwater Quad, third door on the left hand, second staircase.'

As she is moving off hurriedly in the direction indicated her informant adds:

'I am afraid that you will not find him in, ma'am.'

'Not in?' repeats she, in a tone of the most acute astonishment. 'Is not he ill, then?'

'Not that I am aware of, ma'am; he went out about half an hour ago with a lady.'

At the mention of the lady a sudden vermilion flies up into Peggy's face.

'Did you happen to notice,' she asks precipitately—'can you tell me which way they—they went?'

'I think they may have been going to the meadows, ma'am; they went out by the Hall.'

Almost before he can lift his finger to point out the line she is to take she is off upon it. Across the wide quad she speeds, under the exquisite stone umbrella that has held itself for over three centuries above the staircase up which thousands of stalwart young feet have tramped to their dinner in the Hall. Along the still, gray cloisters; past the mean flimsiness of the new buildings, erected apparently as a bad practical joke, out into the sunshine and dignity of the Broad Walk.

She stands for a moment or two uncertainly, looking from the new avenue to the old one. From the stripling rows of limes and poplars which will shade 1900 and 2000—those strange-faced centuries, of which we that are having our little innings willy-nilly now, and will have had them then, think with a certain startled curiosity—she turns to the elm-veterans, who are paying their two-hundredth tribute of amber and tawny leaves to the passing season. Her eye travels the whole length of both long alleys; but in neither does she discover a trace of the two figures she is in quest of. Men in flannels she sees in plenty (*men* they call themselves; but have men such smooth lady-faces? do men laugh like that?)—men by twos and threes and fours and ones going down to, or coming up from, the glinting river. However, she cannot stand hesitating for ever at the top of the diverging avenues; so, since both hold out equally little promise to her, she takes the Broad Walk. It is a bright, crisp afternoon. Above her the elms, thinned of their leaf-crowns, arch their bicentenary heads; the flooded meadow flashes argent on either hand. Merton's gray-gabled front, rose-climbed, and Magdalen's more distant tower lift their time-coloured faces against the blue. On seats beneath the trees, with the shadows, thinner than in high summer, stretching at their feet, climbs here and there a child; rest an old man; sit a pair of lovers. Here and there also— alas, too frequently!—comes a gap in the ancient elm-brotherhood, ill filled by some young puny twig, that shows where the storm laid low the honourable age of a giant whose green childhood the Stuarts saw.

She has reached the end of the walk, and again glances about her uncertainly. There is still no sign to be traced of her truants having passed this way. Whither shall she now bend her steps? She is not long in deciding. On her right a narrower path stretches, following the windings of the Cherwell— narrower, yet delectable too; tree-hung, shadow-pranked, and with the flush river for companion. The country round is all in flood; the fair town sitting among the waters.

Margaret walks quickly along, her look anxiously thrown ahead of her, eagerly asking of each new turn in the walk to give her the sight she seeks. On she goes through the golden weather. A great old willow, girthed like an oak, golden too, stoops over the brimful stream that runs by, in silent strength— stoops with a flooring of its own gold beneath it. There is no wind to speak of; yet the trees are dropping their various leaves on the Cherwell's breast. She, speeding along all the while, watches them softly fall—a horse-chestnut fan; a lime-leaf; a little shower of willow-leaves, narrow and pointed like birds' tongues—softly fall and swiftly sail away. At a better time who would have enjoyed it all so much as she? but she draws no grain of pleasure from it now. She can take none of nature's lovely substitutes in the place of the two human objects she is pursuing. If she does not find them here, where else shall she seek them? What clue has she to guide her?

With a sinking heart she is putting this question to herself when, as the sight of the moored barges, the flash of oars, the sound of shouting voices tell her that she is nearing the spot where the Cherwell and Isis join in shining wedlock, she comes suddenly upon them.

On the seat that runs round a tall plane-tree they are sitting side by side. At least they have not chosen any very sequestered spot. His blonde head is thrown back, and resting against the trunk; while from his lips a stream of mellow words is pouring. He is obviously spouting poetry; while she, in feverish unconsciousness of what she is doing, tears into strips a yellow plane-leaf, her eyes down-dropped, and a deeper stain than even that of Betty's prescribing on her cheeks.

Peggy noiselessly draws near.

Under that holy oak, or gospel tree,
Where, though thou seest not, thou may'st think upon
Me, when thou yearly go'st procession;
Or, for mine honour, lay me in that tomb
In which thy sacred reliques shall have room
For my embalming, sweetest——'''

'Good heavens, Peggy!'

Some slight rustle of her gown must have betrayed her neighbourhood. The lovers both spring to their feet; and for a moment all three young people stand silently eyeing each other. Prue's hot roses have vanished, but they have not travelled far. It is perhaps a sign that there is still some grace left in him, that they are now transplanted to Freddy's cheeks. Margaret is the first to speak.

'I am here to take you home, Prue,' she says in a low grave voice. 'Are you ready?'

'Come, Peggy dear!' cries the young man, recovering his complexion and his *aplomb*, never very far out of reach; 'you need not look so tragic!—you quite frighten us! Do not scold her much,' laying a coaxing hand on Peggy's arm; 'I have scolded her well myself already.'

'You!'

There is such a depth of contempt in this one monosyllable, and it is so elucidated—if indeed it needed elucidation—by the handsome lightning of her eye, that Freddy's colour again changes.

'I was coming home. I should have come home by the next train,' falters Prue, hanging her head; and as this tremulous explanation is received by her sister in a sorrowful silence, she adds with passionate eagerness, 'He was ill, really —very ill. It was not pretence—he was really ill.'

'No doubt,' replies Peggy, in withering quotation from Freddy's own billet; '"the whole head was sick, and the whole heart faint."'

Not vouchsafing him another word or look, she takes her sister's unresisting arm, and leads her away. Without exchanging a syllable, they reach St. Aldate's. Then Peggy hails a hansom, and bids the cabman drive as quickly as he can to the G. W. station. But both her injunctions and his speed are vain. They gallop up only to find the train, reduced by distance to a small puff of smoke, steaming unattainably northwards. There is not a second one for another hour and a half. There is nothing for it but to wait. After all, as Peggy reflects with some bitterness, they are not returning to such a very happy home that they need be in any scrambling hurry to get there.

In mid-October the days are already beginning to close in early, and even before the light goes there comes a sharpness into the air. It is blowing chilly through the draughty station now. Peggy looks apprehensively at Prue. Neither of them have had the forethought to bring any wraps with them. Prue is shivering in a thin summer jacket; her face looks weary, drawn, and cold.

'Had not you better go and rest in the waiting-room?' asks Margaret solicitously, addressing her for the first time, as she takes off her own cloak and wraps it round her.

'Yes, if you wish. I do not mind,' replies Prue apathetically.

When she has been settled in the warmest corner, and her vitality raised a little by a cup of hot tea, Peggy leaves her. There is a painful irksomeness in her company that makes Peggy prefer to it even a silent and solitary march up and down the platform, each footstep beating time to some heavy thought. Her march is not destined to be solitary for long, however. Before she has taken three turns a soft young voice with an intonation of excessive deprecation sounds at her elbow:

'May I take a stroll with you, dear?'

She does not deign him one syllable in answer, but walks along as before, looking straight ahead. He sighs patiently.

'When you come to think it over, dear, I am sure you will acknowledge that you are unjust. I can perfectly see your side of the question. I think that one ought always to try to see both sides; but whether you believe me or not, I can assure you that I never was more horrified in my life than I was this morning, when poor Prue walked in.'

And for once, at all events, Freddy speaks truth.

'Then why,' cries Peggy, blazing around upon him, 'did you write and tell her you were dying? Why did you ask her to come and "lay her little cold white hand upon your burning brow"?'

Freddy winces; and the tone of his charming cheeks rises several degrees.

'I do not quite know, dear, how you justify to yourself the reading of other people's letters,' he says sweetly; 'but if you must quote me, I had rather that you did it correctly.'

'Do you mean to say,' cries she, turning her great honest eyes and her indignant rose face full upon him, 'that you did *not* ask her to "lay her little cold white hand upon——"'

'Oh, you need not say it all over again,' says Freddy, writhing. 'How dreadful it sounds, hammered out in that brutal voice! What a knack you have, Peggy, of turning everything into prose! I did not *ask* her to lay her hand upon my forehead; I said I should like it. So I should; so would you, if your head had been as hot as mine was yesterday.' He pauses; but Peggy has no biting rejoinder to make. 'If I had for a moment supposed,' continues Freddy, 'that poor Prue would have taken it *au pied de la lettre*, I would have cut off my right hand before I would have written it. It is always so much less painful,' he adds thoughtfully, 'to hurt one's self than to hurt any one else.'

But Margaret does not seem much disarmed by this touching sentiment.

'If you did not want her to come, why did you write her that silly letter?' she asks doggedly.

Again Freddy changes colour.

'As I before observed, Peggy dear,' he answers, with some symptoms of exasperation in his soft voice, 'I do not think it would be a bad plan if you confined yourself to your own correspondence.'

The girl's face flushes as much as his own has done.

'Prue left it for me to read,' she says coldly and proudly. After a pause, drawing a long resolute breath, 'Well, next time that you are dying, you will have to look out for some other hand to cool your burning brow; for Prue's will be beyond your reach.'

'So it was now,' rejoins Freddy, showing symptoms of an inclination to lapse into levity. 'Poor Prue! she would have had to make a long arm from the Red House here.'

'As soon as I get home,' continues Peggy, annoyed by, and yet not deigning to notice, his frivolous interpellation, 'I shall put the house into the hands of a house-agent. There is nothing left us—you have left us nothing but to go!'

'To go! Where?'

She shrugs her shoulders dispiritedly.

'I do not know—somewhere—anywhere—out of this misery.'

Her whole attitude and accent speak so deep a despondency that Freddy's tendency to gaiety disappears. He feels thoroughly uncomfortable; he wishes he had not come. He would like exceedingly to slip away even now; but unfortunately it is impossible.

'My dearest Peg,' he cries, in a very feeling voice, 'you break my heart! You are always so self-sufficing, so apt to rebut sympathy, that one hardly likes to offer it; but if——'

'Sympathy!' she repeats, with a scornful lip that yet trembles; '*sympathy* from *you*, who are the cause of all my wretchedness?'

'I?'

'Yes, you!' turning upon him with gathering passion—a passion that is yet not loud in its utterance; that passes unobserved by the few listeners about the station. 'Have not you eyes to see that you are killing her? You might have set yourself a task that would do your philanthropy more credit than breaking an old friend's heart—than turning a poor little childish head.'

Her voice wavers as she utters the last few words, and she stops abruptly. Perhaps it is by accident that Freddy's eye strays furtively to that spot on the platform where 'Way Out' is legibly inscribed.

'When you talk of "childish,"' he says, in an extremely pained tone, yet one of gentle remonstrance, 'you seem to forget that I am not so very old myself. You talk to me as if I were a hoary-headed old sinner. Do you remember that I shall not be twenty-one till Christmas?' She looks at him with a sort of despair. What he says is perfectly true. It seems ludicrous to arraign this pink and white boy as guilty of the tragedy of her own and Prue's lives. 'I assure you, dear,' he says, in a very caressing tone, drawing a little nearer to her side, 'I often have to tell myself that I am grown up; I am so apt to forget it.' Then, as she is silent, he goes on, 'It would make our relations so much easier, Peggy, if I could get you to believe in me a little—mutual confidence is so much the highest and wholesomest basis for human relations. I think we ought all to try and trust one another; will not you'—edging nearer still, and dropping his voice to a very persuasive whisper—'will not you trust me a little?'

Peggy has heard that whisper many times before; has heard it beguiling her into frequent concessions that her judgment has disapproved. It is therefore with a very unbelieving, even if half-relenting, voice that she asks:

'How much the better shall I be if I do?'

'It makes things so much easier if one feels that one is believed in,' he says touchingly, if a little coaxingly. 'Oh, Peggy dear, will not you believe in me? Will not you trust me a little? Will not you wait—wait till I have taken my degree? *Then* you shall see!'

In his eagerness he has seized her hand, unmindful of the publicity of the place; and she, unmindful of it also, is poring in disconsolate anxiety upon his features to see if they look as if he were for once speaking the truth.

'See *what*?' she asks drily; but he apparently does not hear the direct question.

'And you will not let the Red House?' he pursues coaxingly. 'That was only a threat, was not it? Of course, I can perfectly understand your irritation; but you will not let it? Dear little house! if you only knew what a sacred spot it is to me! And you yourself, Peggy—why, you are like a limpet on your rock. You would be miserable anywhere else.'

'Thanks to you, I am miserable there too,' replies she bitterly.

She has withdrawn her hand sharply from him; and they now again walk side by side along the platform, begun to be lit up for the evening traffic.

'I think,' says Freddy reproachfully, 'that if you at all gauged the amount of pain that those sort of speeches inflicted, you would be less lavish of them.' As she makes no sort of rejoinder, he continues, with a heavy sigh, 'Where shall you go? Where shall you take her?'

'That can be no concern of yours,' replies she brusquely. 'It will at all events be beyond your pursuit.'

The moment that the word is out of her mouth she sees that it is an unfortunate one; and, by the light of a gas-lamp which they are at that moment passing, she detects on Freddy's face a curious smile, which denotes the perception in him of a certain humorousness in the present employment of that particular noun.

In this case it is certainly not he that is the pursuer. The station is growing fuller; a train must be expected; not Peggy's, unfortunately, which is still not nearly due. A good many undergraduates have appeared on the platform; several recognise Freddy, and look curiously at his companion. Whether it be their scrutiny that annoys her, or the consciousness of the unlucky character of her last phrase that gives added bitterness to her tone, it is with some asperity that she makes her next observation:

'I hope you are not going to stay to see me off! I had very much rather that you did not.'

'Of course I will not *force* my society upon you,' replies Freddy in a melancholy voice, under which, however, Margaret fancies that she detects a lurking alacrity; 'however much it may cost me, I will go at once, if you bid me.'

'Then I do bid you,' she answers curtly.

'And you—you will not do anything rash?' he says, looking extremely wheedling, and sinking his voice to a coaxing whisper. 'You will let things go on just as they are for a—for a little while? You—you will trust me?'

Her only answer is a derisive laugh.

'You—you will not decide in a hurry; you will take time to consider?' he pursues, with an agitation that seems genuine, following her, for she has already begun resolutely to walk away from him towards the waiting-room. 'You will—you will do nothing *rash*?'

'I do not know what you call rash. I shall write to the agent to-morrow.'

'You will not!' cries he, keeping up with her, and trying to retard her progress. 'You could not be so inhuman. I know that it is a matter of absolute indifference to you what suffering you inflict upon me, but,' with a tremble in his voice, 'you cannot, you must not hurt Prue!'

Again she gives that withering laugh.

'No, certainly not! I should not think of it; I leave that to you! Good-bye!'

So saying she disappears determinedly from his vision within the waiting-room door.

There is nothing left for him but to take the tears out of his smile and the tremor out of his voice, and walk away.

Peggy is as good as her word. On the very next morning she writes, as she had announced that she would, to the local house-agent, putting the dear little Red House into his hands. The deed is done. The letter lies with others in the bag, awaiting the postman; and Peggy goes out of doors to try and dissipate the deep sadness in which her own deed, and much more its causes, have steeped her. Into the garden first, but she does not remain there long. It is too full of pain. Though it is mid-October, the frost has still spared many flowers. There is still lingering mignonette; plenty of Japanese anemones, their pure white faces pearled with the heavy autumn dew; single dahlias also, variously bright. It would have been easier to walk among them with that farewell feeling had the mignonette lain sodden and dead, and the dahlias been frost-shrivelled up into black sticks. But no! they still lift their gay cheeks to the kiss of the crisp air.

How much longer we lure our flowers into staying with us than we did twenty years ago! Perhaps by and by we shall wile them into not leaving us at all.

To distract her thoughts from her sad musings Peggy begins to talk to Jacob; but even he adds his unconscious stab to those already planted in her heart. He can talk of nothing but next summer. To escape from him she leaves the garden, and passes out into the road. She walks purposelessly about the lanes, careless of the splendour of their brambles. She meets a detachment of Evanses blackberry-laden, their plain faces smeared with blackberry juice. They stop her to brag of their booty, and tell her that she must come blackberrying with them next year. *Next year* indeed!

She throws a friendly word of greeting across the hedge to a cottager digging up his potatoes. He tells her they are very bad, but he hopes she will see them better next year. She looks in at a farm to 'change the weather' with a civil farmer's wife, who shows her her chicken-yard, and volunteers a neighbourly hope that she will be able to give her a setting of game-fowl's eggs next summer. They seem to have *se donné le mot* to tease her with their 'next summer.'

She strays disconsolately home again to the little spoilt house, only six months ago so innocently gay, so serenely content, before Freddy came to lay its small joys in ashes. Can it be because she is thinking of him that she seems to see his wavy-haired head lying back in its old attitude on the bench under the Judas-tree, with another head in close proximity to it? She quickens her steps, but long before she can reach the rustic seat Prue has fled to meet her with a cry of joy.

At this now unfamiliar sign of welcoming poor Peggy's heart leaps for a moment up. Can it indeed be she that Prue is so glad to see? But is this indeed Prue? this radiant, transfigured creature, laughing, though her eyes are brimming with divinely happy tears?

'Oh, Peggy, where have you been?' cries the young girl, throwing her arms almost hysterically round her sister's neck; 'I thought you were never coming! I have been longing to tell you! Who was right? Who knew him best? Did not I say it would be all right? No! do not keep me! He will tell you!'

And away she speeds into the house, with Mink yapping his congratulations at her heels, and the parrot rapping out a friendly oath in Sarah's voice at her from the hall window as she passes him.

In an agitation hardly inferior to Prue's, Margaret advances to meet the young man, who has risen gracefully from his lounge, and is coming to meet her.

'What does she mean by saying it is all right?' asks Margaret sternly, and breathing quickly.

'It is very kind of dear Prue to put it that way,' replies he quietly. 'I suppose she means that I have asked her to be my wife. I have run over from Oxford on purpose, without leave, and shall probably be sent down for it. There is something a little comic, is not there, Peg,' breaking into an ungovernable smile, 'in the idea of my having a wife? Does it remind you at all of "Boots at the Holly-Tree Inn"? Well, dear!' lapsing into a pensive and quasi reproachful gravity, 'you see, you might have trusted me! Be not afraid; only believe!'

CHAPTER XX

The autumn is throwing down its red and amber tributes before other feet besides Margaret's; before Betty's, before Talbot's. It does not, however, rain the same shower on both. Betty's famed chestnuts supply no leaf for Talbot's tread. For the first time for five years Harborough Castle gets no share in John Talbot's autumn holiday. This is more through his misfortune than his fault, as Betty, though with angry, thwarted tears, is compelled to allow. From the visit to which after leaving the Manor he had betaken himself, he had been recalled to London with peremptory prematureness by a telegram. A crisis in public affairs—an unlooked-for and unpleasant turn in foreign politics has reft his chief—to that great man's unaffected disgust—from his thymy forest and his amethyst moor back to the barren solitudes of Downing Street. It has kept, if not the big, at least the lesser man bound hand and foot there until the opening of the autumn session, which in any case, even if he had not been defrauded of his legitimate playtime, would have summoned him back to harness. So that Talbot sees no red leaves except those which St. James's Park can show him. To a country-hearted man you would think that this would be a great privation; but this year John is glad of it. To him the country must henceforth mean Harborough. If he has no holiday, he need not, he cannot go to Harborough; and in his heart he says that the loss is well bought by the gain. It is true that Betty has, on various pretexts, run up several times to see him; that he has had to take her to the play; to give his opinion upon her new clothes; to sit on the old low seat beside the old sofa, in the old obscurity of the boudoir, without the old heart. She has even, contrary to his advice, and very much against his wishes, insisted on coming to tea with him in his rooms in Bury Street; and, as a matter of course, has expected him to see her off at Paddington. But on the whole he feels, as he speeds back in a hansom—this last duty punctually done—drawing an unintentional sigh of relief as he does so, that he has got through it pretty well. He has provoked not much anger, and, thank God, no tears. Thank God a hundred times more, too, that he has been miraculously spared any fleers at that other woman, towards whom, perhaps, the completeness of his lady's victory may have rendered her magnanimous. And that other woman! Well, he lets her image tease him as little as he can help it. Whether that is much or little, he himself scarcely knows. Sometimes again he does know, knows that it is infinitely much. But that is only now and then, when some trifling accident has given him a tiny momentary glimpse, such as outsiders often catch, at some keen happiness *à deux*; some two happy souls together blent,

'As the rose

> Blendeth in odour with the violet;
> Solution sweet.'

Then, indeed, he catches his breath with the sharpness of the pain that runs through his lonely heart, saying to himself, before his will can arrest and strangle the lovely, useless thought, 'That might have been Peggy and I.' But this, as I have said, is only now and again. As a matter of fact, his life is too full of genuine continuous hard work, too throbbing with great excitements, too full of the large fever of to-day's hot politics, to have much space for the cherishing of any merely personal ache. Sometimes for a whole day together he keeps his heart's door triumphantly barred against her. For a day—yes; but at night, willy-nilly, she lifts the latch, and cool and tall walks in. In the night she has her revenge. In the day he may think of nations clashing, of party invectives, of discordant Cabinets, and Utopian Reforms; but at night he thinks of Mink, and of the little finches swinging and twittering on *his* ladder; of the mowing-machine's whir, and the pallid sweet lavender bush.

As the winter nears, and such considerable and growing portion of the world as spend some part at least of the cold season in London, refill their houses, he goes a good deal into society, and when there he seems to enjoy himself. How can each woman to whom he offers his pleasant, easy civilities know that he is saying to his own heart as he looks at her:

'Your skin is not nearly so fine grained as Peggy's; your ear is double the size of hers; your smile comes twice as often, but it is not nearly so worth having when it does come'?

And so he seems to enjoy himself, and to a certain extent really does so. It is quite possible not only to do a great deal of good and thorough work, but to have a very tolerable amount of real, if surface pleasure, with a dull ache going on in the back of your heart all the time. He has as little nourishment on which to feed his remembrance of her as she has hers of him; nay, less, for he has about him no persistent little Harborough voices to ask him whether he would not like Peggy to come and live with him always. Sometimes it strikes him with an irrational surprise that no one should ever mention her name to him; though a moment later reason points out to him that it would be far more strange if they did, since her very existence is absolutely unknown to all those who compose his surroundings. Of no one were Wordsworth's lines ever truer than of her:

> 'A maid whom there were none to praise,
> And very few to love.'

One day he meets Freddy at Boodle's, and rushes at him with a warmth of affectionate delight that surprises that easy-going young gentleman. However, as Freddy is himself always delighted to see everybody, he is delighted to see Talbot now; and immediately gives him a perfectly sincere, even if the next moment utterly forgotten, invitation to spend Christmas at the Manor. He has forgotten it, as I have said, next half-hour; he does not in the least perceive the lameness of his friend's stuttered excuses, and he would be thunderstruck were he to conjecture the tempest of revolt, misery, and starved longing that his few careless words, 'Could not you run down to us for Christmas? no party, only ourselves and the Lambtons,' have awoke in that unhappy friend's breast.

Christmas! yes, Christmas is drawing near—Christmas, the great feast that looses every galley-slave from his oar. With how sinking a heart does one galley-slave watch its approach! How much he prefers pulling at his oar, with all the labour and sweat it entails, to the far worse bondage to which his emancipation from it will consign him! There will be no shirking it this time. To all humanity Christmas brings its three or four days of liberation; and these three or four days he must—unless the earth open or the heaven fall between this and then to save him—spend at Harborough. He will have to decorate Betty's church; light the candles on Betty's Christmas-tree; have Betty's children hanging about his neck, and Betty's husband reproaching him for his long absence.

Betty herself accepting his present, thanking him for it, manœuvring to get him alone. Her present! He must be thinking about it. He has not yet bought it. He will have to make time to go and choose it. He yawns. When you are in the habit of giving a person a great many presents, it is extremely difficult to vary them judiciously. If it were a first gift now, how much simpler it would be! Certainly quite without his consent, the thought darts across him that he has never given Peggy a present. How easy, how delightful, how enthralling it would be to make her some little offering! something slight and comparatively valueless that it would not hurt her pride to accept, but that yet would be worth thanking him for. He feels sure that Peggy has not received many presents in her life. He hears her—his sweetheart—thanking him for that ungiven, never-to-be-given fairing; and at the same moment his eye, falling accidentally upon Betty's last letter lying on the table before him, recalls to his mind that it is not Margaret whom it is now a question of endowing with a Christmas gift. His yawn is exchanged for a sigh. Poor Betty! He undoubtedly does not grudge her her present; but how very much it would simplify matters if she could be induced to choose it for herself. So reflecting he takes his hat, and repairing to the great jewellers', turns over Hunt and Roskell's newest trinkets in dubious half-hearted efforts at selection.

Betty is not altogether of the mind of those present-receivers who hold that the cost of the gift is as nothing; the giver's intention everything. Betty likes both; she likes something rather valuable, but that yet has a sentiment attached to it—something that tells of love, and thought, and love's cunning.

To Talbot, a year, still more two years ago, nothing had seemed easier than this combination. To-day, more than two hours elapse before he can cudgel out of his dull heart and fagged brain something that may, if not too closely scanned, bear the semblance of a fond invention. Christmas is now but a week off; but a week, as eager schoolboys, and pale clerks, and worn seamstresses tell themselves. Perhaps it may be because she knows that they will soon meet, that Betty's daily letter to Talbot has now for two whole days been intermitted. It is a lapse that has never before occurred, so far as he can recall, in the whole five years of their connection; her billets appearing as regularly as the milkman. Is it possible that she may have conceived some occult offence against him? That he may have unwittingly committed some mysterious sin against love's code? This thought darts across his mind, presenting itself first as a hope, and then as a dread. When it comes as a hope, it suggests that in the case of her having taken umbrage at any of his doings, or non-doings, she may show her resentment by excluding him from her Christmas gaieties; but this idea does not live beyond a moment. It is not much sooner conceived than it is transmogrified into a fear.

If they have quarrelled they will have to make it up again. Perhaps even his laboriously chosen love-gift will not be held a sufficient peacemaker. Perhaps he will have to expend himself in those expletives and asseverations that used once to come so trippingly, nay burningly, from his tongue, but that now have to be driven by main force from his lips, slow and cold and clogged.

A third morning has dawned. Again no letter. It is certainly very strange.

Talbot walks to Downing Street, pondering gravely what can be the cause of this unprecedented silence. Can it be that she is ill? She must be ill indeed not to write to him! A flash of distorted remorse—distorted, since it is for being unable better to return the tenderness of another man's wife—crosses his mind at the thought of her great love for him. No, if she had been ill, too ill to write, Harborough would certainly have sent him word of it, since no one is ever half so anxious to give him tidings of Betty, to further their meetings and impede their partings, as Betty's worthy, blockhead husband. It is most unlikely that the post, which indeed strangely seldom misbehaves itself, should have erred three times running.

He has reached Downing Street before any solution of the problem has occurred to him. In the course of the day he goes very nigh to forgetting it in the absorption of his work. That work is, on this particular day, specially pressing—specially monopolising. From morning to night he has not a moment that he can call his own. He does not even return home to dress for dinner, but snatches a hasty mouthful of food at the House of Commons, whither he has to accompany his chief, who is to speak on a subject at that moment engaging both House and nation's most passionate attention. The House is thronged to hear the great man. He is for three hours on his legs; and his speech is followed by a hot debate, adorned by the usual accompaniments of senseless obstruction, indecent clamour, and Irish Billingsgate.

It is half-past two in the morning before Talbot finds himself turning the key in his Bury Street door. The whole household has apparently gone to bed; but in his sitting-room the fire has been made up. A touch of the poker upon the coals makes them leap into a blaze, and he sits down in an arm-chair to finish his cigar, and cast an eye over the notes and telegrams that have come for him during his absence. Of the former there are several; of the latter only one. He looks at the addresses of the letters first, to see whether any one of them may be in Lady Betty's handwriting; but such not being the case, he lays them down, and tears open the telegram. He does it without any special excitement. In all our lives telegrams are daily, in his they are half-hourly, occurrences. But not such telegrams as this one. He has been too lazy to light his candles; and now reads it by the firelight that frolics redly over the thin pink paper and the clerkly writing:

'From		'To
LADY BETTY HARBOROUGH,		JOHN TALBOT,
Harborough Castle,		Bury Street,
—-shire.		St. James's,
		London, W.

'Come at once, and without a moment's delay, on receipt of this.'

When the contents of a missive that we receive, or of a speech addressed to us, diverge very widely from anything that we have been at all expecting, it is some time before the meaning of the words, however simple, succeeds in reaching our brain. Such is Talbot's case. He reads the telegram three times before he fully grasps its signification; and it is quite two minutes before it occurs to him to look at its date. 'Sent out at 11.10 A.M. Received at 11.35.' It has been lying waiting for him for fourteen hours and more. He reads it a fourth time. 'Come at once, and without a moment's delay, on receipt of this.' What does it—what can it mean? To obey it now, in the sense in which it meant to be obeyed, is as impossible as to 'call back yesterday out of the treasures of God.' It is true that he can set off, without a moment's delay, on the receipt of it. But as that receipt has been delayed fourteen hours longer than its sender calculated upon, his obedience will be a virtual disobedience.

Why has she sent for him? In any case she would have seen him in five days. What can she have to say to him of such surpassing urgency as cannot brook that short delay? His eye rests doubtfully on the vague yet pressing words. In the mouth and from the hand of any one save Betty, they would certainly imply some grave crisis—some imminent or already fallen catastrophe. In Betty's they *may* mean nothing. More than once before, during the past five years, has she telegraphed for him with the same indefinite peremptoriness; and when—always at great personal inconvenience, once gravely offending his chief, and seriously imperilling his future prospects—he has made shift to obey her summonses, he has discovered that it had been prompted merely by some foolish whim. Once the broken-haired terrier, which he had given her, had had a fit; once Mr. Harborough had spoken sharply to her before the servants; once she had felt so low that she could not get through the day without seeing him. These recollections combine together to form his resolution.

He lays down the paper. He will not go. Accident has made him disobedient; intention shall make him further so. Had she known at what an hour her message would reach him, even she could not have expected compliance with it.

So thinking, his cigar being by this time finished, he rises, and lighting his bedroom candle, turns to go to bed. Only, just as he is leaving the room, some impulse prompts him to read the telegram yet a fifth time. The words have certainly not changed since he last glanced at them; and yet they seem to him to have a more compelling look. Why can't he force them to be more explicit? He pauses; telegram in one hand and candle in the other. What can she want with him? It is just within the bounds of possibility that she may really need his presence; how or why, he is unable to hazard the faintest conjecture. But it is just within the limits of the possible that she may. Various suggestions of what shape that possible may take flit across his puzzled brain. Can it be that her husband has at length made the discovery of what for five years has been the open secret of all his acquaintance? In that case, as he, Talbot, has long known—known at first with leaping pulses, latterly with the cold sweat of an unspeakable dread, she would not have waited for him to come to her—she would have fled to him. It cannot, then, be that. Various other conjectures suggest themselves, but are dismissed as impracticable; but though they are dismissed, the fact remains that the woman to whom he once swore—*once*, nay, millions of times swore a love eternal, unalterable, exclusive—has sent him an imperative summons to her side; and he is preparing entirely to neglect it.

He sets down the candlestick, and takes up an 'A B C' lying on the table, as if officiously close at hand. He will just look to see if there is a train that would take him to her. If there is not, that will settle the matter. He turns to the name of the small station at which travellers to Harborough get out. Of course not. Nothing stops at that little wayside place before eleven o'clock. By that time he will be installed in Downing Street for the day, with his chief's correspondence before him.

He heaves a sigh of relief; and once more turns bedward. But before he has reached the door another thought has arrested him. Though there is no train which could take him to the little station close to her gate, yet there may easily be one which would carry him to Oxford, only five miles away from her.

Again he picks up the 'A B C,' and runs his finger and his eye down the page from the Paddington that heads it. Paddington 5.30; arrives at Oxford 7.40. Yes, there is one. It is, for the last ten miles of its course, a slow crawler; but, if up to its time, reaches Oxford at 7.40. A good hansom would convey him to Harborough in half an hour. He would have twenty minutes in which to learn her will; a second half-hour's drive would take him back to Oxford, to catch the nine o'clock up-train, which would land him in London in time for his day's work. It is possible, then—quite possible. The question is, shall he embrace that bare possibility? Shall he pick out the one chance for, out of the ninety-nine against, there being any real meaning in her message, to build upon it this fool's errand. At all events, he has plenty of time in which to think it over. It is only three o'clock. There are two good hours before he need set off.

He sits down again in his arm-chair, replenishes the fire, and lights another cigar. A year ago he would have gone without hesitation. Two years ago he would have stood on his head with joy at having the chance of going; but *this* year—— Well, it is true that it is no longer the voice of the passionately loved woman calling to him—a voice before whose sound obstacles vanish, space shrivels, time contracts; but it may be the voice of a fellow-creature in distress. *A fellow-creature in distress!* He laughs to himself at the flat pomposity of the phrase. What kind of distress the fellow-creature's can be— a fellow-creature so lapped in cotton-wool, so apparently beyond the reach of most of life's ennuis—he is absolutely at a loss to conjecture! He spends two hours, and smokes three cigars in conjecturing; and at the end, being as wise as he was at the beginning, knocks up his servant, puts on his fur coat, arms himself with as many wraps as he can muster, jumps into a hansom, and through the murkiness—black as midnight—of a hideous December morning, has himself driven to the Paddington Departure Platform; where, for three minutes, he stamps about, telling himself that no such fool as he walks, has ever walked, or, as far as he knows, will ever walk upon God's earth; and is then whirled away.

———————————————

CHAPTER XXI

There are not so many passengers by the 5.30 train as to hinder its being punctual. It is almost faithful to its minute. So far—it can't be said to be very far—fortune favours the one of its occupants with whom we have any concern. He rolls out, cross and furry, still repeating to himself with an even greater intensity of inward emphasis than he had employed at Paddington, that unflattering opinion of his own wisdom with which he had embarked on his present venture. If it had appeared a fool's errand when looked forward to dispassionately from the warmth and ease of his own fireside, what does it appear now? Now that, having picked out the most promising-looking of the few sleepy hansoms awaiting unlikely passengers, and bidden the mufflered purple-nosed driver take him as fast as his horse can lay legs to the ground to Harborough Castle, he finds himself spinning through the Oxford suburbs out into the flat country beyond—ugly as original ugliness, further augmented by a December dawning and a black and iron frost, can make it. At each mile that carries him nearer and nearer his goal, his own unreason looms ever immenser and yet immenser before him. By such a gigantic folly as this even Betty herself may be satisfied. At every echoing step the horse takes on the frozen ground it seems to him less and less likely that Betty has had any real reason for sending for him, any reason that may at all account for or palliate his appearance at this unheard-of hour. Even Betty herself has asked no such insanity of him as this. She had reckoned upon her telegram reaching him at mid-day, and upon his arriving in obedience to it sometime in the afternoon, an hour at which any one may arrive at a friend's house without provoking special comment. But now? At the spanking pace at which, in accordance with his own directions, he is getting over the ground, he will reach the Castle by eight o'clock, just as the housemaids are beginning to open the shutters and clean the grates. When the door is unbarred to him by an astonished footman struggling into his coat, whom shall he ask for? What shall he say? Lady Betty? Impossible! At eight o'clock in the morning! Mr. Harborough? Neither is he, any more than his wife, an early riser; and if, in answer to his, Talbot's, astounding summons, he should drag himself from his couch, and come in sleepy *déshabillé* to meet him, what has he, Talbot, to say to him? What does he want with him? How can he explain his own appearance? Had he better ask for no one, then?—say nothing, but just slip in, trusting to the thoroughness of the Harborough servants' acquaintance with his appearance to save him from any inconvenient questions? Shall he wait in some cold sitting-room in process of dusting, with its chairs standing on their heads, and the early besom making play on its carpet until his half-hour is up, and he can return whence he came, having at least done what he was bidden to do? He laughs derisively at himself. And meanwhile *how* cold he is! He has been up all night, in itself a chilly thing; a hansom is by no means a warm vehicle, at least to one to whom any nipping air is preferable to having the glass let chokily down within a half-inch of his nose. The dawn is being blown in by a small wind—small, but full of knife-blades—and the griding frost that holds all earth and water in the rigidity of death's ugly sleep, has pierced into his very bones. In his life he has seldom taken a colder drive, and yet he dreads its being over. What shall he say to Harborough? The chance of his seeing him is indeed remote; but remote chances do sometimes become facts. If this becomes fact, what is he to say to him? Even through Harborough's hippopotamus-hide there must be some arrow that will penetrate. If anything can open the stupid eyes, so miraculously sealed through five years, surely this insane apparition of his will do it.

They have reached the park gates. The lodge-keeper at least is up and dressed, and runs out with alacrity. She need not have been in such a hurry. He would have been much more obliged to her if she had crawled, and bungled, and delayed him a little. Now he is rolling through the park, by the dead white grass and the pinched brown bracken; under the black arms of the famous chestnuts, beneath which he and Betty have so often strayed; through half a dozen more gates; through a last gate, on leaving which behind them, turf more carefully trimmed, flower-beds now hard and empty, clumps of laurustinus and rhododendron tell of his neighbourhood to the house, which a turn in the approach now gives to his view. His eye flies anxiously, though with little hope, to the front. Does it look at all awake? Are there any blinds up? It would be ludicrous to hope that Betty's could be; Betty who is never seen a moment before eleven o'clock, and very often not for many moments after. He looks mechanically, though quite hopelessly, up at her windows—the three immediately above the portico—and so looking, starts, and gives utterance to an involuntary ejaculation. In the case of all three, shutters are open and blinds up. What can have happened? What can so flagrant a departure from the habits of a lifetime imply? He has reached the door by now, and, jumping out, rings the bell. He will probably have long to wait before it is answered, the servants, expecting no such summons, being probably dispersed to other quarters of the house. But, as in the case of the lodge-keeper, he is mistaken.

With scarce any delay the great folding-doors roll back; nor is there in the faces of the couple of footmen who appear any of that blank astonishment which he had been schooling himself to meet. There is no surprise that he can detect upon their civil features, any more than there would have been had he and his portmanteau walked in at five o'clock in the afternoon.

'Of—of course no one is up yet?' he says, with an air that he, as he feels, in vain tries to make easy and disengaged.

'Oh yes, sir; her ladyship is up! Her ladyship has been up all night.'

Up all night! Then some one must be ill! Is it Harborough? Harborough ill? Will he die? In one thought-flash these questions, with all that for him and his future life an answer in the affirmative would imply, dart through his mind— dart with such a sickening dread that he can scarcely frame his next and most obvious question.

'Is any one ill, then?'

For the first time the servant looks a little surprised. If it is not on account of the illness in the house why has Mr. Talbot presented himself at this extraordinary hour?

'Yes, sir; Master Harborough has been very ill for two days. Sir Andrew Clark and Dr. Ridge Jones came down yesterday to see him, and he was hardly expected to live through the night.'

Master Harborough! Not expected to live through the night! At this news, so entirely unlooked for—since, amongst all the possibilities whose faces he has been scanning, that of something having happened to the children has never once presented itself—Talbot stands stock-still, rooted to the spot, in sad amazement. Poor little Master Harborough! In a moment he is seeing him again as he had last seen him—seen the little sturdy figure that, in its rosy vigour, seemed to be shaking its small fist in defiance at age, or decay, or death. Yes; he sees him again—sees, too, his mother, laughing at his naughtiness, bragging of his strength, smothering him with her kisses. Poor, poor Betty! A great rush of compassionate tenderness floods his heart towards the woman against whom he had just been harshly shutting that heart's doors; discrediting her truth; grudging the service she has asked of him; crediting her even in his thoughts with the indecency of summoning him to her husband's death-bed. Oh, poor Betty! On his heart's knees he begs her pardon.

His agitation is so great and so overcoming that, for the moment, he can ask no more questions, but only follows the butler, who by this time has appeared on the scene, in silent compliance with his request to him to come upstairs—a request accompanied by the remark that he will let her ladyship know that he is here. Having led him to Betty's boudoir, the servant leaves him to look round, with what heart he may, on all the objects of that most familiar scene. How familiar they are—all her toys and gewgaws! Many he himself has given her; some they had chosen together; over others they had quarrelled; over others, again, they had made up—but how well he knows them, one and all! He looks round on them with a triple sorrow—the sorrow of his past love and present pity for her joining hands, in melancholy triad, with his deep and abiding self-contempt. He looks round on the countless fans—fans everywhere—open, half-open; on the great Japanese umbrella, stuck up, in compliance with one of the most senseless fashions ever introduced, in the middle of the room, with Liberty silk handkerchiefs meaninglessly draped about its stem; on the jumping frogs and mechanical mice; on the banjo she has often thrummed to him; on the mandoline she has tried to wheedle him into learning to play, that he may sing her Creole love-songs to it.

He turns away from them all with a sick impatient sigh. How hideously out of tune they and all the fooleries they recall seem with this soul-and-body-biting December dawning—with 'Master Harborough not expected to live through the night!'

He has never seen Betty in the grasp of a great grief. He is as much at a loss to picture how she will bear it as he would be to fancy a butterfly drawing a load of coals. How will she take it? How will she look? What shall he say? How shall he comfort her? That she has had any other motive in sending for him than the child's impulse to show the cut finger or the barked shin to a friend never occurs to him. His poor Betty! No selfish regret enters his mind at having been summoned through the midwinter night helplessly to see a little child die. He can think of nothing but how best to console her. He is very far from being ready with any consolations that even to himself appear at all consoling, when the door opens, and she enters.

At the sound of the turning handle he has gone to meet her, with both hands out as if to draw her and her misery to that breast whose doors are thrown wider to her than they have been for many months; but no answering hands come to meet them. Some gesture of hers tells him that she does not wish him to approach her.

'How late you are!' she says.

If he were not looking at her, and did not see with his own eyes that the words proceeded out of her mouth, he would never have recognised her voice. By that voice, and by her whole appearance, he is so shocked, that for a moment he cannot answer. Even upon the face of a girl in the first flush of youth, and whose only ornamentings come from the Hand of God, two long nights' vigils, extravagant weeping, the careless dishevelment of heart-rending anguish, write themselves in terrible characters. What, then, must they do to a woman like Betty, whose whole beauty is a carefully built-up fabric, on which no sun must look, and no zephyr blow too inquisitively?

For the first time in his life Talbot fully realises what a built-up fabric it is. Through his mind flashes the doubt, whether, if without expecting to meet her, he had come across her in the street, he should have recognised her. She looks fifty years old. Her hair is in damp disorder; at the top all rough and disturbed, where it has evidently been desperately buried in a little counterpane. She is not now crying; but her unnumbered past tears have partially washed the rouge off her cheeks. A dreadful impression of the ludicrous, inextricably entangled with his unspeakable compassion—an impression for which he tells himself that he ought to be flayed alive— conveys itself to Talbot from her whole appearance. But though he ought to be flayed alive for receiving it, still it is there. And meanwhile she has spoken to him a second time. He must say something to her; not stand staring with stupid cruelty at her in her ruin and abasement.

'I expected you all yesterday,' she says in that same strange, dreadful voice.

He gives a sort of gasp. Can that indeed be the voice whose pretty treble has so often run with rippling laughter into his ears? the voice that sang him comic songs to that very banjo—now lying in its irony beside him—almost the last time that he heard its tones? His head is in a grisly whirl between that Betty and this. Which is the true one? Is this only a hideous nightmare? It seems at least to have the suffocating force of one; a force through which it is only by the strongest self-compulsion that he can break to answer her.

'I came as soon as I got your telegram.'

Her eyes, washed away to scarcely more than half their size, are resting upon him; and yet it seems by her next speech as if she had either not heard or not heeded his answer.

'You might have come quicker,' she says.

'But indeed I could not,' cries he, genuine distress lending him at last fluent speech. 'I was at the House till two in the morning; I never received it until I got home to Bury Street; I came by the very next train. Oh, Betty, how could you doubt that I should?'

As he speaks an arrow of self-reproach shoots through his heart at the thought of how near a chance the poor soul's cry for help had run of being altogether disregarded.

'I wanted to speak to you,' she says, a spark of fever brightening the chill wretchedness of her look. 'I have something to say to you; that was why I sent for you.'

'Of course, of course!' he answers soothingly. 'I was delighted to come.'

'I can't stay more than a minute,' she says restlessly. 'I must go back to him; I have never left him for eight and forty hours. He is asleep now—only under opiates—but an opiate sleep is better than none, is it not?' consulting his face with a piteous appeal.

'Much—much better,' replies Talbot earnestly.

'You have heard—they have told you—how ill he is?'

A sort of hard break makes itself heard in her voice; but she masters it impatiently.

'Yes, they have told me.'

'What have they told you?' asks she sharply. 'I daresay that they have told you a great deal more than the truth. If they have told you that there is no hope, they have told you wrong. They had no right to say so; there is hope!'

'They never told me that there was not,' replies he, still more soothingly than before; for it seems to him that no finger can be laid too gently on that terrible mother-ache.

'It all came so suddenly,' says she, putting her hand up with a bewildered air to her damp forehead and disordered hair. 'And yet now it seems *centuries* since he was running about. *How* he ran and jumped, did not he? There never was such an active child. And now it seems *centuries* that he has been lying in his little bed.'

For a moment she breaks down entirely, but fights her way on again.

'It was only a cold at first—quite a slight cold! He was not the least ill with it, and I thought nothing of it; and then on Tuesday there came an acrobatic company to Darnton'—the little neighbouring market-town—'and he was so excited about them, and begged so hard to be allowed to go and see them, that I took him; and he was so delighted with them—he clapped and applauded more than anybody in the house; and all the evening afterwards he was trying to do the things he had seen them do—you know how clever he always is in imitating people—and telling nurse about them. Nurse and I agreed that we had never seen him in such spirits. But he did not sleep well; he was always dreaming about them, and jumping up; and next morning he was in a high fever, and I sent for the doctor, and he has been getting worse ever since; and *now*——'

Again she breaks down, but again recovering herself, goes on rapidly:

'But it is not the same as if it were a grown-up person, is it? Children have such wonderful recovering power, have not they?—down one day and up the next. They pull through things that would kill you or me, do not they? He *will* pull through, won't he? You think that he *will* pull through?'

'I am sure that he will,' replies Talbot earnestly.

It is, of course, an answer absolutely senseless, and in the air; but what other can he give, with those miserable eyes fastened in such desperate asking upon his?

'Oh, if you knew what it has been,' she says, her arms falling with a gesture of measureless tired woe to her sides as she speaks, 'to have been kneeling by him all these two days, hearing him moan, and seeing him try to get his breath!—he does not understand what it means; he has never been ill before. He thinks that I can help him. O God! he thinks I can help him, and that I don't! He turns to me for everything. You know that he always did when he was well, did not he? He is always asking me when the pain will go away? Asking me whether he has been naughty, and I am angry with him? Angry with him! I *angry* with him! O God! O God!'

Her excitement and her grief have been gaining upon her at each fresh clause of her speech, and at the end she flings herself down on the ground and buries her face in the cushion of a low chair, while dry, hard sobs shake her from head to foot.

What is he to say to her? Nothing. He will not insult such a sorrow by the futility of his wretched words. He can only stoop over her, and lay his hand no harshlier than her mother would have done, no harshlier than she herself would have laid hers upon her little dying boy, on her heaving shoulder. But she shakes off his light touch, and raising her distorted face, again tries to address him. But the rending sobs that still convulse her make her utterance difficult; and her words, when they come, scarcely intelligible.

'Do not touch me! leave me—leave me—alone! I—I have not yet said what —what I had to say to you. That—that was not what I had to say to you! I—I —must say what I—sent for you—to say.'

She pauses, gasping. It seems as if the task she had set herself was beyond her present strength.

'Do not tell me,' he says most gently; 'if it is anything that hurts you, do not tell me now; wait and tell me by and by.'

He has withdrawn at her bidding his hand from her shoulder, but has knelt down in his deep pity beside her, and tried to take in his her cold and clammy fingers. But she draws them sharply away.

'Did not I tell you to leave me alone!' she cries in a thin voice. 'Let me—let me say what I have to say to you, and have done with it. I will say it now! I *must* say it now! What business have you,' turning with a pitiful fierceness upon him, 'to try and hinder me?'

'I do not—I do not!' speaking in the tenderest tone. 'Tell it me of course, whatever it is, if it will give you the least relief.'

'I sent for you to tell you that it is all over—all over between us,' she says, having now mastered her sobs, and speaking with great rapidity and distinctness; 'that is what I sent for you to tell you. I wanted you to come at once, that I might tell you. Why did not you come at once? I have been a very wicked woman——'

'No, dear, no! indeed you have not!' he interrupts with an accent of excessive pain and protest.

But she goes on without heeding him:

'Or if I have not, it has been no thanks to me; it has been thanks to you, who have saved me from myself! But whatever there has been between us, it is over now. That is what I sent for you to tell you. *Over!* do you understand? *Gone! done with!* Do you understand? Why do not you say something? Do you hear? Do you understand?'

'I hear,' he answers in a mazed voice; 'but I—I do not understand! I do not understand why, if you want to tell me this, you should tell it me *now* of all times.'

'It is *now* of all times that I want to tell you—that I must tell you!' cries she wildly. 'Cannot you see that it is on account of *him*? Oh, cannot you think what it has been kneeling beside him with his little hot hand in mine! You do not know how fiery hot his hand is! Last night his pulse was so quick that the doctor could scarcely count the beats—it was up to 120; and while I was kneeling beside him the thought came to me that perhaps this had happened to him on—on—account of—*us*! that it was a judgment on me!'

She pauses for a minute, and he tries to put in some soothing suggestion, but she goes on without heeding him.

'You may call it superstition if you please, but it came to me—oh, it seems years ago now!—it must have been the night before last!—and as the night went on, it kept getting worse and worse, as he got worse and worse; and in the morning I could not bear it any longer, and I sent for you! I thought that you would have been here in a couple of hours.'

'So I would! So I would! Heaven knows so I would, if it had been possible!'

'And all yesterday he went on growing worse—I did not think that he could have been worse than he was in the night, and live—but he was. All day and all last night again he was struggling for breath!—think of having to sit by and see a little child struggling for his breath!'

She stops, convulsed anew by that terrible dry sobbing, that is so much more full of anguish than any tears.

'Poor little chap! poor Betty!'

'I have been listening all night for you! I could not have believed that you would have been so long in coming; it is such a little way off! I knew—I had a feeling that he would never get better until you had come—until I had told you that it was all over between us; but I have told you now, have not I? I have done all that I could! One cannot recall the past; no one can, not even God! He cannot expect that of me; but I have done what I could—all that is left me to do, have not I?'

There is such a growing wildness in both her eye and voice that he does not know in what terms to answer her; and can only still kneel beside her, in silent, pitying distress.

'I see that you think I am out of my wits!' she says, looking distrustfully at him; 'that I must be out of my wits to talk of sending you away—you who have been everything to me. Cannot you see that it is because I love you that I am sending you away? if I did not love you it would be nothing—no sacrifice!—it would be no use! But perhaps if I give up everything—everything I have in the world except him' (stretching out her hands, with a despairing gesture of pushing from herself every earthly good)—'perhaps then—*then*—God will spare him to me! perhaps He will not take him from me! It may be no good! He may take him all the same; but there is just the chance! say that you think it *is* a chance!'

But he cannot say so. There are very few words that he would not try to compel his lips to utter; but he dares not buoy her up with the hope that she can buy back her child by a frantic compact with the Most High. Her eyes drop despairingly from his face, not gaining the assent they have so agonisedly asked for; and she struggles dizzily to her feet.

'That is all—I had—to—tell you!' she says fiercely. 'I have nothing more to say!—nothing that need—need detain you here any longer. I must go back to him; he may be asking for me!—asking for me, and I not there! But you understand—you are sure that you understand? I have often sent you away before in joke, but I am not joking now' (poor soul! that, at least, is a needless assertion); 'I am in real earnest this time! I am not sending you away to-day only to send for you back again to-morrow; it is real earnest this time; it is for ever!—do you understand? *For ever*! say it after me, that I may be sure that you are making no mistake—*for ever.*'

And he, looking down into the agony of her sunk eyes, not permitted even to touch in farewell her clammy hand, echoes under his breath, '*For ever!*'

CHAPTER XXII

'Das Herz wuchs ihm so sehnsuchtsvoll
Wie bei der Lichsten Gruss.'

For ever! All through the wintry day they hammer at his ears—those two small words that take up such a little space on a page, and yet cover eternity. There is nothing that does not say them to him. The hansom horse's four hoofs beat them out upon the iron-bound road; the locomotive snorts them at him; the dry winter wind sings them in his ears; Piccadilly's roar, and the tick of the clock on the chimney-piece of the room where he works in Downing Street, equally take their shape to him. *For ever!* They must always be solemn words, even though in the slackness of our loose vocabulary they are often fitted to periods no longer than ten minutes, than an hour, than six months. But one never quite forgets that they can stretch to the dimensions of the great sea that washes Time's little shores. *For ever!* At each point of his return journey there recurs to him the memory of some unkind thought that he had had of her on his way down. Here he had accused her of some paltry motive in sending for him! There he had protested against the dominion of her whims. Here again, he had groaned under the thought of having, within five days, to pass a second time this way in order to spend his compulsory Christmas with her.

Well, that Christmas is no longer compulsory—no longer possible even. He has his will. He may keep for himself that present which he had so grudged the trouble of choosing for her. *For ever!* Those two words are the doors that shut away into the irredeemable past that portion of his life in which she has shared. Only five years after all! He need not have grudged her only five years.

An intense and cutting remorse for the bitterness of his late thoughts of her; for his impatience of her fond yoke; for his weariness of her company, and passionate eagerness to escape from her, travels every step of the way with him as he goes. Well, he may be pleased now. He has his wish. He has escaped from her. But has he escaped? Can that be called escape, not for one moment of that day, or any succeeding days, to get the bottomless wretchedness of those poor eyes, the pathos of those sunk and ghastly cheeks, and of that damp ruffled hair from before his own vision; never for one instant of the whole noisy day to have his ears free from the sound of that thin, harsh mother-voice, asking him whether her boy will live? Between him and the paper on which he writes that face comes. It rises between him and the speakers in the House. It closes his eyes at night. It figures with added distortion in his dreams. It comes with the dull dawn to wake him. He spends his Christmas alone with it in London. To do so seems to him, in his remorse, some slight expiation of the unlovingness of his late past thoughts towards her. He would deem it a crime to join any happy Christmas party while she is kneeling with that face beside her dying child. Since he cannot go to her, he will go nowhere.

Once indeed—nay, to tell truth, twice, thrice, the thought has recurred to him of Freddy Ducane's affectionate invitation to the Manor, and that there is now nothing—no pre-engagement to hinder him from accepting it. But each time he dismisses the idea, as if it had been a suggestion of Satan. Scarcely less ruthlessly does he put to flight a face that, as the days go by, will come stealing in front of the other; a face that—albeit modest—is pertinacious too; since, despite his routings, it comes back and back again. And meanwhile he hears no news from Harborough. To telegraph inquiries would seem to him a contravention of her will—hers, who has so passionately decided that their paths are henceforth to diverge. But he anxiously and daily searches the obituary for that name he dreads to find; looks anxiously, too, about the streets and round his clubs in search of some common acquaintance—some country neighbour—to whom he may apply with probability of success for tidings of the child. But for some days he looks in vain. London has emptied itself for the Christmas holidays, and it appears to him as if he were the only one of his acquaintance left in it. That the boy is still fighting for his life is proved by the fact of his name not having been entered in the list of deaths. Still fighting! He still panting, and she still kneeling beside him! It makes Talbot draw his own breath gaspingly to think of it.

As the days go on, his anxiety to get news—any news, whether it may be bad or good—of how that drama being played out on the narrow stage of a little bed, and the one act of which that he has seen haunts him with such a persistency of torment, grows more urgent and intense. London has filled again. The Christmas holiday week is over, and humanity's innumerable beasts of burden have returned to their yokes. The frost still continues, and the clubs are nearly as crowded as in June; crowded with every one whom he does not wish to see; empty of any one that he seeks. Hitherto, as long as he has had no desire for their company—has avoided it rather, from the associations it has had with his own entanglement—he has met acquaintances made at Harborough, people living in the neighbourhood of Harborough, friends of the Harboroughs, at every turn. They have claimed his acquaintance; have insisted on greeting him; on forcing upon him pieces of local information which have no manner of interest for him. Now, however, that they might do him a substantial service; now that they might, nay, *must*, give him the tidings he is craving for, all such persons appear to have been swept from the face of the earth. Look as he may, in club, and street, and private house, he can find none.

One Sunday afternoon, a cold and ugly Sunday, he is walking down St. James's Street, turning over in his mind how best to obtain some certainty as to that subject, his miserable uncertainty upon which is desolating his life, when in one of the numberless passing hansoms his eye suddenly alights upon a surely very well-known profile. If it is not the profile of Betty's husband, he is deceived by the most extraordinary accidental likeness that ever beguiled human sight. Harborough is in London, then? What does that mean? Does it mean that the boy is better? or does it mean that it is all over? A spasm of pain contracts his heart. Poor little chap! Perhaps his father's presence here only means that he is already hidden away in the grave, and that there is nothing left for father-love, or mother-love either, to do for him.

Talbot's eye has eagerly singled out the hansom, and followed it. Happily for him, it stops at not a hundred yards' distance from him, at the St. James's Club, and a figure—indubitably Mr. Harborough's—jumps out. Talbot hastens after him. It is a club to which he himself belongs, and he enters it not a minute after the object of his pursuit. Some irrational fear that that object may even yet evade him—that he may be even yet balked of that news for which he seems to have been months, years, thirstily waiting, lends wings to his feet. He is so close upon his friend's heels that the latter has not had time to get beyond the hall. One lightning-glance tells Talbot that he looks much as usual; that there is no crape on his hat; and that his insignificant face is as innocent of any expression beyond its ordinary banal good humour as he has ever seen it. Then the child is not dead! That little jolly face that has been so often pressed against his own is not companioned with the dust. Thank God for that! But his one minute's look, though unspeakably reassuring, has not yet so entirely banished his fears that he can delay for one instant putting the question which has been for ten weary days on his lips, unable to be asked.

'The boy? How is the boy?'

Mr. Harborough starts.

'Hullo! it is you, is it? delighted to see you!' shaking his hand with the same prolonged and mistaken warmth under which Talbot has so often writhed.

He does not writhe now. He repeats his eager question:

'How is the boy?'

'Oh! you have heard of our trouble about him?' returns Harborough cheerfully. 'Well, to tell truth, the young beggar did give us a fright! but he is as right as a trivet again now, or at least he is on the high road to be so; but he had a near shave of it, poor little man! not one of us thought he would pull through. Andrew Clark himself did not. We all of us—his mother, I, everybody—thought he was going to give us the slip; but not a bit of it. I never saw such a boy! There he is, shouting and kicking up such a row, they can scarcely keep him in bed; and eat—he would eat an old shoe—he would eat you or me if we gave him the chance.'

He ends with a jovial, if not very wise, laugh; but Talbot does not echo it, though Heaven knows that he is glad enough at heart for any expression of mirth.

'You must run down and see him,' pursues the other hospitably; 'it is a long time since you have paid us a visit. Come now, fix a day; there is no time like the present.' 'You forget,' replies Talbot, with an embarrassment which, however, is not perceived by his interlocutor, 'that I am not one of those lucky fellows like you whose time is their own. I cannot take a holiday whenever I choose; you must remember that mine is just over.'

'Stuff and nonsense!' rejoins Betty's husband, with rough good humour. 'Do not tell me that they keep you as tight as that! I know better! I will take no excuses; only two days ago Betty was saying to me what an age it was since we had seen anything of you.'

Before he can hinder it, Talbot's jaw drops. Betty had said so? *Betty?* Has sorrow then robbed her of her wits?

'By the bye,' continues Harborough, correcting himself, and happily ignorant of the effect produced by his last words, 'it was the other way up; it was I who said so to her. But it is all the same thing; she will be delighted to see you. She will never forgive me if I let you escape us this time; and the boy, you positively must come and help us to keep that boy in order. I never saw such a boy!' (beginning again to chuckle).

It is not without very considerable difficulty, not without some sacrifice of truth, some vague promises, that Talbot at length succeeds in making his escape without having tied himself down to any special day for making his appearance at that house from whose doors the wife has warned him off with as great an eagerness as—it cannot be greater than—the husband now shows to force him into them. As long as he is in Harborough's company, the necessity for baffling his friend's stupid urgencies, the awkwardness of rebutting civilities so well meant, prevent him from realising the full intensity of his relief. But when he has reached his own rooms, when he is alone, then indeed he knows the weight of the burden that has rolled from his shoulders. The boy is *not* dead; riotously alive rather. Thank God—thank God for that! And she is no longer kneeling beside him, no longer out of breath for company. He may drive away for ever from before his eyes that hideous vision of her as he had last seen her, and which has been for fourteen days poisoning sleep and waking for him. He may drive it away; and not only so, but he may replace it by any other vision he chooses. *Any other!* In the first stupefaction of that thought—for joy has her stupefaction as well as pain—he covers his face with both hands, as if, by shutting out all other objects, he could the better bring that astounding change home to his mazed brain and his leaping heart. He is free! He has to say the word over many, many times to himself before he can at all take in its full significance. He is free!—free, too, with a freedom that has been given to him, that has been gained by no violent bursting of bars, and which therefore he may taste with that fulness of joy that those alone can feel who have long lain fast bound in misery and iron. He has been so long a bondman, the irons have cut so deeply into his flesh, that on first coming out into God's good light he staggers blindly as one drunk.

He walks to the window and looks out. The bells are ringing to afternoon church, and the congregations are passing staidly by. He looks out at them all, with a joyous smile at the *endimanché* shop-boys, each with his sweetheart on his arm; at the little children holding fathers' and mothers' hands. He, too, may have a sweetheart. He, too, may be blessed with little children. There are none of the possibilities which make life lovely to other men, to which he, too, may not aspire. The happy tears crowd into his eyes.

From the window he walks to his bureau, and out of a secret drawer takes a tiny tissue-paper parcel, and from it carefully extracts its contents. They consist of only one sprig of dried lavender, thieved from the garden of the little Red House, and at which for five months he has not dared to look. He may look at it now; may pass it lovingly across his lips; may inhale whatever yet lingers of its innocent cottage sweetness. There is enough still left to recall the parent-tree. He may see again that spreading flowered bush; may see again Minky galloping like a little gray whirlwind across the lawn; may hear again the parrot swearing in the cook's voice, and sleepily clacking with his black tongue in the sunshine; may watch the eleven birds—are there still eleven, he wonders?—hopping and quarrelling and twittering up and down upon his ladder; may see Jacob and the mowing-machine; and—*her*. Can any bodily eyes show her to him much more plainly than his spirit's eyes see her now, summoned up before him by that delicate, homely perfume, that is to him so indissolubly associated with her?—see her as he saw her last in the walled Manor garden, standing among the moon-shimmering white gladioli, and saying to him with farewell smile and wavering voice:

'Since you are so determined to go downhill, I suppose I dare not say that I hope our paths will ever meet again.'

But now—but now! God knows how he has long hated his downhill course; and now—and now there is no reason, none in heaven above or earth beneath, why their paths should not for ever merge. His head sinks forward on his clasped hands, still jealously clasped upon the lavender sprig, and his hot tears rain on its little dry buds. In his whole life before he has never cried for joy. At night he cannot sleep for that same troublesome joy; but, indeed, he would grudge any slumber that robbed him for even a moment of the consciousness of his blessedness. He feels no need of that lost sleep all next day as he walks, treading on air, through the murky London streets, that seem to him gold-paved, diamond-shining. He knows that he must look senselessly radiant; for, in the course of the day, several people of his acquaintance meeting him ask what he is smiling at. One inquires whether some one has left him a fortune. Before he can stop himself, he has almost answered, 'Yes.' Is not it true—most true? His state of exaltation lasts, with no perceptible lessening, through all that day, through the night—almost as sleepless as the preceding one—that follows it; but on the succeeding morning there comes a check, a very slight one, but still a check to the triumphal course of his felicity. Amongst that morning's letters is one which, at the first glance, he imagines to be from Betty; and though a second look reassures him on this point, and though, on opening it, it proves to be merely an invitation to dinner from a slight acquaintance, yet the train of thought induced by the shock of that first impression successfully pulls him down from his empyrean. What security has he that Betty may not write to him; that now that her terror and her grief are alike past, she may not deride as superstition the conduct dictated by that grief, and, like a child, ask to have back again her given and repented gift? What security has he—a cold sweat breaks out on his forehead at the thought—that any day, on his return from his work, he may not find her standing by the fire, ready to throw herself into his arms, and tell him with sobs that she cannot bear her life without him, and that they must take up again the old relations? And if she does so—there is such a horrible probability in the idea, that it is as well to face it—what answer is he to make her? Would it be chivalrous, loyal, to take her at that word wrung from her anguish, wrung from her when she was no more her real self than if she had been raving in a fit of madness? To make her keep to it, when with tears and prayers she is begging him to let her resume it? And if not, if not—with what a heart-sinking does he face the suggestion—must he again bow his neck to the yoke? Must he again put on his gyves? God save him from that hard alternative!

And so, in the fear of it, he goes day and night. For weeks it takes the edge off his bliss; for weeks he never glances at the addresses of his letters without a pang of dread; for weeks he never turns the handle of his door on his return home from his work without a shiver of apprehension. But not once does his eye alight on that feared handwriting; always his room is empty of that once so longed-for, and now dreaded presence. Ah, he is not so indispensable to her as he had fancied! She can do better without him than in his self-value had appeared possible. He need not be afraid that her fingers will ever again trace his name upon paper, or hurriedly lift his latch. As he realises this, so unaccountable is human nature, a slight pang of irrational regret mingles with the profundity of his relief and joy. But as the days, lengthening and brightening in their advance toward spring, go by, the pang vanishes as the fear had done; only yet more quickly, and his visions possess him wholly. When—*when* may he make them realities? How soon, without appearing brutally unfeeling towards, prematurely forgetful of, his old sweetheart, may he take his new one by her white hand under the Judas-tree, saying, in the lovely common words that all the world uses and none can improve upon, merely, 'I love you'?

CHAPTER XXIII

No one can be in profounder ignorance than is Peggy of the fact of any one breathing passionate sighs towards her from Downing Street. The only news that she has heard of John Talbot is a casual mention by Freddy of the fact of his having invited him to spend his Christmas at the Manor, and of his having refused without giving any particular reason.

'He does not care for our simple pleasures, I suppose,' says Freddy, with a smile; 'and, on the whole, I am not sorry. He is a good fellow; but we are really much more comfortable by ourselves. I like to have you two dear things all to myself.'

As he speaks he extends a hand apiece impartially to his betrothed and her sister. Peggy is in these days in possession of one of Freddy's hands oftener than she altogether cares about; but, since he is always reminding her that he is now a more than brother to her—in fact, as he has long been in feeling— she decides that it is not worth making a fuss about, and lets her cool and careless fingers lie in that fraternal hand without paying any attention to it. For her the winter has passed *tant bien que mal*. Christmas had brought her love to Prue, and the mumps to the Evanses; and both events have supplied Peggy with plenty of work.

The Evanses are one of those families who have all their diseases bountifully. Their very mumps are severe and simultaneous. They *all* have them—father, mother, schoolboys, old baby, new baby. A hireling tells the Christmas news from Mr. Evans's pulpit, while Mr. Evans sits in his study, with the door locked to hinder the intrusion of his suffering progeny, stooping his swelled features over his *Earthly Paradise*, and thinking with envy and admiration of the institution of a celibate clergy. Both babies bawl from morning to night at this practical joke played upon them by Providence at the outset of their career; and the boys wistfully press their enlarged faces—unnecessarily enlarged, since they were large before—against the frozen panes of the Vicarage windows, in futile longing for the unattainable joys held out to them by the view of the iron-bound Vicarage pond, and the glassy slideableness of the turnpike road.

The calamity to her clergy has thrown the conduct of the whole of the parish charities and gaieties on Peggy's hands. Nor is she without a little nursing on her own account; for Freddy, by dint of keeping his Prue out on the leads till ten o'clock at night, talking to her about himself and the fixed stars, has succeeded in giving her such a cold on the chest, that neither can she hear the

Christmas tidings. However, he is so touchingly repentant for what he has done, says such cutting things about himself, and sits by her side so devotedly for hours, reading poetry to her in a charming sympathetic voice, that nobody can be seriously angry with him—least of all Prue, whose one heart-felt prayer is that her cold may become chronic, or that at least she may have a new one every month.

'He has been reading me such beautiful poetry!' she says in a soft voice one day, when Peggy rejoins her after her lover has taken his daily departure. 'Very deep, you know; so that one had to put one's whole mind to following it. But beautiful, too—like Browning, only better?'

Peggy lifts her eyebrows.

'*Like Browning, only better!*'

'And when I said so,' pursues Prue, with hot cheeks and bright proud eyes, 'he told me that he never knew any one who had such an unerring instinct for what was good in literature as I.'

'And whose was it?' inquires Margaret, a little suspiciously.

'He would not tell me. I could not get him to tell me; but I think—oh, Peggy, I cannot help fancying that it was his own!'

'That would account for his looking upon your instinct as unerring, would not it?' retorts Peggy, laughing.

But she does not always laugh over Freddy and Prue. Though young Ducane repeats to her oftener than once or twice a day that he is now her more than brother, in fact as well as in feeling, he does not tell any one else so. Despite all Peggy's representations, entreaties, protests, he has not yet given the slightest hint of his new situation to his aunt.

'I must insist upon your telling her,' Peggy has said. 'As things now stand, I cannot bear to meet her; I feel an impostor and a cheat. It is putting us all in such a false position; it makes me miserable to think that she has not a suspicion that the old conditions are not quite unaltered.'

'Poor old conditions!' says Freddy dreamily, leaning with thrown-back head in the rocking-chair, and staring up at the ceiling, as in the summer he used to stare up at the sky and the jackdaws. 'It is a sad thought that one never can gain anything in this world without some counterbalancing loss! Life is a sort of compromise; is it not, Peg?'

'If you do not tell her, I warn you that I shall tell her myself.'

Her tone is so resolute that Freddy forsakes his pensive generalities, and sits up.

'I am sorry once again, my Peggy, to have to remind you of that well-known firm who realised a large fortune by minding their own business.'

'It is my own business,' retorts Peggy firmly, though her cheek burns, 'it is Prue's business; and Prue's business is mine. If you do not tell milady, I repeat that I shall tell her myself.'

'I daresay you will,' replies Freddy sadly; 'and if you do, you will give a great deal of pain to a person who has never wittingly given you anything but pleasure in all her life.'

'Why should I give her pain?' returns Margaret, rising in high excitement from her chair, and standing before the fire, with quivering nostril and flashing eye. 'What is there to give her pain in——'

'It would give her pain, acute pain, to hear such a piece of news from any one but myself,' answers Freddy, with the same air of subdued sadness.

'Then why do not *you* tell her?' persists Margaret.

For all answer he rises too, and tries, unsuccessfully this time, to put his brotherly arm about her waist. 'Wait till I have got through my schools,' he says in a melting whisper; 'wait till I have taken my degree. When I have taken my degree she can no longer look upon me as a child, bless her old heart!'

'I see no signs of her looking upon you as a child now.'

'Oh, but she does,' replies Freddy confidently; 'to her' (beginning to laugh) 'I am still the lisping little innocent whom she took to her arms eighteen years ago.' Then, growing grave again, 'I do not think that you quite understand how difficult it is for an old person to realise that we are grown up; as I have told you several times, I find it difficult to realise it myself. Do not you too? No? Well, dear, because you are strong yourself do not be harsh to weaker vessels; but,' sinking his voice to a coaxing whisper, 'be the dear thing I have always found you, and wait till I have taken my degree.'

She has not the slightest ambition to be the 'dear thing he has always found her;' and his beguilements would have been absolutely wasted upon her, nor served to turn her by one hair's breadth from her purpose, had not they been so strenuously backed up by Prue.

'Oh, Peggy, for pity's sake do not interfere!' she has implored, with eyes full of tears and an agonised voice. 'Leave it all to him. He has such exquisite tact that he is sure to choose the best moment for telling her; and if you told her, and anything disagreeable came of it, it might give him a turn against me. He is so finely strung—he knows it himself, and looks upon it as quite a misfortune; the other day he asked me if I thought there was any use in his trying to change it—so finely strung that he cannot bear a contact with anything harsh or violent; and, as he often says, our love now is like a poem; and he thinks that anything that seemed to vulgarise it, or pull it down to a common level, would *kill* him.'

'Very well, dear, very well,' replies Peggy, with a long impatient sigh, stroking her sister's hair; 'have it your own way; only I fancy he would take more killing than that.'

And now Christmas has gone, and the New Year come; and Freddy has returned to his studies, leaving his aunt still in ignorance of those tidings which his exquisite tact has not yet found the right moment to communicate.

And now the spring is coming on with slow green steps. The brown earth is rubbing her eyes, in preparation for her blossomed wakening. Peggy's garden, so long iron-bound, is beginning to turn in its sleep. Jacob and she have gone together round their domain, counting over the dead and wounded that the long frost has left them in legacy. Among the dead, the irrecoverably dead, to which no Easter sunshine or April rains can bring back any little green shoots of life, is the old lavender-bush.

What matter? There are plenty of young ones. And yet, as she stands looking at the dry wreck of last year's fragrance, a hot and foolish tear steals into each eye. Her back is turned towards Jacob, who is examining the mowing-machine, which will soon be again needed.

'It wants fettlin' a bit,' he says in a grumbling voice; 'it has never been the same since that Muster Talbot meddled wi' it.'

Poor Muster Talbot! There is not much fear of his meddling with the mowing-machine ever again. She lifts her eyes, still a little obscured by those tears, to the sky, and they follow a pigeon, its wings silver-white as they turn in the sun. It is flying southwards. She wishes idly that it would fly to him to tell him that the lavender-bush is dead, and the mowing-machine broken; only it should choose a moment when Lady Betty is not by, as such silly news would not interest her.

She strolls away from Jacob, his last remark having given her a distaste for his conversation; strolls away into the little orchard, listening to the birds. How loud they are! and despite the long winter, how many! What a honeyed Babel of strong little voices! There is the thrush, of course:

> 'The wise thrush; he sings each song twice over,
> Lest you should think he never could recapture
> The first fine careless rapture!'

But besides the thrush's dominant harmony, how many others there are! There are the chiff-chaff's clear reiterations; the wren, with a voice so much bigger than her tiny body; the chaffinch's laugh-like notes; the robin's, who, not content with his own pretty song, that perhaps he thinks smacks too much of winter, puzzlingly mimics other singers. She lifts her eyes, shaded by her hand, to look at them, as they swing—jubilant specks—on twig and tree-top. How they are bragging of their happiness! outbragging one another! They are extravagantly gay, and yet their melodies bring the tears to her eyes. Perhaps they remind her that she is alone. Perhaps—more likely, indeed, since she is not very apt to be thinking of herself at all—they remind her of another extravagant gaiety, over which she rejoices or half rejoices in trembling. It is only in trembling that any human soul can see one they love uplifted to such a height of extravagant joy as that on which Prue now sits queening it over the workaday world. 'Can it last?' is the anxious question that Peggy asks herself a hundred times a day; finds herself feverishly asking when she wakes up at night.

If Prue's beauty, such as it is, can keep him, then indeed she has a better chance than ever; for love has put a meaning into the poor soul's insignificant lilies and roses, and made her transiently beautiful. If love, insane and limitless; love at once grovelling and soaring; love that would kiss the dust from his feet, or be burned by a slow fire to give him a moment's pleasure—if love such as this can bind him, then is he bound indeed. But can it?

'I wish you would not spoil him so,' Peggy says grudgingly one day, during the Easter vacation, when her sister has come hurrying from garden to house, on some errand of Freddy's. 'I cannot bear to see you fetching and carrying for him; it is such a reversal of the right order of things. You spend your life in waiting upon him hand and foot!'

'How could I spend it better?' replies Prue, the rapturous colour coming into her face, and the moisture into her radiant eyes.

And so Peggy has to submit, has to overhear ten and twenty times a day:

'My Prue, if you are going to the house—of course, do not go on purpose—my darling, I could not hear of such a thing! What do you suppose that I am made of? Well, of course, if you insist! it is awfully good of you! I will do as much for you when I am as young as you are,' etc. 'Prue, there is a fly on my forehead! I cannot get at my own hands somehow; do you think you could flick it off for me!' 'Oh, Prue! my head burns so! feel it! You do not happen to have any eau-de-Cologne in the room, do you? No? Then do not trouble to go upstairs for it. What? You have been to fetch it! Bad Prue! and I told you not!'

Easter has fallen late this year, and so has come with pomp of pear-blossom, with teeming primroses, with garden hyacinth and field daffodil; has come, too, with a breath like June's. The garden-chairs are set out; and on them, just as if it were midsummer, only that above their heads the Judas-tree holds leafless arms, the lovers sit, through the splendour of the lengthening days.

Freddy has said many a charming thing about the pear-blossom; about nature's awakening; about the hymeneal birds—things that, as Prue says, are almost poetry just as he speaks them, without any alteration. But he will not be able to say any more to-day, since he lies under one of his mysterious obligations—an obligation which he not darkly hints to have been imposed upon him by his aunt—to dine and sleep at a house in the neighbourhood.

'Milady has ignored them for twenty years,' he says of his intended hosts; 'and now she is sending me out as her dove, with her olive-branch. Of course I could not be so selfish as to refuse her. But,' with a heavy sigh, 'I wish she would carry her olive-branch herself!'

'I wish she would,' replies Prue dejectedly, her small face already overcast at the prospect of twenty-four hours' separation.

'It seems hard that one can never be perfectly well off without there coming some element of change and disintegration,' says Freddy, with a subdued sadness. 'Well, God bless you, darling! Take care of her, Peggy! Take good care of my Prue! Be waiting for me, Prue, at the garden-gate at twelve o'clock to-morrow!'

And Prue does wait, is waiting long before the appointed hour; waits—it would be piteous to say for how long after that hour—waits in vain, for Freddy comes not. He does not return all that day; nor is it till late on the next that he comes stepping, cool and smiling, across the evening shadows.

'Do not go to meet him,' says Peggy half crossly; 'he does not deserve it!'

But she speaks, as she had known that she would, to inattentive ears. It was, indeed, only as a relief to her own feelings that she had given that futile counsel. It is some time before they rejoin her, and when they do—

'It was not quite so bad as you expected, I suppose?' Margaret says, a little drily.

'When is anything so bad as one expects?' replies Freddy evasively, throwing himself into his accustomed chair; 'by Jove! how the pear-tree has come out since I left!'

'That was two whole days ago!' says Prue, rather wistfully.

'Two whole days ago!—so it was—

"Measured by opening and by closing flowers!"

165

Prue, do you happen to have a needle about you? No? Of course I do not mean to give you the trouble of going into the house to fetch one; some people have a crop of needles always about them. Oh, Prue!—stop! I am shocked—that is the last thing I meant!'

But poor Prue is off like a lapwing.

'You stayed longer than you intended?' says Peggy interrogatively.

'Yes;—by Jove, Peggy! do not you wish you could paint? Did you ever see anything like the colour of that sky behind the pear-blossom?'

'Did you like them?'

'Oh, you know I like everybody,' answers he vaguely; 'I do not think I possess the faculty of dislike. I think,' pensively, 'that in every human soul, if one gets near enough to it, there is something to love; and,' with a change of key, 'good heavens, are not they rich! They have a yacht of 500 tons; they are going round the world in her next autumn; they asked me to go too. I should like to go round the world.'

'To go round the world!' repeats Peggy, with a rather blank look; 'but by that time you will have taken your degree. You will have settled down to some steady work, will not you?—whatever work you have decided upon. By the bye, are you any nearer a choice than you were when last I spoke to you?'

Freddy agitates his curly head in an easy negative.

'I am afraid not the least; but, after all, there is no great hurry. I think,' with his serious air, 'that one ought to interrogate one's own nature very deeply before one decides on a question of such moment; and meanwhile,' becoming gay again, 'I should like to go round the world with the Hartleys—would not you, Peg? No?—well, I should.'

CHAPTER XXIV

It is May morning, but May morning as yet in early childhood—a radiant infancy that but few persons comparatively are awake to see. It has not struck five; and yet on the top of Magdalen Tower, in Oxford, Talbot is standing. Love has not driven him crazy, as might be the inference drawn from this fact. But those who know Oxford, know too that, as some say, since the time of Henry VIII.—though that overshoots the mark—Magdalen College has observed the rule of sending up her sweet-voiced choir to the summit of Wolsey's Tower on each new May morning, to greet the sun's uprising with a monkish hymn. And there are never wanting those who think it worth while to leave their beds almost before night has withdrawn, to hear those sweet singers greet the dawn with the ancient piety of their Latin hymn; and amongst them, as chance has brought him to Oxford, stands Talbot. He has run down to Oxford for Sunday; and since some of his fellow-guests have willed to rise and be present at the keeping of this unique and old-world custom, the fancy has taken him to come too. Not since the first year of his undergraduate-ship has he stood, as he now stands, on that stern height, looking for once at the world as the birds look, having climbed the steep and endless corkscrew stair. The years that have passed him since then seem to go by him in a solemn procession—solemn as this ante-dawning hour; solemn as the worn pinnacles above his head that have cut the blue of day, and pointed to the planets of night, through three hundred rolling years; solemn as the great and dying moon that is only waiting for her greater brother's upspringing to fade away and be not.

In each interval of the ancient balustrades, and through the opening in the pierced stone, Talbot can see far down a picture differently lovely. Here the world-famous street, taking its way between its schools and stately college-fronts; and with its Mary church's noble spire and the Radcliffe's dome for crown and finish. Here again the low, scarce swelling hills that so softly girdle the fair town, with the morning mists, not yet sun-pierced, streaming across their dim flanks. Here the river stealing; there the bridge, with its black cluster of men and women, waiting to hear the Hymnus Eucharisticus float down. Here a white snow of cherry-blossom in some garden; there, close at hand, so that he can look down, far below, upon their rooks' nests, Magdalen's tenderly greening trees. Infinite gradations of tender green; infinite gradations of delicate blue dying into dreamy gray, all woven into a mantle in which to wrap the yet sleeping city; and above it all, above Talbot, as he stands, lifted half-way to heaven, as it seems, in the august hush of the dawn, is the arch, severely beautiful, of a sky that seems made out of one pale, perfect turquoise.

He has moved away from his companions. He does not want them; does not want any companion. He leans against the parapet; and his eyes rise to the great old pinnacles, whose time-painted gray is married in such marvellous harmony to the cold azure into which they climb. Talbot is thinking of Peggy. She can never be at any very great distance from his thoughts, since there is no fair sight that does not, in one instant, conjure her back to them. There is nothing beautiful whose beauty he does not gauge by its worthiness to be looked at by her. To that height of excellence he acknowledges that the spectacle he is now looking upon attains. He would like her to see it. Where is she now? What is she doing? Doing? Why, asleep, of course; placidly slumbering; or perhaps not so placidly dreaming of Prue. But why is it that on this May morning Talbot is only *thinking* of Peggy? Why, since it is now more than four months since he was set free to seek her, is he still seeking her only in thought? Surely even his busy life may have spared him the necessary moment to put his fortune

> 'To the touch,
> To win, or lose it all.'

He had meant to have sought her at Easter. To put a lesser interval than that which stretches from Christmas to Easter between the decent interment of the old love and the proclamation of the new would have seemed to him a disrespect—a disloyalty to that now dead but once so living passion. Why, by showing such an overhaste to take upon himself another tie than hers, should he cut to the quick her who, not so long ago, was all earth, and all heaven too to him? But when Easter comes, it brings with it the news, borne on the breath of common fame, of the serious illness of that old love; and again his loyalty forbids him—while she, who for five years made sunshine or storm in his life, lies on what may perhaps be her death-bed—to go courting another than she. And before the tidings of her recovery reach him his holiday has been long over. He will have no other worth the name until Whitsun. But to Whitsun there are now only twenty-one days. 'Only twenty-one days!' he says to himself under his breath, still looking up at the pinnacle. He could of course have written to her; but from that he has shrunk with unconquerable repugnance. To put a cold proposition in cold black and white upon cold paper? What could she do but say 'No' to it? He will ask her by word of mouth; if possible under the Judas-tree, with Minky lying on her gown, so that she can't rise up hastily and flee from him. Will ask her by word of mouth, eye to eye; and with such a compelling urgency of look and speech that she shall say 'Yes' to him—if out of nothing else, out of sheer pity for his great and utter need of her. 'Twenty-one days and twenty-one nights!' he repeats to himself once again.

The choristers stand surpliced, looking eastwards to where the sun is rearing his red shoulder. The crowd on the old lead roof is thickening. Undergraduates in cap and gown; fat Fellows, thin Fellows; young ladies, old ladies—every moment a new head, with an expression of relief upon its features at having come to the end of its corkscrew scramble, appears at the head of the ladder that closes the climb. Talbot is not paying much attention to any of them, least of all, perhaps, to his own party, when a voice that has surely a familiar ring in it brings him back to the present.

'You see, dear, you need not have been in such a fuss; we are in plenty of time. The sun has waited for us, as I told you he would.'

Talbot's eyes have sprung to the speaker. Yes, of course it is Freddy Ducane. But after all there is nothing very wonderful in that; for has not he already known Freddy to be pursuing his studies in Oxford? But who is it whom Freddy has addressed as 'dear'? As to that, Talbot is not long left in doubt. Close behind young Ducane, as though afraid of being separated from him by the press, two girls are eagerly following. There are two in reality, but Talbot sees only one. She is not asleep after all; not dreaming of Prue, or of any one else. She is here, wide awake, on the top of Magdalen Tower, not three feet from him, and with her great blue eyes plunged into his. There are some moments in looking back upon which afterwards one wonders how it came about that they did not kill one.

Sometimes, in the retrospect of after-days, Talbot marvels what he could have been made of, not to have fallen dead at her feet on the top of that giddy tower out of sheer joy. He has but just realised her presence, when five grave strokes beat the air. The clock is telling that it is five, the immemorial hour at which the May-Day hymn is wont to soar heavenwards. In a moment a hush has fallen upon the buzzing crowd. Off goes every college cap. All eyes look eastward to where the vanquishing sun has now fairly emerged from night and mist, and sweetly and softly upsails to heaven the ancient monkish hymn:

> 'Te Deum Patrem colimus,
> Te laudibus prosequimur;
> Qui corpus ciborificis,
> Cœlesti mentem gratia.'

The harmony has swelled up skywards, and again died into silence; and no sooner has it ceased than the great bells imprisoned in the belfry below take up the tale. Standing so immediately above them, they do not sound like bells, rather like some loud vague booming music; and to that loud booming music the meeting of Talbot and Margaret is set.

'Talbot!' Freddy has cried cordially, on catching sight of him; 'my dear fellow, I am delighted to see you! Peggy, Prue, are you awake enough to realise that this is Talbot? Who on earth would have expected to find you up here?'

And Prue's little voice has echoed, 'Who indeed?' and Peggy has said nothing; but the touch of her hand in his—the thirsty aching dream of so many empty months—is a reality; and for him too the day is breaking, not less genuinely than is the real day so superbly opening—

'Nor dim nor red, like God's own head,
   The glorious sun uprist.'

The first beam has struck one of the lofty pinnacles, and made laughter and gaiety of its tercentenary gloom. Now it is laying long shadows about mead and street—shadows of noble buildings, of cropping cows, of commonplace yet dawn-ennobled houses, and of vernal trees. Far below on the bridge is the pigmy crowd, with the vulgar din of its May horns, blown thus early, in ill-survival of some Puritan custom, to drown the notes of the Latin hymn. But here, high up above the world, is no music but that august one of the loud bells; no sight but the arch of the perfect sky, and the solid grandeur of God's first best gift to man—new light.

In this stately dawning they stand together, he and she, despite the crowd, virtually alone; for Prue has drawn away Freddy to point out to him what is indeed startlingly obvious, the rocking of the tower under the vibration of the bells. Several undergraduates—more indeed than not—are taking off their college caps, and flinging them down over the battlements. The wind blows colder with the sunrise, but they pay little heed to its chill admonishment. With their bare young heads they stand laughing and leaning down to watch the fate of their mortar-boards. Most alight on the college roofs; one sticks on a pinnacle, greatly to its owner's delight. There is a noise of young voices, exclamations, bets, jolly laughter, on the crisp morning air. And meanwhile Talbot and Margaret stand staring at each other, silent at first; for how from such a torrent of words as he has to pour out before her can he choose which to begin with?

At last, 'I—I—did not expect to meet you here,' he says stupidly.

'Nor I you.'

'Are you staying in Oxford?'

'Yes, at the Mitre. Freddy was very anxious that we should come, and so Lady Roupell brought us.'

She answers him quietly, in a rather low voice, but she does not on her side originate any question. Can it be that she is struggling with a difficulty in any degree akin to his own? Urged by this dazzling possibility; urged still more by the shortness of the time—since what security is there that Prue may not be back upon them at any moment with some fresh discovery about the tower or the bells?—he hazards a speech of greater significance, of such significance in his own eyes that he trembles almost as much as the bell-rocked tower in making it.

'At the moment I first caught sight of you, and before that, I was thinking of

171

you.'

'Were you?'

'I suppose that there are few things in the world more unlikely than that *you* were thinking of *me*?'

She hesitates a second. He sees by a sort of distress in her sweet, candid eyes, that she would like to be able to tell him that she had been thinking of him. But she evidently had not, and is too honest to be able to feign that she had.

'I was not thinking of you at that moment,' she answers reluctantly; 'I was too much out of breath with my climb,' she adds, with a rather embarrassed laugh, 'to be thinking of anything.'

'Oh, Peggy,' cries Prue, breaking in upon them, in realisation of Talbot's fear, 'he has thrown his cap over too! Is not it foolish of him? Is not he sure to catch cold? And I do not see how he is ever to get it again.'

'As to that, dear,' replies Freddy philosophically, gracefully winding his gown about his neck and over his head, 'I am not at all anxious, as it was not mine.' So saying, he again draws away his little sweetheart, or she him, and the other pair are a second time alone. But for how long?

'Are they—are they—*all right*?' inquires John, recalling what strides to intimacy he had formerly made by the agency of Prue's love affairs.

'I think so,' she answers doubtfully; 'it is hard to say; pretty right.'

'*She* looks as if it were all right.'

'Yes, does not she?' returns Peggy eagerly. 'Is not she improved? Is not she wonderfully prettier than when last you saw her?'

Talbot hesitates a second. He knows, of course, that Prue has a face; but whether it is a pretty or an ugly one, a bettered or a worsened one since last he looked upon it, he knows no more than if it had never been presented to his vision.

'Whether you see it or not,' says Peggy, a little piqued at his unreadiness to acquiesce, 'it is so; everybody sees it.'

'But she always was pretty, was not she?' asks he eagerly, trying to retrieve his blunder. 'Could she be prettier than she always was? and happiness is mostly becoming.'

He looks wistfully at her face as he speaks, as if he would not mind trying the effect of that recipe upon his own beauty—so wistfully that she turns away with a sort of confusion; and, resting her hand on the battlement that is still swaying almost like a ship on a sea under the bells' loud joyaunce, looks down. The sun has risen higher. Opposite him his pale sister is swooning away in the west. Before his proud step the spring green grows vivider. The smoke from the morning fires new lit, curls, beautiful as a mist, above the ennobled dwelling-houses, swallowing what is vulgar from sight, as unworthy of the new King's eyes.

The two young people stand tranced for a moment or two side by side without speaking; then Peggy says in a low voice, and with an apparently complete irrelevance to anything that had gone before:

'The lavender-bush is dead.'

'*Dead?*'

'And the mowing-machine is broken,' adds she, beginning to laugh, though a little tremulously. 'Jacob says it has never been the same since you meddled with it.'

'Jacob and I were always rivals. Then he is not dead too?'

'No.'

'Nor the fox?'

'No.'

'Nor Mink?'

'No.'

'Nor the parrot?'

'No.'

How delightful it seems to him to be standing there in the dawning, asking her after them all! He would like to inquire by name after every one of the eleven finches in the big cage. The crowd has very much thinned. There has been for a quarter of an hour a continual disappearance down the ladder of successive anxious human heads.

'Oh, Peggy!' cries Prue, again running up; 'are you ready? We are going down; which way shall you go—backwards or forwards? He says forwards; but I think I had rather go backwards, because I shall not see what is coming. Which way shall you?'

'I shall go forwards,' replies Peggy, with a sort of start. 'I had always rather see the worst coming, whatever it is.'

As she speaks she turns, with what he recognises as a good-bye look, to Talbot. Is it over already, then? Is this to be all? Can it be his fancy that there has come upon her face a sort of reflection of the blankness of his own—that her eyes, lifted in farewell to his, ask his eyes back again, as his are asking hers, 'Is this to be all?' What! let her slip now that God has sent her to his arms on this strange high place in this blessed vernal morning? The thought fills him with a sort of rage that, in its turn, lends him a boldness he had never before known with her.

'Are you going to say "Good-bye" to me?' he asks, with a kind of scorn. 'Then you may save yourself the trouble; for I have not the remotest intention of saying "Good-bye" to you.'

Prue has fled away again to the stairhead, and from it her little voice now sounds in peremptory imploring:

'Peggy! Peggy! come quick! I want you to go down first. I shall not be frightened if you will go down first. I want you to show me which way you mean to go—backwards or forwards. Peggy! Peggy!'

And Peggy, obedient to the tones which, whether querulous or coaxing, have constituted her law for seventeen years, turns to obey. She will slip from him after all! The thought frenzies him. Before he knows what he is doing he has laid his hand in determined detention on her wrist.

'You shall not go!' he says, with an authority which has come to him in his extremity he does not know whence. 'She does not need you a thousandth part as much as I do. Has not she her Ducane? She is greedy! Must she have everything? Let her call!'

Peggy's course is arrested. She stands quite still, with her blue eyes, bluer than he has ever seen them, looking straight at him, in a sort of waking trance.

'But—she—wants me!' she falters.

'And do not I want you?' asks he, unconsciously emphasising his pressure on her wrist. 'Dare you look me in the face, and tell me that I do not want you? You are a truthful woman—too truthful by half, I thought, the first time I met you. Look me in the eyes if you dare, and tell me that you believe I do not want you.'

She does what he tells her—at least half of it. She looks him penetratingly full in the eyes. If the least grain of falsity lurk in either of his, that clear and solemn gaze of hers must seek it out.

'If you do want me,' she says slowly, and with a trembling lip, 'it has come lately to you.'

'Lately!' echoes he, his voice growing lower as the tide of his passion sweeps higher. 'What do you call lately? I wanted you the first moment I saw you; was not that soon enough? How much sooner would you have had it? The first moment I saw you—do you recollect it? when you were so angry at being sent in to dinner with me that you would not be commonly civil to me; that you turned your back upon me, and insulted me as well as you knew how—I wanted you then. I have wanted you ever since—every hour of every day and every night; and I want you—God knows whether I want you—now!'

Prue's callings have ceased; the small laughters, exclamations, appeals, have died into silence. Her and Freddy's pretty heads have both disappeared. Talbot and Peggy are left the last upon the tower-top. Her lip trembles.

'You did not want me last autumn, and you have not seen me since.'

'No, worse luck!' cries he passionately; 'but you need not throw that in my teeth. You might pity me for it, I think. Eight whole months gone, Peggy—wasted, lost out of our short lives! But how dare you stand there and say that I have not wanted you, do not want you, autumn, winter, summer, spring? You are confusing, perhaps, between yourself and me. *You* do not want *me*, that is likely enough. You could not even pretend to have been giving me one poor thought when I asked you. You would have been glad—I saw by your face that your kind heart would have been glad—if you could have told me, with any semblance of truth, that you had been thinking of me; but you had not. I was *miles* away from you.'

Her lip is trembling again, and her chest heaving. She has not had many love-tales told her; not many more perhaps, or of much better quality, than those with which Lady Betty had spitefully credited her. She has let her eyes fall, because she feels them to be filling up with foolish drops; but now lifts them again, and they look with their old directness, though each has a tear in it, into his.

'Why did you go away?'

Why did he go away? That is a question to which, in one sense, the answer is easy enough. 'Because Lady Betty Harborough sent him.' In another—the only one, unfortunately, in which he can employ it—it is absolutely unanswerable.

'Why did you go away?' She has asked the question, and, with her eyes on his, awaits the answer.

And he? He but now so fluent, with such a stream of eager words to pour straight and hot from his heart into hers, he stands dumb before her.

She does not repeat the question; but she does what is far worse, she moves away to the stairhead and disappears, as all the other votaries of the ceremony, as Freddy and Prue have disappeared, down the ladder.

He follows her, baffled and miserable, gnashing his teeth. Is it possible that the gyves he had thought to have cast off for ever are here, manacling him again as soon as he tries to make one free step? Is the old love to throttle him now with the same strangling clasp, dead, that it had done living? Before God, no! Not if he can hinder it. She has not waited for him at the tower-foot; but he overtakes her before she has reached the High Street, and without asking her leave.

The crowd on the bridge has dispersed. The city clocks, with their variously-toned voices, are striking six; to their daily toil the workmen, with tools on back, are swinging along. To them there is certainly nothing unfamiliar, probably nothing lovely, in the morning's marvellous clean novelty, that novelty renewed each dawning, as if God had said not once only but day by day, 'Lo, I make all things new!'

'You asked me a question just now,' says Talbot abruptly.

'Yes.'

'And I did not answer it; I could not. I cannot answer it now. As long as you and I shall live, I can never answer it!'

He stops, pale and panting, and looks at her with a passionate anxiety. O God! Is Betty's shadow to come between them still? Betty renouncing and renounced; Betty gone, swept away, vanished. Is she still to thrust herself between him and his new heaven? Still to be his bane, his evil demon? Still to lay waste that life, five of whose prime years she has already burnt and withered? If it be so, then verily and indeed his sin has found him out.

In passionate anxiety he looks at his companion; but she is holding her head low, and he cannot get a good view of her face.

'Why do you walk so fast?' he asks irritably, his eyes taking in the rapidly diminishing space that lies before him. 'Is not the distance short enough in all conscience without your lessening it? Walk slower.'

She slackens her pace; but still she does not speak.

'You asked me why I went away?' he continues almost in a whisper, and with his heart beating like a steam-ram. 'Does that mean that it made any difference to you? May I make it mean that it did? Stay—do not speak—I will not let it mean anything else. If you say that it did not, I will not believe you. I cannot afford to believe you!'

He has forbidden her to speak, and yet now he pauses, hanging in a suspense that is almost ungovernable—for they have passed Queen's classic front, are passing 'All Souls'—upon her slow-coming words. There is a little stir upon her face; a tiny hovering smile.

'I was sorry that you went without your lavender!'

'I am coming back for it,' he cries passionately, the joy-tide sweeping up over his heart to his lips, and almost drowning his words. 'Coming back for it—for it and for all else that I left behind me!'

The smile spreads, red and wavering.

'You left nothing else; I sent all your books after you.'

'Yes,' he says reproachfully, 'you were very conscientious. It would have been kinder to be a little dishonest. You might have kept back the one that we had been reading out of. I had a faint hope that you might have kept it back.'

'I did think of it,' she answers, under her breath.

'The mark is in it still!' he cries joyfully. 'Shall we take it up again where we left off? Where shall we sit? Under the Judas-tree?'

Her flickering smile dies into gravity.

'You are getting on very fast,' she says tremulously. 'Are you sure that it is not too fast?'

They have passed St. Mary's; noble porch and soaring spire lie behind them.

'Is it worth while your coming,' she continues, with evident difficulty, and with a quiver she cannot master in her low voice, 'when at any moment you may be obliged to go away again?'

'Why should I be obliged to go away again?'

Her voice has sunk to a key that is almost inaudible.

'I am only judging of the future by the past.'

He groans. The past! Is he never to escape from the past? never to hear the last of it? Is it always to dog him to his dying day?

'Are you sure?' she pursues, lifting—though, as he sees, with untold pain—the searching honesty of her eyes to his, while a fierce red spot burns on each of her cheeks, 'that you are not promising more than you can perform when you talk of coming? Are you sure that—you—are free—to come? You know —you were—not free to stay.'

His face has caught a reflection of the crimson dyeing hers, but his look shows no sign of blenching.

'I *am* free,' he answers slowly and emphatically. 'Why do you look as if you did not believe me? Cannot you trust me?'

At his words a shadow passes over her face. Is not Freddy Ducane always inviting her to trust him? She has grown to hate the phrase.

'I am not good at trusting people,' she says plaintively, with a slight shiver. 'I do not like it.'

They have reached the door of the Mitre.

'Over already!' cries Talbot, in a voice of passionate revolt and discontent; 'my own good hour gone before I had well laid hold of it? Who could believe it? Then at least,' speaking very rapidly, 'say something to me—something else—something better! Whether you trust me or not—God knows why you should not—do not let me go away with that for——'

'Peggy dear,' interrupts a soft and rather melancholy voice from an upper window above the door—and yet not very much higher than they, so low and unpretending is the old and famous inn in comparison with its staring towering competitors—'we would not for worlds begin breakfast without you; but I am afraid that Prue is growing rather faint.'

CHAPTER XXV

Whitsun is here. Again the tired workers are let loose. Again the great cities pour out their grimy multitudes over the fair green country, upon which, year by year, day by day almost, their sooty feet further and further encroach. Among the multitudes there are, of course, a good many who are not grimy. Cabinet ministers are, as a rule, not grimy—nor fashionable beauties—nor famous lawyers; but yet they all volley out, too, with the rest, to drink the country air, and smell the cowslips. All over the country the churches are being pranked for Whit-Sunday. It is that festival for which there is least need for devout souls to strip their hothouses and conservatories. In each parish the meadows need only be asked to give a few never-missed armfuls out of their perfumed plenty, and the church is a bower. The brunt of the labour of decorating her church, as of most other parish festivities, falls upon the shoulders—happily vigorous ones—of Peggy Lambton. The Whitsuns, Easters, Christmases, on which Mrs. Evans is not hovering on the verge of a new baby or two, and consequently handicapped for standing poised on ladders, are so few as not to be worth taking into consideration. Prue is willing; but her flesh is weak, and she tires easily. With the aid, therefore—an interchangeable term, as she sometimes thinks, for hindrance—of half a dozen of the best among the young Evanses, Peggy endures the toil, and reaps the glory alone. She has been standing most of the day, and for the greater part of the time with her arms uplifted, so that she is sufficiently weary; but as the work is not yet done, and there is no one to take her place, she treats her own fatigue with the contempt it deserves.

It is tolerably late in the afternoon, and Mrs. Evans has just looked in. Being in her normal condition, she has at once sunk down upon a seat. Mr. Evans has sauntered in after her. He has not much that is beautiful in his life; and the sight of the garlanded church gives him a sort of pale pleasure, something akin to that produced by the luscious flow of his favourite poem. He could not stir a finger to produce the effect himself; but he likes it when it is done for him.

'What a size these gardenias are!' says Mrs. Evans, fingering the blossoms in a box of hothouse flowers reserved for the altar. 'From the Hartleys of course? They are double as big as milady's. I wonder how her gardener likes having all the prizes carried off from under his nose! Dear me! what a thing money is! Burton, the butcher, told me the other day that five and twenty prime joints go into that house every week, beside soup-meat and poultry; and of course they have their own game and rabbits. Five and twenty prime joints, and a yacht that they can go round the world in! Not, I am sure, that I envy them *that*; for I am such a wretched sailor.'

Peggy makes no answer. Perhaps her attention is sufficiently occupied by the management of her long garland of cowslips, catchfly, and harebell; perhaps she has already heard, though not from Mrs. Evans, more about that world-girdling yacht than she cares to hear. She sighs, and her sigh is taken up and echoed in a deeper key by the Vicar; though whether his sigh is caused by regret at the sinful profuseness of a parishioner, or by a reflection upon the inequality of human destiny, that sends five and twenty prime joints into one man's kitchen, and sets a solitary leg of mutton spinning on another man's spit, may be best decided by those most acquainted with Mr. Evans's habitual turn of thought.

'It is a great disadvantage to a neighbourhood having a millionnaire in it,' pursues Mrs. Evans, going on contentedly with her trickle of talk; 'it sends up the price of everything—even eggs. I was saying so just now to Mrs. Bates at the Roupell Arms. I wanted to know whether she could let me have a dozen fresh ones. My hens are all sitting; and you would not believe the number of eggs we get through at the Vicarage—egg-puddings, and so on. Oh, by the bye,' with a change to an alerter key, 'from what she told me, I suppose that Lady Betty Harborough is expected at the Manor.'

The garland, whose dexterous disposition has cost Peggy ten minutes' labour, drops suddenly loose and wavering—a long rope of flowers—in the air.

'Lady Betty Harborough!' she repeats slowly—'with milady away?—most unlikely. Oh, now I see!' with a sudden dawn of relief breaking over her face; 'now I understand how the report has arisen! The children are to arrive to-day, and so it was supposed that she must be coming with them—of course, of course!'

'No; it has nothing to say to the children,' rejoins the Vicar's wife cheerfully; 'and I cannot say that I have heard in so many words that she is coming. It was only' (looking cautiously down the aisle, and lowering her voice)—'I suppose one ought not to talk scandal in a church, but it really is such an open secret—that I concluded it must be so, because a friend of hers is expected.'

'A friend of hers!' repeats Peggy slowly, the blood rushing to her cheek and brow, as she stands poised in space, with the unfinished wreath still dangling forgotten before her.

'Rather more than a friend, I am afraid,' returns Mrs. Evans, with a significance by no means devoid of enjoyment. 'Dear me! I do not half like talking of it here; but, after all, the truth is the truth. To the Roupell Arms of all places, too! and there can be no mistake about it, for I have just seen his portmanteau with "John Talbot, Esq.," in large letters upon it; his man arrived in charge of it this afternoon, and he is to follow by a later train. It really is too barefaced, is not it? I could see that Mrs. Bates herself thought so though of course I did not breathe a word to her.'

Peggy has put out a hand to steady herself on the ladder, since, for a moment, church and heaped flower-baskets, guelder roses and lilac branches, whirl round with her. His portmanteau come, and he coming! It would be a pity then if to-day, of all days, she were to break her neck.

It is nearly three weeks since she had parted from him at the door of the Mitre, in the middle of a sentence which Freddy Ducane never gave him the chance to finish, or her to answer; and since then she has heard neither tale nor tidings of him. Why should she? Of course his octopus has him again. Poor fellow! no doubt from those hundred straggling polypus arms it is harder than she, with her life ignorance, can estimate to tear himself free. And yet he had said he was free; said so—yes. But men's words and their actions are not apt to tally very nicely; at least, the words and the actions of the only man with whom she has any intimacy are not. 'They are all alike,' she has said to herself, and so has gone heavily—a little more heavily perhaps for that bootless, barren morning meeting on the tower-top—about her daily work. And now he is here—as good as here, at least—for does not his herald portmanteau make sure his approach?

'I wonder how he will like his quarters,' continues Mrs. Evans, with a rather malicious laugh. 'The beds are clean, I will say that for Mrs. Bates; but how a man accustomed to a French *chef* will enjoy her chops and rashers, is another question. She is very nervous about it herself, good woman!'

Peggy laughs; a little low laugh.

'Of course Lady Betty will make a pretence of coming to see her children,' pursues Mrs. Evans, warming with her theme; 'and indeed, after the escape that boy had, I cannot think how she can bear him out of her sight. And as milady and Freddy are both away, they will have the park all to themselves to philander in. It really is too barefaced.'

'Too barefaced, is it?' repeats Peggy, softly smiling, and staring at a great sheaf of sweet nancies that she has absently picked up.

'*Is it?*' echoes Mrs. Evans in astonishment; 'why, *is not it*? What other motive could bring him to such a dull village as this?'

'What indeed?' replies Peggy with emphasis, while the thought crosses her mind that she ought to feel mortified at its evidently never having come within the range of the Vicaress's possibilities that any one could visit a dull

181

village in search of her. 'It cannot surprise her more than it does me,' she says to herself.

'One can only hope that he will be too uncomfortable to stay long,' says Mrs. Evans, slowly rising, and preparing to depart. 'Well, I wish I could help you' (this is a formula that recurs as often as do the festivals of the Church); 'but you are getting on capitally. Do you think that the font is quite as pretty as it was last year? I am so glad I sent the children to help you; do not overtire yourself.'

She strolls away, with the contented feeling of having done her part in the church decoration; but it is a couple of hours later before Peggy follows her example. It is nearly eight o'clock when, with stiff arms and tired legs, she enters the hall—embowered in spring blossoms, like the church she has just left—of the Red House. As she comes in Prue springs to meet her.

'Oh, Peggy, Peggy! have you heard?'

The elder sister's heart leaps. Prue understands. Prue is glad—gladder than she had had any conception that she would have been. Kind little Prue!

'Yes,' she falters, grateful surprised tears at her sister's sympathy rushing to her eyes; 'yes, I have heard. Oh, Prue, how nice of you to be glad!'

'Nice of me to be glad!' repeats Prue in a tone of profound wonderment, her eyes growing round. 'Why is it nice of me? It would be very odd of me if I were not glad; but I do not see anything *nice* about it. How did you hear? Has milady come back? Have you seen any one from the Big House? Why, I only got the letter by the second post.'

'The letter?' repeats Peggy stupidly; 'what letter?'

'*What letter?* why, *his* letter of course, telling me that he is not going to stay up for Commemoration after all: he says that without me the balls would be Dead Sea apples to him, so he will be home a week sooner; and the Hartleys are going, and they will not find him there after all. But oh, Peggy! how could you have heard? I do not believe that you did. Why did you say you had?'

The sparkle, but now as bright in Peggy's eyes as in her junior's, dies out; a cold ripple of disappointment rises, and flows over her heart. Prue was not glad for her, after all. It was her own preoccupation that had credited her sister with a knowledge and an interest of which she is quite innocent.

'You shall tell me about it at dinner,' she answers in an altered voice, turning away.

And at dinner Prue does tell her all about it. Too excited to eat, she chatters through their simple repast about the beauty of Freddy's renunciation; his thoughtfulness for others; the irreparable loss that Commemoration will sustain by his absence; the bitter disappointment of Miss Hartley.

Into the middle of her talk, near the close of their short dinner, comes the sound of a railway whistle, announcing the arrival of one of the few stopping trains—in this case the last train of all that touches at their little station. Peggy involuntarily puts up her hand, and cries: 'Hush!'

'The wind must be changed,' she says, reddening at the consciousness of her own motive, though she is safe indeed from having it divined, 'one hears the train so plainly; it is late to-night!'

'What of that?' cries Prue gaily; 'are you expecting a friend by it? Ah, me! how I wish that *I* was! He came by that train last time.'

And so Peggy keeps her tidings to herself. Perhaps if she had had some one to impart them to they would not have made her so restless. As it is, she cannot settle to any occupation. The wheels that will roll him from the station to his inn must pass her door; and through all the trickle of Prue's talk her ear is pricked to catch them. But it is market night, and from the many vehicles noisily passing by, her hearing is incapable of disentangling his. He must have reached the Roupell Arms by now. Is Mrs. Bates setting a very unappetising dinner before him, so unappetising that it will, in accordance with Mrs. Evans's pious aspiration, drive him prematurely away?

'How fidgety you are!' cries Prue, surprised at her sister's unusual restlessness. 'I should have thought that you would have been thankful to sit down, after being on your legs all day.'

'So should I,' replies Peggy, again blushing, and sitting down; 'and I have been upon them since ten o'clock in the morning, have not I?'

'It is quite disgraceful the way in which the Evanses put everything upon you!' cries Prue indignantly; 'though indeed'—with an accent of remorse not very common to her—'I do not think that they are much worse than the rest of us. Why does everybody put everything upon you, Peggy? You do everything for everybody, and nobody ever does anything for you.'

Peggy's eyes brim up at this unexpected recognition of her services by the seventeen-years sovereign of them. Are all good things to come to her together?

CHAPTER XXVI

It is Whit-Sunday. The morning service is over. The parish has had an opportunity of admiring Peggy's nosegays, and of having their nostrils comforted by the scent of her lilac branches and sweet nancies, and of the Hartleys' giant gardenias. Among them a stranger has knelt. Strangers are not very apt to be allured to Roupell Church by the fame of Mr. Evans's sermons; and, indeed, to-day he has preached the same sermon as he did last Whit-Sunday. It would have passed among his flock for a new one, had it not been for an unusual phrase which they remember and recognise. But since they recognise it with pleasure, as an old friend, there is no harm done.

'Did you see that he was in church?' cries Mrs. Evans, hurrying breathlessly out after Peggy, and joining her before she has reached the lych-gate. 'Did you ever hear of anything so barefaced? It never occurred to me that he would come to church. Oh, here are the children! now we shall learn whether *she* has arrived too.'

As she speaks the little Harboroughs, who apparently have hitherto been kept at bay by their nurses, are seen—having broken away from them—to be elbowing their vigorous small way through the press of country people, who smilingly make way for them. In another second, both, with entire disregard of the Vicaress's blandishments, have flung themselves upon Peggy.

'Oh, Miss Lambton, we came last night! How is the fox? I saw Alfred in church. What a lot of freckles he has got! May not I come and see Mink and the kittens? May Franky come too?' asks Lily volubly.

'Of course he may,' replies Peggy kindly, warmly returning the little boy's ardent embrace. 'Why, Franky dear, I have never seen you since you were so ill!—you were very ill, were not you?'

'The doctor thought he was going to die,' answers Lily, officiously replying for her brother before he can set his slower tongue in motion; 'and mammy never took off her clothes for three nights, and father cried; and if Franky had died, I should have had no little brother!' She makes this last statement in a rather triumphant tone, as a fact redounding a good deal to her own credit. 'Why, there is John Talbot!' cries she. 'Franky wanted to go to him in church. Did you ever hear of anything so silly? Now, Franky, who will get to him first?'

But as she dishonestly sets off before poor Franky has had time to withdraw his sturdy body and fat legs out of Peggy's embrace, there is not much doubt as to the answer to her question. However, though Franky is the last to arrive, and arrives weeping at his sister's injustice, and crying, 'You nasty thing, you did not start fair!' yet he has, by much, the warmer welcome.

Is not one welcomed back from the grave's brink deserving of a closer clasp, of tenderer kisses, than one who has only returned from his daily walk? Franky has quite forgotten—if, indeed, he ever, save through Lily's information, knew—how nearly his curly head had been laid in the dust. But Talbot cannot forget it.

'I wish he would not hug those children,' says Mrs. Evans, *sotto voce*; 'it gives me quite a turn. Well, Fanny,' as one of her own offspring plucks her by the sleeve, 'what is it now? Mr. Allnutt wants to speak to me? Dear me! some one is always wanting to speak to me!'

She turns aside reluctantly to interview her parishioner, and Peggy goes on alone. But it can hardly be said to be *tête-à-tête*, or without a chaperone, that she puts her hand in Talbot's under the lime-leaves, young and juicy, stirring in the brisk spring wind.

'Oh, Miss Lambton,' cries Lily, 'may not John Talbot come to the Red House too?'

As she speaks the face of the object of her kind patronage falls perceptibly.

'Are you coming to the Red House?' he asks, with a slight accent of disappointment; 'what, both of you?—now?'

'Miss Lambton says we way,' rejoins she, happily innocent of the motive that had prompted her friend's inquiry; 'and we may stay to luncheon, and all afternoon, may not we?'

Peggy laughs.

'We will see about that.'

'And John Talbot may come too?' urges Miss Harborough pertinaciously, making play with her eyelashes; 'he would like to come.'

'And stay to luncheon, and all afternoon?' adds Talbot, emphasising his apparently playful suggestion by a long pressure of the hand he has forgotten to drop.

He has to drop it soon, however; for it is claimed by Franky, as well as one of his own. Franky insists upon walking between his two friends; where, by dragging well at their arms, he is enabled to execute many playful somersaults, and, from under the ægis of their protection, to make faces at his sister; who, having discovered that she can thereby better watch their countenances, is backing before them.

Under these circumstances, conversation between the elders is not easy, nor is there much of it. But the birds in the thickets they pass make talk for them; and the leaves fresh escaped from their sheaths, and to whom the wind is a new playfellow, rustle their pleasure in his gambols to them, as they walk along beneath; and across the barrier of the little rosy child their hearts cry out to each other. They would be in heaven; but that Lily, by a judicious pull of the skirts, brings them down to earth again.

'Why do you never come to Harborough now?' inquires she, fixing Talbot with the unescapable vigilance of her large child-eyes; 'you used to be always coming. Would not you like to come? I will get mammy to ask you.'

There is a moment of silence. For a second even the kind finches seem cruelly still. Then,

'What are you holding my hand so tight for?' asks Franky plaintively. 'Why have you begun to squeeze it so? You hurt me!'

'I asked mammy the other day,' pursues Miss Harborough, with all her species' terrible tenacity of an idea once grasped, 'why you never came to see us now, and she began to cry; and when I asked her what she was crying for, she boxed my ears: she never boxes Franky's ears!'

This remark is followed by another silence. Peggy is apparently looking straight before her; but yet out of the tail of her eye she manages to see that Talbot is quite beyond speech. She must come to the rescue.

'I have no doubt that you richly deserved it,' says she in a voice that, despite her best efforts, is not steady. 'Why? Oh, I do not know why! because you did. There! run—run away like a good child, and open the gate for us.'

Lily complies, and Franky races after her.

Talbot draws a long breath. For a few moments, at all events, he will have a respite from that terrible catechism. But from the effects of it he cannot at once sufficiently recover to pass into easy speech. Perhaps, too, the sight of the little Red House—the house that has been built into so many of his dreams—helps to make him momentarily dumb.

It is a differently clad Red House from what it was when last he looked upon it. The Virginia creeper and the clematis have laid aside their purple and crimson ardours; and in their place a wistaria is hanging the pale droop of its long clusters. Lilacs push up their blossoms against its casements. The ineffable sappy green of spring everywhere sets and embowers it.

He gives another sigh, a long, low sigh of happiness this time, and turning, wordless at first, clasps her two soft hands—hands no longer claimed by any little dimpled imperative fingers—in his.

She leaves them peaceably to him; but the variations of her colour from red to white, and back from white to splendid red, sufficiently tell him that though she is nearly twenty-three years old, to her a long lover's look, a close lover's clasp, are unfamiliar things.

His heart bounds at the thought; but at the same moment is pierced by an arrow of pain. On what an inequality are they meeting! It is all new to her; while to him! Oh that he had but God's great gift of erasure! that he could sponge out from his life those other looks and clasps! that he could bring to her such eyes, such a heart, such a hand as she is bringing him!

How, save through his own giving to her, could Lily Harborough have had the power to poison these, his fairest moments?

'Will they be here all afternoon?' he asks under his breath.

'I think it is more than probable,' she answers in the same key, while right under his eye, over her cheeks, the lovely carnations and lilies are chasing and dispossessing each other.

It is part of his punishment, perhaps, that across his mind, as he looks, there flashes a recollection of Betty's paint; a comparison that he hates, and that yet he cannot avoid, between that colour and this. Which is brightest?

'Could not you send them away?'

'Lily would not go,' replies Peggy, with a slight shrug. 'And as for him, poor little fellow, I cannot bear to be unkind to him, when he is only just out of the jaws of death. Did you know that he had been at death's door?'

'Yes, I knew,' he answers briefly.

At this reply there comes, or at least it seems to him that there comes, a tiny cloud over the clear blue heaven of her eye; and seeing it, he hastens on:

'Is there no place where we can escape from them—where we can be by ourselves? Oh, Peggy, Peggy! do you think that I came down from London to talk to Lily Harborough?'

The cloud stirs a little, but does not altogether remove.

'Did you know that they were here?'

'I! of course not! How should I?'

A passer-by along the road, throwing in a casual glance between the bars of the gate, gives her a pretext for sliding her hands out of his. It strikes him that she is over-ready to avail herself of it.

'Do they ever go to church in the afternoon?' he asks, catching at this last straw.

A faint ripple of amusement steals over her lips.

'Never.'

She lifts the latch of the door as she speaks, and through the aperture the sun pours in, making a royal road into the cool and shaded interior, where he can catch a glimpse of the birds setting his own ladder aswing; of the Kabyle-pots full of country posies; of the familiar worn furniture he had grown last year to think so beautiful. He follows her with alacrity. It is morally impossible that the children can be inside. He is standing once again on the old Turkey carpet. Here is her sandal-wood workbox, among whose reels he has seen Franky ravaging. Here is the chair whose leg he had helped to mend. Here is the cottage eight-day clock, with the good-humoured moon-face, which they had all agreed to have a look of milady peeping over its dial-plate. Here is Mink, civil and smirking. Here is—herself!

'It is like coming home,' he says softly.

As he speaks a slight noise behind him makes him turn his head. Can it be Lily again? Lily, with more dreadful questions, more terrible invitations to draw out of her armoury of torments? But no! it is not Lily; it is only Prue. Prue, often a little out of sorts, a little sorry for herself, rising with the inevitable poetry-book in her hand, and with a look full of astonishment, from her oak settle by the fireside. He had forgotten Prue's existence.

'Mr. Talbot!' cries she; 'is it possible? I heard a man's voice; I could not imagine whose it could be. Are you staying at the Manor? Is milady back? Is there any one else there? A party?'

He laughs confusedly. 'I have no connection with milady.'

'Are you at the Hartleys' then?' (a greatly increased eagerness); 'do you know the Hartleys?'

'I have not that honour.'

'At the Evanses'? No! impossible! I cannot imagine any one in their right mind staying at the Evanses'.'

'I do not know whether I am in my right mind, but I am not at the Evanses'.'

'Where *can* you be then?'

'I am at the Roupell Arms.'

'The little inn in the village? Not really?'

He makes an affirmative sign. Surely, if the girl is not a perfect fool, she will understand, she will efface herself, she will take herself off, and leave them to themselves, as Peggy has so often left her and her Freddy to themselves. But to a person whose whole being is habitually permeated by one idea, other ideas are slow in penetrating. Prue has not the least intention of effacing herself. Her curiosity—always, save on one theme, a languid emotion—satisfied, she prepares to replace herself on her settle.

'The Roupell Arms!' repeats she; 'what a funny idea! I never heard of any one staying at the Roupell Arms; I am afraid you will be very uncomfortable. Peggy, would you mind covering me again with this shawl? I do not know what any one else feels, but I feel chilly.'

It is clear that to no member of her household has it ever occurred to efface herself for Peggy. Presently the luncheon-bell rings, and the children come bouncing in, delighted at the prospect of dining without pinafores, and the consequent opportunity for beslobbering their best clothes. Talbot's chance of a *tête-à-tête* seems to be retreating into a distance to which his eye cannot follow it. But at least his eye can follow her, as she tries to coax Prue's sickly palate, as she cuts up Franky's dinner. Into this last occupation Lily manages to introduce a slight element of awkwardness.

'When I was little John Talbot used to cut up my dinner sometimes,' says she narratively—'sometimes he cut it up, and sometimes mammy did; but before I was as old as Franky I could cut it myself.'

'You are a very wonderful little girl,' says Talbot angrily, losing his temper at the consciousness that he is reddening, 'we all know that; but suppose that we do not hear any more about you just at present.'

After luncheon they are all dragged out by the children to see the wonders of the stable-yard. It is true that the hayloft kittens have, to Franky's surprise, expanded into sad and sober cats; but this not wholly unexpected metamorphosis has not found Alfred unprepared. He has brought instead, out of his treasure, ferrets new and old; and to see these interesting animals lift their pale noses and hands, and their red topaz eyes out of their box, Talbot has again indefinitely to defer the possession of his love's sole company. Franky is warmly clasping his hand, and Lily is hanging heavily on Margaret's arm.

'How red Alfred's ears are!' says she, in a stage aside; 'and how they stick out!'

Alfred becomes purple.

'Lily,' cries Peggy reprovingly, 'how can you be so rude? You ought never to make personal remarks.'

Lily tosses her head and giggles, and Franky giggles too, simply because he has a faint delighted sense that he ought not. There is an atmosphere of rising naughtiness about them both. Oh that they would but commit some sin big enough to justify their being sent to bed, or packed off home in charge of Sarah! But no. They are wily enough to keep on the hither side of any great iniquity. They are just naughty enough to prevent attention from being ever for more than a moment withdrawn from them; but they avoid incurring any guilt so great as to call down special vengeance on their heads.

Prue has long ago sauntered back to the settle and her rhyme-book. But for these imps he would have Peggy all to himself. He has several times begun eager speeches to her, which have met with interruptions such as these: 'Do you think that they can have fallen into the swill-tub?' 'What *can* they be doing to the parrot to make him swear so dreadfully?' 'They will pull out poor Minky's tail!'

By the end of an hour, Talbot, genuine child-lover as he is, is beginning to feel leniently towards Herod the Great. However, the French proverb says that everything comes to him who knows how to wait. It may be true, though some have to carry their waiting into the dark grave with them. Talbot has not to carry his quite so far. Just in time to save him from such an outrage to chivalry as would be implied by boxing Miss Harborough's ears, appear upon the scene, though late, yet better than never—gods out of the machine—the Harborough nurses. They sweep off both culprits, despite their earnest and sincerely believed-in asseverations that Miss Lambton wants them to stay all day. Franky, indeed, is borne away dissolved in bitter tears at being torn from the friends who, as he honestly thinks, have been so thoroughly enjoying his society. Franky's naughtiness is of a wholly imitative character; but his little warm heart is his own.

Lily, on the other hand, trips away with her head up, having poured one last stage whisper into Peggy's ear: 'Would it be a personal remark if I were to tell John Talbot that I think him handsome?'

The object of this flattering inquiry watches the maker of it with a poignant anxiety, until she, her brother, and her attendants have turned the corner, and are really and entirely out of sight. Then he heaves a sigh of profound relief.

'At last!' he says, sweeping a look round the horizon.

It is quite clear. There is not a living soul in sight. Being Sunday, not even Jacob. Everything comes to him who knows how to wait. He has known how to wait, and now his moment has come.

'Let us sit under the Judas-tree,' he says, and she acquiescing passively, they turn their steps thither.

But before they have gone three yards, there is a light foot on the turf behind them. Prue has fled across the sward from the open window-door, and is whispering something in Peggy's ear. Almost before he has had time to feel aghast at this new interruption, she has fled back again. He looks after her with an irritated inquiry, born of his long tantalisation.

'Well, what is it now?' he asks angrily; 'anything fresh that you are to do or leave undone?'

Peggy reddens.

'It was only that she asked us not to sit under the Judas-tree; she cannot bear any one to sit there—any one else.'

'Any one else!' he repeats, his brief and surface wrath dying away into a smile of passionate happiness; 'any other lovers, you mean. You may blink the *word*, Peggy; but you cannot blink the *thing*: we *are* lovers.'

Peggy does not answer. She has sat down on a seat, above which a great old thorn is just breaking into a foam of blossom. She has taken up this position in all unconsciousness of the advantages it presents, but of which Talbot's eager eye has instant cognisance. The thorn, now thick with flowers, effectually masks all sitters on that seat from the view of any eyes darted at them from the house, the only point whence observation need be dreaded; for what lover minds the robin's round bright eye, or the chaffinch's surveillance?

'We *are* lovers!' he repeats, sitting down resolutely beside her.

The thorn, leaning as old trees will, projects so far beyond their heads as to make a natural arbour for them, and tosses down now and again whiffs of its pungent perfume, which some strange persons affect to dislike.

'Are we?' she says, the words travelling softly out on a long sigh. 'You will think me very stupid'—the red rose of Lancaster for the moment chasing her pale sister of York out of her face—'but, old as I am—twenty-three next birthday—I do not know what love—that kind of love—feels like. I—I—have never had any opportunity of knowing.'

He stares at her in an enraptured astonishment. For such a confession as this, his apprenticeship to Betty has certainly not prepared him. Can it be conceivable that he is the first—the very first—to reap the flowers of this fairest field?

'Do you mean to say,' he inquires, almost with incredulity, 'that you have never given back one small grain of love to any one of the many men who must have showered it upon you?'

'But they have not,' returns she, a slight humorous smile pushing its way through her blushes. 'You are determined that I have had so many lovers, and I have had scarcely any. Two or three people have wanted to marry me—not many. Oh, not at all many! You could count them on one hand, with several fingers to spare; and I do not think that they loved me. They did not give me that impression. They thought I should be a useful wife, strong and active; but love—love—love,' repeating the word dreamily—'no,' shaking her head. 'There are not many women of twenty-three who can say so, I suppose; and I see that you have a difficulty in believing me; but love has never come near me.'

'And are you resolved that it never shall?' he asks, under his breath.

She pauses a moment before answering, while her eyes escape from the tyranny of his, and fix themselves on a row of tulips, rearing their striped and colour-splashed cups upon their strong, straight stalks, in the border before her. With the potent light smiting through them, they look as if they were cut out of some hard precious stone—sardonyx, or beryl, or bdellium—goblets to be filled with fairy wine at the feast of some mage-king.

'I do not know,' she says, with her lips trembling; 'I am not sure. When I see Prue—when I know that it has brought all the pain she has suffered—and she has suffered a good deal—more than you would think, to look at her, that she could bear—into her life—my one prayer is to keep clear of it; and yet—and yet'—with a yearning in her voice—'one would not like to die having quite missed it. Oh, tell me'—with a change in her tone to one of compelling entreaty, bringing back the eyes but now so sedulously averted from him, and plunging them into his under the shade of the hawthorn bough—'were you really speaking truth when you said you had come down from London only to see me? Are you quite sure—quite—that that was your real motive?'

'Quite.'

'Nobody would believe it,' she says, with a sort of wonder in her voice; 'nobody thinks so. They all'—faltering a little—'they all think something quite different.'

'What does it matter what they think?' he cries hotly, the colour which unluckily is equally the livery of brazen guilt and oppressed innocence again mantling his face. 'What have we to do with their blatant suppositions? Are you going to let *them* come between us?'

'You will think me very suspicious,' she says tremulously—'very hard to be convinced of what most women would find it easy enough to believe—but—

but—I care for very few people,' she goes on, beginning a fresh sentence without finishing the former one; 'but when I do care, I care very badly. Do not be angry with me if I say that I have a sort of dread of caring very badly about you.' If he had had his will, the conclusion of that sentence would have found her in his arms; but she holds herself gently aloof. 'If I once let myself love you,' she says, the tears stealing afresh into her eyes, 'I know that I could never unlove you again—never while I lived, try as I might; and if afterwards I found out——'

'Found out what?' breathlessly.

'You know,' she goes on, trying to speak firmly—'I am sure you must know —that when first I saw you, I had heard nothing but what was bad of you. That was my only excuse for the way in which I behaved to you. I had heard things about you—no; do not be afraid,' a writhing motion on his part conveying to her what her words are making him suffer. 'I am not going to ask you whether they were true. I have no business with your past; but what I *must* ask you—what I shall never have any peace until I *have* asked you,' her agitation deepening—'is whether if people said them now they would still be true?'

There is a moment's stillness before he answers—a moment long enough for the hawthorn's perfume to be for ever after wedded in her memory to that pregnant pause. It is almost in a whisper that she has put her question, and it is quite in a whisper that his answer comes:

'If they would be true, should I be here now, Peggy?'

She heaves a deep, long sigh, as one off whose heart a great stone's weight had rolled; and the over-brimming drops roll soft and hot over her cheeks.

'And will they never be true again?' she asks, still under her breath; 'are you sure—quite sure of it? I will believe you if you tell me so. Oh, I *want* to believe you! Dog with a bad name as you are,' breaking into an unsteady laugh—'angry as I was at being sent in to dinner with you—I *want* to believe you.'

The south wind brings a jangle of far church bells to their ears; outside their arbour a starling sits on a tree with its nose in the air, saying odd, short, harsh things; and upon this homely music the souls of Talbot and Peggy on Whit-Sunday float together into love's heaven.

CHAPTER XXVII

'We'll lose ourselves in Venus' Groves of Mirtle,
When every little bird shall be a Cupid,
And sing of Love and Youth; each wind that blows
And curls the velvet leaves shall breathe Delights,
The wanton springs shall call us to their Banks,
And on the perfum'd Flowers we'll feast our Senses;
Yet we'll walk by, untainted of their Pleasures,
And, as they were pure Temples, we'll talk in them.'

The shadows have put on their evening length. Even Minky, as he stands with his little face pushed through the bars of his gate, barking at the servants as they return from church—a mere civility on his part, an asking them, as it were, how they enjoyed the sermon—boasts one that would not disgrace a greyhound or a giraffe.

'Are you there, Prue?' softly asks a voice, coming out of the darkening green world outside; coming with an atmosphere of freshness, of dew, of hawthorn, into the little hall, and peering toward the fireside-settle, which, both from the waning light and its own position, hints but dimly that it has an occupant. 'Are you asleep?'

'I do not know,' replies a disconsolate small treble. 'I tried to go to sleep, to get over some of the time. Oh dear, what a long Sunday it has been! Is he gone?' struggling up into a sitting posture out of her enveloping shawls.

'Yes.'

'And you did not sit under our tree?'

'No.'

'How laconic you are!' cries Prue fretfully; 'and I have not exchanged words with a creature since luncheon. Do come here; turn your face to the light. What have you and Mr. Talbot been talking of for the last four hours? John Talbot, as those horrid children call him. I think it is so impertinent of them; but I suppose their mother taught them.'

A slight contraction passes over the radiant, dewy face, so docilely turned towards the western shining.

'Peggy!' cries the younger girl in an altered tone, forgetting her invalidhood, and springing off the settle; 'how odd you look! You do not mean to say—is it possible? You do not suppose that I do not see—that you can hide anything from me!'

'There is nothing that I want to hide,' replies Peggy with dignity, though the blood careers under the pure skin to cheek, and brow, and lily throat; then, with a sudden change of tone to utmost tender deprecation, 'Oh, Prue, you do not mind? You are not vexed? It will not make any difference to you!'

Prue is silent.

'It will make no difference to you,' repeats Peggy, rather faltering at the total dumbness in which her tidings are received. 'Of course you will go on living with me just as you have always done.'

For all answer, Prue bursts into a passion of tears.

'Oh, do not say so!' she cries vehemently. 'You talk as if I never were going to have a home of my own! Oh, it would be too cruel, too cruel!'

Her sobs arrest her utterance. She has collapsed upon the settle, and sits there a disconsolate heap, with its hands over its face. Peggy stands beside her; a sudden coldness slackening the pulsations of her leaping heart.

'You will not care any longer about him and me,' pursues Prue weepingly. 'You will have your own affairs to think of. Oh, I never thought that I should have to give up *you*. It was the last thing that ever would have entered my head. Whatever happened, I always counted upon having *you* to fall back upon!'

The dusk is deepening. Peggy still stands motionless and rigid.

'I know that I am not taking it well,' pursues Prue a minute later, dropping the fingers wetted with her trickling tears, and wiping her eyes; while her breath still comes unevenly, interrupted by sobs. 'I know that I ought to pretend to be glad; but it is so sudden, such a surprise—he is such a stranger!'

The cold hand at Peggy's heart seems to intensify its chill. Is there not some truth in her sister's words? Is not he indeed a stranger? Has not she been too hasty in snatching at the great boon of love that has been suddenly held out to her—she, whose life has not hitherto been furnished with over-much of love's sweetness?

'I know that you must think me very selfish,' continues the younger girl, still with that running commentary of sobs. 'I *am* selfish, though he says that I am not—that he never knew any one who had such an instinct of self-abnegation; but then he always sees the best side of people. Yes, I *am* selfish; but I will try to be glad by and by—only,' with a redoublement of weeping, 'do not expect it of me to-night.'

And, with this not excessive measure of congratulation, poor Peggy has to be content, on the night of her betrothal. She goes to bed with the cold hand still at her heart; but in the morning it has gone. Who can have a cold hand still at her heart when she wakes at early morning at lilac-tide, to find a little round wren, with tiny tail set on perfectly upright, singing to her from a swaying bough outside her casement, with a voice big enough for an ostrich, and to know that a lover is only waiting for the sun to be well above the meadows to lift the latch of her garden-gate.

Before the dew is off the grass they have met. It is presumable that familiarity with her new position will come in time to Peggy; but for the present she cannot get over the extraordinariness of being—instead of anxiously watching for some one else's tardy lover—going to meet her own. And when they have met and greeted, the incredulity, instead of lessening, deepens. Is it conceivable that it can be *her* whom any one is so extravagantly glad to see? All through the day—all through several after-days—the misty feeling lingers that there must be some mistake; that it must be some one else; that it cannot be the workaday Peggy, whom she has always known, who is being thus unbelievably set on high and done obeisance to.

'Have you told Prue?' asks Talbot, when he has enough got over the ecstasy of that new morning meeting, to speak connectedly.

'Yes.'

'And what did she say?'

Margaret hesitates a moment.

'She—she was very much upset.'

'Upset!' repeats Talbot, his tone evidencing the revulsion of feeling of one who had imagined that all Creation must be rejoicing with him. 'What was there in it to upset her?'

'She said it was such a surprise; she was not at all prepared for it. In that,' blushing, 'she was like me.'

He is silent. It is a mere speck in his heaven; but he would have liked Prue to have been glad too.

'She said that you are such a stranger,' continues Peggy, looking half-shyly up at him, with a sort of light veil of trouble over her limpid eyes. 'When I come to think of it, so you are; if it were not,' laughing a little, 'that I am always hearing the children call you by it, I should not even know what your Christian name was.'

'A stranger!' repeats Talbot, in a rather dashed voice.

'Never mind; you will not be a stranger long,' returns Peggy, laughing. 'She will soon grow used to you; and so' (again with that flitting blush)—'and so shall I. You must tell me all about yourself,' she goes on, a few moments later, when, in order to escape from the aggressive din that Jacob is making with the mowing-machine, as if to assert his exclusive right to that engine, they have passed beyond the garden bounds into the green sea of the adjoining park. 'You must begin at the very beginning; you must tell me *all*.'

Is it his fancy that she lays a slight but perceptible emphasis on that concluding word, which insists on the entirety of his confession? Whether it be so, or that the stress exists only in his own imagination, he winces. They have sat down under a horse-chestnut tree, whose hundreds of blossom-pyramids point like altar tapers to the fleckless sky; at their feet the bracken, so tardy to come, so in haste to go, is beginning to spring and straighten its creases. Far as the eye can reach, the park's green dips and rises are flushed with the rose and cream of flowering thorn-bushes.

'Will you?' with a soft persistency.

'Of course I will,' replies Talbot; 'only,' with a laugh that does not ring quite naturally, 'you do not know what you are bringing upon yourself. Well, where am I to begin? At the very beginning?'

'At the very beginning,' repeats she, with a sigh of satisfaction, settling herself more comfortably with her back against the tree-trunk to listen. 'Tell me where you were born, and,' laughing, 'what sort of a baby you were.'

And so he begins at the very beginning; and for a while goes on glibly enough.

There are worse occupations for a summer's morning than to sit on juicy May grass, with the woman you love beside you; and to read in the variations of her rapt blue eyes her divine compassion for you. For the you, the innocent distant you of six, who had the whooping-cough so badly; her elate pride in the scarcely less distant you of sixteen, carrying home your school-prizes to your mother; her tearful sympathy with the nearer you—the you who still ache at the memory of the loss you sustained when full manhood had given you your utmost capacity for feeling it. Up to the date of his sister's death he goes on swimmingly; but with that date there coincides, or almost coincides, another. It was during the physical collapse that followed that crushing blow that Betty, with her basket of red roses, had first come tripping into his life. He stops abruptly.

'Well?' she says expectantly, looking towards him, and wiping the sympathetic tears from her soft eyes.

'Well!' he repeats, with an uneasy laugh. 'Have not I dosed you with myself enough for one morning? I—I think that is about all.'

'But that was more than five—nearly six years ago,' objects she.

'Nearly six years ago,' he echoes, in a tone of almost astonishment; 'so it was. But—but, as I need not tell you, the importance of time is not measured by its length; there are moments that bring an empire, and there are years that bring nothing, or less than nothing.'

'They cannot have brought *nothing*,' replies she, her luminous eyes, in whose pupils he can see himself mirrored in little, still interrogating his; 'they must have brought *something*, good or bad; they must have brought something.'

'You know that there has been no change of Ministry since then,' he goes on, speaking rather fast, and wincing under the steadiness of her look. 'I have been ——'s secretary ever since—a mere machine, a scribbling machine; and you know that machines have no history.'

She is silent, and her eyes leave his face, as if it were useless any longer to explore it. She presses him no further. It would be both ungenerous and bootless to urge him to a confession which he would never make, and in the effort to evade which he would writhe, as he is doing now. Her breast heaves in a long slow sigh. There is nothing for it. She must submit to the fact of the existence for ever, for as long as her own and his being last, of that five years' abyss between them; an abyss which, though she may skirt it round, or lightly overskim it, will none the less ever, *ever* be there.

There is one subject that, in their moments of closest confidence, must ever be tabooed to them; one tract of time across which, indeed, they may stretch their hands, but which their feet can never together tread; one five years out of the life of him who should be wholly hers, locked away from her to all eternity. Her hand has fallen absently to fondling Minky's poor little gray head, no bigger than a rabbit's. Minky, who has followed them to their love-retreat, and has now come simperingly to offer them his little cut-and-dried remarks upon the fine day.

Talbot's eye jealously follows that long hand in its stroking movement. He would like to take it, and lay its palm across his hot lips. Why should not he? It is his. But that five years' gulf prevents him. A little milky blossom with its tiny stain of red, wind-loosened, has floated down from the horse-chestnut tree, and now rests upon her hair. He would like to brush it off with a kiss. Why should not he? Whose but his is now all that blonde hair? But again the gulf stretches between them.

The sun, steadily soaring zenithwards, sends a warm dart through their tree, which, thick-roofed as it is, is not proof against the vigour of his May strength. The deer gather for shade under the young-leaved oaks. The whole earth simmers in the vivifying heat, and yet they both lightly shiver. Upon Talbot there lies a horrible fancy, as of Betty sitting between them. It seems to him as though, if he stretched out his arm to enfold his new love, it would instead enwrap his old one. Is there no spell by which he can exorcise this persistent vision? Will it always be between them? He is still putting this bitter question to himself, when Peggy speaks:

'Well,' she says, stifling the end of a sigh, and without any trace of resentment in her tone, 'I am very much obliged to you for having told me all that you have. I know that you are not fond of talking of yourself, and if—if'—the carnation mounting even to her forehead—'there is anything in your life that you had rather not tell me, why we—we will let it alone; we—we will not think of it any more.'

Perhaps her words may contain the spell he has been praying for; since, in a moment, the Betty phantom has vanished, and his new sweetheart lies, live and real, in his arms.

'At all events,' she whispers, 'I can contradict Prue, next time that she says you are such a perfect stranger.'

She smiles as she speaks. How lovely her smile is, when he sees it as close as he is doing now! It is not perhaps quite so radiant as the one with which she met him at the gate—but her eyes! He lets himself drown—drown in those heavenly blue lakes. Why should he ever come to the surface again?

'There they are, Franky!' cries a piercing little voice, cutting the summer air from a few hundred yards' distance, 'under that horse-chestnut tree; how close together they are sitting!'

Another minute has brought the owner of the voice, and of another voice more lisping and less shrill, up to their eagerly sought, if not quite so eagerly seeking, friends.

'You are not sitting so close together as you were,' chirps Franky innocently. 'Mammy used——'

'What do you want? What have you come for?' asks Talbot, in a voice a good deal rougher than his little *protégés* are apt to hear from him, and breaking into the middle of a sentence, whose close he can only horrifiedly conjecture, before more than its two initial words have had time to leave its small speaker's lips.

At the extreme and unusual want of welcome in his tone, both children stand for a moment silenced. Then Lily, with an offended hoist of her shoulders, turns pointedly to Margaret.

'Nanny says that my tongue is white,' cries she; 'she is always telling me so. I came to ask you; I thought that you would not mind telling me,' with an insinuating air, 'if it really is.'

'And is not mine white too?' inquires Franky eagerly, and in a minute both red tongues are protruded for inspection; and Talbot bursts, against his will, into a vexed laugh.

It is not always, indeed, to have their tongues looked at; but during the ensuing days of his courtship Talbot finds that he must hold himself in continual readiness against onslaughts in unexpected directions from Miss and Master Harborough, who, finding the little Red House more amusing than the empty Manor, and being troubled with no doubts as to their acceptableness, arrive from every point of the compass at each likeliest and unlikeliest hour of the summer day. The only thing for which he has to be thankful is that their arrival is generally heralded by their eager treble voices; so that he has just time to step down out of his seventh heaven before they are upon him. Perhaps if it were not for this, and for one or two other slight abatements from its complete felicity, the tuliped garden, with its lilac breath, its come pansies, and its coming pinks, would be too like that one when the first he and she felt the heavenly surprise of their new kisses.

For the children's intrusions are not quite the only cloud in Talbot's Whitsun sky. It is oftener than once or twice that the phantom of the past has seated itself between them. It is oftener than once or twice that he has found Peggy looking at him in a pained astonishment, at his having suddenly broken off in the middle of some fond phrase. She cannot know, and he can never tell her, that it is because there has suddenly flashed upon him the recollection, vivid as reality, of some occasion on which he had showered the same words of fire upon her who has had precedence over Peggy in his heart. He would fain cut all such words out of his vocabulary; employ in this new worship nothing that had been desecrated by having been offered on the altars of the old. But it is impossible. He had poured out all his heart's best before the first love. How then can he have anything fresh for the second? The thought cuts him like a knife; but none the less, all the more rather—since it is our knife-thoughts that cling most pertinaciously to us—does it come back and back again. In return for all the wealth of her fresh firstfruits, he has nothing to give her but what is stale, threadbare, sullied. This is a reflection that would sit easily upon most men. If it were not so, there would be but few unembittered love-makings. But upon Talbot's palate it is wormwood. And lest there should be any chance of his escaping from his past, there is always some innocent reminiscence, allusion, or appeal on the part of Lily or Franky to bring it back to him.

Prue, too! On the blue of his heaven, Prue forms another little cloud. Prue makes no pretence of pleasure in the prospect of his brotherhood; and to Prue he is sacrificed oftener than he thinks just. It is, thanks to Prue, that he has so often been sent back prematurely to his pot-house; that he has had prematurely to break off his trance of wonder at the eyes, the only blackness under which springs from some slight and fugitive fatigue; at the cheek, which his doubting finger may rub as hard as it chooses without any other result than that of intensifying its damask; at the hair, from which he has been allowed once to withdraw the pins in order to convince himself by ocular demonstration that though it may come *down*, it can never come *off*.

'I think you had better go now. She has been alone all day,' is a formula whose recurrence he has now learnt to dread.

He shrugs his shoulders.

'I have been alone for thirty-two years.'

'I think if you would not mind going now——'

'I should mind extremely.'

She laughs softly, the happy low laugh of the consciously well-beloved, rich in the prospect of a whole lifetime of love ahead.

'Whether you mind it or not, I am afraid you *must* go. She had been crying this morning.'

'More shame for her. What has she to cry about? Now if *I* were to cry— Peggy, you like her much better than you do me' (taking her half angrily in his arms). 'Pah!' with a change of tone, perceiving, for the first time, a gardenia pinned upon the breast of her gown; 'why do you wear that horrid thing?'

'Franky gave it me. He begged it from the gardener at the Manor for me.'

'Throw it away!' cries Talbot, with more energy than the occasion seems to warrant. 'I detest the smell. It is like a fungus.'

'It will hurt his feelings if I do.'

'It will hurt mine if you do not,' returns Talbot with emphasis; and suiting the action to the word, he snatches the blossom almost violently from her breast, and tosses it away.

She looks at him, her eyes tinged with a faint surprise.

'What a thing it is to have rival admirers!' she says, laughing; and then she sends him reluctantly away.

If it were a scheme of the most deep-laid coquetry, instead of the result of a lifetime's habit of self-sacrifice, she could not have hit upon a better method of inflaming his passion. All through the long light evening, whose yellow at this sweetest season is so late in changing to night's blue, he prowls about outside her garden-fence, peering between her lilac-clusters and laburnum-droops for a glint of her white gown; shaking his fist at Prue's selfish little head, and counting, through the fevered night, the strokes of the leisurely church clock as they carry him nearer and nearer to the dewy morning hour, when he may again hold his red rose of Lancaster in his hungry arms.

And meanwhile his short holiday is racing away. Scarcely has it seemed to have begun when the end is already at hand. The date of the reassembling of Parliament, of his chief's return to Downing Street, and his own consequent reappearance there, looms nearer and nearer.

To return to Downing Street without her! He has been without her all his life, and until the last six months has never looked upon himself as particularly an object of commiseration on that score; but *now* his whole soul swells with a disgusted self-pity at the idea of his lonely return to his Bury Street lodgings.

He has extracted from Peggy without much difficulty a promise that his last evening shall be indeed and wholly his; that for once it shall be Prue, not he, that goes to the wall; that he shall neither be dismissed to his public-house, nor left to disconsolate moonings about the inhospitable roads and fields, until it is time to betake himself to his truckle-bed; that, on the contrary, he may for once have his fill of her fair company, that should by rights be always his; may sit, and saunter, and sweetly stray with her; and at length, when the stars ride high, may leisurely bid 'God bless her!' at the garden gate, and dismiss her to dream of him.

But lovers propose, and freakish chance disposes.

Talbot has returned to his inn to dress for dinner, and has jumped into his dress-clothes, in miserly grudging of the moments stolen from his final hours. He had left Peggy with eager injunctions to be equally quick, so that a few more moments may be squeezed out before Sarah, with her clamorous dinner-bell, breaks, with life's loud prose, into the whispered poetry of their *tête-à-tête*. And apparently she has been obedient to his behest, for she is—though he would have thought it impossible—beforehand with him, and stands awaiting him, with arms resting on the top of the gate.

But how is this? She has made no change in her dress, but is still in her morning cotton.

As he draws near to her she stretches out her hand to him deprecatingly.

'I hope you will not be very angry!'

A slight chill of apprehension passes over him.

'But I am sure that I shall,' he answers, with a hasty instinct to ward off the impending blow. 'What is it? What do you mean? Not,' with an accent of incredulous indignation, 'Prue again?'

'It is not her fault,' replies Peggy apologetically, and yet defensively too; 'nobody *enjoys* being ill. But you know how finely strung she is; something must have upset her.'

'Something is always upsetting her!' returns Talbot brutally.

'I am afraid she must have taken a chill,' pursues Peggy, wrinkling up her forehead into anxious lines. 'I am sure I do not know how, but I think she must; she has had to go to bed.'

The young man's brow clears. If Prue's illness involves only her absence from the dinner-table, he will not very violently quarrel with it after all.

'Very wise of her,' he says in a lighter voice; 'the best place for her! Poor Prue!'

'But——,' begins Peggy, whose brow has not smoothed itself in sympathy with her lover.

'But what?' inquires he sharply, his apprehensions returning. 'You are not going to tell me that on my last evening I am to be sacrificed to a *malade imaginaire*!'

'She is not a *malade imaginaire*,' answers Margaret half indignantly; 'her cheeks are as hot as fire, and her pulse has run up to ninety.'

'I believe she runs it up on purpose. Are you barring the gate for fear I should force my way in?'

'Oh, no, no!' cries she, hastily dropping her arms from their resting-place on the top rail, and flinging her portals hospitably wide. 'Come in! come in! how could you dream of such a thing? Do you suppose that I am going to send you away without your dinner? But after dinner——'

'After dinner?'

'When she is ill, she likes me to sit beside her, bathing her forehead and her hands. I have always done it, ever since she was a baby. When you are ill, I will bathe your forehead and your hands. Oh!' clasping her fingers soft and fast upon his arm, and looking up with brimful eyes into his angry face, 'do not look so cross at me! Do not you think that it is hard enough for me without that?'

CHAPTER XXVIII

The dinner is over—the first *tête-à-tête* dinner that John and Peggy have ever shared. To dine *tête-à-tête* with her in her own still house, amid her old and homely surroundings, with the summer evening tossing them in its lavish perfumes through the wide-opened windows, would have seemed to him, a month ago, the realisation of his fairest and most hopeless dream. But in their translation into the bald language of reality—the jejune prose of fact—our dreams have a way of losing their finer essence. It has escaped, without our being able to tell whither or by what channel. Over both a sort of wet blanket has fallen. Try as he may, Talbot's temper cannot recover from the poignant disappointment of his lost last evening; and try as she may—broken in, as she is, by a lifetime's habit of self-sacrifice—Peggy cannot hinder the lump from rising in her throat, and the tears from crowding into her eyes, at the reflection that her own hand has cut off, and flung away, the blossoms of these final crowning hours. How many things she had saved to say to him on this last evening—things too tender for her shamefacedness to utter, save under the justification of an imminent severance—things that he would have liked to have heard all through these days, but that she had laid up in the storehouse of her heart as too close and sacred for aught but to sweeten their parting! How can she say them now across a dinner-table, with Sarah coming out and in, Prue sending peevish messages to her, a score of trivial interruptions forbidding any but the most banal talk? It was only with her head on her love's breast, in the dusk of the starshine, that she could ever have found courage to utter them. When will they be uttered now? The present, the brave solid present, is our own, to caress or misuse; but who dares say to the future, that formless form wrapped in uncertain gray, 'Thou art mine'?

And now the dinner is over, and they have separated, with spurious coldness. Peggy has vanished upstairs to her sister, and Talbot is left to employ the hours of his last evening as he best may. It is true that Margaret has eagerly begged him to take possession of house and garden, and has held out tearful hopes of snatching here and there a moment from Prue's sick exactions to give him. But his ireful restlessness will not allow him to accept this concession. It would be worse to be within apparent reach of her, yet just beyond her eye and touch, than to be quite outside her domain. He tells her so, half harshly; and opening the gate into the park, takes himself and his ill-temper to the oaks and the deer for consolation.

At first he walks along over the dew-freshened sward, under the isolated oak giants, or between the more gregarious beeches and limes of spinny and copse, without seeing them. He has no eyes, save those angry inward ones that are turned upon his own disappointment. His last evening!—his last evening! If it had been any but the last! Henceforth, in retrospect, this holiday of his will take all its colour from this bitter last evening. It is the end that stamps anything as bad or good. Oh, cruel Peggy! He has had so few really good hours in his life; and now she has ruthlessly robbed him of his best. And for what?

With the answer which he is compelled to give himself to this question comes his first dawn of consolation. Certainly to no personal gratification has she sacrificed him. He can hardly, in his most aggrieved moments, picture her as better amused than himself as she stoops—with the tears called up by his ill-tempered words scarcely dried upon her cheek—over her equally ill-tempered invalid, bathing her forehead, holding her jealous hands.

Poor Peggy! He will go back at once, and beg her pardon. But no. The consciousness of his being hanging wrathfully about will only further complicate her difficulties. He will take a lesson out of her book, and efface himself wholly for this one evening, even though it is the last. The last in one sense, but in another——?

He has sat down on a felled trunk, stripped of its branches, but not yet removed by the wood-cutter's cart. The hawthorn comes in *âcre* whiffs to him. His heart, though he is alone for the whole evening—though he will probably have to go back to his alehouse without one more glimpse of her damask-textured face, gives a great bound. The last? For him and her there will be no last evening until—for God, who has given him so much, will surely give him, too, the supreme boon to die first—until, bending over him as she now bends over Prue, her voice and her hands smooth his passage to the easy grave.

The revulsion of feeling from his earlier ill-humour, produced by this thought, brings the moisture to his eyes. What is this parting in comparison with that six-months-ago one—when he had taken leave of her with no rational hope of ever having his eyes enriched by her again—when he had been afraid to trust his tongue to any speech, lest it should drift into tendernesses he had believed for ever prohibited to it? That parting in the walled garden! Why should not he go thither now, so that, surrounded by the mute witnesses of his former despair, he may the better gauge the extent of his new felicity? The idea, once conceived, approves itself so instantly to his imagination that he starts up; and, exchanging his former purposeless saunter for a quick walk, sets off in the direction of the Manor gardens.

The evening is falling, in late May's best serenity, weighted with the innocent sweetness of country odours. The deer—their mottled sides growing indistinct

—are browsing wakefully among the bracken. The throstles have reached their song's last verse.

He has gained the pleasure-grounds, just as the vanguard of the stars take possession of the emptied sky. He hastens along, almost as hurriedly as if it were to a rendezvous with the real Peggy, instead of with the six-months-old memory of her, that he were speeding; between the burnished laurels; past the fresh-blown splendours of the great rhododendron-beds, on fire with red, and pale with cream and blush and lilac; narcissus and may taking his nostrils by storm as he brushes past them to his goal, the still walled garden.

As he nears it, a misgiving seizes him that he may perhaps find himself locked out—that he may perhaps have to content himself with the mutilated satisfaction of peering in at it, between the wrought iron of its gate; and it is with a trepidating hand that, standing at last before it, he tries the handle with fingers not very confident of success. But for the first time to-night Fate is kind to him. The gate yields to his touch; and pushing it, he walks in. He has not been inside the enclosure's quiet precincts since the night of that parting, whose bitterness he has now come, in the wantonness of his new joy, purposely to revive. He must indeed be happy that goes, of his own accord, courting a dead misery. He draws a long luxurious breath, as he looks round in search of the landmarks of that past woe. They are here, but they wear a changed aspect. Through the wrought-iron railing, indeed, the church tower and the yews, its brothers in age and gentle gravity, still rise in the friendly dusk; but another race of flowers has sprung in the place of those that witnessed his despair. The ghostly white gladioli are gone, and the autumn-faced asters. The winter winds have dispersed the down of the traveller's joy; and the penetrating breath of the mignonette has long ago died off the air. But in their place another nation has arisen; a better, he says to himself, as he stands with all spring's scented hopefulness crowded about his feet.

He walks slowly along, seeking to recover the exact spot where that parting had taken place; seeking to recover it by the aid of the small landmarks that bear upon it. There had been a moon, a section of a moon, to light it. There is none now.

He is glad. She has been the accomplice of half the world's crimes. He wishes that the outward conditions should be as altogether changed as the inward ones. He is glad that the trees, then wrapped in the heavy uniformity of late summer, are now showing the juicy variety of their early leafage. He is glad that the creepers are in bud, instead of in lavish flower; glad of the fresher quality of the light air; glad of anything that marks the fact that that bad old night has gone, and this good young new one come. For so changed is his mood since the time that he set off from the Red House gate, that his evening, though spent in solitude, does seem eminently good to him, and his heart bounds with almost as high an elation as if she were pacing beside him in the starlight, with her head on his shoulder, as she will do in the future, many hundred happy times.

He has paused in his walk. It was here that she stood—just here. He knows the exact spot, by a comparison of the distance from the long bed of violets, which, alone unchanged of all the flowers, still stretches beneath the south wall, and mingles its odours with that of the new-come flowers, as it had done with the departed ones. Just here! And he himself had stood here. She had been facing the gate, and he with his back to it. Thus, thus. The little crafty half-moon had shone into her eyes, as she made him her last wistful speech:

'Since you are so determined to go downhill, I suppose that I dare not say I hope our roads will ever cross again.'

Six months ago, only six months between the moment when he had in dumb hopelessness acquiesced in the fact that their paths must for ever diverge, and this in which they are, for all eternity, merged in one. His eyes have dropped to the gravel, as if seeking the print of her dear feet, that he may stoop and kiss it. His back is, as on that former occasion that his imagination has so potently summoned from its grave, turned towards the gate. He is alone. There are no witnesses to make him ridiculous. Why may not he be as foolish as he pleases? He has actually dropped on his knees, and is stooping his lips towards the pebbles, which may or may not be the very ones her light step pressed half a year ago, when the sound of the click of a latch behind him makes him raise his head and spring to his feet. Who, at this late hour of the evening, can be turning the handle of the gate? Who but one? She has forsaken Prue for him after all. Love's instinct has told her the path he took; and here, on the spot where he had for ever renounced her, she has come to him under the stars. What welcome can he give her that will be thankful and joyful enough for such an unlooked-for grace? He turns—his whole face alight with ecstasy—towards her, but his feet do not move to meet her.

By a refinement of love's cunning he will await her here; and, on the very foot of ground that witnessed their separation, he will receive her into his arms again. She has pushed the gate now, and, like himself, she is within the enclosure; her white gown (he has often praised her in white, and she must have put it on since he left her) flitting like a snow-winged dove, along the dusky walk towards him.

'What an odd place you have chosen to say your prayers in!' cries a high-pitched voice.

'BETTY!' For, by one of Fate's juggles, it is the old and not the new love to whom his radiant greeting is addressed. It is the old and not the new love whom, if his arms clasp any woman under the stars to-night, they must enfold. They do not, indeed, show much readiness to do so. They hang as if palsy-struck at his sides, while his voice repeats in a horrified whisper that he would fain, if he could, make one of incredulity, '*Betty!*'

'Do not trouble yourself to repeat it a third time,' says she, with a flighty laugh that has yet no tinge of mirth in it. 'I do not need convincing that *I* am *I*, nor need you.'

'*You* here?'

'I may return the compliment—*you* here?'

He is staring at her with wide, shocked eyes that are also full of an astonishment he is powerless to master. Is *this* the Betty he had parted from on that awful Christmas morning? *this* the wretched woman, clammy-handed, dishevelled, reckless of all save her own mastering agony, who—her haggard mother-eyes unable to attain the boon of any tears—had hoarsely forbidden him her presence for ever? Can this be she—this hovering vision of lace and gauze—that has floated towards him on the wings of the night, and now lifts to his, eyes that in this light look as clear as Peggy's—cheeks whose carnations seem no less lovely and real? Before his confused consciousness, the two visions—of *that* Betty and of *this*—inextricably entangled, and yet irrevocably separated, pass and repass; and he continues standing, wordlessly, stupidly staring, in a horror and a wonder that are beyond the weight of his volition to conquer, at the woman before him.

After her last sentence she is wordless too, and also stands looking at him, mute and full, as if she had forgotten his face, and were learning it off by heart again, her factitious gaiety for the moment died down and gone in the silent starlight. It is he who first speaks.

'You—you came here to see your children?'

'To see my children?' repeats she. 'Ha! ha! Yes, that was the reason I gave at home; and a very pretty and laudable one too, was not it? To see my children! But, as it happens, a woman has often more than one reason. I had more than one.'

She has lapsed into her flippant gaiety again, and now pauses as if expecting him to inquire into the nature of the other reason to which she alludes; but if so, he does not gratify her. He is still fighting with the horror of that double consciousness. Can this be the woman to whom in that icy winter dawning his whole soul had gone out in such an overpowering passion of pity? And if it be indeed she, has she clean forgotten the sacred agony of their last farewell?

Her laugh is still dissonantly jarring on his stunned ear, when, finding it hopeless any longer to wait for questioning on his part, she resumes:

'It is always well to kill two birds with one stone—is not it?' says she, looking hardily into his eyes. 'Pardon the homeliness of the expression! You know that reports reach even quiet places—Harborough, for instance. Well, such a report—a *canard* probably, but still there was something oddly circumstantial about it—was spreading there yesterday about a—person—I—used—to know—rather well—have some interest in—in fact——'

She pauses again; her words have, for the last half of her speech, come draggingly, with a little break between each, and not for one instant does her eye release him. But again he makes no comment. Her breath is coming perceptibly quicker when she next takes up her theme.

'You do not ask what the report was? No? I fear my little tale does not interest you. It would perhaps be civiller on your part if you could pretend that it did; perhaps you will think that it improves as it goes on. Well, the subject of the report is a man; and the report itself—do not you think that it was the simplest plan on my part to come and verify it in person?—is that he is going to take to his bosom a—ha! ha! I never can help laughing when I think of it—a—guess! No; you would never guess—*a sack of pota*——'

'Do not call her names,' says Talbot, for the first time finding his voice, and stretching out his hands, but now hanging so nervelessly at his sides, in authoritative wrathful prohibition; 'do not dare to call her names!'

'Then it *is* true?'

Her laugh, little kin as it had ever had with real merriment, is dead—strangled in her throbbing throat; and she puts up her hand as if she were choking.

'Until you can speak of her with the respect that is her due, I will answer no questions,' he replies sternly.

The next moment he sees her stagger in the starlight, and his heart smites him for his cruelty. He makes a hasty movement towards her, thinking that she is going to fall; but before he can reach her she has steadied herself, and faces him, livid, it is true, under her paint, but firm and collected beneath the stars. She has even recovered her laugh.

'Thank you,' she says, in a low but distinct voice, 'for the information that you have incidentally given me, even though you refused to let me have it direct. I have no further occasion to trouble you, and need only offer you my congratulations and my hopes that you and your bride will meet with some one to sweeten your married lives as you have sweetened mine.'

So saying, she turns to leave him. If he were wise he would let her go—would set no hindrance in her way; but which of us, in the crucial moment of our lives, is wise? Before his reason can arrest him, following only the impulse that forbids him to let the woman who for five years had sat crowned and sceptred in his heart thus leave him, he makes two hasty steps after her.

'Betty!'

At the sound of his voice, there comes a sort of wavering; but she does not stop or turn her head.

'Betty!' he repeats, overtaking her, and preventing her egress by setting his back against the wrought-iron gate; 'after all that has come and gone, are we to part like this?'

'How else do you wish us to part?' she inquires in a steely voice of the bitterest irony, while her eyes glitter, but not with tears; 'do you expect me to dance at your wedding?'

'There is no reason why you should not,' he answers firmly, looking steadily back at her. 'I have done you no wrong. Have you forgotten how, and with what solemnity, you sent me away from you for ever?'

'So I did,' cries she, breaking into a hard laugh. 'Do not tell any of my friends, or I should never hear the last of it. What an *accès* of superstition I had that cold morning! I will do myself the justice to say, the first and last of its kind. I thought to save Franky by renouncing you, was not that it? If I had known how little there was to renounce, I might have spared myself the pains, might not I?—ha! ha!'

Again her merriment rings harshly on the soft air, and he can find no word of rejoinder.

'How you must have been laughing in your sleeve!' pursues she, still with that arid, withering mirth. 'Though the joke is against me, I cannot help laughing at myself when I think of it.'

But at that he breaks in:

'I looked so like laughing in my sleeve, did not I?' he asks, panting, and in a voice which emotion of the most painful quality he has ever felt renders indistinct.

'No one would believe it,' she goes on, unheeding, apparently unaware of his interruption, 'of a woman of my age, and who, as they say, has lived every minute of her life—I *have* done that, have not I? But it is nevertheless Gospel truth that I was such a greenhorn as to be almost as sorry for you as I was for myself. I suppose,' with a sort of break in her dry voice, 'one gets into a stupid habit of thinking one's self indispensable!'

She pauses, and making no further effort to depart, stands silent, with set teeth and hands that unconsciously twist and tear the slight lace pocket-handkerchief between her fingers.

What can he say to her? By what words—save words of entreaty to her to put again the chain about his neck and the fetters upon his limbs—can he appease or comfort her? And sooner than utter such words, he would fall dead at her feet.

'Wretched superstition!' she says between her teeth, still rending the morsel of lawn in her fingers; 'how could *I*, of all people, have been such a fool as to be conquered by it? What did it matter to the Powers above—what did they care whether I kept or threw away the one miserable bit of consolation I had in my hideous life? The child would have got well all the same, while I—I—but perhaps' (her tone changing to one of alert suspicion), 'perhaps even then you had come to an understanding, you and she. Perhaps even then you were hoodwinking me. I was so easy to hoodwink—I, of all people, who had always thought myself so wide awake—ha! ha!'

Again that dreadful laugh assails his ear, and makes him shiver as if it were December's blasts that were biting, not May's breezes kissing his cheek.

'I never hoodwinked you!' he answers, in an agitation hardly inferior to her own; 'it was always plain-sailing between us. I went away because you sent me.'

'And you took me at my word?' cries she wildly. 'Yes, I know that then, at that moment, I meant you to take me at it; but I was out of my mind. Hundreds of people less mad than I was then are in Bedlam. You might as well have listened to the ravings of a lunatic as to mine that day; and—you—took—me—at—my word!'

Her speech, which in its beginning was shrill and rapid, ends almost in a whisper.

'I thought you meant it,' he says miserably; 'before God, I thought you meant it!'

'The wish was father to the thought,' she says, again breaking into that laugh which jars upon him far more than would any tears or revilings; 'you believed it because you wished it. I showed you a handsome way out of your dilemma. I played into your hands. Without knowing it—oh, I think that you will believe it was without knowing it—I played into your hands. Without hurting my feelings—without quite giving the lie to all your glib vows—without any disagreeable shuffling—you were free! I set you free! *I!* Oh, the humour of it!

I wonder how you could have kept any decent countenance that morning! and I—I—never saw it. Oh, I must have been blinder than any mole or bat not to have seen it, but I did not!'

She pauses, as if suffocated; but in a moment or two has recovered breath and composure enough to resume:

'And I was *sorry* for you. I do not know why I have a pleasure in showing up my own folly to you; but, as you say, it has always been plain-sailing between us, and one does not easily shake off an old habit. Yes, *sorry* for you! Not at first. At first I could think of nothing but *him*; but he took a turn for the better very soon—God bless him! As long as he was only getting well, it was enough for me to think that I had him back—oh, quite enough!' some tears stealing, for the first time, into her scorching eyes; 'but when he was on his legs again, and everything going on as usual, then I began to see what I had done.'

Her voice has sunk to a low, lagging key of utter dispiritedness.

'You never sent for me; you never wrote to me,' says Talbot hoarsely.

'Did you expect it?' she cries, a sudden eager light breaking all over her face. 'Were you waiting for me to write? Did you watch the post for a letter from me? Oh, if I had only known! Did you—did you?'

She has laid her hand convulsively on his coat-sleeve, and is looking up, with all her miserable soul in her eyes, into his face. What can he answer? He had watched the post indeed; but with how different a motive from that with which her passionate hopes have credited him!

'No! I see that you did not,' she says, dropping her hand from his arm with a gesture of disgust, as if she had touched a snake, a horrible revulsion of feeling darkening all her features; 'or, if you did, it was with dread that I should make some effort to get you back. At every post that came in, without bringing you a specimen of my handwriting, you drew a long breath, and said: "It is incredible! I could not have believed it of her; but she has let me go, really!" Come, now,' with a spurious air of gaiety, in ghastly contrast with her drawn features and burning eyes, 'you were always such an advocate for truth; you used to be so severe upon my little harmless falsehoods. Truth! truth! Let us have the truth!'

'Have it, then!' he says desperately, stretching out his arms towards her, as if transferring from his keeping to hers the weight of that murderous confession. 'I *was* glad!'

Again, as once before, she reels, as though it were some heavy physical blow that he had struck her; and again his heart smites him.

'I—I—thought that we had both come to our right minds,' he says, stammering, and seeking vainly for words that will soften the edge of that bitter sword-thrust, and yet not incur the deeper cruelty of bringing again that illusory radiance over her face; 'I—I—thought we might begin our lives again —different, better! We had been most unhappy!'

'*Unhappy!*' she repeats, in a voice that, if he did not with his own eyes see the words issuing from her lips, he could never have believed to be hers —'*unhappy!* Are you telling me that you were unhappy all my five years? Has she made you believe even this?' She stops, and fixes her glittering look upon him with an expression so withering that he involuntarily turns his away with a sensation as of one scorched. 'No!' she continues, her voice rising, and growing in clearness as she goes on; 'she may persuade *herself* of that—what do I care what she persuades *herself* of?—but she will never really persuade you. No! no! no!' a ring of triumph mixing with the exceeding bitterness of her tones. 'There is one superiority that I shall always, to all eternity, have over her; one that neither she nor you, do what you will, can ever rob me of: I shall always—always have been *first*! There is nothing you can give her that will not be second-hand!'

He has clenched his hands in his misery till the finger-nails bite the palms. Is not this the very reflection that has been mingling its drop of earth's gall with the honeyed sweetness of his heaven?

'Yes!' he says, panting; 'do I deny it? I can never give any one better love than I gave you.'

'*Gave!*' she repeats, her voice dropping again to a husky whisper, and casting her parched eyes up to heaven, as if calling on the stilly constellations to be witness to her great woe—'*gave!* He himself said *gave!* And I am alive after hearing it. Oh, poor I!'

Her voice shudders away in a sigh of intense self-pity; and she hurriedly covers her face with her hands as if to shut out the view of her own fate, as too hideous to be looked upon with sanity; while long, dry sobs shake her from head to foot. The sight of her anguish is more than Talbot can bear. Two steps bring him to her side; and before he can realise what he is doing, he has taken her two hands and drawn them forcibly away from her face.

'Betty!'

'Well!' she says dully, leaving them in his, as if it no longer mattered where, or in whose keeping, they lay; 'what about Betty?'

'Betty!' convulsively pressing her small, burning fingers, 'you break my heart!'

'I wish I could!' rejoins she fiercely. 'I wish to heavens I could! But I must leave that to *her*. Tell me about her!' changing her tone to one of factitious temperate interest. 'She is a good soul, I am told; *bonne comme du pain*. There is nothing so pleasant as complete change, is there? How does she show her goodness, by the bye? Does she say her prayers every night, and make a flannel petticoat for the poor every day, eh?'

He attempts no answer to her gibes; only, in his intense and mistakenly shown compassion, he still holds her hands, and looks down, with a pity beyond speech's plummet-line to sound, into the eyes whose beauty he has long ceased to see, but whose agony has still power to stab him.

'I suppose,' she goes on, her mood changing—it is never the same for two minutes together, and her mockery giving way to a tone of condensed resentful wretchedness—'that if I loved you properly, as people love in books, I should be glad to see you march off triumphantly, with drums beating and colours flying, to be happy ever after; but I am not! I tell you fairly I am not! If I had my will you should be as miserable—no, *that* you never could be; I would let you off with less than that—as I am!'

He looks at her sadly.

'Even if I were so happy as you fear, a couple of hours ago, I think you have cured me of it.'

'You used to be a kind-hearted man,' she says, scanning, as if in dispassionate search, his sorrowful features; 'perhaps you are still, if happiness has not hardened your heart. It does harden the heart sometimes, they tell me; it is a long time since I have had a chance of judging by experience. But, if you are, try not to let me hear much of your happiness—try to keep it as quiet as you can.'

Her last words are almost inaudible through the excess of the emotion that has dictated them.

'Perhaps you will have your wish,' he says gloomily, for the last half-hour seems to have shaken all the fabric of his prospective Elysium; 'perhaps there will not be much to hide.'

'That is a very civil suggestion on your part,' she answers, relapsing into biting sarcasm; 'so likely, too. Go on. I am cheered already: find out some more equally probable topics of consolation for me. Why do not you remind me that I still have my husband—my husband whose society *you* have taught me so much to enjoy; my visiting-book; my—my——'

'You have your *boy*,' he interrupts sternly, goaded into anger out of compassion by her tone.

Her hands drop from his, and a light shiver runs over her shuddering body.

'*I—have—my—boy,*' she repeats slowly; 'so I have. God forgive me for having even for one moment forgotten him! Yes, I have him—bless him! but for how long? Even if he lives—oh, he *will* live! God cannot take *him* too from me—I was a fool ever to fear it; but even if he lives to grow up, he too will go from me. People will tell him things about me; or if they do not tell him, he will pick up hints. I shall see it in his eyes, and then he—too—will—go—from me!' breaking into a long moaning sob. 'I suppose,' looking in utter revolt up to heaven, 'that *They* will be satisfied then. I shall have nothing —*nothing*—NOTHING left!'

She has broken into a storm of frantic tears, that rain from her eyes and career unheeded down her white gown. He can only look on miserably.

'But at least,' she says deliriously, every word marking a higher stage in the rising sea of her frenzy, 'I shall always have been *first*! Neither you nor she can take that from me. It may make you both mad to think so, but you cannot. I shall always—always have been there first. You may tell her so from me, if you like,' with one last burst of dreadful laughter; 'it will be no breach of confidence, for I give you leave.'

Then, in a moment, before he can divine her intention, or—even if he had the heart to do so—arrest her, she has flung her arms convulsively about his neck; and in a moment more she is gone, leaving him there dazed and staggering in the starlight, with the agony of her good-bye kiss on his lips, and his face wet with her scorching tears.

CHAPTER XXIX

If there is one hour of the day at which the little Red House looks conspicuously better than another, it is that young one when the garden grass is still wet to the travelling foot, and the great fire-rose in the east has not yet soared high enough to swallow the shadows. So Talbot thinks, as he takes his way next morning to his love's little russet-coloured home. She has promised over-night to rise betimes, to give him an early tryst before he sets off on his dusty journey back into the world without her. He is of course by much too early; and though he tries to hasten the passage of time by looking at his watch every two minutes, yet he is compelled, if he would not be at her door long before it is opened to him, to journey towards her at a very different rate from that at which his heart is doing. He walks along, drawing in refreshment of soul and body with every breath. He has not slept all night, and his eyes are dry and feverish; but the air, moist with the tears of the dawn, beats his lids with its soft pinions, and all the lovely common sights of early morning touch healingly upon his bruised brain, and heart still jarred and aching with the ignoble pain of that late encounter.

At every step he takes some sweet or gently harmonious sight or sound steals away a parcel of that ugly ache, and gives him an atom of pure joy instead. Now it is a stray wood-pigeon beginning its day-long sweethearting in the copse. Now it is a merry din of quiring finches, all talking together. Now it is a glimpse of a sprinkle of cowslips in an old pasture, shaking off their drowsiness. Now it is only a stout thrush lustily banging its morning snail against a stone, the one instance of gross cruelty amongst the many that the scheme of nature offers, which the most tender-hearted cannot fail to admire. And now a turn of the road has given him to view her house, and the tears, cleansing as those of the morning, leap to his eyes at the sight of it. Dear little wholesome, innocent house, giving back the sun's smile from each one of its shining panes; giving it back, as *her* mirroring face will give back his own love-look, when she comes—so soon now, oh, so soon!—across the dew-drunk daisies to his arms. With what a feeling of homecoming does his heart embrace it—he that, for so many arid years, has had no better home than Bury Street lodgings, or Betty's boudoir!

He looks eagerly to see whether, by some blessed accident, she may even now be ahead of him in time, awaiting him with sunshiny face uplifted, and firm, fair arms resting on the top-rail of the gate. He knows how early she rises, and that no coquettish punctilio as to being first at the rendezvous will hinder her, if she is sooner ready than he. But apparently to-day she is not. There is no trace of her.

A slight misgiving as to Prue's illness, which until this moment he had indignantly dismissed from his memory as imaginary, having a more serious character than he had credited it with, makes him glance apprehensively towards the young girl's casement. The blind is down, it is true; but over all the rest of the house there is such a cheerful air of everyday serenity, that, considering the earliness of the hour, he cannot attach much importance to the circumstance.

Prue is always—how unlike his fresh Peggy!—a lie-a-bed. Mink and the cat are standing airing themselves on the door-step, and, by the suavity of their manner, obviously invite him to enter.

The hall-door is open, and he passes through it. It is the first time that he has had to push uninvited into her sanctuary—the first day that she has not met him at the gate. He checks the rising chill that the reflection calls forth, and hurries on into the hall; meaning to hurry through it, for surely it will be in the garden that he will find her. Perhaps, by one of love's subtilties, she has chosen to bid him farewell under the very hawthorn-tree where he had first called her his. But he has not made two steps into the hall before he discovers that his calculations have erred. Can it be by another of love's subtilties that she is sitting here indoors, away from the morning's radiance, sitting quite idle apparently by the table; and that, on his entry, she does not even turn her head?

'Peggy!' he cries, thinking that she cannot have heard his step, though it has rung not more noiselessly than usual on the old oak boards; and that Mink, with a friendly afterthought, is firing off little shrill 'good mornings' at his heels.

There is no change of posture in the sitting figure, no movement, unless, if his eyes do not deceive him, a slight shiver running over it.

'Peggy!' he repeats, alarmed; and, in a second, has overleaped the intervening distance—has fallen on his knees at her feet, and grasped her hands. 'What is it? Quick—speak to me! Is Prue worse?'

There is no answer. She has averted her face, so that he can see only the outline of her cheek's oval, at his approach; and—what is this? She is drawing her hands with slow decision, not with any petulance or coquetry, but as one irrevocably resolved, out of his. Then she rises slowly to her feet, and, having put three paces between them, turns and looks full at him. Looks full at him, this tall, risen woman, who will not lend him the custody of her hand! But who is she—this woman? Not his Peggy! Nay, surely not his Peggy! His Peggy, cheeked like the dawn, with eyes made out of sapphires and morning dew—his kindly, loving Peggy—what has she in common with this pale austerity that is facing him?

'What is it?' he repeats huskily, a vague horror making his knees knock together; 'is she——'

He breaks off. The idea has flashed across him that Prue is dead! What lesser catastrophe can account for this horrible unnamed change?

'She is better,' replies Peggy hoarsely.

'Better!—thank God for that!' drawing a long breath of relief. 'What do you mean by looking like this? You made me think—I do not know what; but,' his agony of perplexity returning in profounder flood, 'if so—if she is better, what is it?—what else? For mercy's sake answer me!—answer me quickly! Do not keep me waiting! You do not know what it is to be kept waiting like this!'

He has risen from his kneeling attitude; but that unaccountable something in her face hinders him from making any effort to bridge the distance she has set between them. Across that distance comes her reply, in a voice that seems to set her continents and seas away from him:

'Are you—quite—sure—that—I—need answer you?'

'Sure that you need answer me?' repeats he bewildered, struggling against the ice that is sweeping up over his heart; 'why, of course I am! Why else should I have asked you? We must be playing at cross-purposes,' with an attempted smile. 'Of course I am sure!'—reading the disbelief in her white face—'quite sure! What can I say to asseverate it? As sure as that I stand here—as sure as ——'

'Oh, stop!—stop!' she cries vehemently, thrusting out her hands towards him as if in passionate prohibition, while a surge of colour coming into her face restores her to some likeness to his Peggy; 'do not—do not let me have to think that I have been the cause of your telling any more falsehoods!'

'Any *more*?' echoes he, putting up his hand to his forehead, and feeling as if she had struck him across the eyes.

'Yes,' she says, gasping, while he sees her hand go out in unconscious quest of the table-edge, as if to steady herself. 'Yes!—do not I speak plainly? Any *more*!'

Again he passes his hand over that brow that feels cut and furrowed by the lash of her words.

'You—must—explain,' he says slowly; 'apparently I am dull this morning. What other falsehoods have I told you?'

Both her hands are clutching the table now; nor is its support unneeded, for her body sways. Only for a moment, however. In a moment she is standing firm again.

'What other?' she repeats, half under her breath; 'what other? Oh!' with a long shuddering groan, 'how many, many you must have told before you could grow to do it with a face that looks so like truth!'

But at that the insulted manhood of him awakes, goaded into life, and shakes off the paralysis engendered by his horrible astonishment.

'Come!' he exclaims, disregarding her unspoken veto, going close up to her and standing before her, with folded arms and flashing eyes; 'this is intolerable!—this is more than man can bear! Let me hear what you have to say—speak your accusation; but do not tell me to my face that I am a liar, without bringing a rag of evidence to support it!'

She looks back at him, taking in, with a startled air, his changed demeanour—the command of his attitude—the authority of his eyes. Then—

'You—are—right,' she says, panting, while he sees her poor heart miserably leap under the pink cotton gown he had praised yesterday—was it yesterday, or before Noah's flood? 'I—have no right to bring vague accusations, as you say. Will you—will you—let me wait a minute?'

She sinks upon a chair as she speaks; and, resting her elbow upon the table, passes her pocket-handkerchief once or twice over her face, wiping away the cold drops of anguish that, despite the morning's radiant warmth, are gathering upon it. He waits beside her, in a black suspense, pushing away from him the fear that he refuses to formulate.

'There!' she says, after a year's interval, which the clock falsely calls sixty seconds; 'I—I—beg your pardon for keeping you waiting.' She has banished, as far as she can, all signs of emotion, and begins in a level low voice. 'Prue got better almost immediately after you went away last night—was it really only last night?' with a bewildered look; then, immediately recovering herself, 'so decidedly better, that I thought I might safely leave her.' She pauses. 'I—I —thought I—I—would follow you.'

Another pause. It is evidently killing work to get on at all. Angry as he is with her, clearly as he now sees what is coming, he cannot help a compassionate wish to help her, and make it easier for her.

'I—did not know which way you had gone,' she resumes, after another battle with herself; 'no one had seen you. But I thought—I guessed—I fancied that it might have been to the walled garden, because—because we had—had—

said good-bye there last year.' Her voice wavers so distressingly that he thinks she is about to lose all control over it; but no!—in a moment she has recovered her self-mastery, and taken up her thread again. 'As I drew near the garden, I saw that the gate was a little open, so I knew that I had guessed right. I—looked—in; I—saw—oh!' with a burst of indignant agony, 'are you going to make me tell you what I saw?'

'Yes,' he says breathlessly, 'tell me!—what?' A hope, faint, and yet tenacious, lingers in his mind that it may have been any one moment of his last night's interview except that of the supreme embrace which she had witnessed. He has not long to wait before this last prop is knocked from under him.

'I—I—saw—you holding—a woman in your arms, and, a moment after, she ran past me—and I saw—who she was!'

The answer he has insisted upon reaches him in a broken whisper; and her strained eyes are fastened upon him, as if, in the teeth of a certainty as absolute as that of her own identity, she were nourishing the hopeless hope of his uttering some impossible, yet convincing, denial. But he attempts none such. He stands before her silent, with his arms still folded and the tide of a shoreless despair washing over his heart. Betty has put the crowning touch to her work.

'It is true then?' Peggy asks, in a voice of such bitter suffering as if she were realising it for the first time; as if she had not already known it for twelve endless hours.

'What is the use of denying it?' he replies blankly; 'you say that you saw her!'

She has risen to her feet again, risen to her full height (how tall she is!); and once again stands confronting him, not even asking the table-edge for any support.

'And—you—told—me—that—you—were—free!'

The words drop wonderingly from her mouth, barbed with an icy contempt that makes him writhe. But at least he thanks God that she does not treat him to such mirth as Betty's.

'I told you the truth,' rejoins the poor fellow doggedly—'I *was* free; I *am* free!'

But the consciousness of the impossibility of really clearing his character, save at the expense of her whom he must for ever shield, lends a flatness and unreality to his assertion, which, as he feels through every aching fibre, will only serve the more deeply to convince Peggy of his guilt. It is not long before he sees that he has divined justly.

'You need not make a laughing-stock of me,' she says with dignity, turning towards the door. But at that, the despair which has been paralysing him awakes, and cries out loud, giving him motion and a voice.

'You are not going!' he cries in a tone whose agony stabs her like a knife, flinging himself upon her passage.

'What is there to stay for?' she answers, choked. But she pauses. Can he, even yet, have anything to say?

'Do you think that I met her there *on purpose*?' he asks, his words pouring out in a hoarse eager flood, as if he had but little hope of commanding her attention for long to them—'by appointment? Ask yourself whether it is possible? Was I so anxious to leave you? Was not it you that drove me away? I tell you I had no more idea of meeting her than I had of meeting——' he hesitates, seeking for a comparison strong enough to emphasise his denial —'as I had of meeting one of the dead. I did not even know that she was in the neighbourhood. I had held no communication with her for months. It was an accident—a mere accident!'

He breaks off suffocated. At the intense sincerity of his tone, a sincerity which it is difficult to believe feigned, a sort of stir has come over her face; but in a moment it has gone again.

'Was it,' she asks with a quietness that makes his hopes sink lower than would any noisy tears or tantrums, 'was it *by accident* that she was in your arms?'

He is silent. In point of fact, he is as innocent of that embrace as Peggy herself; but from telling her so he is, being a man and an Englishman, for ever debarred. He must stand there, and bear the consequences of that supposed guilt, whatever those consequences may be. There is a little stillness while he waits his sentence—a little stillness broken only by the eight-day clock's tick-tack, and by the distance-mellowed sounds of the village rising to go about its daily work.

'Have you nothing to say for yourself, then?' she asks at last, in a voice which she dares not raise above a whisper for fear of its betraying her by altogether breaking down—'no explanation to give?'

'I tell you that it was all an accident,' he repeats, with a doggedness born of his despair. 'I can give no other explanation.'

'And that is none,' she replies, a wave of indignation sending back the colour to her ashy cheeks, and steadying her shaking limbs as she again turns to leave the room.

He does not, as before, throw himself in her way; he remains standing where he is, and only says in a dull voice:

'Are you going?'

'Why should I stay?'

'Going without saying good-bye?'

'I will say good-bye if you wish.'

'Going for—*for good*?'

'Yes.'

He makes no effort to change her resolution—vents no protest—if that indeed be not one, and the strongest he could utter, that long groan with which he flings himself on a chair beside the table, and covers his face with his hands. She has reached the door. No one hinders her from opening it and leaving him, and yet she hesitates. Her sunk blue eyes look back at him half relentingly.

'Are you sure,' she says quaveringly, while her pale lips tremble piteously —'are you sure that you have nothing to say—nothing extenuating? I—I should be glad to hear it if you had. I—I—I—would try my very best to believe you.'

There is no answer. Only the mute appeal conveyed by that prone figure, with its despairing brown head fallen forwards on its clenched hands. Is it possible that he has not heard her? After a moment's vacillation, she retraces her uncertain steps till she stands beside him. Feeling her proximity, he looks up.

At the sight of his face, she gives a start. Can it be she herself—she that had thought to have loved him so kindly—who has scored these new deep lines on brow and cheek? At the relenting evidenced by her back-coming, his dead hopes revive a little.

'Do you know what I did when I reached the walled garden last night?—I am afraid that you will not think the better of my common sense—I knelt down and kissed the place where I thought that your feet might have trod last year.'

'You did?' she says, with a catch in the breath; 'you did? and yet five minutes afterwards you were—oh!' breaking off with a low cry; 'and this is what men are like!'

He sees that his poor plea, instead of, as he had faintly hoped, a little bettering his position with her, has, read by the light of her mistaken knowledge, only served to intensify in her eyes the blackness of his inconstancy. Well, it is only one more added to the heap of earth's unnumbered injustices. It is only that Betty has done her work thoroughly this time. But he cannot bear to meet the reproachful anguish of the face that is bent above him, knowing that never on this side the grave can he set himself right with her. If only it might be for ever, instead of for these few hurrying moments, that he could shut out the light of day! The clock ticks on evenly. It sounds unnaturally loud and brutal in his singing ears; but its tick is not mixed with any light noise of retreating footsteps. She is still lingering near him, and by and by a long sob shudders out on the air.

'If you could persuade me that I was wrong,' she wails; 'if you could persuade me that it was some hideous delusion of my eyes—people have had such before now—that it existed only in my wicked fancy! Oh, if you could—if you could!'

'I cannot,' he replies hoarsely; 'you know that I cannot. Why do you torment me?' He has answered without looking up, still maintaining the attitude dictated by his despair; but when a little rustle of drapery tells him that she is really departing, he can no longer contain himself, but falls at her feet, crying out, 'Tell me how bad my punishment is to be!'

For a moment she looks down on him silently, her face all quivering as with some fiery pain; then in a very low voice:

'Punishment!' she says; 'punishment! There is no question of *punishment*. It is only that you have killed my heart.'

'Killed—your—heart!' he repeats blankly, as if too stunned to take in the meaning of the phrase.

'Yes,' she says, breathing fast and heavily; 'yes. I do not think you knew what you were doing. I believe it was a sudden madness that seized you—such a madness as,' with a touch of scorn, 'may be common to men. I know but little of them and their ways; but—but—what security have I against its seizing you a second time?'

He writhes. A second time? Oh, if she did but know how little it had seized him the first!

'If I married you now,' she goes on, her voice gaining a greater firmness, and a new and forlorn stability coming into her white face, 'I should love you, certainly. Yes,' with a melancholy shake of her head, 'I think that I shall never leave off loving you now. But if I married you, I should make you very unhappy; I should not take things easily—I should not be patient. And however happy we might be when we were together, since you have killed my trust in you, you would never be out of sight that I should not be fancying that you were—as—as—as I saw you last night.'

Her voice has dropped to an almost inaudible pitch. He has risen to his feet again, and some instinct of self-respect helping him, stands silently before her, accepting the doom which, as he hopelessly feels, can be averted by no words that he has leave to utter.

To her ears has come the noise of nearing wheels—the wheels of the fly he had ordered over-night to take him to the station, allowing the smallest possible margin of time in which to get there, so that as little as possible might be robbed from the poignant sweetness of his last farewells.

The poignant sweetness! He almost laughs. That sound must have hit her ears too, judging by the long sob that swells her throat, and by the added rush of anguish in her next words:

'I ought to have believed what they told me of you, but I would not; I would believe only you—only *you*; and this is how you have rewarded me!'

He locks his teeth together hard. For how much longer can he bear this? There comes over him a rushing temptation to try to buy one soft look from her to take with him, by the hypocrisy of asking her forgiveness; he whose whole smitten soul stands up in protest against the need of any forgiveness.

But no. Sooner than descend to such an equivocation he will depart on his lonely way uncomforted.

'I must go,' he says steadily, though his lips are livid. 'Will you—would you mind shaking hands with me?'

He is going. She had known what the wheels meant, and yet there seems a murderous novelty in the idea. She has put her death-cold hand into his;

speech is almost beyond her; but she mutters some poor syllables about not wishing him ill.

'Peggy,' he says, with a solemnity such as that of those who are spending their last breath in some sacred utterance; 'Peggy, you are wrong! Any one to whom you told your story—any one who had to judge between you and me, would say that you were right; but you—are—wrong! If I have killed your heart, you have killed mine, so we are quits. Good-bye!'

The next moment she is alone in the room.

CHAPTER XXX

The Whitsun garlands that had so gaily wound about the pillars of Roupell Church have long ago been taken down, dead and faded. Poor Peggy has once again stood all day on her ladder, and decked aisle and chancel and font and altar with the manifold roses and the May lilies that by Trinity Sunday are bountifully ready to her hand. Once again has Mrs. Evans sat in a pew and helped her with moral suasion, and with easy suggestions of alterations that would entail her undoing half her work.

The scent of the lilies is too much next day for the youngest church-going Evans, and he has to be carried out, with his boots in the air, to the great delight of the schoolchildren, and enlivenment of the congregation generally. Not one of the civil parishioners, dropping in now and again to observe her progress and offer help, would think that the Peggy they see smiling down upon them from her ladder had been lately treading on hot ploughshares. But yet she has. The worst is over now, she tells herself. Which was the worst hour? Which the worst moment? she asks, with what she thinks to be a perfectly dispassionate inquiry. That one when she had found his glove lying quite naturally, and as if at home, on the hall-table? That one when she had had to tell Prue that it was all over; when through the obstinacy of the young girl's disbelief she had had to asseverate and re-asseverate it, until she had almost screamed out loud in the agony of that reiteration? That one when scarce two days after the blow had fallen, going on some necessary business to the Parsonage, Mrs. Evans had met her with the triumphant announcement that she—Mrs. Evans—had been right after all in her conjecture as to Lady Betty Harborough? that though it might not be known to many persons, yet the fact was none the less certain that she had paid a flying visit to the Manor: Mrs. Evans's nurse having had the information from the very flyman who had driven her from the station; adding the circumstance, that so little sense of shame did she manifest that she insisted upon an open fly.

'Of course the children were the pretext,' pursues the Vicar's wife, with a shrug; 'it is so shocking to think that they should be made accomplices, as it were. One always feels,' looking affectionately round at the various Evans specimens—old and new baby, little girl with a cold, middle-sized boy with a stomach-ache, kept indoors by reason of these ailments, and now littering the worn carpet—'one always feels that one's children are one's best safeguard.'

And Peggy remembers to have smiled. That a hideous knife is cutting her own heart in two, does not make the fact of Mrs. Evans's virtue requiring a safeguard at all the less funny. The worst is over, so she assures herself. The wren that sang at her chamber-window, waking her to tell her that Talbot was at the gate, that waked her all the same when it had no such news to tell her, is happily silent.

The pungent hawthorn-blossoms are discoloured and dead. She smiles drily as she sees them swept up, and rolled away in Jacob's barrow. What a mercy it would be if she could sweep up the dead brown love they emblematise, and get Jacob to wheel it away too!

After all she is but where she was before Whitsuntide, where she has been all her life. She has only a few, such a few steps to retrace. Ah, but the retracing of those steps! The nights are worst. All the great nations of the variously woeful on this sorrowful earth's face, know that the nights are worst. Oh, the agony of that crying out of strong souls for earth's supreme good just shown them, and then for ever snatched away! She had thought herself happy before —quite sufficiently happy, and had walked smiling and content along her path, until suddenly one had taken her by the hand, and had led her into God's paradise; and having just given her time to have her astonished eyes for ever dazzled by the shining of that great light, had pushed her away into the darkness, where she must stand henceforth with blind hands beating on the unopened door. She had thought herself happy before. In the darkness she laughs out loud. She had mistaken that wretched farthing rushlight for day.

All night she struggles in the deep waters, foothold slipping from under her. All night she fights with dragons, with noisome, baleful creatures, like stout Christian in the Valley of the Shadow; wrestles with temptations unworthy of her; with base longings to have him back, even though it be to go shares with another in his love; to cry 'Come back, come back! fool me, cheat me again— only come back!'

She had told him but the truth in saying that when she cared for any one, she cared very badly. She is caring very badly now, and it goes hard with her. What wonder that the wakening birds and the uprising wind of morning find her daily staring dry-eyed, watchful, languid, at the rose of dawn!

> 'Once drinking deep of that divinest anguish,
> How can she seek the empty world again?'

But through the day no one finds out her languor; no one knows that she is going about her daily work unfortified by sleep. Happily for her there is no one to observe her very nicely. If there were any one to steal anxious glances of sympathy at her to see how she is bearing it, she must break down; but, as I have said, happily for her, there is no one.

Prue, indeed, is quite affectionate and sorry; rather remorseful, in fact, at the consciousness of having but grudgingly given that kindness which, as it turns out, would have been needed only for one week. Her method of compensation for former shortcomings, that of repeating many times how unworthy she had always thought Talbot of her sister, is perhaps scarcely judicious. The assertion of his unworthiness cuts Peggy like a lash, but she bears it with set teeth and a sort of smile. It is true. He is unworthy. And after a while—but a little while—this part of her ordeal is over; for Prue, swallowed up in the sea of her own coming troubles, forgets to remember that there is any one else struggling in the waves.

And so, by and by, Peggy grows to walk her ploughshares with as unshrinking a foot as if they were velvet turf; grows to thank God again for her garden, and to be able to thank Him even for that one glimpse of the supremest good, though given but to be withdrawn; last of all, to acquiesce in that withdrawal. Since she is so urgently needed by the poor little life beside her, it is as well, so she tells herself, that she should have no distracting life of her own to pull her two ways. Whatever else her Prue loses, she can now never lose her.

And as time goes on, it seems as if Prue, too, were to have her losses. The first of these is perhaps but a little one, merely the loss of that promised company of her betrothed through those rich June days when Oxford is holding her yearly riot of pleasure—the riot from which he had joyfully engaged to steal away to her quiet side. But, as has happened not unfrequently before in Freddy's history, as it may be confidently predicted will happen not unfrequently again, he has promised more than when pay-day comes he is able to perform. After all, it seems—and at that poor Prue would be the last to wonder—Commemoration cannot get on without him.

Strange as it may appear, among the crowd, unusually large this year, that throngs to the fair city for her saturnalia, and extensive as is the acquaintance among undergraduates of the Hartley family—two of the sons, indeed, being at the present time members of the University—there is no one who is found capable of doing the honours of the festival to these comparatively new acquaintance with the exception of Mr. Ducane. He is therefore compelled, in compliance with his own creed of, as he very nobly says in his letter to Prue, 'making Self march last in the Pageant of Life,' to forego the simple joys he had planned in his sweetheart's company, and carry his absent, yearning heart through the bustle of theatre, ball, and *fête*. It is not until the last moment that he has announced to Prue his change of project, not until all her little preparations for his reception had been made, all the flowers gathered to be laid on the altar of the poor soul's God.

'He might have told you before,' says Peggy indignantly, when one morning the news of this defalcation is brought her by a trembling-lipped pale Prue.

'He did not know it himself,' replies the other, in eager defence; 'he says so somewhere, doesn't he?' (turning over the pages in feverish search); 'or if he did know, it was out of consideration for me that he kept me in the dark, that I might have less time to be disappointed in; and he was right. I have had all these weeks—all this hope and looking forward—to the good.'

Her under-lip quivers so piteously, as she makes this cheerful statement of her gains, that she puts up her hand in haste to hide it. But after all, Commemoration is only a matter of four days; and perhaps it is worth while to have the pleasure of his company deferred for that short interval, for the sake of the still higher pleasure she receives on his return, of hearing him read aloud to her a choice little poem he has found time to write on the subject of his own distraught wandering through the gay throng; questioning every maid he meets as to why she was not Prue. After he is gone, Prue repeats it—she has already learnt it by heart—with sparkling eyes to her sister. It is not only that it is so beautiful, as she says, but it is so *true*. Nobody could write like that, unless he felt it, could he now? Peggy is spared the pain of a reply by her sister's hurrying off to copy out the lines into that gold-clasped, vellum-bound volume, in which, written out in his sweetheart's best hand, the productions of Mr. Ducane's muse find a splendid shelter, until that surely near moment when rival publishers will snatch them from each other. She has plenty of time to devote her best penmanship to them, as it turns out; since after two days at the Manor, Freddy has to be off again. It is to London this time that a harsh necessity drives him. Freddy never 'goes,' or 'wishes to go.' He always 'has to go.'

'Whatever happens, we must not lose touch with the Great World-Heart beating outside us!' he has said, looking solemnly up at the stars over his betrothed's head, hidden sobbingly on his breast.

And she, though she knows little, and cares less, about the Great World-Heart, acquiesces meekly, since *he* must be right. So the Red House relapses into its condition of female tranquillity; a tranquillity of two balked young hearts beating side by side. The one pastures her sorrow on the name that now appears almost daily among the titled mob that crowds the summer columns of the *Morning Post*. The other digs hers into the garden; paints it into pictures for the workhouse; turns it into smiles for the sorrowful; stitches it into clothes for the naked.

The stillness of high summer is upon the neighbourhood; all the leafy homes around emptied of their owners; the roses, ungathered, shedding their petals, or packed off in wet cotton-wool to London. Milady is in London. So are the Hartleys. So is everybody; everybody, that is, except the Evanses. The Evanses are at home. They mostly are. A family of their dimensions, even in these days of cheap locomotion, does not lend itself to frequent removals. A couple of years ago, indeed, milady good-naturedly whisked off the Vicar for a fortnight's Londoning. But he came back so unaffectedly disgusted with his cure, his offspring, and his spouse, that the latter cherishes a hope, not always confined to her own breast, that this act of hospitality may never be repeated. And hay-harvest comes. The strawberries ripen, and jam-making begins. The Evans boys are home for the holidays; and one of them breaks his leg. The threatened baby arrives; and all the little events, habitual in the Red House's calendar, happen punctually; for even the Vicarage fracture is not more than the usual and expected outcome of the summer holidays. But neither hay-time, nor hot jam-time, nor holiday-time bring back Freddy to the Manor, whither his country-loving aunt has hastened back joyfully to spud and billycock and shorthorns, a round month ago. He does not even write very often. How should he? as Prue says. How could any one who knows anything of London expect it of him? But in all his letters, when they do come, there is invariably an underlying ring of sadness, that proves to demonstration how cogent though unexplained are the reasons which alone keep him from that dear and sacred spot, where alone, as he himself says, his soul reaches its full stature. But at length, apparently, the occult causes relax their hold of him; and when August has begun to bind her gold stooks, and the cuckoo has said good-bye, he comes. In August. It is a month to whose recurrence Peggy has looked forward with dread: to her a month of anniversaries. Happily it is only to herself that they are anniversaries. Who but she will remember that on such a day the fox bit Talbot? Dingo himself has certainly forgotten it; though he is as certainly quite ready to do it again, if the chance is afforded him. Who will know, or even suspect, that such and such days are made bitter to her by the fact that on their fellows in last year he drove the mowing-machine, or gathered the lavender, or cut out the new flower-bed? She smiles half sarcastically, wrapping herself securely in the cloak of her little world's entire indifference to her epoch-making moments.

'One has no windows in one through which one's friends can look in at one,' she says philosophically, 'even if they would take the trouble. Mrs. Evans perhaps would take the trouble; I do not know any one else that would. As long as one is not foolish outside, it does not matter; and I am not foolish outside.'

August is here; and the sacred seat under the Judas-tree, the seat that had been forbidden to Peggy during her one triumph-hour, is again occupied: save in the dead of the night has, for the last five days, been scarcely a moment unoccupied; and Prue's little cup—the cup that had run as low as mountain-springs in a droughty summer—again brims over.

'It is so much better than if he had never gone away,' she says rapturously, 'for then I might have thought that he liked me only because he had never seen anything better; but now that he has had all the most beautiful ladies in London at his feet——'

'Has he indeed?' rejoins Peggy, smiling; 'does he tell you so?'

But she has not the heart to suggest that the present emptiness of the Manor of all inmates, except himself and his aunt, may count for even more in Mr. Ducane's assiduities than his indifference to the London beauties.

One afternoon she has left the young pair cooing on their rustic seat as usual, and has betaken herself to the Manor, on one of her mixed errands of parish business and individual friendliness to its mistress. She finds the old lady surrounded by all the signs and symptoms of a new hobby—plans, encaustic tiles, designs for the decorated pans and skimmers of an ornamental dairy.

'I have a new toy, my dear!—congratulate me!' says she, looking up from the litter around her, almost as radiant as Prue; 'an ornamental dairy-house! I cannot think how I have lived without it for sixty-five years! After all, there is nothing like a new toy; you would not be the worse for one,' she adds, glancing kindly at the girl's face, a little oldened and jaded since this time last year, its beauty lending itself even less than it had then done to Lady Betty's sarcasm about being improved by being bled. 'And Prue?—how is Prue? She is not in want of a new toy *par hasard*?—still quite satisfied with the old one, eh? Well, he is a very ingenious piece of mechanism!'

'Very!' replies Peggy drily.

'And when are the banns to be put up?' inquires the old lady abruptly, resting her arms upon the heap of her plans and estimates, and pushing up her spectacles on her forehead, in order to get a directer view of her young *vis-à-vis*. 'I should like to have a week's notice, in order to get myself a new gown; Mason was telling me this morning that I have not one that can be depended upon to hold together.'

'The banns?' repeats Peggy, a flush of pleasure spreading over her face; 'then he has told you! Oh, I am so glad! I was afraid that he would not!'

'Told me!' repeats the elder woman, with a withering intonation; 'not he!— trust him for that! No doubt he has some high-falutin' reason for not doing so; it would wound my feelings!—it would be dangerous at my age! He had rather efface himself and his own interests for ever than roughen, by one additional pebble, my path to the grave!' mimicking, with ludicrous insuccess, Freddy's round young tones. 'Told me?—not he!' The tinge brought into Peggy's face by that emotion of transient satisfaction of which milady's words have proved the fallaciousness, dies out of it again. 'Nobody has told me,' continues the old lady tranquilly; 'I have only taken the liberty of seeing what was directly under my nose. No offence to you, Peggy; but I had quite as soon not have seen it.'

'Of course—of course,' replies Peggy, flushing again.

'I suppose that we have no one but ourselves to thank,' says milady, with philosophy, her eye returning affectionately to one of the designs for the front of her hobby. 'I do not care about that one; it is too florid—it would look like Rosherville. Throw two selfish idle young fools together, and the result has been the same since Adam's time!'

Peggy's heart swells. Idle and selfish! Never, even in the most secret depths of her own mind, has she connected such epithets with her Prue; and here is milady applying them to her as if they were truisms.

'I must send him away somewhere, I suppose,' pursues Lady Roupell, with a rather impatient sigh. 'He is an expensive luxury, is Master Freddy, as your poor little Prue would find; but no doubt it will come cheaper in the end. Give him a couple of hundred pounds, and pack him off on a voyage round the world! Believe me, dear,' laying her hand—whose tan, contracted by an inveterate aversion for gloves, contrasts oddly with its flashing diamonds—compassionately on Peggy's shoulder, 'he would have clean forgotten her before he had got out of the chops of the Channel.'

A great lump has sprung into Peggy's throat, constricting the muscles.

'And she?'

The old woman shrugs her shoulders.

'When we are forgotten, child, we do the graceful thing, and forget too. I suppose we all know a little about that.'

Margaret has picked up one of the Dutch tiles that are to line the walls of milady's new plaything; but it is but a blurred view that she gets of its uncouth blue figures.

'She would not forget,' she says in a low voice, that, low as it is, has yet been won with difficulty from that seeming mountain in her throat; 'she has put all —everything into one boat! Oh! poor Prue, to have put everything into one boat!'

'And such a boat!' adds milady expressively.

For all rejoinder, Peggy fairly bursts out crying. The accumulated misery of weeks, so carefully pent and dammed in the channels of her aching heart, breaks down her poor fortifications. Her own life-venture hopelessly perished! Prue's foundering on the high seas before her very eyes! She had not cried for herself; she may, at least, have leave to cry for Prue.

'God bless my soul, Peggy!' says the elder woman, taking off and laying down her spectacles, and speaking with an accent of pronounced surprise and indignation; 'you do not mean to say that you are going to *cry*! There's an end to all argument while you are sniffing like that.' Then as the girl rises to go, but imperfectly strangling her sobs, she adds in a still vexed but rather remorseful voice: 'You make me feel quite choky too. You have no right to make me feel choky! Run away! run away! What do I care for any of you? I have got my dairy-house!'

CHAPTER XXXI

'And such a boat!' The words ring in Peggy's ears through her homeward walk. After all, she had heard no new thing. That Freddy was an unseaworthy craft to which to commit the precious things of a life, the gems and spices of a throbbing human soul, has long been a patent fact to her. But there is a wide difference between a fact that has only been presented gently to one by one's self, and the same fact rudely thrust under one's eyes and into one's reluctant hands by some officious outsider.

'And such a boat!' She is unconsciously repeating milady's simple yet pregnant commentary on her nephew's character as she re-enters her own garden. Almost as she does so she is aware of Prue flying past her without seeing her, a condition of things explained by the fact of her handkerchief being held to her eyes in obvious passionate weeping.

Prue, too, crying! An idea dazedly flashes across her brain that Prue must have overheard, and before common-sense can correct it, the girl is gone.

With a still more uncomfortable feeling at her heart than that which had been already there, Margaret continues her course to the Judas-tree. One of the pair she had left smiling beneath its shade is still there, and still smiling; or, if not actually smiling, at least in a mood that has no relation to tears.

He is lying all along on the garden-seat—Prue's departure, though no doubt deplored, has at least given him more room to stretch his legs—and is murmuring something, apparently of a rhythmic nature, half under his breath, as he stares up at the clouds.

'What have you been making Prue cry about?' asks Peggy, abruptly stopping before him.

Freddy starts a little, and reluctantly begins to draw back his legs, which, being too long for the bench, are elevated upon and protruding beyond its rustic arm.

'I am sure you are not aware of it, dear,' he says pleasantly, 'but your question has taken rather an offensive form. Prue *is* crying, I regret to say; but why you should instantly conclude that it is I that have made her cry, I am at a loss to imagine. I think, Peg, I must refer you to 1 Corinthians xiii.'

'You used to tell me that *I* always made her cry,' returns Peggy sternly; 'that *I* was hard upon her; that she "needed very tender handling."'

'Did I indeed?' says the young man, with a sort of wondering interest. 'It shows how cautious one ought to be in one's judgment of others. Thank you for telling me, Peg!'

'What have you been talking about to make her cry?' repeats Peggy, with a sad pertinacity. 'She was not in the least inclined to cry when I went away. I never saw her more joyous, poor little soul!'

'I may return the compliment, dear,' retorts Freddy, carrying the war into the enemy's quarters, and staring up with a brotherly familiarity into her still flushed and tear-betraying face from under the brim of Prue's garden-hat, which, as being more comfortable and wider-brimmed than his own, he has worn all afternoon. 'What have you been talking about to milady to make *you* cry?'

She puts up her hand with a hasty gesture. She had not known or thought about the ravages wrought on her face by her late weeping; but now that the consciousness of it has been brought home to her, she is for a moment put out of countenance. But in a second she has recovered herself.

'We were talking of *you*,' she replies gravely. 'Milady knows; she has found out about you and Prue.'

Freddy has abandoned his prone posture; he is sitting up, lightly switching the end of his own boot with a small bamboo; Prue's hat, being capacious, veils his face almost entirely.

'I should have thought that the information would have come more gracefully from you,' continues Peggy coldly. 'I should have thought it would have been better if *you* had told her.'

'If I had told her,' repeats Freddy dreamily, without looking up; 'after all, Peggy, there was not much to tell: "I love;" "I am loved." The whole scheme of Creation lies in those two phrases; but when you come to telling—to putting it into brutal words——'

It is a warm evening, but Peggy feels a slight sensation of cold.

'It will have to be put into *brutal words* some day or other,' she says doggedly, with an indignant emphasis on the three syllables quoted from Mr. Ducane's speech.

'"Some day, some day!"' echoes he dreamily, humming the refrain of the hackneyed song. 'Of course it will,' lifting his head again, and staring at the heavens. 'Good Lord, Peggy, what a pace that upper strata of cloud is driving at! there must be a strong current up there, though it is so still down here. You know, dear, you and I have never been quite at one upon that head. I have always thought that it took the bloom off one's sacred things to blare them prematurely about.'

There is such a tone of firm yet gentle reproach in his voice, that, for a second, Peggy asks herself dazedly, 'Is it possible that he is in the right?'

'And what did milady say?' inquires the young fellow a moment later, in a lighter key, growing tired of watching the racing vapours in the upper air, and bringing his eyes back to earth again. 'You have not told me what milady said. Did she recommend my being put back into long-clothes?'

'No.'

'I am not at all sure that I should not be more comfortable in a white frock and a sash,' continues Freddy, laughing; 'I do feel so ridiculously young sometimes. I do not think that either you or dear Prue quite realise how young I am. You take me too seriously, Peggy. It is rather terrible to be taken so seriously.'

He has risen while speaking, and drawn coaxingly nearer to her. She looks at him with a sort of despair. It is quite true. He is terribly, ridiculously young. As her glance takes in the beardless bloom of his face, the Will-of-the-wispy laughter of his eyes, it comes home to her with a poignant force never before fully realised how ludicrous it is—ludicrous if it were not tragic, that commonest of earthly alternatives—for an agonising human soul to trust its whole life-treasure, without one thrifty or prudent reservation, into his butterfly keeping. Probably her thought translates itself into her sad eyes; for Freddy fidgets uneasily under them, slashes at a tree-bough with his bamboo, shifts from foot to foot.

'You *are* young,' she says sorrowfully, 'but you are twenty-one; at twenty-one
____'

'At twenty-one Pitt was Prime Minister, or nearly so; that is what you were going to say, dear, was not it? Do not! I shall never be Prime Minister. I am like port wine,' breaking into a smile like sunshine; 'I should be better for a couple of voyages round the Cape!' and he is gone.

Though Margaret has been unable to extract from Freddy the occasion of Prue's tears, she has no great difficulty in learning it from the sufferer herself.

'It was very stupid of me,' she says, though the fountain shows symptoms of opening afresh at the bare recollection, 'and very cruel to him; he always says that the sight of tears unmans him so completely, that he cannot get over it for hours afterwards' (Peggy's lip curls). 'And of course it was only out of kindness, for my own good that he said it; as he told me,' blushing with pleasure at the recollection, 'when one is in possession of a gem, one naturally wishes to have it cut and polished to the highest pitch of brilliancy of which it is capable. Was not it a beautiful simile?'

'Yes, yes; but that was not what made you cry, surely?'

'Oh no, of course not; what made me cry,' clouding over again, 'was that he said—he spoke most kindly, no one could have spoken more kindly—that he was afraid that I had no critical faculty.'

'Was that all?' says Peggy, relieved. 'Well, a great many people go through life very creditably without it. I do not think I should have cried at that.'

'He was reading me some new poems of his,' continues Prue, not sensibly cheered by this reassurance; 'and when he had finished, he begged me to point out any faults I saw in them. And I told him what was the truth—that there were not any—that I thought them all one more beautiful than another; and then he looked rather vexed, and said he was afraid I had no critical faculty.'

Peggy smiles, not very gaily.

'He had better show them to me next time.'

'Do you think that he would have been better pleased if I had picked holes in them?' inquires Prue anxiously. 'But how could I? They all seemed to me to be perfectly beautiful; I did not see any holes to pick.'

'Do you happen to have them by you?' asks Peggy. 'If so, we might look them over together, and provide ourselves with some criticisms to oblige him with when next he calls.'

'No—o,' replies Prue reluctantly; 'I have not. He took them away with him, I think—I suppose that he wanted to read them to somebody else—somebody more intelligent. Peggy'—after a pause—'do you suppose that Miss Hartley has a critical faculty?'

The sisters are sitting, as usual after dinner, in their little hall. Prue stretched upon her favourite oak settle; Peggy on a stool at her feet.

'My dear,' with an impatient sigh, 'how can I tell?'

'I dare say it must be very tiresome to be always praised,' pursues Prue, after a pause, in a not very steady voice—'particularly if you are, as he is, of a nature that is always struggling up to a higher level—"agonising," as he said to-day, "after unrealisable ideals."'

Peggy coughs. It passes instead of a remark.

'I have often thought how terribly insipid he must find me,' pursues Prue, with a painful humility. 'But I suppose, in point of fact, the more brilliant you yourself are, the more lenient you are to other people's stupidity; and, after

237

all,' with a distressingly apparent effort at reassuring herself, 'he has known it all along. It is not as if it came fresh to him; and I do not think that I am any duller than I was last year. Of course, if I had profited by all the advantages I have had in his conversation, I ought to be much brighter; but at least I do not think that I am any duller—do you?' eagerly grasping her sister's arm as if to rivet her attention, which, in truth, is in no danger of wavering.

'No, dear; of course not,' very soothingly.

'Come and sit on the settle by me,' cries Prue restlessly; 'we can talk more comfortably so, and I can rest my head on your shoulder. It is such a nice roomy shoulder.'

'Yes, darling—yes.'

There is a pause. The moon looks in from the garden. A startle-de-buzz booms by on the wings of the night, and once an elfin bat sweeps past on the congenial dusk.

The night is in Margaret's soul too, and not such a bland white night as that spread outside for elves to dance in.

'I am going to say such a silly thing,' says Prue presently, heralding her speech by a fictitious laugh. 'If it were not rather dark, I do not think that I should dare to say anything so foolish. I am going to ask you such a stupid question; I am sure you will not consider it worth answering. Do you think it possible—ha! ha! I really am idiotic to-night—that he might ever—not now, of course—if you had seen how distressed, how heart-broken he was to-day at my crying, you would not have thought there was much danger of its happening now—but,' her speech growing slow, and halting with quick feverish breaths between, 'do you think it is just possible that sometime—many years hence—twenty—thirty—he—might grow—a little—tired of me? There! there!' her utterance waxing rapid and eager again; 'do not answer! Of course, I do not mean you to answer!'

Peggy is thankful for the permission to be silent thus accorded to her; but she does not long profit by it.

'I think I had rather that you did answer, too,' says Prue, with a quick uneasy change of mind. 'It seems senseless to ask questions and get no answer to them; and, after all, there can be but one answer to mine.'

Peggy shivers. There can indeed be but one answer; but how dare she give it?

'Why do not you speak?' cries Prue, growing restless under her sister's silence. 'Did not you hear me say that I should like you to answer me after all? I believe you are asleep!'

'How can I answer, dear?' replies Peggy sadly. 'I have so little acquaintance with men and their ways; and I am not sure,' with a small bitter laugh, 'that what I do know of them is very much to their credit.'

There is a ring of such sharp hopelessness in her tone as to arrest the attention of even the preoccupied younger girl.

'You were not very lucky either, Peggy,' she says softly, rubbing her cheek caressingly to and fro against Margaret's shoulder. 'Why do I say *either*?' catching herself quickly up. 'As if I were not lucky—luckier than anybody; but you were *un*lucky. Oh, how unbearable to be unlucky in that of all things! And I was not very kind to you, was I?'

Peggy's heart swells. Her lips are passing in a trembling caress over her sister's hair.

'Not very, dear.'

'Somehow one never can think of you as wanting any one to be kind to you,' says Prue half-apologetically; 'it seems putting the cart before the horse. But,' with a leap back as sudden as an unstrung bow to her own topic, 'you have not answered my question yet! Oh, I see you do not mean to answer it! I do not know what reason you can have for not answering; but, after all, I do not mind. I ought never to have asked it. I had no business. It was not fair to him. Of course he will not get tired of me,' sitting up and clasping her hands feverishly together; 'and if he does,' with a slight hysterical laugh, 'why, I shall just die at once—go out like the snuff of a candle, and there will be an end of me, and no great loss either.'

CHAPTER XXXII

In order perhaps to give an ostensible reason for her last flying visit to the empty Manor, or more likely (since she is not much in the habit of testing the value of her actions by the world's opinion) for her own solace and consolation, Lady Betty Harborough had taken her little son with her on her return home; had taken also her daughter, though the latter's company is a matter of much less moment to her maternal heart.

The departure of the children had, at the time, been an unspeakable relief to Margaret. The recollection of the poignant pain and inconvenience she had endured last year from their questions upon John Talbot's departure, such as, 'When was he coming back?' 'Would not she like him to come and live with her always?' make her look forward with dread unutterable to a repetition of such questions, to which her new circumstances lend an agony lacked by her former ones. How shall she answer them if they ask her now whether she would like John Talbot to come back and live with her always? Shall she scream out loud?

It is, then, with untold relief that she hears that they are gone, whipped off with such promptitude by their parent as to be unable to make their adieux to the Red House, the fox, and the fondly loved though freckled Alfred. That they have again reappeared on the scene, she learns only a couple of days after her interview with milady, by coming upon them and their nurses suddenly at a turn of the Road. The shock is so great—Lily is wearing the very same frock and Franky the same hat in which they had burst into her love-dream on the first morning of her engagement—that she cuts their greetings, to their immense surprise, very short, and, under the pretext of extremest haste, breaks away from their eager little hands and voices.

Her conscience smites her when the sound of sobbing overtakes her, and she turns her head to see Franky fighting with his nurse to get away and run after her, in order to rectify the, to him, unintelligible mistake of her want of gladness at meeting him. Poor Franky! She has not so many lovers that she can afford to rebut the tenderness of even so small a one as Master Harborough. She will make it up to him next time. It is not long before she is given the opportunity. On the following morning she is sitting at her writing-table doing the weekly accounts, when a rapping as of minute knuckles on the outer door is followed—before permission to enter can be either given or refused—by the appearance of a small figure, that of Miss Lily, who advances not quite so confidently as usual.

'Oh, Miss Lambton!' she says rather affectedly, obviously borrowing a phrase she has heard employed by her mother, 'how fortunate I am to find you! We have come to see you. Franky wants to know whether he was naughty yesterday that you would not speak to him. He thinks he must have been naughty. He has sent you a present; he did not like to give it you himself, so he has asked me. He took a bit of Nanny's letter-paper when she was not looking, to wrap it up in. It is not hers really; it is ours, for there is "Harborough Castle" on it. Nanny always likes to write to her friends on paper with "Harborough Castle" on it.'

During her voluble speech, she has come up to the table and deposited in Peggy's hand a tiny untidy parcel, piping hot, evidently from the pressure of anxious small fingers tightly closed over it, all the way from the Manor to the Red House. Peggy begins to unroll it; but before this operation is nearly completed, a second little voice is heard, in intense excitement from the door.

'It is my knife that father gave me after I was ill; it has five blades, and a scissors, and a button-hook, and a corkscrew, and a file. It cost ten and sixpence; and I like you to have it: it is a present.'

The next moment Master Harborough and the object of his affections are in each other's arms. It is a long time before she can persuade the little generous heart to take back its offering; before, with the tears in her own eyes, she can succeed in forcing it back to its natural home in the pocket of his sailor trousers; before general conversation can be introduced by Lily.

'Just as we were setting off we saw Freddy going out riding,' says she agreeably. 'He would not tell us where he was going; but Nanny thinks it was to Hartley's. Why does she say "*Hartley's*" instead of "Mr. Hartley's"? She always talks of *Mr.* Richards, the butcher!'

Simultaneously with this unanswerable query about her, Nanny herself appears with a note in her hand, which she has been commissioned by Lady Roupell to give to Miss Lambton, and which, when she is once more alone— the children having scampered off to embrace Alfred—Miss Lambton opens. She does so with some slight curiosity. The envelope is so large as to imply the certainty of an enclosure. Milady's own notes are not apt to require much space, nor is the present one any exception to her general rule. It runs thus:

'DEAR PEGGY,

'This woman has asked me to forward you the enclosed. I do not quite know why she could not find out your address for herself. Freddy has worried me into saying I would go. It is such a long while off that we shall probably all be dead and buried first. Meanwhile, do not order a fly, as I can take you and Prue.

'Yours,

'M. R.'

With a heightened interest Peggy turns to the enclosure. It reveals a large and highly glazed invitation card, on which Mrs. Hartley announces her intention of being 'At Home' on the evening of the 15th of September, and which holds out the two lures—each lurking seductively in its own corner—of 'Theatricals' and 'Dancing.' While she is still looking at it, Prue comes up behind her and reads it over her shoulder; and as she does so, the elder sister hears her breathe quicker.

'Oh, Peggy!' she cries, with agitation, 'then I shall see her at last. I shall be able to judge for myself. It is so odd that we should never have met her, living in the same neighbourhood; it shows how little we go out, does not it? *He* has always been so anxious that we should know her, almost ever since he knew her himself. How long is that ago?' stifling a sigh. 'Oh, a long time ago now! He says he is always trying to make the people he likes clasp each other's hands.'

'And is he very successful generally?' asks Peggy drily.

But Prue's eyes have lit upon Lady Roupell's note, and her attention is too much absorbed in it for her even to hear her elder's sarcastic question. Peggy would fain have spared her the pain of reading the sentence that refers to Freddy. But it is too late. Margaret becomes aware of the moment when she reaches it by the slight colour that rises to her eager face.

'He was always so good-natured about the Hartleys,' she says, in hasty explanation; 'he would have been just the same to any one else in the same position. He thought that people left them out in the cold; he never can bear any one to be left out in the cold.'

'This does not look much like being left out in the cold, does it?' says Margaret, rising, walking to the chimney-piece, and setting up the card against the dark background of the old oak; 'since it is our only invitation, it is well that it is such a smart one. What an odd fashion it is, when one comes to think of it, that a woman should consider it necessary to send these magnificent bits of pasteboard flying half over the country, merely to tell us that she is at home!'

'There is no need for us to do that,' rejoins Prue rather disconsolately; 'we are always at home.'

'We shall not be at home on the night of the 15th of September,' says Peggy, laughing, and passing her arm fondly round her sister, who, unable to keep away from the magnet of Mrs. Hartley's invitation, has followed it to the fireplace.

'The 15th of September,' repeats the other, dismayed; 'is it possible that it is not till the 15th of September? Oh, what a long time off! How I wish that I could fall asleep now, and only wake up on the very morning!'

Peggy sighs. There is to her something terrible in her sister's eagerness, knowing, as she does, how little it has in common with the wholesome hearty hunger for pleasure of her age. But she speaks cheerfully:

'The play will be the better acted; the floor will be the better waxed.'

'I am sure that it was *he* who reminded them to ask us; I am sure that they would never have remembered us but for *him*,' pursues the young girl, colouring with pleasure. 'He used to say—indeed,' still further brightening, 'he said it again not so long ago, that he always felt a sensation of emptiness about a room that I was not in.'

'Oh, Miss Lambton!' cries Franky, bursting into the room, and bringing with him a somewhat powerful agricultural odour, 'we have been having *such* fun! we have been helping Alfred to fork manure. Nanny is *so* cross; she is coming after me—oh, do not let her find me! do hide me somewhere!'

But unfortunately Master Harborough's attendant is able to track him by another sense than sight, and from the shelter of Peggy's petticoat, magnanimously extended to protect him, he is presently drawn forth, and carried off, in company with his sister, to a purification profoundly deprecated by both.

For the next four weeks the Hartley card of invitation remains enthroned in the place of honour on Peggy's chimney-piece. Festivities are not so rife in the neighbourhood of the little Red House that it runs any risk of being dethroned, or of even having its eminence shared. Freddy has been affectionately taxed by his betrothed with having been instrumental in its despatch, but he has delicately denied.

'I always think,' he says prettily, 'that there is a magnet in the heart of all good people, drawing them towards each other; so that you see, dear, there was no need for me.'

The magnet of which he speaks must be in great force in his own case just now, judging by the frequency with which the ten long miles—always charged by the flymen as eleven—between the Manor and the home of the Hartleys are spanned by him. Prue does not always hear from himself of these excursions, though, indeed, he makes no great secret of them. Oftener an officious young Evans thrusts upon her the fact of having met him going in the accustomed direction; oftener still, the little Harboroughs innocently mention it as a thing of course; oftenest, her own heart divines it. And after all, what can be more natural than that at such a juncture his services should be needed and asked; than that he whose mouth has always been so full of the beauty and duty of living for others, should give them readily and freely? And again, what can be more natural or obvious than that his presence should be needed, should be indispensable in fact, in the endless discussions as to the choice of a play, interminable as the ever famous ones in 'Mansfield Park;' and that with him it should rest to adjust the jarring claims of the young Hartleys, of whom some pipe, some harp, and some do neither, but are none the less resolved to display themselves in one capacity or another before the ——shire public? And, later on, when the stage with its decorations arrives from London, what can be more natural than that those among the scenes which do not commend themselves to the actors' liking should be painted afresh; and that again Freddy's unerring taste and illimitable good-nature should be called into play?

'You really are too good-natured, Mr. Ducane,' Mrs. Hartley reiterates; 'you let them impose upon you. You really ought to think of yourself sometimes; it does not do not to think of one's self sometimes; one has to be selfish now and again, in this world.' And Freddy, aloft on a ladder with a large brush in his hand, and smouches of paint on his charming face, smiles delightfully, and says he should be sorry to have to think that. And when he does make time for a visit to the Red House, he is so affectionate; brings with him such an atmosphere of enjoyment; is so full of interesting pieces of news about the progress of the preparations, of pleasant speeches as to the intense eagerness on the part of the whole Hartley family to make Prue's acquaintance, that for twenty-four hours after each of them her spirits maintain the level to which the fillip of his easy tendernesses has lifted them.

'It would be tiresome if it were to last for ever, I grant you,' she says to Peggy one day, with an assumption of placid indifference; 'but as it is a temporary thing—so very temporary—why, in less than a fortnight now it will be over, how silly I should be to care! In less than a fortnight' (her face growing suffused with a happy pink) 'we shall go back to our old ways; and the Hartleys will be off in their fine yacht round the world—and good luck go with them! I *like* him to help them. I tell you I like it,' reiterating the assertion as if knowing it to be one not very easily to be believed; 'it would not have tallied at all with my idea of him if he had refused.'

And Peggy only rejoins despondently: 'Well, dear, if you are pleased, so am I.'

Not, indeed, that Margaret contents herself with this depressed acquiescence in her sister's eclipsed condition. She has on several occasions, and despite many gently conveyed hints on his part that she is not judicious in her choice of opportunities, endeavoured to tackle Mr. Ducane on the subject of his future, to obtain some definite answer from him as to the choice of a profession, etc. But her unsuccess has been uniform and unvaried. It is not that he has ever refused to discuss the question with her. Indeed, in looking back upon their conversation she is always puzzled to remember how it was that he had eluded her. She has generally ended by tracing his escape back to some exalted abstraction; some sentiment too delicate for the wear and tear of everyday life; some bubbling jest.

'You know, dear,' he says to her very kindly one day, when she has been pointing out to him, with some warmth, the entire frivolity of his present mode of life; 'you know, dear, that you and I are always a little at odds as to the true meaning of the word "education." I have always felt that the soul's education can be more furthered by what the world calls "play," than by what it has chosen to define specially as "work." There is no use in forcing one's spirit, dear Peggy. One is much more likely to learn the lines that one's true development ought to follow by sitting still and listening humbly to the voice of the Erd Geist.'

'And the voice of the Erd Geist tells you to paint drop-scenes for the Hartleys'?' replies Peggy witheringly; but her sarcasm furthers her cause as little as do her more serious reasonings.

At the end of the month that intervenes between the arrival of the Hartleys' invitation and the fulfilment of its promise, that cause is exactly where it was. By milady Peggy has been spared any further reference to the subject of her sister's engagement; nor, as far as is known to the girl, has Lady Roupell taken any step such as she had threatened for the separation of the lovers.

With a stab at her heart Peggy recognises the reason of this inaction. The shrewd old woman sees how needless is her interference; and, being kind as well as shrewd, refrains from giving the last unnecessary shove to the tottering card-house of poor Prue's felicity.

CHAPTER XXXIII

'At Charing Cross, hard by the way
Where we, thou know'st, do sell our hay,
There is a house with stairs;
And there did I see coming down
Such folk as are not in our town;
Forty at least in pairs.'

On the night of the 15th of September a great many more than forty pairs of feet were passing up and down the stairs of that magnificent specimen of Jackson's domestic architecture, the Hartleys' new palace in ——shire. Amateur theatricals are, strange as it may appear, since going to see them is almost invariably the triumph of hope over experience, always an attractive bait to hold out to a country neighbourhood. Apart from the pleasure of thinking how much better than do the actors, one could have played their parts one's self; and that opposite and more good-natured, if not quite so acute pleasure, of wondering with Miss Snevellici's patroness, 'How they ever learnt to act as they do, laughing in one piece, and crying in the next, and so natural in both,' there is, in the present case, an element of curiosity which adds an additional poignancy to the expectation of enjoyment usual in such cases.

It is the Hartley *coup d'essai* in hospitality in the county, and there is a widespread interest manifested as to how they will do it. Almost as widespread is the comfortable conviction that they will do it well.

An old-established squire who has been seated on his modest acres for a couple of hundred years may venture to invite his friends to dance on a sticky floor to the sound of a piano, and to wash away their fatigue in libations of 50-shilling champagne; but the millionaire, who has only within the last year set an uncertain foot upon the land, is not likely to try any such experiments upon the county's patience. It is, then, with a confident hope of Gunter and Coote and Tinney that the occupants of most of the carriages step out on the red cloth—a hope that the first glimpse of the banks of orchids that line the entrance-hall goes far to make a certainty.

From the minds of the occupants of one carriage, to whose turn, after long waiting in the endless string, it at length comes to set free its load, Gunter, Coote and Tinney, and orchids are equally distant. Milady's head is still running on her Patience, which, by the aid of a carriage-lamp and a pack of tiny cards, she has been playing contentedly during the whole of the long ten miles. The little portion of Peggy's heart that is not filled with an aching compassion and anxiety for her sister is pierced by the fear of the extreme likelihood, in so promiscuous a gathering of three-fourths of the county, of her finding herself face to face with the one woman whom she would compass sea and land to avoid, and with the man whom that woman habitually carries in her train.

And Prue?

'I think he is sure to be at the door to receive us, do not you?' she has whispered to her sister, under cover of milady's absorption in her solitary game, while they are still waiting in the string; 'not that I shall be so silly as to attach any importance to it if he is not; but after a whole week!' stifling a sigh. 'Oh dear!' letting down the glass and craning her neck impatiently out, 'shall we never get there? I see carriage-lamps for half a mile ahead of us still!'

A whole week! It is true. For a whole week the Red House has been favoured with no glimpse of Mr. Ducane. How should it, indeed, since he has been compelled by the exigencies of his situation to take up his abode entirely at the scene of his labours? Of what use to waste upon the long ride there and back time so precious in a last week? the time of one upon whose inexhaustible stock of ability and good-nature every one thinks him or herself entitled to draw.

But though he has been unable to present himself in person to his betrothed, he has had time to scribble her a tiny pencil-note, just a word—but then how little can the value of a letter be measured by its length!—praying her to keep a place for him by her side at the theatricals.

'If my Prue refuses, it will be all over with my pleasure,' he ends simply.

The carriage, after many tantalising halts opposite dark laurels, draws up finally before a blaze of electric light, a crowd of powdered footmen, an arching of palm-boughs; and milady steps deliberately out in her fur boots and her diamond 'fender,' followed by her two *protégées*. Freddy is not at the door to receive them; and the moment that she has discovered this fact, Prue sees the irrationality of the hope that had led her ever to expect that he would be. He is naturally not in the cloak-room, where milady seems, to the girl's passionate impatience, to loiter unconscionably long, tugging at the strings of her *sortie de bal*, which have got into a knot, and talking to the numerous friends she meets there. To do her justice, it is not any care for her toilette that detains her. She would quite as soon have the famous tiara—her 'fender,' as she always calls it—which the county has admired for fifty years, on crooked as straight. The county expects to see it on great occasions, and so she puts it on; but if Mrs. Mason were to dispose it behind before, the circumstance would disturb but very slightly her lady's equanimity. Mr. Ducane is not, as far as can be made out by a first glance, in the magnificent music-room, to-night arranged as a theatre, and at whose door Mrs. Hartley stands, smiling and splendid, to receive her guests. But though Prue's eye has as yet to fast from the sight of her betrothed, her ear at least is gladdened by his praises.

'Oh, Lady Roupell, I do not know how we ever can thank Mr. Ducane enough!' she hears Mrs. Hartley exclaim. 'My girls say they do not know what they should have done without him—so kind, so clever, and unselfish is not the word!'

Milady grunts.

'No, I do not think it is,' she says, half *sotto voce*, as she passes on.

At the first look, the room, superb as are its proportions, seems already full; but a closer inspection reveals at the upper end several still vacant rows of arm-chairs, reserved by the host and hostess for those among their guests whom they most delight to honour. To this favoured category belongs milady, and she is presently installed with her two young friends by a *sémillant* papa Hartley, in the very middle of the front rank. For the present, nothing can be easier than for Prue to keep the chair at her side vacant. She has already anxiously and surreptitiously spread her white frock over it. Each of earth's glories has probably its attendant disadvantages; a warm and consoling doctrine for those to whose share not much of life's gilding falls; nor is a seat in the front row of synagogue or playhouse any exception to this rule. It has the inevitable drawback, that except by an uncomfortable contortion of the neck-muscles, it is impossible for its occupants to see what is going on in the body of the room; and the view of foot-lights and a drop-scene is one that after a while is apt to pall.

Prue's head is continually turning over her shoulder, as, from the body of the long hall, all blazing with pink-shaded electric lamps, comes the noise of gowns rustling, of steps and voices, as people settle into their seats. At first she had had no cause for uneasiness. The people, as they tide in, conscious of no particular claim to chief places, pack themselves, with laughs and greetings to acquaintances, into the unreserved seats. But presently Mr. Hartley is seen convoying a party of ladies and men to the top of the room with the same evidences of deferential tenderness as he had shown to milady; and no sooner are they disposed of, according to their merits, than he reappears with the same smile, and a new batch. This continues to happen until the human tide, like its prototype in its inexorable march over swallowed sands and drunk rocks, has advanced, despite the piteous protest in Prue's eyes, to within three chairs of her. Yes, including that one so imperfectly veiled by the poor child's skirt, there are only three vacant seats remaining.

'Oh, I wish he would come! Oh, I wish he would come!' she repeats, with something that grows ever nearer and nearer to a sob in her voice. 'Oh, Peggy, do you think he will not come after all? You are longer-sighted than I am; do look if you can see him anywhere! Oh, I wish he would come! I shall not be able to keep this chair for him much longer, and then——'

Her words are prophetic. Scarcely are they out of her mouth before the vision of the radiant host is again seen nearing them, with a fresh freight—a freight that rustles and jingles and chatters louder than any of the previous ones.

'Oh yes, do put me in a good place!' a high and apparently extravagantly cheerful voice is heard exclaiming; 'I always like the best places if I can get them—do not you? and I mean to applaud more loudly than anybody. I have been engaged by Freddy Ducane as a claque; and I assure you I mean to keep my word.'

Although she has been expecting it—although she has told herself that to hear it is among the most probable of the evening's chances, yet, at the sound of that clear thin voice, Peggy turns extremely cold. It has come then. In a second she will certainly be called upon to hear another voice. Let her then brace herself to bear it decently. Her hands clasp themselves involuntarily, and she draws in her breath; but she cannot lift her eyes. She sits looking straight before her, waiting. But instead of the tones that with such sick dread she is expecting, she hears only milady's voice—milady's voice not in its suavest key.

'Oh! it is you, is it? How many of you are there?—because we are pretty full here; and I suppose you do not mean to sit upon our knees.'

'There is nothing I should like better!' cries Lady Betty friskily. 'You are looking perfectly delightful to-night; all the more so because your fender is quite on one side. Come now, do not be ill-natured, but make room for me; you know I am not very——'

Peggy hears the voice break off abruptly; and involuntarily her eyes, hitherto glued to the back of the chair in front of her, snatch a hasty glance in Lady Betty's direction. She has turned away, and is addressing Mr. Hartley in an altered and hurried key.

'After all, I hope you will not think me very changeable, but I believe I should like to sit a little farther back; one sees better, and hears better, and gets a better general idea.'

'She is going away!' whispers Prue, with a long quivering sigh of relief. 'Oh, I was so frightened! I thought she was going to take my chair. Why did she go? She could not have seen us!'

But this is not quite the conclusion arrived at by Peggy, as her eyes follow Betty's retreating figure—Betty, with her

> 'Little head
> Sunning with curls'

that go to bed in a box—Betty, with the docile Harborough and a couple of Guardsmen at her heels; and—without John Talbot! That for one chance evening she should happen to lack his attendance is, after all, but small evidence against his being still riveted with her fetters; but Peggy's heart swells with a disproportionate elation at the discovery. There is, alas! not much likelihood of poor Prue's feeling a like expansion; for scarcely has she finished drawing the long breath caused her by Betty's retreat, than the seat which the latter had spared is approached, settled upon, and irrevocably occupied—poor Prue's barriers politely but ruthlessly swept away.

She has attempted a hurried protest, but it has not been even heard; and now it is too late, for a bell has rung. The curtain has swept aloft, with less of hesitation and dubiousness as to the result than is generally the case with amateur curtains, and discloses to view the second Miss Hartley seated under the rustic berceau of a wayside Italian wine-shop, in peasant's cap and bodice, soliloquising rather nervously and at some length. What is the drift of that soliloquy; or of the dialogue that follows with a person of a bandit nature, whom it takes some moments for his acquaintance to decipher into a young man Hartley; or of the jiggy catchy songs with which the piece is freely interspersed, Peggy will never know to her last day.

Before her eyes, indeed, there is a phantasmagoria of people going and coming in a blaze of light—of more be-peasanted Misses Hartley, with more banditted brothers; in her ears a brisk dialogue that must be funny, judging from the roars of laughter coming from behind her; of smart galloping quartettes and trios that must be humorous and musical, from the storm of applause and encores that greet them. But to her brain penetrate none of the gay and smiling images conveyed by her senses. Her brain is wholly occupied by the painful and impossible effort to calm Prue, whose agitation, rendered more unmanageable by the weakness of her state of health and the lack of any habit of self-government, threatens to become uncontrollable.

'Oh, Peggy, why has not he come? What has become of him? Where can he be?' she keeps moaningly whispering.

Peggy has taken hold of one of her sister's feverish hands, whose dry fire is felt even through her glove, and presses it now and again.

'He will be here directly,' she answers soothingly; 'no doubt he could not get away. You heard how useful he has been! Probably he is helping them behind the scenes. Do not you think that you could try to look a little less miserable? I am so afraid that people will remark it.'

'If he is behind the scenes,' moans Prue, not paying any heed to, evidently hardly hearing, this gentle admonition, 'he is with her. You see that she is not acting either! Wherever they are, they are together! Oh, Peggy, I think I shall die of misery!'

The close of her sentence is drowned in a tempest of riotous applause, and Peggy's eyes involuntarily turn to the stage, to learn the cause. One of the performers, who has been throughout pre-eminently the funny man of the piece, is singing a solo, accompanied by many facetious gestures. The drift of the song is the excessive happiness of the singer—a theme which is enlarged upon through half a dozen successive verses:

> 'The lark is blithe,
> And the summer fly;
> Blithe is the cricket,
> And blithe am I.
> None so blithe, so blithe as I!'

Peggy happens to have some acquaintance with the singer off the stage; knows him to be sickly, melancholy, poor; to-night racked with neuralgia, yet obliged to do his little tricks, and go through his small antics, on penalty of banishment from that society, his sole *raison d'être* in which is his gift of making people laugh.

'La Comédie Humaine!' she says to herself—'La Comédie Humaine!'

251

CHAPTER XXXIV

'We men may say more, swear more; but indeed,
Our shows are more than will, for still we prove
Much in our vows, but little in our love.'

The Hartleys are wise enough to avoid the error so common amongst amateur actors and managers, of prolonging their treat until pleasure is turned into weariness. They are obviously mindful of the fact that among their audience are a number of dancing feet, whose owners not even the acting of Rachel or Mrs. Siddons would indemnify, in their own opinion, for having the fair proportions of their dancing hours thrown away. The operetta has only three acts, and is followed by no farce or afterpiece. In point of fact, it is contained within the limits of a couple of hours. Yet to two of its auditors it appears practically interminable. To two amongst them it seems as if there never would be an end to its songs, its facetious misunderstandings, and jocose makings up; and when at length the curtain falls amid a hurricane of applause, only to be instantly drawn up again in order that the whole of the final quartette may be repeated, it appears as if they must have sat watching it for nights. At last the curtain drops finally. At last there is an end to the endless encores. The performers, in answer to the shouts which demand them, have appeared in turn before the curtain, and made their bows, and picked up their bouquets, with such differing degrees of grace and *aplomb* as their native gifts, or more or less familiarity with the situation, allow.

The sad little merryman has cut his final caper, and made a grimace of so surpassing a ludicrousness as will allow him to be peacefully melancholy for the rest of the evening.

And now all eyes are turned away from the stage; all tongues are loosed. The doors at the end of the hall are opened, and a stream of people is beginning rapidly to issue through them. Every one has risen and is looking about, glad to shift their position, say 'how do you do' to their friends, and exchange comments on play and actors.

There is a general stir and buzz; a seeking out of expected friends, and delighted greeting of unexpected ones; a reciprocal examination of gowns, now first possible; and a universal aspiration for supper.

Milady and her girls have risen with the others. Prue, indeed, has been the first person in the room on her legs. She is looking round, like the rest of the world; at least, so to a casual observer it might appear. But, alas! what is there in common between the smiling careless glances, lighting with easy

252

amusement on indifferent objects, and the tragic searching—terrible in its one-ideaed intentness—of those despairing blue eyes? Peggy has firm hold of one burning hand, and is murmuring broken sentences of comfort into her inattentive ear.

'Yes, dear, yes! I will go with you wherever you like; but you know we cannot quite leave milady; and he is more likely to find us here. I dare say he has been looking at us all the while from behind the scenes, trying to see how you were enjoying yourself.' She leaves off hopelessly, since Prue is not listening to her. Snatches of talk, disjointed and mixed, reach her ear.

'Jackson was the architect; built the new schools at Oxford; they always strike one as rather like a splendid country house.'

'Thoroughly well built; made all his own bricks; sent them up to London to be tested; best that ever were made!'

'Really nearly as good as professionals; better than some professionals; might easily be that. They say that the one who acts best of all did not act to-night— the eldest.'

'Why did not she, I wonder?'

'Better employed perhaps—ha! ha!'

At the same moment Peggy feels a convulsive pressure on her arm, and hears Prue's passionately excited voice:

'There he is! at the far end of the room; he is looking for us! Oh, how can we make him see us?'

She has raised herself on tiptoe, and is sending a look of such agonised entreaty down the hall as, one would think, must penetrate even the mass of shifting, buzzing humanity that intervenes between her and its object. Perhaps it does. Perhaps the magnet that Freddy once prettily suggested to be in the hearts of all good people drawing them together is exercising its influence on his. At all events, in a few minutes they see him smilingly pushing his way, stopped at every step by greetings and compliments—for it has somehow become generally diffused through the room that to him is to be ascribed most of the glory of the entertainment—through the crowd. In a moment more he is before them.

'Here you are, you dear things!' he says, taking a hand of each, looking flushed and handsome, and speaking in an excited voice. 'Did not it go off wonderfully well?—not a hitch anywhere. Did you hear the prompter once? No? Neither of you? I thought not; and yet if you had seen us half an hour before the curtain drew up, you would have said that the whole thing was going to be a fiasco.'

He stops to draw a long breath of self-congratulation.

'I kept the chair beside me as long as I could,' says Prue, in a faltering voice; 'I did my best.'

His eye rests on her for a moment with a puzzled air—on her small face, flushed like his own; but, alas! how differently! It is evident that for the first second he does not comprehend her, having entirely forgotten his own request. Then recollecting:

'How good of you, dear!' he says affectionately. 'Of course, it was a bitter disappointment to me, too; but on occasions of this kind,' with a slight resigned shrug, 'one must, of course, give up all idea of individual enjoyment.'

He is such an embodiment of radiant joy as he speaks, that Margaret cannot help darting an indignant look at him—a bolt aimed so full and true, that it hits him right in his laughing eyes.

'Of course,' he says, reddening under it, 'I do not mean to say that there has not been a good deal of incidental enjoyment; but *you*, dear,' turning to Prue, with lowered voice—'you who always see things intuitively—you will understand what a distinction there is between pleasure and happiness —*Innigkeit*!'

She has lifted her eyes, cleared for the moment of their agonised seeking, to his, and is beginning a little trembling eager speech to assure him of her complete comprehension; but his own mind having meanwhile flown off at a tangent, he breaks in upon it:

'Was not that song excellent—

> "The lark is blithe,
> And the summer fly"?

Quite as good as anything of Grossmith's—do not you think so! Did not it make you laugh tremendously? Oh, I hope, dear,' with an accent of rather pained reproach, 'that it made you laugh!'

Prue hesitates. In point of fact she had not heard one word of the jocose ditty alluded to; as, during the whole of it, she had been keeping up a conversation in heart-broken whispers with Peggy.

'Oh yes; of course,' she answers nervously; 'it was very funny—excessively funny! I—I—should like to hear it again. I—I—am sure that it is one of those things that one would think much funnier the second time than the first.'

'It is as good as anything of Grossmith's,' repeats Freddy confidently. Then, beginning to hum a valse, 'You can have no idea what a floor this is! Be sure, dear, that you keep quantities of dances for me!'

'Oh yes; of course—of course,' replies she, with tremulous ecstasy. 'Which—which would you like?'

But before Mr. Ducane has time to signify his preferences, a third person intervenes. Poor Prue has often expressed a wish to see the eldest Miss Hartley; but the mode in which our wishes are granted is not always quite that which we should have chosen.

'Oh, Mr. Ducane,' she says, hurrying up, 'I am so sorry to interrupt you; but it is the old story,' laughing, and with an apologetic bow to Prue—'we cannot get on without you. We are so puzzled to know who it is that papa ought to take in to supper! Is it Lady Manson, or Lady Chester? We thought you could tell us which is the oldest creation.'

Freddy has not an idea, but instantly volunteers to go off in search of a 'Peerage' to decide this knotty point; and Miss Hartley, having civilly lingered a moment to excuse herself to the Miss Lambtons, and to remark in almost the same words as her mother had used upon the extraordinary unselfishness of Mr. Ducane, flits away after him.

'It was too bad of her,' says Prue, with a trembling lip. 'She might at least have let him tell me how many dances he wanted; but'—brightening up—'he said "quantities," did not he? You heard him?'

Peggy's rejoinder is prevented by her attention being at the same moment claimed by milady, and by a general forward movement of the company, which has been requested by Mrs. Hartley to vacate the hall in order that it may be got ready for dancing.

In the slight confusion and pushing that follows, Peggy finds herself separated from her sister and her chaperon; and a few minutes afterwards, the joyful tidings having spread abroad that the supper-room doors are open, an acquaintance offers her his arm to lead her thither. She looks around anxiously once again in search of Prue; but not being able to catch a glimpse of either her or Lady Roupell, can only hope that both have reached the goal of supper before her.

The room is of course thronged—when was a just-opened supper-room not crowded?—and it is some little while before Peggy's partner is able to elbow a way for her to the table, which, when she reaches it, is already robbed of its virgin glory. She looks down the long rows of moving jaws; catches milady's eye—milady eating *pâté de foie gras*, which always makes her ill; snatches a

255

far glimpse of Mr. Evans setting down a champagne-glass, with the beatific smile of one who, drinking, remembers the Vicarage small-beer; and has a nearer, fuller view of Lady Betty, rosy and naked as Aphrodite, laughing at the top of her voice, and pulling a chicken's merry-thought with one of her Guardsmen to see which will be married first.

Peggy quickly averts her eyes; and, bringing them home, they alight upon Mrs. Evans, whom, by a singular accident, she finds next door to her.

Mrs. Evans, as we know, cannot come under the condemnation of those who 'have not on a wedding-garment,' since she never wears anything else. Despite her old dyed gown, however, she is obviously enjoying herself with the best.

'This is not the sort of thing that one sees every day,' cries she, in a voice of elated wonder, surveying the ocean of delicacies around her. 'I only wish I could get hold of a *menu* to take home with me! I am so glad we came. I was not at all anxious to come, on account of the distance; in fact, I yielded entirely on Mr. Evans's account. He is in one of his low ways; you know what that means! He wants change; we all want change. Did you hear the mistake he made last Sunday in the Psalms? He said, "In the midst were the damsels playing with the *minstrels.*"'

Peggy laughs absently.

'It sounds rather frisky.'

'I only hope that nobody noticed it,' pursues the Vicaress; 'he always makes those kind of mistakes when he wants change. Dear me!' casting a look and a long sigh of envy round the room; 'if I had a house like this, I should never want change for my part; and to think that it is to be shut up for the whole of the winter—for a whole year, in fact!'

The Hartleys' house has not, so far, afforded Peggy such a large harvest of pleasure that she is able very cordially to echo this lamentation.

'What can possess any one to go round the world passes my understanding,' continues her interlocutor, pelican-like, as she speaks, forcing some nougat for her offspring surreptitiously into a little bag under cover of the table-edge; 'not but what they will do it in all possible luxury, of course—cheval glasses, and oil-paintings, and Indian carpets, just as one has in one's own drawing-room.'

At this last clause, sad and inattentive as she is, Peggy cannot forbear a smile of amusement, as the image of the Vicarage Kidder rises before her mind's eye; but it is very soon dissipated by her neighbour's next remark.

'By the bye, some one was telling me to-night that Freddy Ducane is to be of the party. I assured her, looking wise, that I knew better; but she persisted that she had had it upon the best authority—one of the family, as far as I could understand.'

She may continue her speech to the ambient air; for, when next she looks up from her larceny of bonbons, Peggy is gone. The hall, meanwhile, has been cleared of its innumerable chairs, and its theatrical properties generally, and converted into a back-room, with that surprising rapidity that unlimited money, with practically unlimited labour at its beck and call, can always command.

No sooner have the guests well supped, than, with no tiresome interregnum, no waiting and wondering, they may, if they list, begin to dance. A smooth sea of Vienna parquet spreads before them, and established on the stage, the British Grenadiers themselves—no mere piano and fiddle—are striking up the initial quadrille. It is some little time before Peggy is able to make her way between the forming sets to where milady sits, her coronet more hopelessly askew than ever, and an expression of good-humoured resignation on her face.

'My mind is braced for the worst,' she says good-naturedly; 'get along both of you and dance. Not that there can be much dancing in this silly child,' pointing to Prue; 'she must be as empty as a drum. She has not eaten a mouthful.'

She shrugs her shoulders, since it is evident that Prue does not hear. In a state of preoccupation so intense as that of the young girl's, it would be difficult for anything presented by the senses to make its way into the brain. She is standing stiffly upright, her head and chin slightly advanced, as one looking with passionate eagerness ahead. Her lips are moving, as if she were saying some one thing over and over to herself. Whatever of her face is not lividly white is burning; and her eyes——

As she so stands, an acquaintance comes up, and asks her for the dance, now well begun. She does not understand him at first; but, on his repeating his request, she refuses it curtly.

'Thank you, I am engaged.'

'If you are neither of you going to dance,' says milady, seeing both her *protégées* remaining standing beside her, and speaking with a slight and certainly pardonable irritation, 'I may as well go home to my blessed bed.'

Go home! Prue has caught the words, and cast a glance of agony at her sister. *Go home!*

'Do not be impatient, dear milady,' says Margaret, trying to speak lightly and look gay; 'you will be crying out in quite another key just now. I am engaged for nearly all the programme. Ah, here comes my partner!'

For by this time the quadrille has come to an end, and a valse has struck up. To join it, Margaret walks off reluctantly, looking behind her. She is profoundly unwilling to leave her sister in her present state; but, since to dance is the only means of averting milady's fulfilment of her threat of going home, there is no alternative.

To most girls of Peggy's age the joy in dancing for dancing's sake is a thing of the past; but to her, from the innocency of her nature, and her little contact with the world, which has preserved in her a freshness of sensation that usually does not survive eighteen, the pleasure in the mere movement of her sound young limbs, in the lilt of the measure and the wind of her own fleetness, is as keen as ever.

Peggy loves dancing. To-night she has a partner worthy of her, in her ears brave music beyond praise, under her light feet a Vienna parquet of slippery perfection; and she is no more conscious of these advantages than if she were dancing in clogs on a brick floor. Whenever she pauses—and, long-winded as she is, she must pause now and again, in whatever part of the pink-light-flooded room her partner lands her, whether by the great bank of hothouse flowers at the lower end, or near the blaring Grenadiers at the top, or beneath one of the portraits of famous musicians that line the side walls—it seems to her that absolutely nothing meets her eyes but that one tiny burning face, stretched always forward in the same attitude, with its lips moving, and its eyes turning hither and thither in forlorn and desperate search. Prue is not dancing.

As Peggy, answering absently and *à bâtons rompus*, the civil speeches of her companion, watches, in a pained perplexity, the features whose misery has so effectually poisoned her own evening, she sees a fresh expression settle upon them, an expression no longer of deferred and piteous expectation, but of acute and intolerable wretchedness. She is not long in learning the cause. Following the direction of Prue's glance, her own alights upon a couple that have but just joined the dance. It is needless to name them.

Peggy's partner catches himself wondering whether it can be any of his own harmless remarks that has brought the frown that is so indubitably lowering there to her smooth forehead, or that has made her red lips close in so tight and thin. He wonders a little, too, at the request that immediately follows these phenomena.

'Would you mind taking me to Miss Hartley and her partner? I want to speak to them; we might dance there.'

A minute of smooth whirling lands her at Freddy's side, and fortunately for her, at the same moment some one addressing the daughter of the house from behind takes off her attention.

'Are not you going to dance with Prue?' she asks in a stern breathless whisper. 'Have you forgotten that you are engaged to Prue?'

He looks at her with a gentle astonishment.

'What are you talking about, dear? Is it a thing that I am likely to forget? Of course I must get through my duty-dances first. Dear Prue is the last person not to understand that. You are looking *splendid* to-night, Peg! perhaps because you are so ill-tempered—evil passions always become you. You have not a dance to spare me, I suppose? What a floor! Tra la la!'

Away he scampers with Miss Hartley, and Peggy, curtly resisting all her ill-used swain's entreaties to take another turn, insists upon being led back there and then to her chaperon. Prue shall not, through her fault, have one second's more suspense to endure.

'It is all right!' she says eagerly, under her breath, into the young girl's ear; 'he is getting through his duty-dances first. It is all right.'

CHAPTER XXXV

But the execution of Mr. Ducane's duty-dances is apparently no short task, nor one lightly or quickly accomplished. But few of them, as it turns out, are danced in the ball-room in the eye of the world, and of the electric light. A far larger number are danced on sofas, in obscure corners of little-frequented boudoirs, on steps of the stairs, and under the palm-fans and tree-ferns of the conservatory.

And meanwhile the night swings on. Dance has followed dance. The feet fall pat to the perfect time of the soldiers' music: valse, galop, polka, mazurka, Lancers—Peggy dances them all.

In the Lancers chance brings her close to Lady Betty, who is romping through them with a staid County Member, whom to the petrifaction of his wife, watching horror-struck from afar, she makes romp flagrantly too. Her voice throughout the evening is heard, penetratingly high, above the band; her laugh seems to be ringing from every corner of the room, accompanying her extraordinary antics. For Lady Betty is by no means on her best behaviour to-night, and permits herself such innocent and humorous playfulnesses as putting a spoonful of ice down the back of one of the young Hartleys, popping a fool's-cap out of a cracker on the head of a bald old gentleman perfectly unknown to her, etc. She is evidently not fretting very badly at Talbot's absence. So Margaret thinks, as with a sort of unwilling fascination she watches her.

Lady Betty is evidently in precisely the same mood as she was on that evening when she had favoured milady's guests at the Manor with her remarkable song. It would take uncommonly little persuasion to-night to induce her to sing—

'Oh! who will press that lily hand?'

'I think she is *drunk*!' says Mrs. Evans charitably. 'I am sure she acts as if she were. If *I* were to behave like that, I should expect men to take any kind of liberty with me. I should not feel that I had any right to complain if they did.'

Peggy laughs. The idea of Mrs. Evans dancing the can-can, and getting kissed for her pains, is so irresistibly comic that for a minute or two she cannot help herself.

Lady Roupell has grown tired of scolding Prue for her obstinate refusal of all invitations to dance. Milady has happily fallen in with an old friend, whose path hers had not crossed for thirty years. With him she fights o'er again the battles of her youth, and forgets her 'blessed bed.' She goes in to supper a second time, and has more *pâté de foie gras*. Peggy sees it in the guilt of her eye when she comes out.

And meanwhile Peggy herself dances on indefatigably, returning, however, rigorously at the end of each dance to her chaperon, in order to assure herself that there is no change for the better in the position of Prue.

None! none! none! Always standing on precisely the same spot; the poor little figure rigidly upright; the flushed cheekbones; the straining eyes. Always? No, thank God, not always! At last it is gone! At last she finds its place vacant.

'Where is Prue?' she asks eagerly, forgetting her usual gentle good manners so far as to break with her question into milady's *tête-à-tête*.

'Prue!' repeats the other, looking round rather tartly from her interrupted conversation; 'God bless my soul, child! how can I tell?' and so resumes her talk.

But though this is not a very lucid explanation of her sister's absence, Peggy returns from it with a considerably lightened heart. Since it is a matter of certainty that Prue would never have consented to dance with any one but Freddy, he must have come at last. They are nowhere in sight, therefore he must have carried her off to some retired corner, where he is persuading her— so easy of persuasion, poor soul—of how much he has been suffering all evening, and how extremely loftily he has behaved. Of whatever he is persuading her, her long agony is for this evening at least probably at an end.

Peggy draws a deep breath at the thought, and for the first time becomes aware how good the floor is, and how pleasant the long swallow-swoop from end to end of the ball-room. The crowd is growing much thinner. People who have a long distance to drive are already gone. Mrs. Evans, bulging at every point with the result of her thefts, and driving the reluctant Vicar before her, takes herself off, having indulged herself in one parting whisper to Peggy, to the effect that she 'shall not bow to Lady Betty, even if she looks as if she expected it.' For Betty is still here, and having run up the whole gamut of her schoolboy follies, having grown tired of throwing tarts at her admirers, and pelting them with lobster claws, has settled down into a steady audacious open flirtation with a Rural Dean, the sight of whose good lady's jealous writhings seems to afford her a great deal of innocent joy.

Lady Roupell's old friend has been reluctantly reft away from her by his party, and she is beginning to show signs of uneasiness, as Peggy can see from a distance. But since Prue's place beside her is still vacant, the elder sister is resolved that no action of hers—however apparently called for by the ordinary rules of politeness—shall tend to shorten the few brief moments of happiness that have come, however tardily, to sweeten her evening's long bitterness. She has deliberately dodged milady's messengers sent in pursuit of her, has evaded them behind doors, and has slipped past them in passages; and it is not until she catches a distant glimpse of Prue returning to her chaperon on Mr. Ducane's arm, that she at length allows herself to be captured. Milady receives her rather testily.

'Come along! come along!' cries she fussily; 'why did not you come before? I do not want to help blow out the lights.'

But Peggy does not answer. Her eyes are fixed in a shocked astonishment on Prue. Instead of the radiant transformation she had expected to find in her—a transformation hitherto as certain under three kind words from Freddy, as the supplanting of night by red-rose day in the visible world—she sees her livid, and with an expression of hopeless stunned despair, such as never before in her saddest moments has been worn by it, on her drawn face. Her hand has fallen from Freddy's arm, and her sister snatches it.

'What is it, Prue? What is it?'

The girl does not seem to hear at first; then:

'Nothing, nothing!' she says stiffly. 'Home; let us go home.'

'She is tired!' cries Mr. Ducane—he too looks pale—caressingly lifting her other hand, which lies perfectly limp and nerveless in his clasp, and pressing it to his lips; 'our Prue is dead-beat. Dear milady, you know you never can recollect that we are not all Titans like yourself. She is worn out. Are not you, Prue?'

'She would have been all right if she had had some supper,' says milady gruffly, probably thinking in bitterness of spirit how greatly to their reciprocal advantage it would be, if a balance could be struck between her own past refreshments and Prue's. Then she adds very sharply, and with an obvious disposition in her tone to hustle her graceful nephew, 'I do not know what you are dawdling here for? Why do not you go and look after the carriage?'

He does not require to be told this twice, and by the alacrity with which he obeys the command, Peggy knows that it comes at this moment most welcome. No one could enjoy looking in a face with an expression such as Prue's now wears, knowing that he himself has brought it there; and for one so especially partial as Mr. Ducane to wreathed smiles, it is doubly painful and trying.

The footman and carriage are long in being found. Our party have to wait what seems to them for a good half-hour in the hall, cloaked, and, as far as concerns milady, fur-booted, while through the open hall-door streams in on the mist the flash of carriage-lamps; the frosty breath of horses—frosty though it is only mid-September—the noise of gravel kicked up under hoofs; the sound of other people's shouted names.

Freddy comes back, and stands beside Prue, and addresses her now and again in coaxing undertones, to which—a fact unparalleled in her poor history—she makes no rejoinder. She is standing right in the full draught from the open door. Her cloak is unfastened at the neck. She has evidently not taken the trouble to tie it. The keen north-wester blows in full upon her thin collar-bones; but when Peggy remonstrates with her, she does not seem to hear.

'Lady Roupell's carriage!'

Thank God, the welcome sound at last! Milady, who has been nodding, bounds to her feet and seizes the arm of her obsequious host, who has been struggling under difficulties to give her a pleasant impression of her last moments under his roof; under difficulties, since she has been more than three-quarters asleep. Peggy hurries after her, and Prue and Freddy bring up the rear. There are too many impatient carriages behind Lady Roupell's for there to be any moment for last words. The footman bangs the carriage-door, jumps on the box, and they are off.

Milady does not light her lamp or shuffle her Patience cards again on the homeward drive. She is fast asleep before the Hartleys' park gates are reached; nor does any jolt or jar avail to break her slumber, until she finds herself being bidden good-night to, and thanked by Peggy, at the door of the little Red House. Not one word is exchanged during the whole ten miles between the three occupants of the brougham. Prue has thrown herself into her corner, beside milady. Peggy, sitting back—she always sits with her back to the horses, and has so long pretended to like that position best, that she has at length almost persuaded herself that she does so—leans forward every now and then and peers into the blackness, trying to catch a glimpse of her sister's face or attitude. In vain at first. But after a while—once at a turnpike-gate, once at a flat railway-crossing—a ray of light streams in, and reveals her cast prone and hopeless in her corner, with her face pressed against the cushions.

Before they reach the Red House, though the dawn has not yet come, it is heralded by its dim, gray forerunner—a forerunner that gives shape to the still colourless hedges as they pass, and an outline to the vague trees looming out of the dim seas of chilly vapour, that a couple of hours more will turn into rich green meadows and yellow stubbles. But the light is not strong enough to reach the recesses of the carriage, to touch milady's sleepy head, rolling about in the tiara which makes so uncomfortable a night-cap, or to throw any cruel radiance on the blackness of Prue's despair.

The stopping of the carriage, which partially rouses the old lady, seems not to be even perceived by the younger woman; and it is not until Margaret has stooped over her, pulling her by the arm, and crying in a frightened voice, 'Prue! Prue! we are at home. Do not you hear, dear? at home. Come, come!' that she slowly stirs, and lifts her head. Peggy has given her latch-key to the footman, and herself jumping out of the carriage, stands in the raw dawn wind, and receiving into her arms her staggering and half-conscious sister, carries rather than leads her into the little house, whose door that sister had left with so bounding a heart, such towering hopes of enjoyment seven or eight hours ago. In a moment more, milady—her slumbers already resumed— is borne swiftly away.

Peggy had forbidden the servants to wait up for her. She wishes now that she had not. It is very eerie here alone in the little dark house, whose darkness seems all the blacker for the faint, unsure glimmer of coming day that here and there patches the night's garment; alone with her half-swooning sister. Thank God! there is a lamp still burning in the sitting-hall, though the fire is out, and the air strikes cold. She staggers with her burden to the settle, and laying her gently down upon it, snatches up a flat candlestick, and lighting it at the lamp, hastens away upstairs to the closet where she keeps her drugs for the poor, medicine for the dogs, and her small stock of cordials; and taking thence a flask of brandy, hurries back with it, and pours some down Prue's throat. It is not an easy task to get it down through the girl's set and chattering teeth; but at length she succeeds, and is presently rewarded by seeing signs of returning animation in the poor body, whose feet and hands she is chafing with such a tender vigour.

'I am cold,' says Prue, shivering; 'so cold! May not I go to bed?'

'Do you think that you can walk?' asks Peggy anxiously; 'or shall I carry you?'

'Walk!' repeats the other, with a little dreary smile. 'Why not? There is nothing the matter with me.'

She rises to her feet as she speaks, but totters so pitiably that Peggy again comes to her rescue.

'Of course you can walk,' she says soothingly; 'but I think we are both rather tired: had not we better help each other upstairs?'

And so, with her strong and tender arm flung about her poor Prue's fragile, shivering figure, they slowly climb together—oh, so slowly!—the stairs, down which Prue had leaped with such gaiety eight hours ago.

In the bedroom, which they at last reach, the fire is happily still alight, and only needs a few fresh coals to blaze up cheerfully. But since Prue still shivers, long shudders of cold running down her limbs and convulsing her frame, Peggy wheels an arm-chair close to the fire, and wrapping a warm dressing-gown about her sister, holds her cold feet to the flame, rubbing them between both her hands. For some time Prue's only answer to these attentions is a low moan which, after awhile, shapes itself into articulate words:

'To bed! Let me go to bed!'

And so Peggy, unlacing with a sick heart the poor crumpled gown that had been put on in such pride and freshness over-night, carries its drooping wearer to her bed, and laying her down most gently in it, covers her with the warm bed-clothes, tucking them in, and bidding God bless her, as she has done every night for nigh upon eighteen years.

Prue lies exactly as she had laid her down, with no slightest change of posture, with no attempt at turning over and nestling to sleep; her eyes wide open, with that long shudder recurring at first at intervals. But then this ceases, and she lies like a log—the very dead no stiller than she—staring blankly before her. Peggy sits beside her through the remnant of the night, watching in impotent pain, to see whether the eyelids will never mercifully fall over those wide rigid eyes; watching the insolent light march up and take possession of the curtained room; watching its daring shafts push through chink and cranny even to the dying fire. The clock has struck seven. The servants are up and astir; and—oh, God be thanked!—at length Prue's eyes are closed, and her head has fallen a little sideways on the pillow. Having waited awhile, to assure herself of the blessed fact that she is asleep, Peggy rises noiselessly, and, turning with infinite precaution the door-handle, passes out.

The light seems unutterably glaring in the passage, and her tired eyes blink as they meet it; meeting at the same moment the astonished look in Sarah's face, called forth by seeing her still in her torn and tumbled ball-gown. She has not the heart to spend much time in explanations, but, passing quickly to her own room, tears off the crushed finery, associated in her mind with an evening of such acute misery; and having washed and again dressed in her usual chintz morning-gown, returns to Prue's door, and listening at it for a moment, cautiously enters. But her caution is needless, as her first glance into the room shows her. Though she has not been absent more than half an hour, its aspect is completely changed. The curtains are drawn back, and the blind pulled up to the top; and Prue, sitting up in bed, with blotting-book and ink-bottle before her, is rapidly writing. As her sister hastens up to her, with an exclamation of surprise and dismay, she puts her two hands over the page to hide it.

'I am writing a letter,' she says hurriedly. 'I do not wish you to see what I am writing; you have no business to look!'

'I should not think of such a thing!' cries Peggy, drawing back pained. 'But why are you writing *now*, darling? It is only eight o'clock in the morning.'

Prue's trembling fingers are still clutching her pen.

'It—it—is as well to be in good time,' she says. 'This is a letter that ought to be written; the—the person to whom it is addressed will—will expect to get it.'

Peggy is standing by the bed, tall and sorrowful. She has taken the poor hand, pen and all, into her protecting clasp.

'Is it—is it all over then?' she asks chokingly.

'He is going round the world with the Hartleys,' says Prue, not answering directly, and beginning feverishly to fidget with her paper and envelopes. 'Of course I should like this to reach him before he sets off.'

Going round the world with the Hartleys! The blow has fallen, then. Peggy had known that it was coming, as surely as she knows the fact of her own existence. She had seen it approaching for months; and yet now that it has come, she stands stunned.

'I suppose that that was what he was talking to her about all evening,' pursues Prue, looking blankly away out of the window, to where, on the top of the apple-tree outside, a couple of jackdaws are sitting swinging in the fresh wind. 'That was what made him forget all about his dances with me. Of course, there would be a great deal to arrange; they are to be away a whole year. It was quite natural, quite; only it showed that it was all over with me. Even I could see that.'

She says it quite calmly, and with a sort of smile, her eyes still fixed on the jackdaws. Peggy is still too choked to speak.

'No one would have guessed last night that it was *I* who was engaged to him, would they?' pursues Prue, bringing home her straying look, and resting it in a half-uncertain appeal upon her sister. 'And yet I was, was not I? It was not my fancy; he did ask me once to be his wife—*his wife*,' dwelling on the word with a long, clinging intonation—'standing there by myself all those hours. I am sure that if he had known how it hurt me he would not have done it; he is too kind-hearted willingly to hurt a fly.'

Peggy's only answer is a groan.

'But of course I must write to him,' continues the younger girl, beginning again to draw her half-written sheet of paper tremblingly towards her. 'And—

and it is not altogether an easy letter to write; you understand that. It requires all one's attention.'

'Lie down and rest first, and write afterwards,' says Peggy, in a tone of tender persuasion.

'No, no!' returns the other, pushing her sister away. 'I will lie down and rest afterwards; there will be plenty of time. But I could not rest before it was written; and do not disturb me; do not speak to me. I should be sorry if there were anything ridiculous—anything that she could laugh at in my last letter to him.'

CHAPTER XXXVI

Though she has begun so early, Prue is writing nearly all day; writing sitting up in bed—writing when the eastern sun is pouring in his rays from the gates of day—writing when he has climbed the zenith—writing when he is reddening westwards. She has asked to be left alone, so as to be quite undisturbed; and when, at intervals, unable longer to keep away, Peggy returns from her sad and aimless rambles about the dahliad garden, and, pushing the door, looks softly in, the same sight always greets her eyes. Prue, with a fire-spot on each cheek, writing—writing. And yet when the postman comes to take the letters, it is only one small letter that he carries away. She is very loth to let it go, even then. No sooner is it out of her hands than she would have it back. There is a phrase in it that she would fain have altered, that he may think unkind. It vexes her all through the night, that phrase. It keeps sleep away from her, even if the oppression on her chest, caused by the heavy cold she has contracted through standing in the draught at the Hartleys' hall-door, would allow slumber to approach her eyes. In the small hours, indeed, she wanders a little; and would be up, and walk after the postman to take her letter from him. At dawn she falls into a broken doze; and Peggy, who has sat by or hung over her all night, poulticing, giving her drink, holding her hand, and assuring her with tears that there is nothing in her poor sentence that could wound Freddy's feelings, rises, stiff and cold from her vigil, and sends Alfred off on the pony for the doctor.

He comes, and prescribes, and goes away again, leaving behind him that little fillip of cheerfulness that the doctor's visit always gives; and another day wears on. Prue talks a great deal throughout it, though her laboured breathing makes speech difficult. She is very restless: would get up; would go down into the hall; out into the garden; would sit under the Judas-tree. She sheds no tears, gives no sign of depression; indeed, she laughs many times at recollected absurdities told her by Freddy. But the fire-spots blaze on her cheeks, and the fever-flame glitters in her eyes.

Another night follows; sleepless as the previous one, and with stronger delirium. She is going out riding with her lover. He has lent her the bay mare, which he has taken from Miss Hartley for her sake! He is waiting for her!— calling to her! and she cannot find her whip or her gloves. Oh, where are they? Where can they be? Will not Peggy help her to look for them? And Peggy, with death in her heart, feigns to search, through the chill watches of the night, for that whip and those gloves whose services it seems so unlikely that their young owner will ever need again. With morning her delusions die;

and, as the forenoon advances, she falls into a heavy sleep. Such as it is, it is induced by opiates.

Peggy has not been in bed for three nights, and an immense lassitude has fallen upon her. It is not that she is conscious of feeling sleepy; but her head is like a lump of lead, and her hands are ice-cold. She would be all right if she could get into the open air for five minutes. A greedy longing to drink in great draughts of the fresh wind that she can hear outside frolicking so gaily, yet gently too, with the tree-tops, lays hold of her; and, since Prue still sleeps heavily, she gives up her place by the bedside to Sarah, and walks drearily out into the garden. It is only two days since she had been last in it; but it seems to her as if years had rolled by since she had last trodden that sward, seen Jacob digging, and watched the birds pecking at the sunflower-seeds, and the wasps pushing their way through the netting into the heart of the peaches. It appears to her a phantasmal garden, with an atmosphere of brilliance and joyousness that may have their home in that realm where Thomas the Rhymer lived; but can have no relationship to her bitter realities. But when she reaches the seat under the Judas-tree, the kingdom of Thomas the Rhymer is gone, and reality is here in its stead. As she looks at it, her hands clench themselves, and a tide of rage and misery surges up in her heart.

'You have killed her!' she says out loud; 'killed her as much as if you had cut her poor throat! When she is dead, I will tell you so!'

She walks on quickly; rapid motion may make her burden easier to bear. But, alas! her domain is small; and no sooner has she left Prue and the Judas-tree behind, than the hawthorn bower and Talbot face her. The creamy foam of flowers that had sent its little pungent petals, shaped like tiny sea-shells, floating down upon their two happy heads, has changed to lustreless red berries.

'They are not more changed than I!' she says; and so sinks, helplessly sobbing, upon the rustic bench, her cheek pressed against the gnarled trunk. 'They are all the same!—all the same!' she moans. If it were not so, would she be lying with her head achingly propped against this rough bark? Would not it have been resting on her love's breast? Would not he have been telling her that Prue will get well? She has no one now to tell her that Prue will get well; and when she tells herself so, it does not sound true.

The tears drip from under her tired lids. One moment she is here, with aching body and smarting soul; the next she is away—how far, who shall say? Away, at ease; all her sorrows sponged out, for God has sent her His lovely angel—sleep.

It is two hours later when she wakes with a frightened start, and springs—half unconscious of her whereabouts at first—to her feet. The position of the sun in the sky, the altered angle of the shadow cast by her may-bush, tell her to how much longer a period than she had intended her five minutes have stretched. She begins to run, with a beating heart, back towards the house. Prue will have missed her! Prue will have been crying out for her! How stupid, how selfish of her to fall asleep!

She has entered the hall, when the noise of a closing door—her ear tells her Prue's—reaches her; and by the time she gets to the foot of the stairs she is confronted by a person coming quickly down. It is not Sarah, nor yet the doctor. It is the person to whom, beside the Judas-tree, she had framed that bitter message. She can give it now if she chooses. Freddy's hair is all ruffled, and the tears are streaming down his face—real, genuine salt tears.

'Oh, Peggy!' he cries, in a broken voice, as he catches sight of her, seizing both her hands; 'is that you? Come and talk to me! Come and say something nice to me! I am *so* miserable! Oh, how dreadful these partings are!'

As he speaks he draws her back into the hall with him; and throwing himself on the settle, flings his arms down upon the cushions, and his head upon them.

'Have you seen her?' asks Peggy in a shocked stern voice. 'Do you mean to say that you have seen her?'

The answer comes, blurred and muffled, from among the pillows.

'Yes, yes.'

'You are not satisfied, apparently, with the way in which you have done your work,' rejoins Peggy, with an intonation of icy irony, though her voice trembles; 'you are anxious to put the finishing-stroke to it!'

'I do not know what you are talking about,' says Freddy, lifting his tossed head and his tear-stained face, and looking at her with his wet eyes. 'I can see by your look that you mean to be unkind—that you have some cruel intention in your words; but you may spare yourself the trouble. I am so wretched that I am past feeling any blow you may aim at me. I knew nothing of her illness; her letter reached me only an hour ago. I came to see her; she heard my voice. Oh, Peggy, you do not realise how keen love's ears are! She asked to see me; she was lying on the sofa in her dressing-room. My Prue!—my Prue! What have you been doing to her? Oh, that word "Good-bye"! What long reverberations of sorrow there are in it!'

At the sight of the young man's emotion, so overpowering and to all appearance so genuine, Peggy's heart has been softening a little; but at this last sentence, uttered with something of his old manner of lofty and pensive reflection, it hardens again. Bitterness, such as had seized upon her by the Judas-tree, is rising again in her.

'You keep to your plan, then? you are going?' she asks, breathing hard, and with a sort of catch in her voice.

'And leave her as she now is?' answers Freddy, with an accent of wounded reproach, which perhaps in his opinion may exempt him from answering the question directly. 'Oh, my Peg, if I could but teach you to credit your poor fellow-creatures with at least bare humanity!'

'Then I am to understand that you are *not* going? that the idea is given up?'

She is still standing inexorably over him.

'I do not know why we should discuss the subject at all to-day,' returns Mr. Ducane, again interring his head in the cushions; 'I have not the heart to discuss anything to-day.'

'Then you did not mention the subject to her?'

'She introduced it herself; she has quite come round to think it a good plan— if you do not believe me, you may ask her—a year's probation to make me fitter for my Prue'—in a voice of dreamy tenderness. 'Oh, Peggy, cannot you understand what a sacred deposit the care of such a soul as Prue's is? cannot you comprehend that I do not feel yet worthy of it? You know, dear, I am very young, though you never will own it; and you cannot put gray heads upon green shoulders. Be merciful to me, little friend! be merciful to me!'

As he makes this coaxing request, he takes her reluctant hand and presses his wet cheek against it. But she feels no mercy in her heart, and promises him none even when she leaves him stretched full-length upon the settle, shaken with real sobs. For her, he may sob as long as he pleases; while in one panic-stricken bound upstairs she reaches her sister. She finds her—the Prue upon whom the doctor had enjoined such a strict confinement to bed and maintenance at one temperature—sitting, not even lying upon the dressing-room sofa, breathing labouringly, with every symptom of imminent bronchitis, with racing pulse and burning hands, but with heaven in her eyes.

'You have seen him,' she says pantingly, as Margaret comes in. 'You have heard—oh, do not scold me for getting up! I know that I ought not, but I will go back to bed as soon as you like; and—and it *is* real, is not it? it *is* true? I am not wandering. I was last night, I know; but I am not now, am I? Give me something of his, something to hold that I may be sure that it is true!'

Peggy has sat down upon the sofa beside her, and gathered up the little quivering figure into her arms.

'I will go back to bed now,' says Prue restlessly; but oh, with how different a restlessness from that of three hours ago! 'If I do not, I shall be longer in getting well, and I want to get well quickly. If I do not get better he will not go, and it would be selfish to hinder him from doing what is so much the best thing for him; yes, and for me too—for me too! Take me back to bed, Peggy.'

So Peggy takes her back to bed, and as she lays her down the thin arms close gratefully round her neck.

'You dear old soul! It is your turn for a bit of luck next.'

And when the night comes—the night dreaded by watchers beside sick-beds, the night that doubles fever and sharpens pain, and accentuates grief—Prue, clasping to her feverish breast an old glove, left behind by careless Freddy on some former occasion, wakes repeatedly with a jump from her broken slumbers to ask in a terrified tone, 'Is it true? Is it real?' And Peggy is always there, always awake, always beside her to answer reassuringly that it is. It would have been too flagrant a violation of the laws of nature and disease, if poor Prue had escaped scot-free from her infraction of both; and, in fact, her escapade is followed, as the meanest observer might have predicted that it would be, by a very sharp attack of bronchitis.

For a few days her illness is so acute that it seems as if Mr. Ducane would be placed in the painful dilemma of either leaving his betrothed fighting hand to hand with death, or of abandoning his cherished project. He arrives at the Red House in the morning, almost before the shutters are opened; he strays for hours about the garden with his hands clasped, his head bent forward, and his charming face as white as a sheet, till even Jacob's bowels yearn over him; though the style of observations by which he elects to show his sympathy are not perhaps precisely of a cheering nature, consisting chiefly of remarks such as that 'his missis says she never see any one go downhill so quick as Miss Prue—never.'

One day when Prue is at her worst, Freddy lies on the floor at her threshold, with his face buried in the mat, to the intense admiring compassion of Sarah and the nurse; but he really is not thinking of them. By and by the disease yields to treatment. Perhaps the patient's determination to get quickly better— her eagerness to return to a life once more become joyous and valuable to her —counts for much in the quickness of her rally.

Whatever be the cause, Prue is certainly better—is able once again to sit up; to shake milady's hearty hand, and eat her excellent jelly. But by the time that she is able to do so, the Hartleys' monster yacht is getting up her steam at Southampton; and all her passengers, with the exception of Mr. Ducane, are off to embark upon her. Within two days the die must be cast as to whether

Freddy is to be of that ship's company or not.

'It is for you to decide, sweet,' he says, in his south-wind voice with all the joyousness taken out of it, as he half-lies, half-sits, beside the dressing-room sofa, upon which she is stretched in her shadowy convalescence, while his head rests on the pillow beside hers. 'Yes—no! go—stay! I have no will but yours. You know that the only reason I ever had for wishing it was that I might come back a little less unworthy of you—with wider experience and larger horizons. As to *pleasure*'—with a small disdainful smile—'there can be no question of *that*! I think that my worst enemy will own that pleasure and I have waved farewell to each other of late.'

Prue has been lying prostrate and languid; but at his words she draws herself up into a sitting posture, and into her little face, not much less white than her dressing-gown, has come a faint pink flush—the flush of a generous effort.

'And, after all, it is only a year,' she says bravely. 'How absurd to make a fuss about only a year! When one was a child, one used to think it endless—an eternity; but now—why, it is gone by like a flash!'

'*Only* a year!' repeats Freddy, with a moan. 'Oh, Prue, can you say *only*? How do you do it, dear? Teach me—teach me!'

'And when it is over,' continues Prue, the colour deepening in her thin cheeks with the pain and labour of her sacrifice, 'and you come back, perhaps you will find me, too, changed, and not quite for the worse. Perhaps—perhaps if I do my best—if I try hard to educate myself between now and then—you will find me better able to understand your thoughts, and enter into your ideas, and say something besides the stupid praise—which I know has often vexed you, though you have tried not to show it—of your poems.'

She stops exhausted, and her faint head droops on his breast. The tears have sprung again to Freddy's eyes. Before he can make any rejoinder, she has lifted her face, and is again speaking.

'You say that I am to decide?' she says, in a firm tone. 'Well, then, I have decided. You are to go. I send you. No one,' her voice breaking a little, 'can pity me if I send you myself—can they?'

Two days later he goes. Upon the solemnity of his last parting with his sweetheart no one intrudes; but he prolongs his leave-taking so unreasonably that he is within an ace of losing his train; and it is not till after many vigorous rappings at the door, strong remonstrances, and nervous apostrophes through the keyhole, that he at length issues from Prue's room, livid and staggering.

'Oh, Peggy!' he says hoarsely, wringing her two hands; 'surely—surely the bitterness of death is past! Take care of her—in God's name take care of her for me! Do you hear?—take care of her for me!'

But Peggy answers never a word.

CHAPTER XXXVII

'Weep with me, all you that read
   This little story,
And know, for whom a tear you shed,
   Death's self is sorry.'

It is Sunday. The *Lapwing* is ploughing her way through a short chopping sea in the Bay of Biscay; and here at home, at Roupell, the people are issuing in a little quiet stream from afternoon church. They are coming out rather later, and with rather more alacrity than usual, both which phenomena are to be accounted for by the fact of Mr. Evans—never churlishly loth to yield his pulpit to a spiritual brother—having lent it to a very young deacon, who has taken a mean advantage of this concession to inflict fifty minutes of stammering extempore upon the congregation.

The Vicar has sat during this visitation in an attitude of hopeless depression, and has given out, with an intense feeling born of the excessive appositeness of the words to his own case, the hymn after the sermon—

'Art thou weary,art thou languid?'

Peggy sits alone in her pew, and her mind straying away from the fledgeling curate's flounderings, she asks herself sadly for how many more Sundays will this be so?

Mrs. Evans overtakes her as she walks down the path after service, to tell her that she and her whole family are to set forth on the following Tuesday in pursuit of that change for which she has been so long sighing.

'Mr. Evans is off on his own account!' cries she in cheerful narration. 'He does not like travelling with so large a party; it fidgets him, so he is off on his own account. The Archdeacon wanted him to go with him to the Diocesan Conference; but, as he justly says, what he needs to recruit him is an entire change of ideas as well as scene. So he is going to run over to Trouville or Deauville, or one of those French watering-places.'

'Indeed!'

'It seems very unkind of us—I am so sorry that we are leaving you here alone,' pursues Mrs. Evans, her elated eye and tone giving the lie to her regretful words. 'And they tell me that you are to lose milady too; she talks of a month at Brighton. She does not much fancy being at the Manor at the fall of the leaf.'

'Thank you,' replies Peggy civilly; 'but we never mind being by ourselves.'

'Oh, I know that you do not in a general way,' returns Mrs. Evans. 'But of course just now it is different; Prue so far from well. I only thought—I was only afraid—in case——'

'In case what?' asks Peggy curtly, while a cold hand seems crawling up towards her heart.

'Oh, nothing! nothing! I was only going to say, in case—in case she—she had a relapse.'

'And why should she have a relapse?' inquires Margaret sharply, in an alarmed and angry voice, turning round upon her companion.

'Why indeed!' replies the other, looking aside, and laughing rather confusedly. 'And at all events, you have Dr. Acton. He is so nice and attentive, and yet does not go on paying his visits long after there is any need for them, just to run up a bill as so many of them do.'

She is interrupted in her eulogium of the parish doctor by the appearance on the scene—both of them running at the top of their speed, as if they more than suspected pursuers behind them—of Lily and Franky Harborough. They, too, being on the wing home to-morrow, have come to bid their friend, Miss Lambton, good-bye; a ceremony which they entirely disdain to go through either in the churchyard or in the road, or indeed anywhere but under her own roof.

'Well, then, if you come you must be very quiet; you must make no noise,' she has said warningly.

She repeats the caution when they have reached the hall of the Red House, upon the settle of which there is no Prue lying; for though she is so much better—oh, so much—she has not yet been moved downstairs from the dressing-room.

'You must be very quiet,' Peggy repeats; 'you must remember that Prue is ill!'

Franky has climbed upon her knee, and is playing with the clasp of her Norwegian belt. He pauses from his occupation to ask her gravely, and in a rather awed voice, 'Is she *very* ill? Is she going to die?'

'God forbid!' cries Peggy, starting as if she had been stabbed. What! are they all agreed to run their knives in their different ways into her? 'My darling, do not say such dreadful things!'

'People do not die because they are ill,' remarks Lily, rather contemptuously; 'you did not die!'

'No, I did not die,' echoes the little boy thoughtfully.

He sits very quietly on Margaret's lap for a while, and when at length he climbs down, walks about the room on ostentatious tiptoe, speaking in stage-whispers.

It is only at the moment of parting, in the eagerness of pressing upon his friend once more for acceptance his five-bladed knife, and self-denyingly rebutting her counter offer of the largest ferret, that he forgets himself and Prue's invalidhood so far as to raise his little voice above the subdued key which he has imposed upon himself.

Peggy stands leaning against the gate, watching, until it has turned the corner out of sight, the tiny sailor-dressed figure disappearing down the road, with its refused love-gift reluctantly restored to the custody of its white duck trousers-pocket, with its small shoulders shaken with its sobs, and with its hand dragging back in petulant protest against the relentless grasp of its nurse.

'Poor little fellow! I almost wish that I had taken his knife,' she says regretfully.

And now they are all gone, dispersed their different ways: milady in her brougham, the children and maids in the omnibus, and the Evans family squeezed into, packed all over, and bulging out of their own one-horse waggonette and the inn fly. They are all gone—gone a week, a fortnight, now a month ago.

At first Peggy is glad of their departure, even milady's. What security has she but that, with all her hearty rough kindness, with her good sound human heart, and her plentiful kitchen physic, she may not at any moment stick another knife into her, with some well-intended word, as Mrs. Evans, as little Franky have already done? She would fain see no one—no one. The fox, swishing his brush in lazy welcome to her, and raising his russet head to be scratched through the wires of his house, poisons their intercourse with no insinuation that Prue is not really better. Minky does not ask her with the terrible point-blankness of childhood, 'Is Prue going to die?'

She will confine herself, then, to their kind and painless company.

But as the days go by, each dwindling day with the mark of night's little theft upon its shorn proportions; as the wind's hand and the frost's tooth make ravine among dear summer's leaves; as the beautiful blue and green year swoons in November's damp grasp—a change comes over her spirit, a famine for the touch of some compassionate hand, for the sound of some humane brave voice bidding her be of good cheer. It is a forlorn and rainy autumn. As in the days of St. Paul's shipwreck, so in those of Peggy's, 'neither sun nor stars in many days appeared.' When the rain-sheets are not soaking the saturated ground, the thick, dull blue mists reign everywhere. They have left their legitimate distant province, and have advanced even to the very walls of the Red House, swaddling the laurels and the naked lilacs, and the China roses that offer the delicate pertinacity of their blossoms to the autumn blast.

The garden has not yet been done up for the winter, as Jacob is waiting until 'they dratted leaves' are all down; and the rows of frost-blackened dahlias looming through the fog, the tattered garlands of canariensis, the scentless ragged mignonette, seem to Margaret's fancy, inflamed and heightened by grief and sleeplessness—for she seldom now has an unbroken night—to be the grinning skeletons of her former harmless joys.

The park is a fog-swathed swamp, here and there quite under water. Once or twice when she has passed by the Manor, its shuttered windows have appeared to scowl sullenly at her. Even the silence of the Vicarage seems hostile, as does the shut gate, upon which no pea-shooting boys or long-legged down-at-heel girls are swinging and shouting.

To the village, usually so often haunted by her charitable feet, she scarcely ever now goes. She dares not enter the cottages, because she knows what their inmates will say to her. It is no longer only Jacob's 'missis' to whom the rapidity with which Miss Prue is going downhill is matter of outspoken compassionate wonder. They mean no unkindness. They do as they would be done by. How many times has Peggy heard them calmly discussing in the very presence of their dying, the probability or improbability of their holding out until Christmas, or Candlemas, or Whitsun, as the case may be! But the first time that a kind-hearted cottage wife suggests to her, as in like case she would wish to have it suggested to herself, 'What a sad thing it is to think that poor Miss Prue will never see the primroses again, she as was allers so fond of flowers!' Peggy has stumbled away, half-stunned, as if some great and crushing weight had fallen on her head. And this Prue, about whom her village friends are making such sad prophecies, how is it with her? If you had asked her, she would have said, 'Well, very well, excellently well!'

Every day for the last month she has been going to be moved down next day to her settle in the hall; but whenever the new morning has come, that move has been deferred to the next. 'There is nothing the matter with her, really nothing; only she does not feel quite up to it; and, after all, there is plenty of time for her to get well in. Twenty-four hours will not make much difference, and she is so happy and comfortable up here.'

Up here, lying on the dressing-room sofa, with the fire flickering on the hearth beside her, talking to her cheerfully through her bad nights and her drowsy days; with every little present given her by Freddy ranged round her, within easy reach of her eye and hand, like a sick child's toys, and with his letters—they are not very many, for he is but a poor correspondent, though he says such beautiful things when he does write—kept delicately blue-ribboned in a little packet under her pillow, or oftener still held in her hot dry hand.

Their number has lately been swelled by the addition of a bulky one from Southampton, over which she has rained torrents of blissful tears. Hanging on the wall opposite to her, so that her look may rest continually upon it, is a large card, upon which she has had the number of the days of her lover's intended absence marked in black strokes. Every morning at her waking she has it brought to her, in order to put a pen-line through one more day. There are over thirty already thus scored out, as she shows to Peggy with a radiant smile.

At the beginning of the month, her sofa had been always covered with books. Freddy's own poems—these indeed stay to the last; the 'Browning' he has retrieved for her from Miss Hartley; books of criticism, of history, of verse, over which she pores laboriously, in pursuance of her promise to him to be more able to enter into his thoughts and understand his ideas upon his return. But by and by she has to cease from the attempt.

'I am afraid I cannot quite manage it,' she says to her sister, with an apologetic intonation; 'my head does not seem very clear. Sometimes I am afraid'—the wistful tears stealing into her blue eyes—'that it is not in me; that when he comes back he will find me just where he left me; that he will have to put up with me as I am.'

She does not suffer much actual pain, only her nights are increasingly broken, and her cough teases her sadly, which only makes her say that she is quite glad Freddy is not here, as a cough always fidgets him so. One morning in early November, after a night of more than usually wakeful unrest on the part of her sister, Peggy, who has had a bed made for herself on a sofa at the foot of the sick girl's, and has been up and down with her all night, is standing at the open hall door, trying to get a little freshness into eyes and brain. Her eyes are stiff with watching, and her brain feels thick and woolly, so thick and woolly that you would have thought it incapable of framing a definite idea. And yet across it there comes shooting now and again with steely clearness a torturing question—a question that is dressed sometimes in her own words, sometimes in Freddy's childish lisp, sometimes in the villagers' rough Doric; but that, however dressed, is yet always, always the same.

She has mechanically picked up the morning paper, and her languid eye is wandering carelessly over the daily prosaic list of the born, the wed, and the departed. As well that as anything else, though even as she makes the apathetic reflection, the question darts again in a new and hideous guise before her mind: 'How long will it be before there is another entry among these?'

With a great dry sob, she is in the act of dashing down the journal, when her glance is arrested by the letters of a familiar name, *Harborough*. It seems that there is a Harborough dead. Can it be that Betty has gone to her account? or that her complaisant husband has carried his complaisance so far as to take himself out of the world, and leave the field clear for that other? She has time to taste the full bitterness of this new thought, in the half second before her eye has mastered the advertisement:

> 'On the 3d inst., at Harborough Castle, ——shire, after a few days' illness, Francis Hugh de Vere Deloraine, only son of Ralph Harborough, Esq., aged 6 years.'

Even now that she has read it, she does not at once understand who it is that is dead. The string of high-sounding unfamiliar names sets her at fault. 'Francis Hugh de Vere Deloraine.' Is it—can it be *Franky* that is dead? Can it be that neither father nor mother have trodden the universal road, but that it is the little blooming child who has led the way? Why, it is impossible! There must be some mistake. It was only yesterday, as it were, that he was here; that she saw him passing through that very gate. In the confusion of her ideas, she has hurried out along the damp drive to the entrance-gate, and, standing there, gazes irrationally down the road, as if she expected once again to see the tiny sturdiness of the sailor figure, the tear-washed roses of the little face turned back over its shoulder in such fond and pouting protest at having to leave her; but the mist-bound road is empty—empty, save of its mire and of its rotting leaves. 'Franky dead! Little Franky dead!' She says it out loud, as if the idea could gain entrance into her brain more easily by her ears; and then she leans her forehead against the damp gate-post, and bursts out crying.

'I wish that I had given him another kiss! I wish that I had gone to the turn of the road with him, as he asked me! I wish that I had taken his knife!'

Her tears seem to make her intelligence clearer, to render sharper her power of suffering.

'Is there *no one* to be left alive? Is Death to have it all his own way?'

Her dimmed eyes rest on a drift of leaves blown by the last blusterous wind against the hedge-bank outside; a discoloured pile—the yellow poplar leaf, the black-brown pear and the bronzed beech, the ribbed hazel and the smooth lime—one fate has overtaken them all. Dead—dead!

At her foot is an elm-leaf half-dragged underground by the dark industry of some blind earthworm. Underground—underground! That is the bourne of us all; of the young green leaf, aloft two months ago on the tree-top, visited by the voyaging birds and the gamesome airs, as of the little bounding joyous child.

The searching vapour has penetrated her clothes, and made her shiver with cold; but she dares not yet go indoors again, dares not yet face her sick Prue, with those sudden tidings written on her face.

She retraces her steps along the drive, and turns into the garden—the empty garden; empty to-day of even Jacob's presence, as he is kept at home by his rheumatism. It is profoundly silent. The fog has got even into the robin's throat. It is profoundly silent; and yet to Peggy, the air is full of voices—the voices of her dead, her lost, and her dying. Her mother, Talbot, Prue, and now little Franky. He was not much to her, perhaps you may say; and yet she can ill spare his little drop of love out of her empty cup. Along the walks they hurry to meet her, and yet, as they come up to her, they pass her by with averted faces.

'I am certainly very lonely,' she says to herself, with a sort of astonishment; 'it is a very unusual case. There has happened to me what happens commonly to people only at eighty: I have outlived everything! I was given very few people to love, to begin with; but I did love them well. I gave them my very best. Oh, you cannot say, any of you, that I did not give you my very best, and yet not one of you will stay with me. Not one of you. God—God! What have I done to be picked out of all the world for such a fate? Is it fair? Is it fair?'

Her voice goes wailing out into the mist; but the dying world around her has no answer to give to her riddle. It is awaiting that to its own. She has thrown herself down on the seat under her hawthorn bower, and from its dull berries and sharp thorns, and few still-clinging yellow leaves, the cold drops drip on her bare head, mix with the scalding drops on her cheeks; but she feels them not as she lies there, huddled up, collapsed, and despairing. Not for long, however. By and by her soul, as is the way with souls habitually brave, puts on its courage again. She raises herself, and lifts her drowned and weary eyes, as if through the fogs and exhalations they would pierce to Him who, as all the world once thought, as many still hold to be a truth far dearer than life, sits in judgment and mercy beyond them.

'Shall not the Judge of all the earth do right?' she says solemnly. 'Shall not the Judge of all the earth do right?'

CHAPTER XXXVIII

'I am not mad,—I would to heaven I were!
For then 'tis like I should forget myself:
Oh, if I could, what grief should I forget!
Preach some philosophy to make me mad,
And thou shalt be canonised, cardinal;
For, being not mad, but sensible of grief,
My reasonable part produces reason
How I may be deliver'd of these woes,
And teaches me to kill or hang myself:
If I were mad, I should forget my son;
Or madly think a babe of clouts were he.
I am not mad; too well, too well I feel
The different plague of each calamity.'

In the days that follow, the death of Franky Harborough, which at an ordinary time would have been the sorrowful main occupation of Peggy's thoughts, has to retire into the background of her mind. In the foreground there is room for but one absorbing topic. Prue is decidedly worse. In an illness such as hers—which is less a definite disease than a decline all round, a bowing to its final ruin of a building whose foundations have been sapped for more than a year—there is very often, for a considerable period, but little change to be noted from day to day; and then suddenly—no, not suddenly—in a progression rather, as natural as that from seedtime to harvest, on some morning, at some noon or night, there is a step down to a lower level of vitality; a travelling along that lower level, until the time for a new and farther descent. It would seem impossible that any breath of the chilly fog outside could have thrust its pestilent way into the atmosphere, regulated with so passionate a nicety, of Prue's room; and, indeed, there is no sign of any return of that bronchitis which had been the ostensible beginning of her illness. Nor is there any very perceptible aggravation of any one of her symptoms.

The signs of her approaching dissolution are rather negative than positive. It is only that Miss Prue is going downhill rather quicker than before—that is all. There is now no longer any question of the oak settle in the hall. Even the sofa in the dressing-room has been abandoned. Prue no longer stirs from her bed; but she lies there quite happily, quite as happy as she was before; for Freddy's gifts are within as easy reach of her hand, spread on the counterpane before her, as they were on the table in the adjoining room; and her card with its 365 black strokes hangs quite as full in her eye, on the wall opposite her bed.

However bad her night may have been, there is always something to look forward to at dawning, in having it brought to her to put her triumphant pen through another day.

'I shall be glad when we have got up to forty,' she says to Peggy, with a faint but cheerful laugh. 'I shall feel quite differently when we have reached forty: there will be all but a ninth of the time gone then.'

It is a day on which the officious dusk of the winter afternoon—always in such haste to shoulder away its pale brother—has already settled down. For sixteen long hours there will be no more glint of light. This dreary thought is passing through Peggy's mind, as she nods drowsily over the fire. She is roused from it and from her semi-sleep by hearing the room-door open cautiously and seeing Sarah making signs—evidently not intended to be seen by Prue—through the aperture.

In obedience to them, Margaret rises languidly, and goes out upon the landing.

'What is it?'

'If you please, 'm, there's a lady wishes to speak to you.'

'Oh, Sarah, you know that I can't see any one; why did not you tell her so?'

'I did tell her so, 'm, but she would not take "No"; she says if she stays all night she must see you.'

'What does she mean?' cries Peggy, in a voice of astonished indignation; 'who can she be? Who is she?'

'Well, 'm, I really did not recognise her until she spoke—dressed in deep mourning and that; and she asked me not to mention her name. She said she was sure you would not see her if I did.'

Dressed in deep mourning! Peggy's legs have been somewhat shaky under her of late, through long standing upon them. Perhaps that is why she now catches at the banisters. It has flashed upon her who her visitor is. What has brought her hither? Why has she come? Has she gone mad?

'Go and sit with Miss Prue, while I am away,' she says to the servant; and so walks slowly downstairs. Outside the door of the hall she pauses a moment to pull herself together. She is trembling violently, and her teeth chatter.

What has brought her here? What can they have to say to each other? She enters. Beside the table is standing Lady Betty Harborough; for it is she who is Peggy's visitor. The lamp is lit, and burns brightly, though nowadays there is never any one to read or work by its gentle glow. A flourishing fire sings on the hearth; but their joint cheerfulness serves only to throw up into higher relief the inky gloom of the figure they illuminate. She makes no movement to go to meet Peggy, but awaits her coming; and for a moment the two women look at each other in silence.

As they do so, a doubt—a real, serious doubt flashes across Peggy's mind, as to whether this is Lady Betty. Coupled with the doubt comes a darted recollection of the two last occasions on which she has seen her; the very last of all, sitting under a date-palm in the Hartleys' conservatory, in the full flush of her *décolleté* beauty and impudent folly, out of sheer love of mischief, turning the head of a foolish parish priest; and the time before—oh! that time before—when her own heart had lain down and died, on that star-strewn night, when through the gate of the walled garden she had seen her with her arms laced about John Talbot's neck.

There is no veil to disguise the ruin of Lady Betty's face. Under her heavy crape bonnet, her hair, uncurled by the damp of the winter night, hangs in pitiful little tags upon her sunk forehead. There is no trace of rouge on her pinched cheeks; nor any vestige of black, save that painted there by agonised vigils, under her hopeless eyes. Her mouth—that mobile mouth so seldom seen at rest, always either curved into a smile, or formed into a red pout, or playing some pretty antic or other—is set like a flint, and around it are drawn lines deeper and more, many more, than those cut by old age's chisel. Can it be this forlorn and God-struck creature that she, Peggy, has been hating so long and so well? Beneath this dual consciousness—the same consciousness under which Talbot had confusedly laboured once before—beneath the waning influence of that old hostility, and this new and immeasurable compassion, Peggy finds it impossible to speak. But her visitor saves her the trouble.

'I must apologise for intruding upon you at such a time. I know that I have no right to do so; I should not have taken such a liberty, only that—that I had a message to give you—a commission from a—a person who is dead.'

Her voice is perfectly clear and collected, without a quiver in it. It is only by the slight hesitation before a word here and there that it could be conjectured that it was not a matter of perfect indifference to her of which she is speaking. There is such a lump rising in Peggy's throat, that she could not answer if she were to gain a kingdom by it.

'Perhaps you are aware,' continues the other, quite as collectedly as before, 'that I have lost my son. He died, after a few days' illness, on the 3d; and when he was dying, he was very anxious that you should have *this*,' holding out to Margaret, in a hand that does not shake, the knife that had been so eagerly urged upon her acceptance by poor little Franky on his last visit to her. 'He wished me to tell you that it has five blades; and that though there is a little notch out of one of them, it does not cut the worse for that.'

Peggy has taken the knife, and is covering it with sad and reverent kisses.

'God bless him!' she says brokenly. 'God in heaven bless him!'

The tears are raining in a torrent down the face of Franky's friend; but his mother's eyes are dry.

'Not long before he died,' she resumes, in that awful collected voice, 'he asked me to give it into your hands; that must be my excuse to-night. I believe you refused it once before. I told him that I thought you would not refuse it now. He begged you to keep it. He said he should not want it any more; it was quite true,' her eye wandering round the room, and speaking as if to herself, as if having forgotten Peggy's presence—'he will never want anything any more!'

Peggy has lifted her swimming eyes upwards.

'They are in God's hands, and no evil shall touch them!' she says solemnly.

It is not only the little innocent who has already crossed the flood of whom she is thinking, but also of that other one in the room upstairs, whose feet are so fast nearing the ford.

'He was very fond of you, very!' says the mother, her parched eyes noting with an expression of surprise and envy the agitation of her companion. 'And he was not one to take a fancy to everybody either; he had his likes and dislikes. Yes, he was very fond of you; but,' with a sort of hurry in her tone, 'you did not come before me; no one did that. Mammy was always first. Last time he was staying at the Manor he wrote me two little letters; how do you think he signed them?' with a pale, wild smile: '"Your loving friend." Was not that an odd signature? "Your loving friend!"'

Peggy's sobs have mastered her so completely, that she can make no answer beyond that of once again convulsively pressing her poor little legacy to her quivering lips.

'He suffered a good deal,' continues Betty, with that terrible composure of hers; 'but he made no fuss about it. He asked me once or twice whether I could not take away the pain; but when I told him that I could not, he quite understood. Children are so patient; and he always was a plucky little chap.'

'You *poor* woman!' cries Peggy, in a voice almost unintelligible through her tears. 'Oh, I wish I could do anything for you! Oh, you poor woman!'

She has caught both Betty's icy hands into her own warm compassionate clasp. She has clean forgotten that they are the hands of the woman who has slain her life. She knows only that there is a most miserable creature struggling in the deep waters beside her, to whom all her large pitying heart goes out. The other accepts indifferently that strong and sorrowful clasp, as what would not she so accept?

'You seem to be very kind!' she says, with a sort of stupid wonder. 'And yet, if you come to think of it, we have no great cause to love each other; you have no great cause to be fond of me.'

'You poor soul!' returns Peggy, looking back, with all the perfect honesty of her sad eyes, into the other's disfigured face. 'I bear you no malice for any harm you may have done me; and I have never wittingly done you any.'

'*Never wittingly done me any!*' repeats Betty, with a dull and dragging intonation. 'Have not you? There were only two things in the world that I cared about. You took one of them from me, and now God has taken the other.'

Peggy lets go her hands in a revulsion of feeling strong beyond the power of words to express, and steps back a horrified pace or two. Is it possible, is it conceivable that in this most sacred hour of holy mother-grief, she can think or speak of her own lawless passion?

'You are shocked!' says Betty, perceiving this movement on the part of her companion. 'I do not know why you should be. If I were to pretend that I had always been a good woman, it would not give me back my boy; and what does anything else matter?'

Then there is silence for a minute or two. It is broken by Betty.

'When you had taken him from me, why did you send him away again?' she asks abruptly.

For a moment it seems as if all the blood in Peggy's body had sprung to her brain, and was hammering at her temples, and dinning in her ears in a surge of passionate indignation. But at sight of the stricken face before her, her anger dies down again.

'I could not say anything harsh to you to-night,' she replies gently; 'but you must know that you are the last person who has any right to ask that question.'

'I know it,' replies Betty, with a stony indifference; 'any right, or any need either, since I know the answer. Do not I know that you were in the walled garden on that night last June? Did not I see you as I ran past? I knew what you would think, and I knew, too, that I could trust to him not to undeceive you.'

Peggy is trembling like a leaf. Must she bear it? Does Christian charity command her to endure this ruthless, purposeless tearing open of her scarcely cicatrised wound?

'There was no question of undeceiving,' she says brokenly, yet with dignity. 'I did not trust to hearsay—I should not have been likely to do that; but I could not distrust the evidence of my own eyes.'

Betty's sunken look is fixed on the girl's quivering features.

'It was a pity for your own peace of mind,' she says slowly, 'that you did not come a moment earlier, or stay a moment or two later! You would have seen then how much the evidence of your own eyes was worth. It would have saved you a good deal of pain; for I suppose you have taken it to heart—you look as if you had. I thought that you looked as if you had when I saw you at the Hartleys' party the other night. *The other night*'—putting up her hand to her head with a confused look—'was it the other night! or a year ago? or when?'

Margaret's heart has begun to beat so suffocatingly fast that she can hardly draw her breath. What is Betty saying? What is she implying? Is it—is it——

'I suppose,' continues Lady Betty, in the same level, even, absolutely colourless voice as before, 'that you thought we met by appointment? Poor man!' with a catch that is almost like the echo of a ghost's laugh in her voice; 'if you had seen his face when he first caught sight of me, I think you would have exonerated him from that accusation. What do you suppose that he was doing when I came upon him? Why, kissing the spot of ground that he fancied your feet might have touched! I suppose that that was what sent me mad! There was a time, you know, when he used to kiss the print of *my* feet. Yes, I suppose it was that, though it seems odd now. If I had known how differently things would look from the other side of my Franky's grave, how little I should have cared!'

The oppression on Margaret's breathing is heavier than ever—the thundering of her heart more deafening; but she *must* master them—she *must* speak.

'But I *saw*!' she cries, gasping; 'I *saw*!'

'You saw my arms round his neck,' returns the other, in that terrible level voice of hers, out of which despair seems to have pressed all modulation, not a shade of colour tinging her livid face as she makes the admission. 'I know that you did. Do you wonder that I can own it? If you only knew of how infinitely little consequence it seems to me now, you would not wonder. Yes, you saw my arms round his neck; but do you suppose that it was by his will or consent that they were there? Poor man!' with the same ghastly spectre of a laugh as before; 'if he is as innocent of all other crimes at the Day of Reckoning as he is of that, he will come off easily indeed.'

Is Peggy's breath going to stop altogether? Is her heart resolved to break altogether out of its prison in the agony of its springing? She presses her clenched hand hard upon it. It *must* let her listen. It *must not*—must not burst in two until she has heard—heard to the end.

'I wish you to understand,' goes on Betty, relentlessly pursuing her confession, 'that it was I—I—who forced my last good-bye against his will— oh, most against his will—upon him! I knew that it was good-bye; he had not left me much doubt upon that head. I knew that his one wish was to be rid of me—to hear no more of me—to have done with me for this and all other worlds; and so, as I tell you, I thrust my last good-bye upon him, and you saw it, and misunderstood, as how should not you? I do not know whether you will believe me—it matters little to me whether you do or not.'

Her hopeless voice dies away on the air, and her sunk look wanders aimlessly round the room. Peggy is reeling as she stands. Is it the fog from outside which has come in and is misting her eyes? She puts up her hand stupidly to them, as if to wipe it away.

'I—I—I—am sure you are speaking truth,' she says, in an almost unintelligible broken whisper; 'but as yet—as yet—I—I—cannot take it in.'

'I would be quick about it if I were you,' answers the other stonily. 'I would not waste any more time. You have wasted five months already; and we are none of us allowed much time to enjoy ourselves in. We none of us keep our good things long. Any one would have thought that I might have kept my Franky a little, would not they? He was only six. Did you know that he was only six? Many people took him for seven; he was so big for his age. What, crying again? Well, I do not much wonder; he was a very loving little fellow, was not he? and had a great fancy for you. He prized that knife almost more than anything he possessed, and yet he was determined that you should have it. You will take care of it, will not you? Good-bye!'

CHAPTER XXXIX

> 'Part of the host have crossed the flood,
> And part are crossing now.'

She is gone—passed out into the blackness of the winter evening—gone before Peggy, paralysed, half-stunned as she is, can arrest her. Was she ever here? The doubt flashes into the girl's mind. Of late, in her long vigils, she has seemed to be parted from the spirit-world by but the consistency of a spider's web. Has that fine partition been broken down? Has she been seeing visions, and dreaming dreams? Did that crape-gowned figure ever stand really in the body beside the table? Did she herself ever look across the lamplight into the still and bottomless despair of its eyes? Did it really give her Franky's knife, and tell her—oh no, it is incredible! God can never have granted to her —to her of all people, sunk so low as she is, far beyond the reach of any joy to touch—to hear such things as her ears seem to have heard. She looks wildly round the room.

'It was not true!' she says out loud; 'it was hallucination. It comes of sleeping so little.'

And yet it must be true, too; for here, clasped in her hand, is the poor knife, the object of the mother's journey. If that be real, then must all the rest be real too. As the splendour of this inference breaks in dazzling overpowering light upon her soul, she sinks on her knees beside the table, lays down her head upon it at the same spot where Talbot had laid his head in his heart-break five months ago, while she had stood over him pronouncing her unjust and inexorable sentence.

'Oh, love, love!' she sighs out; 'dear love! poor love! forgive me! come back to me! how could I tell?'

And then she lifts her face up to him, as if he were there; her face irradiated with a joy like that of morning. Yes, though Prue is dying upstairs, though Franky's pathetic bequest is still held between her fingers, her heart is leaping. Has not one of her dead been given back to her? Why, then, shall they not all? In that moment of supreme elation, it seems to her as if all things were possible; it seems to her as if Prue must get well, as if all her other dead joys must come crowding back to welcome that exceeding great one, that has flown to her with widespread arms out of the night of winter and despair. Prue will get well. God will make her well. With God all things are possible. There is a smile of wet radiance on her pale lips, and in her tired eyes; and she is repeating over and over again to herself, as if by repetition she would ensure their fulfilment, these lovely promises, when the door opens and Sarah looks in.

'If you please, 'm, could you come back to Miss Prue?'

'Oh yes, this minute—this minute! How has she been? how is she? Better? a little better?'

There must be something strange about her own appearance, for her servant is looking at her in undisguised amazement.

'Better, 'm?' she repeats in a wondering key; 'whatever should make you think she was better? She has had a bad bout of coughing since you left, and it has tired her out, so that it quite frightened me. That was partly why I came for you.'

Before her sentence is ended Peggy is upstairs again and at her sister's bedside; the transfiguration all dead out of her face.

'You have been a long time away,' says the sick girl feebly, and with a little of her old querulousness; 'why did you go?'

'I will not go again, darling.'

'But why did you go?' repeats the other with the pertinacity of sickness; 'where have you been?'

Margaret hesitates a moment; then:

'I have been with Franky Harborough's mother,' she answers gently, the tears rushing afresh to her eyes, as she holds out the legacy of the dead child before the faint eyes of the dying one; 'he sent me his knife; his mother brought it me.'

'Poor Franky!' says Prue softly, but she does not manifest any curiosity. She only turns her wan face upon the pillow, and closes her eyes. In the watches of the night, however, she recurs more than once to the subject, waking up to cry, 'Poor Franky!' and to say, 'How sad it is when young people die!'

And Peggy acquiesces.

The tired servants have gone to bed. They, too, have had their share of watching on former nights. Peggy keeps her vigil alone. In the intense silence of the dark, in the intense silence of the little lonely country house standing fog-muffled through the enormous November night, beside its unfrequented country road, she keeps her vigil alone. Not even an owl calls from the tree-tops, nor does a star look through the murk. In her night-watching of late she has been tormented with a cruel over-mastering drowsiness, which has filled her with a remorse such as those must have felt to whom it was said, 'What, could ye not watch with Me one hour?' but against which offended nature, being yet stronger than she, she has once and again contended in vain.

To-night, however, through all the hours of her vigil, she is broadly, acutely awake. Awake! Yes; but is she sane? That is the question that over and over again she puts to herself. If she be, what are these voices that keep calling to her out of the noisy silence? What are these faces that are becking and mowing at her? What are these flashes of light, dreader than any darkness— flashes that have the blasphemy to look like joy—that dart now and again across the sorrow-struck confusion of her soul? How dare they come? God-sent, or devil-sent; messengers from heaven, or fiends from hell, how dare they come? They shall not, shall not thrust themselves between her and her Prue.

When the tarrying dawn comes, it finds her almost as exhausted as it does her whose stock of mornings and evenings has so nigh run out. It has come, that tarrying dawn; and Prue, waking up with a start, as by some infallible instinct she always does as soon as the east has sent her first weak arrows against the great target of the dark, feebly calls to her sister to bring her her card that she may erase the one more parted day from the calendar. But when Peggy's strong and tender arms have propped her up, when Peggy's fond hand has put the pen into hers it escapes from her disobedient fingers.

'I do not know what has come to me,' she says with her little smile; 'but you must do it for me—that will be just as well, will not it? You do not think,' with an anxious catch in her voice, 'that it is ill-luck your doing it this once, instead of me? If you think so, I will try again.'

As morning advances there comes a slight renewal of strength—a slight revival to the dying girl. The servants and the doctor—the kind doctor who still makes a feint of prescribing—urge upon Margaret to take advantage of this slight amendment to snatch an hour or two of sleep; but she pushes away their advice almost rudely. Is not the text still ringing in her ears, 'What, could ye not watch with Me one hour?' And Prue, as it turns out, needs her more to-day than most days. For she is less drowsy and lethargic than she has been of late, able even to plan a new arrangement of all Freddy's presents, a new grouping round her of his photographs.

'Had ever any one so many portraits of the same person?' she says with a tiny white smile, looking contentedly at them, when the new arrangement has been effected. 'I am very silly about him; but he is silly about me too, is not he?' with a look of intensely wistful asking in her blue eyes.

When evening draws on, she begins to grow heavy again.

When evening draws on! Can it be again approaching? already again approaching—the grisly nightmare night? Why, it seems as if not more than half an hour had elapsed since day had begun to deal out her avaricious dole of light! and now she is again withdrawing it. The night is approaching. The night has approached. The night is here, in dominant black supremacy. And again Peggy watches. It is not the fault of the servants that she does so. At any crisis—a sickness, a catastrophe, a death—servants are almost always kind; and Margaret's are more than willing to shorten or forego their rest in order to share with her, or replace her in her vigil. But she dismisses their offers promptly, yet with a resolution that shows that it would be vain to press them. She will call them if there is any need. They go reluctantly, and once again night settles down upon the sad little Red House.

The drowsiness that used to frighten Margaret with its threatened mastery she has no longer any need to keep at bay. On the contrary, the preternatural wakefulness which had been with her all last night is with her still. With her, too, is the thundering silence, beating in her ear like a loud drum. All her last night's enemies are here again—all but one, the worst. She has no longer to contend with those flashes of dreadful incongruous joy. They at least are gone —extinct, dead! He that had called them forth is massed in her despair with her other dead. They are all gone irrevocably. The only difference is that God took the others, and she herself has thrown him away. But they are all equally gone—gone! If it were not so, if she had any one left, would she be kneeling here, in this overpowering loneliness, watching Prue go, and asking God over and over again, in the same stupid agonised words, to let her go easily?

Yes, it has come to this. We begin by asking such great things for our beloved —honour, and wisdom, and long life, and riches; and we end in this, 'Give them a short agony, an easy passing!' Is it a sign that God has heard her prayer, that as the hours go by Prue begins to talk out loud, with little laughs between? to talk—not of her cough, and her physic, and her short breath—but of gay and lovely things. She is talking to one who is not here, of fair sights that are not before her dying eyes.

Peggy holds her breath to listen. She is sitting in the garden with Freddy. She is riding with him through the woods. From what she says, it must be springtime. What a sheet of harebells! Never any May that she remembers have they been so many before! And the birds! how loudly they are singing! She would like to know the note of each, but she is so stupid, he must teach her!

A great dry sob breaks from the listener's breast.

'Oh, Prue, Prue!' she moans; 'take me with you! Let me, too, see the flowers and hear the birds!'

But Prue does not heed. She babbles happily on. By and by her wanderings die down into a sort of semi-stupor, that is neither sleep nor waking. The silence that her voice had broken is not again wholly restored. It is exchanged for those indefinite noises of the night which, to timid souls, seem to share the dominion of terror with its stillness. There are definite noises too. A mouse gnaws behind the wainscot; the wind has risen, not into a loud and roaring storm, but into a plaintive piping and muttering and whistling. A loose rose-branch that in summer sends its petals flying in through Prue's casement to her feet, is now tapping pertinaciously on the pane. It seems as if it would not take 'No' for answer, as if it were crying to her with summoning fingers, 'Come, come! it is time!'

The night has reached the dreariest of her little hours, that one that seems equally remote from the comfortable shores of the gone day and the coming one. The clocks have just struck two, and Peggy kneels on, still reiterating that monotonous prayer that God will take her Prue gently. To her ears, though not to her senses, come the noises of the night; come also noises that do not rightly belong to the province of the night, that are rather akin to the noises of the day: the sound, for instance, of wheels outside upon the lonely road, a sound that does not die away, gradually muffled and fading into the distance, but that ceases suddenly on the air—ceases, only to be succeeded by the noise of a vague, subdued stir in the house itself. But Peggy kneels on. The only noise that she heeds is that of the beckoning rose-branch that calls continually, 'Come, come!'

She has buried her face in the bed-clothes, praying always; and as she lifts it again she becomes aware that in the doorway, left ajar to give Prue more air and ease in breathing, some one is standing, some one standing at the dead of the night, looking in upon her. But still she kneels on. She is quite past fear. Is she wandering, like Prue? Is it some heavenly messenger that has come out of pure pity to her help? If it be so, it wears the homely human form, the form of one with whom she once sat under a hawthorn bower, with her happy head upon his breast.

As her solemn, haggard eyes meet his, he advances into the room, and kneels down beside her. They exchange no word. Their hands meet in no greeting; only they kneel side by side, until the morning. And at morning, when the first dawn-streak makes gray the chinks of the window-shutters, Prue, true to her infallible instinct, wakes up out of her trance; and, opening her eyes, cries with a loud, clear voice:

'Is it morning? Then there is another day gone. Forty days gone—forty days!' and so, lifting her face to Peggy to be kissed, as she has done all her life, before addressing herself to sleep, she closes her eyes, and turns her face on the pillow with a satisfied sigh; and on that satisfied sigh her soul slips away.

Speak softly, for Prue is asleep—asleep as Franky Harborough sleeps, as all they sleep, the time of whose waking is the secret of the Lord God Omnipotent.

———————

Her little world have long prophesied that Prue would die, and now she is dead—dead, and, restless as she was, laid to rest in her moss-lined grave. With the live green moss environing her, with the bride-white flowers enwrapping her from dreamless head to foot, she has gone—gone from sofa and settle and garden—gone soon from everywhere, save from Peggy's heart. And he who is the alone lord and owner of that great heart does not grudge its place to the poor little figure seated for ever by that warm fireside; and if, as time goes on, he knows that the Prue so perennially enthroned there—the Prue of whom in after-days Peggy's children are taught to talk with lowered voices, as of some thing too sweet and sacred for common speech—is not the real Prue who fretted and repined, and loved to madness here on earth, he does not own it even to himself.

———————

Postscript.—About six months after the death of Prue Lambton, the attention of the readers of one of the graver monthlies was arrested by the appearance in its pages of a short ode, the melody of whose versification, the delicate aroma of its fancy, the quaint beauty of its imagery, and the truth and freshness of its feeling, called to their minds the best of the Elizabethan lyrics. It was anonymous, and was addressed 'To Prue in Heaven.'

———————

THE END.

Lightning Source UK Ltd.
Milton Keynes UK
UKHW010642291222
414571UK00004B/288